Daniel Polansky

TOMORROW'S
CHILDREN

ANGRY ROBOT

ANGRY ROBOT
An imprint of Watkins Media Ltd

Unit 11, Shepperton House
89 Shepperton Road
London N1 3DF
UK

angryrobotbooks.com
twitter.com/angryrobotbooks
No escape

An Angry Robot paperback original, 2024

Cover by Alice Coleman
Edited by Paul Simspon and Travis Tynan
Set in Meridien

ISBN 978 1 91520 285 7
Ebook ISBN 978 1 91520 284 0

Printed and bound in the United Kingdom by TJ Books Ltd.

9 8 7 6 5 4 3 2 1

MIX
Paper from
responsible sources
FSC   FSC® C013056
www.fsc.org

For L

A While Back...

1

Hem and the Serpent

Hem followed the blood trail to a den on the banks of the Huddy and to half a dozen newborn pups. One look and you could see why you bred dogs for meat but you caught them for war. Savage, howling mutts with big paws – they'd go for fifty a head in Midtown, but first he had to kill their mother.

"Go quiet, girl," said Hem. The bitch had left a leg in his snare trap five blocks back, but still she blocked the burrow with her body and snapped furiously at his approach. "Go easy." Hem picked up a rusted pipe in case she tried to charge but planned on waiting until she bled out. "Dim comes for all of us."

The weeds in Inwood Hill Park rose over Hem's head, and high above both, the Henry Hudson Parkway sat still and silent. Inwood was as barren a spot as could be found on the Island, abandoned for generations, fallow since the funk. Hem's father had been a hunter. His whole life he had lived off the things what lived off men, hunting cat and dog, hunting wild pigeon and sewer snake, and even he didn't fancy being so far from civilization. But lately, with every Bubba and Lamont thinking they were hunters, a man had to range wide to have a hope of profit.

And look at how his audacity was rewarded! Six pups, plus what he'd fetch for the mother's skin, as rich a catch as he'd ever bagged, excluding an alligator he had once clubbed to death what had gotten lost topside.

The bitch growled, the pups yelped, Hem shifted back a step. "Lay those cares down now, girl," he said. "There's none carry 'em forever."

Hem took a quick gander at the wall of gray which floated a few hundred feet out onto the Huddy. Downtown, the funk seemed certain, a smeary dome splitting the sky and the towers in two, separating the Island from the World-Writ-Large; but by the coasts, and this far north especially, it had a way of moving faster than you'd think possible. Stare down at your shoes and look back up to find it next door, shapes in the firmament like, like, like–

Hem dodged back. "Clever thing," he said. "Almost caught me napping!"

The bitch was a fighter, no doubt, and her pups would be the same, but that last lunge had exhausted her. She dropped over her injured limb, eyes going dark. Hem raised his pipe above her skull...

...and then stopped stiff and stared off at the water.

Hem was a brave man. He had hunted beneath the Hi Line, and once chased a succulent-seeming Pekinese to the very borders of ruined TriBeCa. The knife on his left hip was for skinning, but the knife on his right hip was wide and wavy, a man-killer, and they had both known work. A brave man, but watching it emerge from the funk and beach itself on the shoreline, oblong and black like a necrotic phallus, Hem's eyes went wide and his pants turned damp.

"Hell and High Towers!" he screamed, sprinting off east.

The bitch died just then, and so it was only her pups left to bear howling witness to the end of the end of the world.

Dimtime Last…

2

The Death of Don DeAndre

The Kid Makes His Appearance

He came in as the bright faded through the windows overlooking Mulberry. Nothing special going on in the clubhouse, and most of the I's were out on business, clique or personal. Krill and Hammet were smoking flower below the mural of the old fathers done up on the lobby walls – the Scarred One, the Father and the Son and the Father as Son, so on and so forth. They weren't guarding the place – that was Silo's job – just hanging around, but in practice these amounted to much the same thing.

"I'm here to see your man," he said. He was a kid. He had high cheek bones and bright eyes. His hair was red coxcomb. His pants were very tight and his jacket hung loose and he wasn't wearing a cutter. If he was eighteen, he was eighty.

Krill licked shut the seam on his smoke. Hammet farted. "You're here to see who?"

"Your man."

"Somebody in here rutting you?" Krill asked.

"Not my man," said the kid. "Your man."

"You mean the Don?" Krill asked.

"Don DeAndre is *the* man," Hammet said.

"He's not my man," said the kid.

"Won't be seeing no man," said Silo from his stool by the elevator. There weren't many cliques with enough juice to keep the lights on, let alone power a lift, but the I's weren't just any clique; they were the I's. For that matter, there weren't many cliques could afford boom, but damn if Silo didn't have two in the scattergun on his lap. "Out with you."

"This is Mulberry and Broome, right?" asked the kid.

"Yeah."

"That makes you the I's?"

"The one and only," said Hammet.

"The Eternal I's," said Krill, "our thing never dies."

"That's a grand ambition," said the kid.

Two quick steps and Hammet loomed over him. Krill set his joint behind his ear and pulled his hatchet from where he had stuck it into the wall and joined his partner beside the new arrival.

"You got a mouth on you," said Krill.

"Thanks! It was my mother's."

"You been huffing funk?' asked Hammet.

"Not a wisp," said the kid.

"What do you want?"

"Like I said, I've got a meeting with the Don."

"The Don don't have time to waste with every scab off the street."

"I'm sure we have a meeting now," said the kid, seeming perplexed. "I even made a note–"

He was reaching into his jacket when Krill slapped him and Hammet pinned his wrist against his back. Just that quick and easy; the boy didn't even put up a fight.

"Move, and I'll break your arm," said Hammet.

"What you got in there?" asked Krill.

The kid sagged helplessly. "Just getting my appointment book."

"Mutt-rutting fool," said Silo. "What was he going for?"

Krill reached into the kid's jacket and came back out with a slender black book. Opening to its ribbon, he frowned, puzzled, then bent it back so Hammet could see…

The front windows erupted, flecks of glass scattering. Hammet looked down to discover a knife in his chest which had not previously been there. He sat down on the floor.

The window had been busted by a smiling killer wearing spiked red leathers and enough steel to arm a mob, and Krill went at him screaming. From his vantage point, Hammet couldn't see much of what happened, just this guy in red dancing a bit and then Krill had joined Hammet on the floor. I's came streaming in, Talon and Giuseppe and Alto the Tall and a bunch of others, armed and furious, but before they could turn the tide an explosion echoed from the doorway, a billow of black smoke dissipating to reveal a strange cannon carried by a fierce-looking woman.

"Monster!" Hammet screamed, for surely this could only be a funk-born familiar of the leering child-devil who had knifed him. Hammet had lost a lot of blood by this point. "Demon!"

"He's got your number, Chisel," said the kid.

"Only in temperament," said Chisel, sending a second shot through Alto the Tall.

Things went on like that for a while, and then, between the boom and the man in red's cutters, suddenly there weren't no I's left, Silo and Talon and Giuseppe and all the rest strewn about the lobby like the toys of a spoiled Uptown child.

"Did you see that entrance?" asked the man in red. "What timing! What dash!"

The kid retrieved his journal from where Krill had dropped it. "Yes, Ael, it was magnificent. Where's Hope?"

"Outside flirting with a junk seller," said Chisel.

"It's not just enough to do it; you gotta do it pretty," said Ael, cleaning his cutters.

Hammet supposed Ael was talking to himself until a flash of color streaked in through the windows and began to squawk agreement: "Do it pretty! Do it pretty!"

"Bacon and Bliss," Hammet said, "a hypebird!"

"Sweet, right?" asked Ael.

Chisel made her way to the lift, and when the up button didn't respond she pried open the control box and began to splice together its nest of wires.

The kid opened the lobby door for a short, pretty girl his bare senior in age, caramel skin and very black hair. She wrinkled a button nose. "I hate the smell of boom," said Hope.

"It was underhanded, that last throw!" Ael told his hypebird. "And I had to draw it from my offside!"

"Fast as lightning!" the hypebird agreed.

The lift opened, and they all filed in.

"Wait!" yelled Hammet, rapidly exsanguinating on the floor. "Wait!"

"Yeah?" asked the kid, popping his head out of the elevator.

"Who are you?" asked Hammet with his last words.

"I'm the Kid," said the Kid.

A Brief Ascent

It was cramped inside the lift, but it got better after Ael tore out a roof pane and hoisted himself topside.

"You got him?" asked the Kid.

"I had him from three blocks out." Hope took a tin from her pocket, pulled out a battered wad of pink and started to chew. "I told you; I could've taken care of this without leaving the café."

"But then we'd never have gotten to share this experience," said the Kid.

"I'd have survived," said Chisel, reloading one chamber on her weapon and spinning to the next.

"You ready up there, Ael?" asked the Kid.

The hypebird fluttered back down and squawked, "Born ready!"

"Why did you buy him that thing?" Chisel asked.

"It keeps him entertained," said the Kid.

"Oh, I hear you, bald man," said Hope. She was not talking to Chisel or the Kid or the hypebird or anyone else in the elevator. "You're no mystery to Hope. Hope got the scuttle on you, bald man. Hope gonna make a meal out your brain."

"How long?" asked the Kid.

Chisel undid the clasp on a fat brass chronometer that hung from her belt. "Ninety tics."

The Kid counted thirty off silently, and then he said, "Go."

"Quit worrying," said Hope, crossing her arms against her chest and popping her gum. "I got this bagged like a pecker in a whorehouse."

So High As You'd Care to Be...

Once upon a time, from Bowery to Centre Street and from Canal up to Broome, there had lived a race of giants, warrior-kings what reigned supreme across Downtown. Long ages since they had passed, since before even the funk had come, but still their descendants held proud sway. Don DeAndre was a true child of the I's – a small, fierce, dark man, wise in counsel, terrible in war. From his office on the eighth floor, he awaited the assault untrembling.

"The Honey Swallowers?" Don DeAndre speculated.

"Nah," said the Button Man, Don's bodyguard and the I's champion. "You know how those fanatics are. They'd have sent a trumpeter and set a challenge."

Don DeAndre grunted. "How many?"

"Four," the confessor said. "No, three."

"Which is it?"

"Three," said the confessor.

"You sure?"

The confessor drew his fur cape tight over his shoulders. "Unequivocally."

Don DeAndre grunted. Don DeAndre did not like the confessor – his head like a pigeon egg, his smarm, his power to control the minds of others. Most especially, Don DeAndre did not like the hundred in bonds he paid weekly to enjoy the confessor's presence. Don DeAndre did pay the confessor, of course. Everyone who was anyone kept one on retainer – an expensive armistice, but it beat the alternative, and just then Don DeAndre felt happy for the back-up.

A guard opened the office door. "They're coming up the elevator."

"We got people on the stairs?" asked the Button Man.

"We got people on the stairs."

"The elevator might be a trick," said the Button Man.

"I just said we got people on the stairs."

"Say it again," said Don DeAndre.

"Again," said the guard.

"You tell the boys anyone got boom is free to use it," said the Don. "I won't be docking wages for loose fingers."

"Got it," said the guard.

There were twenty-two floors in the I's headquarters – at least, there were that many buttons on the elevator – but Don DeAndre kept his office on the eighth floor. The I's were heavy hitters, sitting members of the Council since your momma was in bloomers, and few among them had gone any higher. Once, on a dare the Button Man had climbed all the way to the twelfth, but even he wasn't mad enough to visit the false thirteenth, not with the funk hovering close overhead.

"Could be the Widow Makers," said Don DeAndre, "or the Anarchs."

"Could be a lot of people," said the Button Man. He had a chest like a keg of house brew and carried an axe twice as large as any of his soldiers'. "We'll keep one alive to tell us."

"I assure you, whomever it is will be spilling their secrets soon enough," said the confessor. "For a graduate of the Cloister like myself, it's nothing to make a man offer up his innermost confidences. Such invaluable assistance, I might add, is impossible to put a price on, although after this we might well need to reneg–"

He began screaming then, seamlessly between syllables, then dropped to his knees and shoved his fingers into his face, two through his sinuses and a thumb in the white glob of his eyes, howling louder and louder until the Button Man severed his neck, a quick spurt of red and the confessor's head rebounded off the wall.

"That was a lot of money wasted," said the Don, but he didn't have time to say anything else; one of their boom echoed from up front, and then a boom that wasn't theirs, and then a boom that was louder than either – much louder. So loud that it shattered the windows and dropped glass onto Broome Street.

The door opened to reveal a scene of bloody devastation only partly obscured by a wave of smoke, the ceiling wrecked from explosives, the I's reduced to component parts. The presumable architect of said destruction slipped in triumphantly, a big man in leathers twice stained red.

"Hiya!" said Ael. "I guess you must be the Button Man! I'm Ael! You ain't heard of me yet, but you would have."

The hypebird was swift in beside him. "Fight to the finish!" it crowed. "Fight to the death!"

A trickle of red leaked out of the Button Man's ear. He had dropped his axe when the boom erupted, but he picked it up slowly. "Take the back lift to the basement," he said.

"We go together," answered Don DeAndre, drawing a long knife from his belt.

The Button Man turned one thick hand on Don Deandre's shoulder and shoved him towards the back door. "Do it now!" he bellowed. "So long as you survive, we survive! The I's are eternal! Our thing never dies!"

They looked at each other. There wasn't enough time to say everything that needed to be said, but some portion of it, at least, was said with that look. Don DeAndre turned and bolted.

The Button Man watched him leave for a stricken instant, and then turned to face Ael.

"About that axe," Ael remarked, apparently indifferent to Don DeAndre's disappearance, "it's the wrong tool for the circumstance. Point of a thing like that is its *reach*, and how much use is that indoors? Plus, it's slow to get going. Easy way would be to do you quick-quick, get ahead before you can even put that thing into play. Or drop a knife in your side and run you around a while. You favor your left foot, yeah? Yeah." Ael carried two cutters and a hand hatchet and a bunch of sharp things to toss, not to mention a sling band wrapped around his forearm, a set of spiked knuckles, and a chain which swung from his waist, six and a half feet of bristling scrap steel. From off his back, he loosed a club with barbed wire curly-cued round the business end and took a quick practice swing.

"What about the knife?" asked the Button Man.

"Whoever got great doing things easy?"

...And Still a Bit Higher

Don DeAndre hit the button to call the service elevator, then turned to face whatever was coming. From back inside his office, the Button Man screamed and then stop screaming. Don DeAndre's hand closed white around the hilt of his knife. He'd be avenged. They'd lost a lot of good men, but not all of them; there were plenty of I's left to rally. In the basement far below, the ancient machinery whirred into motion, the lift rising, third floor, fourth. He was the Don, Don DeAndre reminded himself, heir to Vito and to blessed Lucky himself. Sixth floor, seventh. Revenge is best eaten as a leftover, or so the proverb went, and the Don would savor his. The door opened. He backed into it and pushed the $ button. The door closed, the elevator descended. First thing would be to set up another headquarters, get the word out to the rest of his brothers. So long as the Don was alive, they could still regroup.

And when the time came, they would pay back whoever had done this a hundredfold, a thousand, a hundred-thousand-fold. A moment, now, and he'd be in the basement and out to freedom, the first step in a savage saga of violence which would echo across the Island for generations – retribution so terrible as to become a byword from the East to the Huddy, something to curse by, something to frighten children, something to–

"Hell and High Towers," Don DeAndre gasped suddenly, "I'm going up."

Up! Up, up, up towards the funk! Don DeAndre tossed himself against the walls like a maddened animal, but the elevator rose indifferent, to the ninth floor, then the tenth. The Don thought to use the knife, but by that point he couldn't make his hands move. By the eleventh floor Don DeAndre's throat was raw from screaming and still it rose, to the twelfth floor and then the terrible thirteenth!

Silence.

Behind Door Number One

Back down on the eighth, Chisel was hunched over the lift's control box. "Are you sure this is wise?"

"Entirely," said the Kid, lighting a cigarette.

"Why not leave him up there?"

"Because we need to use the elevator."

"Why?"

"Because I said so," said the Kid.

"The big ones are never as good as you'd hope," Ael told his hypebird, "'cause it's speed, you see, it's all speed."

"Gotta be quick!" the hypebird agreed.

"Still, I'd have hoped he'd have lasted a little bit longer. Hardly worth the trip downtown." Ael began to shadow-box, a flurry of jabs and a quick hook. "That wasn't half bad with the knife, Kid. You've got the makings of a pretty good killer."

"Your opinion means the Island to me."

"You've got speed, which, as I said, is the most important thing. Nothing like me, of course, but then…"

"Nothing like you," the Kid agreed.

"Nothing like you!" the bird repeated, at that point a full quorum.

Hope came out of the Don's office feasting on a cud of bubblegum, her fingers garnished with gold. "You believe I found all of these in one drawer? How many rings does a man really need?"

The elevator began its descent.

"Ael," the Kid said.

"Remember that throw I made downstairs?" Ael asked his bird.

"Cleanest toss I ever saw!"

"Ael," the Kid snapped, "stop talking to the bird and get over here. Chisel, keep your cannon ready; and Hope, get behind Ael."

"All right, all right," Ael said, unsheathing his matched pair of cutters. "Maybe there's still time for this to get interesting."

Generally, a bath in the funk only means an inconceivably painful death. The unlikely alternative is much worse, and the Kid and his gang awaited it in nervous anticipation. Tics ticked past. Ael flourished his weapons. Chisel cocked back the hammer on her cannon. Ash grew along the Kid's cigarette. Hope's bubble swelled.

The doors opened.

Pop! went Hope's bubble.

"Shame," Ael said.

"You'd have had him easy," said the hypebird.

There was nothing recognizably human in the elevator. Though if you were to take the time to look, you might have an unstrung inch of intestine or perhaps a stray ear lobe.

"Gross," said Hope. "I'm taking the stairs."

"Hope," the Kid snapped.

They stuffed themselves into the lift, all scowling except for

Ael, who did not seem to mind the gore. His hypebird alighted on his shoulder. Hope spat her gum through the closing doors.

"Classy," said Chisel.

The Next Bright...

3

The Spreading Scuttle

The scuttle came to Abner Wiles, Senior Newsboy, early next bright. In a wide room on the first floor of the Times building, Abner and twenty-five other runners waited, notebooks out, pens inked. An editor entered, walked wordless to the chalkboard, and began to sketch.

There were gasps from the more junior staff, but Abner snarled, and they went silent. He'd have words with them later; that kind of bunk might pass at one of the rival establishments, but a runner for the Times ought to be able to trace out a second apocalypse without batting an eye. At the board, the editor continued with…

…and before he had finished the last symbol, Abner Wiles was up from his chair and out of the hallway and down the stoop into the street, a full fifteen tics ahead of his swiftest colleague.

Two blocks east and the Way opened, wide and crooked and true, and Abner lengthened his stride. Out on the Eff-Dee-Ar, a grinder with a decent cycle could triple his pace. But here in the heart of the Island, dodging overloaded pedicabs, roaming children, and desperate touts, it was sprint or be carried; and heading downtown on foot, there was no one to match Abner Wilkes.

"What's the scuttle, Abner?" asked one of a line of bow-legged pedalers shuffling north to JuiceTown, a bright spent on a stationary so some Enclave banker could take a warm bath.

"Got something good for us?" asked a peddler, carrying his store of kitchen knives and scoured pots up to Times Square. Abner ignored them both, as both had known he would, their request merely a form of greeting which Abner was too busy to answer with his usual abuse. The suggestion that a Senior Newsboy would betray his faith remained unthinkable, even in these sad times.

Just south of the Empire State Building, a crew of salvagers towed a four-door to some Uptown foundry, and Abner swerved down 6th to avoid the bottleneck. This meant leaving the safety of the Way, the sanctity of which was the Island's most potent taboo, but 6th Avenue, running north for sixty blocks, was the empire of the Honey Swallowers, all yellow paint and yellow flags, and the worst Abner risked was a sermon. To be a Newsboy was to have an infallible mental map of the Island, every block colored by clique, with notes in the margins explaining who was at war, who was about to be, what cowardly warchiefs or cuckolded spouses might hold some unjust grievance against the Times News Co., the enemies of a free press no less prevalent than before the coming of the funk.

Falling into his easy inimitable rhythm, Abner coasted south past the Flatiron, Honey Swallower-yellow disappearing once he hit 14th Street. The West Village was Antiquarian territory, tie dyed rags and the thick rank of budding flower, a riot of sound and color running all the way to cursed TriBeCa.

Abner had started to feel it a bit in the lungs, but all was forgotten as soon as Washington Square came into view, the neat rows of crops, kids practicing with wooden cutters, old men playing chess at two bits a game. Crake waited below the great stone arch, doing vocal warm-ups. Being the best Newsboy in the service, Abner was partnered with the best broadcaster, and there were grinders who came from as far as Alphabet City to hear their scuttle, passing by a dozen rivals because they couldn't stand a second-rate word. It was a responsibility Abner took seriously, and he had his sketch out before he had reached a full stop.

"Tall buildings and buried corpses," Crake said, looking over the symbols. "Are you sure you got this right?" But before Abner had caught his breath enough to curse – as if a Times Newsboy, let alone a Senior Newsboy, would have misdrawn a symbol – Crake leaped nimbly atop his speaking box and began to bellow. "Mass slaughter in I-town! Bloody knives and pierced bodies!"

Did they listen? Oh, they listened – the counting house clerks, the peddlers and shopkeepers, toughs coming back bloody from dimtime work, hunters carrying slings and snare traps, Boromen looking to trade for rubber or spokes, outright degenerates sinking into an early drunk. Crake roared the scuttle a second time, loud enough for the whole square to get to panting, and then he dropped into a practiced silence.

"Who done it?" asked an oysterman in from the Huddy.

"Yeah, who done it?" asked a Gansevoort Goon wearing a well-holed shirt.

"Before I tell you that, friends," Crake continued, "allow me to say a few words about Edaman's Mystery Meat."

A collective of good-humored groans from the crowds. Of course, this was to be expected; the Times had to make their scrip, same as anyone else, and you couldn't charge for the scuttle – how would that even work?

"*Mmmmmm*, that smells good!" Crake said, dipping into his Father Just Got Home voice. It was a common trope, one every broadcaster had down, though there were few that managed it with such gusto.

"Yeah, Mom, that's some good-looking dog!" Crake did a

passable Well-Behaved Son also – not as strong as some of his colleagues, but then, he was hampered by his natural baritone.

His Doting Mother, a low falsetto, was universally regarded as unequaled south of Midtown: "Not dog!"

Back to the Father: "Is it cat?"

"Not cat!"

"Pigs?"

"There aren't any pigs left, Dad!" yelled Crake the Son.

Crake the Father laughed.

"If they can't tell," said Crake the Wife, "why should I? Edaman's Mystery Meat! Because we don't have any more pigs!"

"I'll buy a tin, if you get on with your story!" said a bleary-eyed pedaler, just come off the first shift.

"I'll buy a vat!" said a scavenger on his way to the far reaches.

Crake returned to his full height and his normal speaking voice. "Just before dimtime last, the I's suffered an assault! Cutters and boom! Don DeAndre is missing and presumed dead!"

"Who done it?" asked a Wall Street Widowmaker.

"Yeah, who done it?" repeated a dung-harvester.

"Bet it was the Honey Swallowers," said the pedaler, finishing his cup of stoneroot tea.

"Excuse me, gentleman," said Crake, interrupting the interruption, "but I don't go up to where you work and kick the bike out from between your legs."

The crowd laughed and then shouted the men to into silence, and Crake resumed his rightful and unchallenged role. "As to who killed him," he let the moment run long, "there is no information at this time." One final, climactic groan of annoyance from the crowd. "But the Council will be making an announcement regarding the spot in their ranks left vacant by the death of Don DeAndre, and as soon as we know, so will you. Remember: if you aren't listening to the Times, you aren't hearing the scuttle."

It was big news! Bones in the tunnels, it was big news. Whoever managed to snatch up the I's territory would go from second tier to the top of the heap, knee deep in scrip, supping on roast dog and fresh oyster. Practically every soul in Washington Square took to wondering aloud as to who was responsible for the Don's death, and who would most benefit by it, because the Honey Swallowers were always hungry, but one could not discount Alphabet City out of hand.

The sole exception to the general bemusement sat on a far bench, a dark-skinned, plain-faced, lean-limbed woman in a battered trench coat and a faded hat. Her name was Gillian[1], and Gillian didn't wonder for nothing.

---

1   The Arbiter, the Banshee, the Doom What Came to TriBeCa. A nasty woman.

4

The Most Dangerous Man in the World-Writ-Large

The Way changes as you head south, the streets grittier and more vibrant, the Force leaving security to the local cliques. From Houston till Broome, the Devastators held sway, offering security and hawking the pleasures of their bordering bordellos. South to Walker, the Sacred Band took over, hairy men in black leather chains, both cliques sharing space without menace. If taboo and the certain penalty of the ban weren't sufficient guarantee of good behavior, pragmatism would serve. Operating protection on the Way was a guaranteed fortune, grinders from the far borders and Enclave tourists swarming to take part in the festivities.

Gillian turned east on Canal, stopping at a small brothel located between a dram shop and a woman selling grilled skewers of rat. The pair of catamites at the bar were not quite so hungover as to mistake Gillian for a john, and she passed into the back like a vapor. The lifts were of course juiceless, and she allowed herself the tiniest expression of displeasure before beginning her ascent.

The last time Gillian had been inside, the loft had been freshly painted and filled with furniture scavenged from an Uptown condo. The walls were still there, but the sofa and all the rest had been reduced to kindling, save for a mattress on which the author of this ruin lay in stupor, a pillow pressed tightly against his head.

"Swan," said Gillian. "Get up. It's Gillian."

"I know who it is," said Swan. What could be seen of his body was unimpressive: a faint coil to the biceps, but his stomach was sallow and unmuscled. "And I don't want to. Go away. Come back later."

"Get up," Gillian repeated.

Swan groaned.

"Where's your sword?" Gillian asked.

"Stop yelling."

"I can get a lot louder."

Shank Alice, owner/proprietor, so called for her long legs, not the weapon – though, incidentally, there was one in her boot – came in then, carrying a tray with a few slices of plain toast and a steaming pot of spoor blossom tea.

"Where's his sword?" Gillian asked.

Alice gestured to the walls, pocked like the face of a teenager. "We had to take it away from him. It's in the downstairs cabinet, next to the pigeon stock."

"Go fetch it."

"Ignore her," said Swan. "I'm not working now. Maybe next bright. Not next bright. Go away."

"He's cut off, you hear?" Gillian said to Alice.

"What rot you talking?" Swan asked. "I'm flush from clearing the Bruisers out of the Battery."

"That was ages ago."

"No it wasn't." A rustle beneath the blanket. "Was it?"

"He's done," Gillian said to Alice. "The teat is dry, savvy? No more smoke, no more drink, nothing until I say otherwise."

"Don't listen to her," Swan said.

"And as for you," Gillian continued, "you'd best get off your ass if you don't fancy a life of strict sobriety."

"Alice, if you don't bring me that tea I will kill you with my fingers," said Swan. "It wouldn't be the slightest trouble. Come to think of it, I'll kill you too, Gillian."

"You do either and there's no more money to get high with."

"I'm owed for the walls," Alice said.

"Fine," said Gillian.

"And the furniture."

"Fine." She turned back to Swan. "I'll need you by evening. Wring yourself out and wait for my message."

"No. It's loud out there. Aren't you too old to still be doing this nonsense? You don't need the money. Just buy a condo and rot away like the rest of us. It's pathetic, is what it is. Running around like a child."

"We can't all spend our lives comatose and reeking of piss. Be ready for my call come dimtime, or I'll come back with a brass band and shivaree you into the river."

Swan moaned more. Gillian pulled out a coil and slipped a chunk of change into Alice's waiting hands. "Bring him tea with just tea in it, and see if you can't force some bread down his throat. And by the Bear and the Bull, find his sword."

5

A Brief Recess

"I'm a loser," said Newton.

"Say it again," said Kev.

"I'm a loser," Newton said a second time.

Kev laughed.

"How big of a loser are you?" asked Doyle.

"A big one?" Newton guessed.

"You're such a loser that you don't even have any parents."

Even Kev blanched a little at the awfulness of this insult, but when the funk did not collapse down on him, he laughed again.

"Maybe," said Newton.

"They ditched you because you're such a loser," explained Doyle.

"I got it," said Newton. "Can I have my pen back?"

Kev broke it first, but not so badly that Newton couldn't use it if he choked up on his grip. They'd done a more thorough job with his sketchpads, but sketchpads also were replaceable. When Newton had first started at school, he had brought in one of his panel books, an antique that his uncle had bought him, where a champion in black fought a harlequin, only missing three pages. After stealing it, Doyle had told everyone he had used it to wipe his ass, though Newton suspected he had just sold it.

"That was a nice building I drew, though," said Newton to

himself. And indeed it had been: the tower of Virgil the Wise himself, the Great King of Old Hypernia. It was from that tower that Virgil's son, Cinder, wielder of the living flame, would lead the forces of light to victory over the dreaded Last Wyrm, though Newton had not yet gotten around to illustrating this part of his story.

"You can draw another tower," Newton consoled himself.

Serah pointed and laughed, and then Jeana did also.

6

The Hard Sell

Waiting outside of Gillian's[2] apartment building was the Mayor's aide, young and clever and spitting the predictable cloak-and-dagger patter. At brightest, the traffic into Midtown was its usual miserable morass, and their pedicab crawled up the Way. At least they didn't need to wait once they got to the Enclave, the patrolman on duty waving them inside.

Stone and pavement and scrap, the walls of the Enclave rose to the second story and ran from Amsterdam East to Park, and went north all the way to 120th. It was an oasis of civilization, a beacon of light in a sea of darkness, a parasite leeching off the rest of the Island. Inside the Enclave, there was a pigeon in every pot and the Force on every block. Through the gates was a world removed from Downtown's anarchy. The sidewalks were busy with smiling women and square-jawed men, but the phalt was left to wheel or the occasional hoof, and they made it to Columbus Circle in no time.

Alighting from the pedicab, Gillian was eyeballed and searched, then walked swiftly through the lobby and into an atrium beyond. Anywhere else, so much space would have been turned over for crop, but the Enclave had Central Park, enough green to feed themselves and half the Island, so the garden, bright wildflowers and a small pond, had been left undisturbed.

---

2   Scowling, hard-eyed, full of secrets.

The triumvirate waited for her beneath the boughs of a tree seeded before the coming of the funk. They were the three most powerful souls on the Island. The Commissioner was a square man wearing the same dull blue as when he had first walked a beat. The Pope hadn't had time to shave that morning, and wrapped in ceremonial mink, there was a sheen of sweat on her stubbled head. The Mayor was a good-humored fellow; his bushy beard was gay, his biceps were cheery, and the hard knobs of his knuckles were positively jovial.

They were the three biggest dogs on the Island. Which one was biggest? Good question. They spent a lot of time trying to figure out that one themselves.

"I'm not interested," said Gillian.

The Mayor laughed. The Commissioner bristled. The Pope remained inscrutable.

"Long way to come to turn down a job," said the Mayor.

"There's nothing you can say would convince me to take the badge a second time."

"Who said anything about the badge?" the Commissioner asked.

"I did," said Gillian. "I said I wouldn't take it."

"Surely, you would at least listen to our request? As a courtesy." The Mayor's smile threatened at any moment to spill over his face and onto the floor.

Gillian sat.

"No doubt you heard the scuttle," said the Mayor. "The I's were slaughtered last dim, the Don and all his top people. They're finished as an outfit."

"Since when has it been against the law to kill someone?" Gillian asked.

"Since the Council said so," said the Commissioner.

"What my esteemed colleague means," the Mayor continued, "is that, had the I's been defeated in honest combat, we would be welcoming their successors onto the Council with open arms. But this naked assassination has us all concerned."

"Sure," said Gillian, "the dagger's fine so long as you know the hand that's holding it. Not interested."

"Gillian, please. Perhaps this is just some up-and-comer, or a personal matter within the ranks of the–"

"Maybe he choked on a rat bone," Gillian interrupted. "Maybe he fell in the shower."

"See?" the Commissioner said. "Even she knows it's the Honey Swallowers[3] what did it."

"Maybe," Gillian countered, "or maybe the Widow Makers[4] started thinking their borders might look better a way's east. For that matter, Commissioner, it doesn't do you any harm for the I's to shake hands with their grandfathers. The counting houses, JuiceTown – going to be a lot of dry eyes at the Don's wake. Only certainty is that whoever did the I's could do the same to me."

"Five thousand in Goldman bonds," said the Mayor, "or your preferred currency."

"You could make it ten; what's it matter if I'm not around to spend it? Putting the ban on TriBeCa was enough for me. You'll can find some other sucker to play sheriff."

"Who said anything about the badge?" asked the Commissioner, and this second time it had a whiff of exasperation.

"Surely, Gillian, you would be willing to come on board as an adviser," the Mayor attempted, "simply to–"

"How do I know where this trail goes? Maybe at the end of it all, you heavies get to thinking that bygones are best left bygone, and I'm best left holding the bag. No thanks," Gillian said, standing once more.

The Mayor set something on the table just then: a star in white gold with the Council's crown worked into it. "Fifteen," he said.

---

3   Fanatics, worshipers of the Queen in Yellow, their domain running from
     Chelsea to the Upper West Side.
4   Of Wall Street and the surrounding territories.

"Twenty," Gillian answered, slipping the badge into her pocket.

"Done," said the Mayor. "I deputize you as Sheriff, the Council's left eye and right hand. No action performed in furtherance of your duties will be held against you, nor may any claim revenge afterward, on penalty of the ban itself."

"That's ten thousand up front," said Gillian.

"Fine," said the Mayor.

"I'll be in touch when I have a reason to tell you something," said Gillian.

"Very well."

"And don't think to be offering any unsolicited assistance. I'll have enough to worry about without dragging your cleverest halfwit around like a lead shadow."

"The badge is yours," the Mayor assured her. "We'll do nothing to hamper your efforts."

Gillian grunted and left without further word.

"You were carrying that?" asked the Commissioner.

"I assumed she'd ask for it," said the Mayor.

"I didn't expect you to offer it," said the Pope. It turned out her voice was a weak, reedy thing, less than her position seemed to warrant. "Who knows what trouble she'll get into as Sheriff? This is not the time to be turning over stones."

"This is exactly the time," said the Mayor. "We'll need something to appease our tourist."

The Commissioner looked nervous. "Why would he care what happened to the I's?"

"Because it's unexpected. He won't like that, and he'll blame us for it, and we'd best have something for him."

"And what do we do," the Pope began, scratching at her stubbly pate, "should the dog catch the cat we set on the rat?"

"Simple," the Mayor answered. "We poison the dog."

7

Stumbling Towards Tomorrow

Eight chambers hung like a honeycomb from the bottom of the Brooklyn Bridge, cages made of tarp and scavenged plastic, the very lowest of which was Chisel's[5]. In one corner a Null on a stationary bike peddled furiously. A twist of copper attached to the wheels carried his efforts to where Chisel tested the current against a pile of light bulbs, tossing dud after dud into the water below. The Nulls lived in dorms lofted in the bridge's suspensions, but full Bridge Brides had the honor of occupying individual chambers suspended from the structure itself. Apart from the bike and the table and a single chair, there was a mattress and a scratchy blanket, and things Chisel was building and things with which Chisel was planning to build.

Chisel found a functioning bulb, finally, and she hung it above her workstation. "You can look," she said, "but sweat on anything and I'll unman you."

Her Null wiped his face with his shirt and leaned over, legs jogging along untroubled. Not long past he had given up his old name and sworn the three oaths: to serve his superiors, to cherish knowledge above his own life, and to labor to hasten tomorrow. In that time, he had winnowed himself down to firm muscle, but learned few of the Bridge Brides' secrets, and he was anxious for whatever tidbits Chisel might offer.

5   Last seen killing the Don with an elevator.

She pulled a blackish cube from a pile at her feet and set it below the light. "This is from a kind of car that's different from most of them. There isn't really a better way to explain it. It's probably a battery. I think it's a battery, Adze thinks I've been sniffing funk. Adze has more muscle than brain; I know a battery when I smell one. But it doesn't look like the other batteries we have, and thinking on it a while, I still can't figure how it works, and so I'm going to break it open and see what's inside. This is what we've been reduced to, like busting up a bike wheel for the spokes." Chisel grabbed a hammer and shattered the black cube with one firm blow, then augured a moment with its metallic entrails.

"Hmph," she said. "This is not what I thought would be in here."

There was a rap from the roof, which was the floor of the cage above. "Chisel! Adze is calling!"

Chisel tossed the hammer onto the table and walked smoothly through a slit in the tarp that served as a door, catching hold of the neighboring rope ladder and clambering upward. Her Null was off his bike and after her a moment later, the towers of Downtown to one side, the great wall of funk to the other, and the waters of the East River waiting far below. Chisel was sure-footed as a squirrel, but the Null, given his relative inexperience, was cautious, and he came late to the bridge and the conversation.

"The guy from last time or another guy?" Chisel asked.

"Same guy." Adze was actually only twice as tall as Chisel or the Null, but with his multicolored mohawk, he looked taller. Overtop of his muscle was more muscle and a faded brown apron roughly the color of his skin. He wielded the maul, which hung at his side, like a ball peen hammer, and when he spoke, his voice could be heard from one end of the bridge to the other.

"I hate that guy," Chisel said. "He's too lazy to lean."

Walking funkways from Chisel's cell would take you to

the laboratories, where only senior members had access and strange sounds could be heard from bright through dim. The Null had never been funkways. The Null followed the two of them phaltways, past smithies and distilleries and workrooms, past the communal cafeteria and the hanging nets of greenery which fed it, past an armory with stout pikes and quick-firing X-bows. They were stopped three times before reaching the gates by Bridge Brides with questions for their leader – about tech or policy or personnel. Each time, Chisel listened closely, once nodding and once saying "no," and once saying "of course he thinks that, he's an idiot," and always moving on afterwards without a backwards nod. Just inside the walls of the compound, a pack of Adze's soldiers watched over a pedicab shipment and the men who had brought it.

The caravan guard wore a serviceable cutter and a patch on his jacket. "Same as last time," he said. Making his way up from the abutments had required a crooked jaunt through a labyrinth of barricades and sentries, false phalt, and snares. As a rule, it was his assistants' job to pedal the bike, but their laborious ascent had demanded he take a turn, and he looked winded and unhappy. "You want to go through it piece by piece?"

"What do you think?" Chisel asked.

"It's just that it's getting late, and I'd like to get to the Way before dim."

"Then you should stop wasting time."

The guard scowled harder but didn't argue, gesturing to his assistant to help unbox the merchandise while Chisel engaged Adze in a quick aside.

"You set that thing up with the hunter?" she asked.

"Yeah," said Adze.

"We'll go after this."

Adze grunted.

"You got something to say?"

"I said it, didn't I?" said Adze.

"And I ignored it. Remember, I'm a lot smarter than you are."

"What happened with that thing I told you wasn't a battery?"

"Rut a mutt," said Chisel.

Adze spat over the side, watched it tumble towards the river. "Smart isn't always right."

8

A Giant of a Man

Maryland Slim was a big fellow. His neck was big, and his cheeks were quite large. His fingers were like sausage links, his arms were like legs and his legs like the trunks of a tree. He had a fat philtrum. His eyelids were oversized. His tailored suit used enough fabric to rig a sailboat. His perfectly tied cravat was the size of a newborn babe. His hat – which, being a gentleman, Maryland Slim had hung on the side of his chair – was the rough radius of a manhole cover. When he had first sat down, Slim's chip stack had been of similar stature, though at present, it looked lamentably gaunt. "Raise thirty," he said.

"And fifty more on top of it," Shkreli said. Shkreli was a VP for the Wall Street Widow Makers, slick-haired and slick-tongued and slick with the cutter they'd made him leave at the door, house rules. He'd been on a hot streak since sitting at the table, the Bull filling out every flush and blessing him on the turn, his winnings rising like barricades.

Slim pushed in his fifty.

The dealer sweated and flipped over the seven in blood. Outside it was less bright, but inside 💰 🎩 it was always dimmest, the place busy with hatchet-boys and blade-carriers, courtesans of both sexes, dream merchants, second-rate prophets, first-rate conmen, so on and so forth, most all focused on the table and the game which was then reaching its climax.

"Not what you were hoping for, was it Slim?" Shkreli asked,

good fortune swelling an already rotund self-regard. "Nothing to save you there?"

"I'll raise you the table," said Slim.

"The table?"

"The table."

"Meaning everything that's on it?"

"Whatever you got."

"What I got is what I got," said Shkreli, "and it's a lot more than you got. Unless all that fat is resting on a mountain of change, you've no business–"

Slim's fingers tapped loud beside his desiccated stack, amethyst and sapphire and a dull diamond winking in the juicelight. "The rings."

"The rings?"

"The one on my pinky is worth a hundred, at least."

"First, I'd have to get them off those fat fingers of yours," said Shkreli.

"Jeffy?"

Jeffy was the bartender.

"Yeah, Slim?"

"Bring me a knife," said Slim.

"Slim," the dealer began, "the house can cover–"

"It's no trouble," Slim said.

Jeffy came back from the kitchen with the knife they used to joint dogs.

"On from the pinky," Slim said, "until you decide we're square."

Gillian[6] entered just then, though no one noticed.

Shkreli ran his hands through his hair, slicked back with fish oil, as was the style in FiDi at the time. "If you was anybody else, I'd say you must be holding pocket commissioners; 'cause who's got the stones to bluff themselves to stubs? And the answer is: Maryland Slim." Shkreli pushed at the base of one of his towers,

---

6   Sheriff once more.

and a shower of chips scattered over the stained cleaver. "I'm going to give your rings to my girl, and fry your fingers up for supper." He turned over his cards, revealing a second Pope to join her sister on the table, and it was the rare soul in the bar who did not think Shkreli would make good on his boast.

A drop of sweat slipped free from Slim's nose and broke against the green below. "Not commissioners," he said, flipping over two mayors, gold crowns and hard eyes.

The bar hooted. The bar hollered. Shkreli went from shock to despair to fury as if shuffling through a deck. "Balls of the Bull," he spluttered, "this is garbage. You don't have any business sitting at an honest game."

"You knew who he was when you bet," the dealer said.

"Why don't I?" Slim asked, ignoring the dealer.

"You know why; wouldn't let a confessor play, either," said Shkreli.

"I'm not a confessor," Slim said, smiling, picking at his tangled black mane.

"No, but you're a head case. How do I know you didn't poke into my brain, make me go all in on that last hand?"

"What would the fun be in that? The point of gambling is that I might lose – not often, certainly not to Downtown dimwits don't know skill from luck, but sometimes; and when I do, I smile graciously and find a friend to buy me a drink. I could have made you go all in, though. For that matter, I could make you stuff phalt in your pockets and walk smiling into the East River. I can do a lot of things." Slim's chair sagged reverentially. "I'm Maryland Slim."

Shkreli exited amid general jubilation. Slim tipped the dealer a small fortune and told him to bring over his winnings with his supper, though it required several congratulatory drinks among the crowd of well-wishers before he could join Gillian at his regular corner table.

"Gillian," he said, with a perfect bow of greeting. "A social visit, I assume?"

"No doubt."

"Nothing to do with the scuttle."

"Did you hear the scuttle, locked inside a bar?"

"We send a boy out for it. 'I's go blind,' was how the News At High Bright phrased it."

"They must have had that one gathering dust."

"Yeah."

Their conversation was interrupted by the arrival of two dog haunches crisped in garlic, a mountain of potatoes and onions, an admirable stack of fry bread, a bucket of the house brew, half a dozen boiled pigeon eggs, various sorts of pickles, and a bond for four hundred and twelve in change, redeemable at 💰 🔷's preferred counting house.

"Say for the sake of argument," Gillian said, "it did have something to do with the scuttle."

"I'd wonder what the scuttle had to do with me."

"Say it didn't. Say it had something to do with me."

"I'd say I was getting lost in hypotheticals." The fingers Slim had nearly lost dabbed up a bit of fry bread in grease and brought it to his mouth.

"I'll get concrete: feel like making money?"

Slim gestured at his check. "Not really."

"It's light work," Gillian promised. "I just need you to come along and give me a read on the scene."

"And after that?"

"Probably nothing."

Slim severed a piece of dog and swirled it in gravy. "Where have you been? I figured you'd have found me by now."

"Midtown traffic. Plus, I had to rustle up Swan."

"I thought you said it was light work?"

"I did, but you didn't believe me."

"I've got a party later in Greenwich."

"Those things don't get started till dimmest; you'll be fashionably late."

"Doesn't do to arrive at a place on time," Slim acknowledged, swallowing a pigeon egg, "but my retainer's doubled."

"I thought you said you didn't care about money."

"I said I didn't *feel* like making money – that doesn't mean you shouldn't give me any."

"You're a greedy bastard, Slim."

Maryland Slim tilted back his cup of house brew, guzzling till it was gone. "What can I say? I've got a lust for life."

9

Several Discussions

The Way ends at the Bull and the Bowling Green, and just past that was 😵🐦, an institution since Ahmed Sigverson and the Mayor before the Mayor before this Mayor, that Mayor what got murdered by his wife. Marble steps and frescoed walls, a warren of bars and stages and private rooms gussied up with brass railings and heavy carpets. True, the decor had faded, and all the hip young things had long since moved on – nothing lately but counting house clerks and second-rate courtesans – but all the same, there is something to say for tradition.

For generations at the Drunken Hen, in juice-lit alcoves and above battered porcelain urinals, the fate of Downtown had been decided, hushed conversations which would reshape the Island, several of which were going on just then:

In the South Gallery

The three Stuymen squeezed into the booth beside the Kid[7]. They looked like they all do in Stuyvesant Town: flat heads and broad shoulders – there aren't but so many parents in those towers.

"It's still on," said the first Stuyman.

"There's just been a hiccup," said the second.

---

7   Sower of discord.

"The elders are nervous," said the third.

"They want to call another quorum."

"We've got the votes."

"It won't be a problem."

The Kid took a tiny sip from the glass of house brew in front of him.

"It's just a formality."

"Stuy word is solid."

"Stuy keeps its promises."

"Stuy don't rattle."

The Kid was not really one for drink.

"Just a couple of dims."

"Not much longer."

"Good as done."

The Kid pushed over his glass in the direction of the Stuy boys. One and Two got away, but Three found his lap soaked for his sluggishness.

"Walk to Jersey!"

"Why did you do that?"

"Bust up your face to match your hair!"

"Checking to see you weren't statues," said the Kid.

"What you're asking–"

"It's never been done before–"

"Ruined my pants, by the–"

"Nothing's been done until someone does it, and then everyone looks round and wonders why they didn't do it first. How long has the feud between Peter Cooper Village and Stuyvesant Town been going?" the Kid asked rhetorically.

"Forever."

"Since the funk come."

"Forever."

"Forever till next bright," said the Kid. "Then things get decided, one way or the other. You don't want what I'm selling, I can peddle my wares to your neighbors up north. Make sure you thank your graybeards when the Coop are sleeping in your beds."

Number Three leaped furiously at the Kid, but One and Two restrained him.

"We'll get it."

"It's a deal."

"Arrogant, funk-huffing–"

"Good," said the Kid. "And no more of this nonsense about your sainted grandfathers. Your grandfathers done had plenty; they ate until their stomachs couldn't stand it. Don't let them feast off your plate likewise. You play your hand right, it'll be you they talk about, your name that rings out, not some wrinkly old sack of spoor hasn't been able to hold a pike since forever." He turned suddenly towards the bar. "Hell and High towers," he said.

In the West Gallery

Used to be there was a whole brass band in the West Gallery, a proper twelve-piece, folks dancing and laughing – Uptown folk too, Enclave folk, people with class. Now they just let anyone inside, any cheap grinder or scuzzy hunter, like the one over in the corner; probably try and pay in rat pelt.

"You have to order if you want to sit," said the bartender to Hem[8].

"I'm waiting on someone," said Hem.

"You can wait while you drink."

Chisel[9] came in then, with Adze[10] and Chisel's Null[11] in tow. They stood for a moment in front of a mural, long-haired cavalry with spears pursuing the Bull through vast fields of green, a yellow disc above. Adze pointed at Hem, and then they all headed over.

---

8   Hunter turned harbinger of the second apocalypse.
9   Leader of the Bridge Brides.
10 Head of security for the Bridge Brides.
11 The lowest ranking member of the Bridge Brides; at current, undeserving of a name.

"You him?" Chisel asked.

"Maybe," said Hem. "What do you want him for?"

"If you're going to stay at the counter, you need to order something," growled the bartender, who felt association with Hem was sufficient to warrant discourtesy.

Chisel wasn't paying attention. "I hear you have a story."

"Don't know why three of you had to come," Hem said. Hem had sold his traps and most of his lures, but he had not yet sunk so low as to sell the man-killing knife on his hip. "Why you so interested in this, anyhow?"

"You don't order, you gotta go," said the bartender.

"Repeat that," said Adze.

"My reasons are my business," Chisel told Hem. "You don't need to know my reasons; you just need to see my change."

"Repeat that," Adze repeated angrily, swelling over the increasingly frightened bartender.

"I don't owe you nothing, girl," Hem began reaching for his weapon, "and you'd best–"

"Four house brews," interrupted the Null, "and then you can find somewhere else to stand." The Null had a deep voice, and a handsome face. The Null would be something once he stopped being nothing.

"That scrip, bond or–?" the bartender began.

Nulls weren't allowed money, but Adze slapped a disc of loose change on the table. "You bite it and I'll break your jaw," he said, and the bartender flustered off.

"What was it made you decide to meet here?" Hem grumbled.

"We don't come to FiDi a lot," said the Null. "Don't worry about it."

"This place sucks."

"It's not our scene neither."

"Uppity bartenders, treating you like trash 'cause you had a bad run."

"There's an idiot every block," said the Null.

Said idiot returned with their drinks, then skedaddled.

The house brew at ⊗🐤 was dark and rich, and Hem drank his as if searching for a prize hidden in the bottom.

"What about this story?" Null asked.

"No one liked hearing that story," said Hem. "First they laughed, then they got angry."

"Last pays for all," said Chisel. "Tell us about the snake."

"Never said it was a snake," said Hem. "Said it *looked* like a snake. Wasn't a snake. Don't know what it was." He had finished his house brew, so Chisel passed him hers. Then she uncoiled three discs off her change ring.

"Start from the beginning," she said.

"I was following this bitch uptown," Hem began, "near the GeeDubya..."

Back in the South Gallery

"He's with the Anarchs, and he uses a club." Ael[12] was at the counter. He was supposed to be keeping an eye on the Kid, but he'd gotten distracted by his conversation.

"A cutter," said Standford. Standford worked middle management at a counting house, and probably should not have been drinking distil before dimtime.

"No, he doesn't."

"Not a cutter," the hypebird[13] agreed, pecking at a bag of popcorn.

"He uses a war club," said Ael. "And anyway, he's only got a couple of kills. So even if he used a cutter, the suggestion of mentioning him as one of the best in the Island, like he was Swan himself–"

"You guys are like a cult or something," said Standford. "Swan this, Swan that, Swan can walk to Jersey. If he was so good, why didn't he never make it to the Mad?"

---

12 Wears red, likes weapons.
13 Enthusiastic avian supporter of [12].

"Hell and High Towers," the Kid cursed from where he sat in a corner with the three men from Stuy. "I gotta go." He rose and slid to the counter and did his best to interrupt the brewing trouble. "Say, Ael–"

"None of the best ones made it to the Mad," Ael continued, growing angry. "Any real fan knows that. Bighead what axed his way through Meat Packing, that Boudicca whose Boudicca got killed by the Force and so she took her bow up to Carnegie and started wasting blues till they had to use boom on her, all three of the Isley Brothers; didn't none of them ever get on the court!"

"Don't let this old idiot–" the Kid attempted.

"Say word!" advised the hypebird.

"The Mad is for second-raters," Ael continued, swelling like a spider bite, "for never-will-bes! No real killer would ever lower themselves to such spectacle."

"Say word!" the hypebird repeated.

"I know this place is a rathole," said the Kid, "but I'd rather not get banned and–"

"Talking about Swan while you sit with a pedi tire for a gut, probably go bust if I made you run up a staircase – Swan what never lost a single fight, Swan what never even been touched, not once, and who knows how many kills he's got?"

"Say word!" the hypebird insisted.

"Word!" Standford exclaimed, frightened enough at this point to swear that his mother was a Maltese. "Word. Swan's it. Swan's the one and only."

"Actually, I'm a little bit better," Ael said, "but still, you got no business talking him down. What was that, Kid?"

"I was saying we're done. I'll meet you outside."

"Oh," said Ael. "Okay. Just let me pay for the popcorn."

"Better than Swan!" insisted the hypebird as it finished off the bag, "best on the Island!"

Outside the Bathrooms...

They bumped into each other. "An unlikely coincidence," said the Kid.

"What's that supposed to mean?" asked Chisel.

"It means what are you doing here?"

"Grabbing a drink," said Chisel. "What are you doing here?"

"Likewise," said Kid.

They glowered a while.

"Still on for..." the Kid began.

"Yes."

"Fine."

"Fine."

10

Manifest Destiny

They marched in perfect lockstep down 41st Street, boots echoing against the phalt. First the pages, scattering yellow confetti and blowing chartreuse plastic horns; then the shield-bearers, their master's eponymous aegises on their backs, war clubs in their hands; then the Paladins themselves, wearing gold-painted lamellar and holding long swords aloft; and finally the priestesses with some of the Queen in Yellow's lesser relics – a shoe she had worn, a scrap from a dress, her image gilded in pure leaf atop a pole covered in the same.

Left to defend against this surging sharp-edged river were twenty-odd Midtown Maulers, some wearing indigo leathers, the others only T-shirts of faint purple, all carrying a mixed variety of things pointed and things sharpened. A boy judged too young to fight kept up a shrill dirge on his recorder, but apart from him and a few scattered grunts, the Maulers awaited death silently.

As the Honey Swallowers crossed over 6th Avenue, the front ranks executed a quick turn, aligning on the sidewalk. Unspooling from the heart of it, surrounded by a lifeguard carrying halberds, came Alvin, War Chief of the Honey Swallowers, first servant of the Queen in Yellow. The man almost single-handedly responsible for making the Honey Swallowers masters of the West Side from South Riverside Park to Chelsea had short hair and big shoulders and didn't really look like anything – unless his eyes were open, in which case, he looked like a great force bearing down on you. "All hail the Queen in Yellow!" he cried.

"All hail the Queen in Yellow!" roared the assembled, loud enough to shift the edges of the funk.

Behind their barricade, the Maulers held firm. "You sure you brought enough men, Alvin?" asked their War Chief. "A full muster to deal with our little corner of the Island? I guess the Hive doesn't feel so sure of themselves unless they fight you ten to one."

"Your insults ring hollow," said Alvin. "We will face you man to man, without use of boom or clever tactics, steel against steel, nothing more."

"Why come at all?" The Mauler's War Chief towered over the barricade, and there were strong men who could not have raised his great cleaving cutter. He chewed anxiously over a fork of his beard. "The Queen in Yellow can't rest without adding five blocks more to her empire?"

"It is hers already!" shouted the high priestess, a woman of prodigious and withered bosom. "All the Island, from the Battery to the Devil, and any who stand upon it without giving her due worship are trespassers!"

"All hail the Queen in Yellow!"

"All hail the Queen in Yellow!"

"If it's a matter of tribute–" the Mauler's War Chief began.

"What cares the Queen in Yellow for scrip?" the High Priestess interrupted. "And what care her servants for ought but the cares of the Queen in Yellow?"

"The only tribute which interests the Queen in Yellow is the willing, permanent submission of your soul," said Alvin. "Were you to drink the lemonade, I would hold you tight and call you brother, I would anoint your head with all the honey of the Hive. But with blasphemy, there can be no quarter."

"All hail the Queen in Yellow!"

"All hail the Queen in Yellow!"

Alvin snapped his fingers, and a page lifted aloft an oversized chronometer. "You have five tocs to come to a decision; may the Queen in Yellow grant you wisdom."

On the Island, war was a public spectacle, and it took a while for Gillian to push her way to the front. In the crowd were not only the Maulers' civilians – shopkeepers and peddlers who would soon be paying protection to the Honey Swallowers – but tourists following the commotion in from the Way, gamblers offering prop bets on the action, vendors hawking roasted oysters and sweetened distil, and of course, scouts from every gang in the surrounding territories: the West Forty Thieves, the Garment District Gallants, even a lieutenant from the South Chelsea Chosen, all anxious for a look at the force which would soon be brushing against their borders.

Someone noticed Gillian, and shortly thereafter, two severe-looking soldiers in yellow arrived to escort her to the front.

"War Chief," said Gillian.

"Gillian," said Alvin.

"It's Sheriff, in fact."

"A sheriff can only be made with the full consent of the Council," said Alvin, "and I would surely recall having offered it."

"Then you object?"

Alvin shrugged. "No. The Mayor is bent, but he is not a fool. He had no right to give you the badge, but it's in the Hive's interests to have our innocence proved as swiftly as possible, and you are the best one to handle it."

"Innocence," said Gillian. "I don't run into a lot of that."

A cat lounged on a window ledge on the second story of a neighboring building. Behind the barricade, the Maulers sweated, cursed, prayed, swallowed hard, muttered to one another, lamented their sins and hoped for the chance to add to their tally.

"The Hive had no role in the tragic death of Don DeAndre," said Alvin.

"Laying it on a bit thick, aren't you? The Don getting done leaves you with a free hand Downtown. You wouldn't be so quick swallowing these small fish if the I's were still swimming about."

Before Alvin could respond, the clock began to ring, and he turned back towards the barricades and repeated his ultimatum in a voice which rattled all the way to 7th Avenue. "The Queen in Yellow has waited long enough," he said. "She will have worshipers in her choir, or skulls set at her feet."

The Mauler youth had stopped playing his recorder. A near twin, barely any older, held a trembling spear beside him. It took a stretch for their War Chief to answer. "My father was a Mauler," he said, gaining a gradual crescendo, "and his father, and my mother's kin likewise. I'll die before I betray them. The only thing I've got for your Queen in Yellow is fresh spoor."

"As a man," said Alvin, "I applaud your courage. As a servant of the Queen in Yellow, I'll have your limbs distributed to the four corners of your former domain, so that your civilians learn the consequences of blasphemy."

"Walk to Jersey, you self-righteous runt!"

Alvin began a slow clap in response, one that was soon picked up by the army of men which he led until all the block rung in perfect syncopation. The Paladins in the front row echoed it, banging their long swords against their shields and marching forward to the beat, a wall of steel closing around the Maulers.

"You do me a disservice, Sheriff," said Alvin, turning back to Gillian, his voice loud enough to be heard above the clamor. "I desired nothing more than to come to grips with the I's – oh, the plans I had formed, the strategies, the feats I might have accomplished in the Queen's name!"

The Mauler's War Chief did not wait for his line to be breached, leaping nimbly over the barricade and burying his great two-handed cutter in the thick kite shield of a Paladin, who buckled from the blow but remained upright.

"This is how the Hive makes war," said Alvin, "for the Queen's glory, chanting the Queen's name. I mourn the death of Don DeAndre as sincerely as his own mother, for now I will never be able to offer his skull to She whom I serve."

"All hail the Queen in Yellow!" barked the high priestess who had maneuvered her way into the corner of the conversation.

With his cutter still trapped in the kite shield, the Paladins were quick to surround the Mauler's War Chief. He died bloody and screaming, clutching a bubble of pink intestine for long tics before being put out of his misery.

"May the Queen in Yellow guide your hand," Alvin blessed Gillian, "and crown your efforts with swift justice."

"All hail the Queen in Yellow!" agreed the high priestess.

"Glory to her name," added Alvin.

Over the barricades the Paladins scrambled, the Maulers failing to show the mettle of their War Chief, screaming for the far corners of their modest territory, the Hive swarming after them, onward, ever onward.

11

Up, and Down

Dim had gathered before an overtaxed pedicab finally deposited Maryland Slim beside a grumbling Gillian in front of what had been, the dim prior, the headquarters of the Eternal I's. Guarding the scene were two members of the Force[14], armed with pikes, and one of the Mayor's aides[15], dressed fine and carrying a swell cutter and a cannon clean enough to perhaps hold boom. A tabby cat scowled from a windowsill. Gillian flashed her badge and they let her into the lobby.

"Damn, Gil," Slim said. "How'd you talk them into giving you that?"

"I'm persuasive."

"Getting desperate, are they?"

Gillian didn't answer. Inside the lobby was a lot of dried blood, but at least the Council's goons had gotten rid of the bodies. The elevator opened, and out from it, hairless and wearing their heavy furs, came the Pope[16] and her lifeguard.

"Can't catch a break with both hands," muttered Gillian. Then, "Hold the door!"

But for once, no one seemed to be listening to Gillian. The

---

14 The Enclave's army, with the Commissioner at the head.
15 Self-explanatory.
16 Head of the confessors, member of the Council, can do strange things with her brain.

lift closed, and the Pope and her people eyeballed Maryland Slim like huskies fighting over a hydrant.

"What is the apostate doing here?" she asked.

Slim's bushy mane fluttered pleasantly. "Beautiful word, apostate. Has such a pleasant feeling coming off the lips."

"Maryland Slim is assisting me in the investigation that you insisted I conduct," said Gillian.

"The Mayor insisted," said the Pope, "I sat silently."

"In any event, what are *you* doing here?" asked Gillian.

"A confessor was among the victims upstairs. The Cloister is conducting its own inquiry into his death."

"I'll pour a house brew out in his honor," said Maryland Slim.

"You should be more careful with whom you associate," the Pope told Gillian. "Any assistance you need, the Cloister would be more than happy to provide. Better then trusting to this... dropout."

"Those who can't do..." said Maryland Slim.

As protection, the Pope had a cardinal and two bishops, enough backup to walk to Wall Street, but Slim seemed unimpressed.

"You'd best watch your tone," said the Pope. "We agreed to suspend your sentence as a courtesy to the Sheriff, but the Cloister has a long memory."

"Long, perhaps, but spotty." said Slim." As I recall the circumstance, you were tired of your people washing up in the Huddy and Gillian was kind enough to offer a save face."

"Whatever the specifics," Gillian said, growing exasperated, "I did get the two of you to agree to a truce, and I've got some other things to take care of right now. And for that matter, Slim, so do you. Professional obligations take priority over personal enmity." Gillian excused herself to call the elevator.

"Her abiding code," Slim said, smiling. "And she's right, I'm on the clock – but I'm not always. You can find me at Money Talks after dimmest, assuming you've forgotten what happened to the first six of your colleagues came knocking."

"Rotund rodent," snapped one of the bishops.

"Keep a leash on your pup, Pope," Slim said, "or I'll muzzle the lot of you."

The elevator buzzed unhappily at the delay. "Slim!" Gillian snapped. "You're wasting juice and time."

"It's the I's juice."

"But it's my time."

Slim tipped his hat and slid past the Pope etc. with surprising grace.

"Was that necessary?" Gillian asked when Maryland Slim had finally strutted into the elevator.

"I've got a reputation to keep up," said Slim, scratching at his double chin.

Gillian grunted. There was no call to judge the obsession of another. She had her own, after all.

"They don't have any idea who killed their confessor," Slim added.

"How do you know?"

"Because I don't have any idea either, and I'm a lot better at this than they are. There's sort of a… style to how each of us works, like a signature they leave behind. This one is odd. Different."

The eighth floor was in ruins, more holes than there were ceilings or walls.

"That's a lot of boom," Slim observed.

Gillian saw no need to confirm the obvious. She made a slow circuit of the room. "You think a scattergun could do this?"

"No."

"Or a hand cannon?"

"Nope."

The Don's office had been stripped predictably clean of its valuables, first by neighborhood scavengers, then by the Force who had chased them out. Nothing to be seen there. Gillian headed to the service elevator, opened it, and spent a while peering at the remains of Don DeAndre.

"They sent him into the funk?" said Slim.

"Looks like it."

"That's a bad way to go."

"Not easy," Gillian agreed.

"Who was it knew how to jury-rig the elevator?" Slim asked.

"Same person was using that boom, if I had to guess. Force say, when they got here, it was in the basement."

"Meaning whoever did this used it to get back down?"

"That's how that would work."

"The things I do for you," said Slim, following her into the lift, careful to keep his suit jacket away from the red-stained walls. "How did things go with the Honey Swallowers?"

"Protestations of innocence and the usual cant."

"Yellow is a hideous color."

"Be slow to tell them that."

"Void bacon and piss champagne!" Slim cursed all a sudden.

"What's wrong?"

"I stepped in gum."

"Just scrape it off."

"You can never really get gum off your shoes," Slim, said with sad wisdom. "There's always some little bit left behind."

The juice was down in the basement. Gillian took a torch out from her trench coat, swiveling it about until they found footprints leading through the dust. Slim did his best to clean his shoe with his handkerchief, and then they followed the tracks into a side room and up to an open manhole cover.

"Have fun, Gil," Slim said.

Someone other than Gillian might have cursed. "Can you make contact with Swan?"

"Depends on how smashed he is."

"You'll have to make do. Give me a buzz in..." Gillian thought through the near future. "Ninety tocs or so."

"Will do," said Slim as he helped her into the sewer.

"And don't get so occupied that you forget."

"A veritable monument to sobriety," Slim promised.

The trail led through an access chamber and into another tunnel, much wider and with rails running through the middle. Gillian scanned about a bit, then sighed and turned her torch off and settled down to wait.

It wasn't long. First came the faint rustle of their movements, then the smell of half-tanned leather and fungi and something else, something dank. Presenting no threat and offering no resistance, still, it was a hard tumble Gillian took into the muck, and they weren't careful in trussing her.

The light from her stolen torch revealed a familiar face. "Hello, Gillian," said Daedalus. "Can you give me any reason not to eat you?"

12

Box Seats at the Mad

In attendance for the main event were representatives from almost every clique on the Island: Two Bridge Twins and some Felons from Five Points, Widow Makers come uptown in customized pedicabs, Honey Swallowers despite the Queen in Yellow's disapproval, a dozen Boudiccas howling against the railings, even a few boys from Stuytown and the Coop, who had scraped themselves away from the feud for an evening. Registered soldiers got in free, but the rest of the Island had to buy a spot in the cheap seats – counting house clerks cheering off a shift, Uptown beaus and their squealing gals, Enclave tourists with their grandchildren, peddlers, pedalers, fortunate hunters of dog, gamblers smiling and unsmiling, oystermen, tillers, courtesans, catamites, and in a private room at center court, the Mayor and Mr Simpson.

"Should be a good show," the Mayor said. "Three on three, a real grudge match. The Stanton Street Slayers claim one of the Anarchs stole a woman. They were set to unfurl banners, but we convinced him to keep it a matter between champions. That big clubber with all the hair is the one to watch – a real up-and-comer."

"I prefer tennis."

"Excuse me?'

But Mr Simpson did not clarify.

"Would you like something to drink?"

"No."

"Something to eat? My chef prepared a cut of poodle roasted in garlic."

Mr Simpson shuddered, and the Mayor was saved further awkwardness only by the buzzer and the roar which followed. The court was shifted before every match, barricades and barbed wire and sudden breaks in the wood, and the combatants entered the maze warily from opposite sides.

"We're handling it," the Mayor assured him.

"Handling what?"

A too-bold Anarch fell victim to a jaw trap, a *snip* and a scream and space below the knee. The crowd erupted in enthusiastic disapproval, though Mr Simpson ignored it, as disinterested in human flesh as he was canine.

"It's nothing to be concerned about," the Mayor said.

"What isn't?"

"Don DeAndre had many enemies."

"Something happened to DeAndre? Should I send flowers?"

The first clash of arms, the long-haired Anarch pinning a Slayer against a wall, a feint and then not a feint and then it was all evens.

"He was murdered," the Mayor said.

"Gosh," said Mr Simpson.

"Last dim."

"In one of these big fights you guys are so keen on?"

"Not in open combat. An assassination."

"Golly."

"Things happen, Mr Simpson. The Island is a dangerous place."

Wandering too close to the boards, an Anarch got a bottle broke over his head, courtesy of a Stanton supporter, or just a fellow eager with a bottle. The Anarch howled and jabbed his spear at a likely target, and the team of Force working security came sprinting down the aisles, clubs swinging.

"It doesn't seem so rough to me," said Mr Simpson.

The wounded Anarch, stumbling and skull-shocked, proved easy prey for the Slayers, up then two to one. A virtually insurmountable lead, though the remaining Anarch seemed keen to surmount it, appearing suddenly to foul his club off an enemy's skull, the sound echoing into the nosebleeds.

"In any event, Mayor, I'm pleased to hear you so confident. I can see how it would be a source of concern for you, Don DeAndre being a member of your little... consortium."

"We've contracted out the investigation to a specialist. I've every confidence in her abilities."

A fight for the ages! A champion in the making! Oh, to be in the Mad that dim! Almost worth the price of the house brew.

"I sure hope it works," said Mr Simpson. "Where I come from, it's bad business to let people kill people you're in business with."

Honest fans, whatever their personal allegiance, admired the Slayer for his boldness in making the cast, with his spear better suited to melee and a miss meaning certain death.

"I gather our ways seem a bit savage, to you, Mr Simpson, but they suit us well enough, and–"

"Yes, that's what they seem like, savage. Savage, exactly; savage, as in barbaric, idiotic, sub-fucking human, your monkey parliaments and delusions of grandeur. Poodle meat, for cunt's sake. I don't give a rat shit about Don DeAndre, and I don't give a rat shit about anything else here either. The only thing I give a rat shit about is the tunnel. The rest of you can chop yourself into mince, if it makes you happy. What are you waiting for?"

Back on the court, the victor held a severed head aloft, waiting for the official verdict, him and a capacity crowd. The Mayor grabbed his megaphone and delivered it. "We find for the Stanton Street Slayers! Alphabet City is to forfeit their bond, return the woman and foreswear further vengeance. Hail the Stanton Street Slayers! Hail their new champion!"

The Mad went wild, the entire building roaring and surging to their feet, except for Mr Simpson. who had to yell to make himself heard. "Do you still grow carrots here?"

"Yes."

"Good, because I'm all out. If there's more to this than your usual Ren Faire fuckwittery, best figure out what it is, and fast. Any delays and you're going to meet my stick."

13

Under the Phalt

They only took the bag off Gillian's head once she was tied to a chair, in a utility closet they had turned into a safehouse. Outside, three rangers rolled knuckles for her coat and its contents. Inside, Daedalus scowled, and the girl standing as his second scraped aimlessly at the dirt with a long hook. Gillian's shoulder hurt, and her eye had started to swell like the wall mushrooms, a cultivated crop that bathed the chamber in a faint green glow.

"It's on the cuff," Gillian said.

"Once more?" Daedalus was handsome – for a man what lived below ground – except for the stump of his right hand and a couple of other places. The labyrinth in black ink which ran up his corded arms and neck marked him as clan royalty, and his face was hard as cellar stone.

"I wouldn't charge an old friend."

"You don't have friends, Gillian, just convenient pawns. What are you doing down here?"

"Looking for you, obviously. The IRT goes below Mulberry, and I knew the Green Line wouldn't miss my trespass."

"Crone keen for kettle," spat the girl. Daedalus had wandered topside, but she was pure tunnel, her skin pale and her eyes enormous. Her maze tattoo covered half her face and spread over her hands like gloves, more ink even than Daedalus.

"Rat simmer," Daedalus snapped, then turned back to Gillian. "Ariadne has a point, though. Why shouldn't we eat you?"

Gillian slipped out of the restraint, then took the badge from a hidden pocket and tossed it to Daedalus. Being double jointed was one of her many secrets. "I'm on the council's tab."

Ariadne hissed and flourished her hook, and the rangers quit their dicing and mustered in the doorway. Daedalus had seen the trick before and wasn't impressed. "I guess congratulations are due."

"I guess."

"Getting all those cats lined up and walking in the same direction – the Mayor, the Pope, the Honey Swallowers..."

"Kettle the Honey Swallowers!" Ariadne snapped.

"Oh, that's right," Daedalus said. "We hate them down here, don't we?"

"But the fear is a little worse than the hate, isn't it?" Gillian asked. "Or have you forgotten what happened to the Orange Line?"

The girl's hook twisted high, but Daedalus set his stump against her chest. "I remember," he said softly. "Down here, we all remember – those who made slaughter, those who stood aside and watched..."

"You didn't have a chance of helping them, and I told you that. If you'd have listened to me, then you might still have your hand. If you listen to me now, you might still save your people. You hear about the I's getting done?"

"We get the scuttle below the phalt."

"Whoever killed him trespassed on your lines dimtime last."

"Not our fault, some topsider using our rails," said Daedalus.

"What's fault to do with it? Council looking for an excuse to smoke you out."

"Fix trouble," advised Ariadne, "kill Crone."

"Stitch a lip," Daedalus said.

"Whoever hit the I's isn't done, not with the Council or with your tunnels. Killing me solves nothing; a simpleton could follow the trail down here, and it'll be that same simpleton which lays the guilt around your neck."

"Mazed need naught from topside," said Ariadne, "and Dade not need naught from Crone."

"You might be fool enough to believe that, but Dade isn't," Gillian countered.

"There were four of them," Daedalus said after a while, "one carrying boom. They headed uptown and transferred west at 14th Street, and left a trail so clear you might suppose they didn't mind it getting found."

"West towards the Honey Swallowers?"

"Could be."

"Fine," Gillian said, "give me my coat back, and have a ranger show me where they went. I'll take care of the rest, and the Council won't never hear your name. That's my word, Dade. I haven't forgotten what was, even if you have."

Daedalus scratched faintly at a scar on his face that hadn't been there the last time Gillian had seen him. "You know the only thing worse than being not clever?"

"Tell me."

"Being too clever. That was always your problem, Gil: you can't leave well enough as is."

"What's that mean?"

"It means you over-convinced me. You're right, Green Line got trouble. The Council will be looking for a scapegoat, and they'll take us if we don't give them someone better. So, we had better give them someone better, and sweet words aside, I don't trust you to oversee our interests."

"You want to go rambling again?" Gillian asked, smiling crooked.

Daedalus waved his stump. "I'm pretty well retired. Best leave this sort of business to the next generation."

Something dripped somewhere. This was often the case below the phalt. Something squealed in the walls. This was not uncommon either.

"By the Sixth Bridge," said Gillian. "No way."

"Dade gone light mad?" asked Ariadne. "Rats in the tunnels, and the tunnels for the rats."

Daedalus snatched up his claw and turned on the girl as if to use it. "Rat or mouse? Clan or cur? Loyal to the labyrinth? Shelter in burrow but balk at business? Line call, rat stay silent?"

Ariadne bore the dressing down so long as she could stand it, then turned furious eyes in Gillian's direction and nodded mute acquiescence.

"And you, Gillian," Daedalus said, calmer, though still gesturing with his hook. "This isn't the first time I heard you run someone backwards with your tongue – don't be thinking you've got me muddled. I'm conductor, got to carry all clan safe through the tunnels, and that means figuring out who's behind this. Not for you, not for the Council; for us. Ariadne goes as proxy. Isn't a mazed alive knows the tunnels any better. And anyway, it's past time she saw the funk. She'll hear you like it was my mouth speaking, and she'll come back with whoever it is been thinking on bringing us harm, bring them back trussed and well-seasoned. Nostalgia don't move me; this is business, pure and simple. You get someone to fill our pot, Gillian, or you'll be heading right back into it."

14

The Kid in Exile

The Borofolk had kipped on the Eff-Dee-Ar just south of
Belleview, taking the usual precautions, a strong line of pedicabs
northward, a strong line of pedicabs south. Schenectady was
on guard, along with a dozen hounds, not one of them raised
for meat. They gave warning as the Kid[17] came up the off ramp,
Ael[18] lanking easy beside him.

"Yo," said the Kid.

Schenectady looked at Ael a while, and the metal that Ael
carried. "Too late to trade, tinker, or talk. You'd best be off till
first bright."

What could you get from a Boroman? Your knife sharpened
and your clasp fixed; a patched tire that collapsed as soon as you
were out of sight; the best flower outside of the West Village;
your future read in the swirls of your skin, if you believed that
sort of thing; sewn in a bag and dumped in the Huddy, if you
weren't careful.

"You mistake me for a local," said the Kid.

"What you know about the bridge's shadow? Or the house
where Babe played?"

"I'm kin to Big on my mother's side."

"Your mother's side?"

---

17 Bringer of troubles.
18 Amiable murderer.

A wooly mongrel bayed into the funk above.

"That's what I said."

"Once there was a ship," said Schenectady, "a ship that took you to a second island, not gray but green." His voice grew misty. He fingered faintly the knife at his belt, though surrounded by his savage pack, he would scarce need to use it. "So I've heard tell."

"What was the cost of a berth on this ship?"

A great black mastiff raised its lip. A hunting poodle snarled fierce.

"Nothing," the Kid said, "in ages past, a man might reach paradise for free."

"What was will be once more," said Schenectady. His hand was off his weapon, and the hounds were likewise content. "Kin are always welcome, but your friend has to stay outside."

"It's all right," said Ael, "maybe bring me a bowl of whatever I smell." He knelt down to scratch the ears of a St Bernard the size of a tandem bike. "Say, did you hear how the fight went?"

"The Slayers on top," said Schenectady.

"I knew it! Everyone talking up that Anarch like he was some phenom–"

"Second-rater, second-rater!" squealed Ael's hypebird, from its perch on a lightless lamppost, safely out of reach of the dogs.

"Never going to be any good only using a club," agreed Schenectady.

"That's what I said!" Ael said. "That's just exactly what I said!"

The Kid left them to it and headed into the ring of brightly colored wagons, canvas tents and scattered furniture. There was a small fire for cooking and a large fire for gathering around, on tire stools or the honest phalt. Dinner was most of the way over, the Borofolk lounging and gossiping, rolling dice, picking teeth, breaking wind. Someone tuned a string. An old woman argued with an older woman about something that had happened before either had been born. A girl chased a boy through the outskirts of the camp, on the cusp of when play becomes serious and cousins turn spouses.

Kid found Hope[19] lying on the skeleton of a sofa, puffing flower while a gallant massaged her feet. Her septum was pierced with one of the rings she had taken from Don DeAndre's desk. "You like it?"

"Not to the slightest degree," said the Kid.

"I think it's beautiful," said the guy by Hope's feet.

"You look like every chick in FiDi," said the Kid.

"You dress like a counting house clerk, and your tops never fit."

"Tell your new friend to bring Ael a bowl of stew," said the Kid.

"I ate already," said the guy, looking hard at Hope, "but I've always room for dessert."

"That's what passes for clever at this end of the Ring?" Hope withdrew her feet. "Go play host."

Hope's dandy left, and the Kid slipped into his spot. A tabla took on a rhythm, and the guitar found its melody.

"Bit of flower?" Hope asked.

"No," said the Kid.

"Did you take care of everything?" Hope asked. "I'll need you around less bright."

"Fine."

"And bring 'dessert' over there, and a couple of his friends to pedal."

Braced by the firelight, a dusky-hued starveling rose to sing:

'Neath the towers of Midtown we wept,
sat and wept,
dreaming of the Boros.
On lamp posts we unstrung our guitars,
though our captors howled for music.

---

19 Likes bubblegum, can kill people with her mind.

Who can sing a song of Brooklyn in foreign lands?

Hope tugged at her nose ring. "Am I walking them off a cliff?"

"Do I look shook?" asked the Kid.

"How can I tell with your shirt so big?"

"That's why I wear them like that."

"Really?"

"No, it's because it makes it easier to hide things, and it makes people think I'm smaller than I am."

"Not much chance of that, the way you're going."

"What's the point of this, Hope?" the Kid asked. "The dice are tossed. You're in it and I'm in it, Chisel's in it, and so is... everyone else."

"I'm not worried about me, and I'm not worried about everyone else, and I'm certainly not worried about Chisel. You sure your judgment there is as clear as it ought to be?"

"Cold certain," said the Kid.

Cripple my hand, should I forget Staten!
Rot my tongue if I omit Queens!
Ruin every moment with memory of the Bronx!

"In the midst of all this elaborate strategizing, the complexities of which halfwits like myself can only dimly surmise, did you get around to planning yourself a party?" asked Hope.

"For what?"

"Don't you have a thousandth dim coming up?"

The Kid shuddered.

"You're just a barrel of laughs all the time," said Hope. "How can you even stand it?"

Hateful Manhattan,
blessed is your tormentor!
Blessed she who hurls your children from the bridge!

Hope bobbed along, the ember of her joint pirouetting through the darkness. "I like the old songs," she said. "Something comforting about them."

"Not if you're a toddler," the Kid pointed out.

15

A Well-Earned Reputation

-32:17:89

They followed the rails west by the flickering light of Gillian's[20] torch, stopping occasionally so Ariadne[21] could double-check the tracks. After a long stretch, the trail wandered off the main tunnels and into a side sewer, ending below a grate.

"Topside?" Ariadne asked.

"Quiet as mouse," said Gillian.

"Like Crone know from quiet," Ariadne smirked. And indeed, she went up the ladder like a shadow and she shifted the lid in practiced silence, a crack for her leering eye and then back down again.

"Washington and Little West 12th," she said.

"Okay," said Gillian. Then she didn't say anything for a while.

"Well?" Ariadne asked.

"What?"

"Shrooms growing."

"They do that."

The silence in the tunnel seemed almost its own sound.

"Crone napping?"

"Study patience."

---

20 Troublemaker/troubleshooter, depending.
21 Tunnel-dweller and occasional cannibal.

-20:12:18

"Blessed Mother," said Mountain Girl, arching her back and laughing out loud. "Five bridges and three tunnels."

"Only two tunnels, baby," said Maryland Slim.

"You deserve an extra one."

The Greenwich Village Aquarians resided in a sprawling castle on 6th Street, red brick long painted over in their preferred particolor. From below Mountain Girl's window wafted flower smoke and the sound of accordion and xylophone, beat freaks in the garden jamming till first bright. Slim took a brass timepiece from the pocket of a vest which hung off the bedpost.

"Off so soon?"

"Nothing like, baby; I just want to make sure that if anyone ever asks, "Maryland Slim, when was the moment of your greatest and most complete happiness, the peak by which all previous and future experiences paled so miserably?" I can give them the exact tic and toc."

"Where you been forever, Slim?"

"Been busy," said Slim. With his head to the window, there were none to notice that his eyes had turned inward.

"Can you do that thing with your tongue again?" asked Mountain Girl. Mountain Girl was a round woman with freckles and scarlet hair and the faintest pleasant sag to her breasts.

"I can do lots of things," said Slim.

"I never felt anything like that."

"Whatever you need."

"I say this to all of them, but you're the best I ever had."

"Yeah, well, you're knee-deep in sewage, about to kill a bunch of people, so maybe quit throwing stones."

"What?"

"Nothing," Maryland Slim said, turning to face Mountain Girl. "Sorry. You want to do me a kindness I'll repay swift and twice over, and go get me a glass of water?"

"Of course, baby." Mountain Girl pulled on a slip the same color as the hair beneath, then descended from her turret and into the revelry below. On the second floor she found home brew and distil and some spoor blossom punch, but not honest tap, and so she had to go all the way down to the kitchen, past yippies disputing on the nature of the cosmos, a line of soldiers waiting outside of a bedroom, and two separate drum circles. Rough times in Greenwich lately, with the Honey Swallowers pushing south and NoHo always looking for their bite, but at least the Aquarians could still hurl a hootenanny.

Slim was waiting for her on the edge of the bed when she returned. He set the glass on the table and cupped his broad hands around the small of her back.

"What about the water?"

Slim loosened her sash. "I'd prefer something sweeter."

-20:06:04

"What the hell took you so long?" Gillian asked.

"What?" asked Ariadne.

"Can you get in touch with Swan?"

"Who's Swan?"

"Tell him I need him at Washington and Little West 12th. Tell him in the event of my death, I've arranged a band of Boromen to follow him around playing fiddle. Are you talking to me while you're still slick with some West Village skank?"

"Crone gone light mad."

But Gillian had snapped back into focus an instant before, and she returned fire. "Rat young to know everything."

"We going topside?"

"Eventually," Gillian said.

"Why tarry?"

"We're waiting for the reserves."

"Crone gone cur."

"You been topside?"

"I been."

"You been topside twice?"

"Been plenty."

"Rat pinker than dog tongue," Gillian said contemptuously. "Rat rosy."

"Crone withered. Crone gray to her privies."

"Rat jealous?" Gillian asked, not quite incredulous. "Simmer. I don't spoor in my stew."

"Rat don't worry. Dade been mine. Dade be mine. But Dade don't know everything."

"No, Dade don't," Gillian said. "You better hear the scuttle – I owe Dade from way back; I haven't forgotten. I let you follow so long as you keep quiet and don't shame yourself, but I don't give a loose toenail for your pride, or your ink."

"Topsiders waste words."

So Gillian fell into the cant. "Rat hear, rat obey, or rat get her maze solved but good."

The most terrible insult a subterranean could swallow. Ariadne went for her hook but found Gillian's hands fastened on her wrist.

"Rat far from clan," Gillian reminded her. "Simmer or be spoor."

Ariadne freed her hand but kept it away from her weapon, conciliating herself with thoughts of vengeance and roast long pig.

-07:35:78

"Maryland Slim," said Mountain Girl, "you're the one and only…"

-05:34:92

When Ariadne and Gillian finally climbed the ladder up to

Meat Packing, it was dimmest and there was nothing to be seen but phalt and shuttered windows. The east end of Little West 12th had been barricaded, scrap metal atop a rusted Chevy, a common sight on the Island, each neighborhood its own fiefdom. Some distant trickle of music wafted up from the Village. A gray cat watched them from the transom of a neighboring building. A whippoorwill hooted its eponymous sound, and a moment later a group of men sauntered out of the shadows and up Washington.

"Recollect," warned Gillian, "Crone is conducting, rat rides along."

This admonishment proved useless, and Ariadne freed a crooked dagger in one hand and raised her claw with the other.

"And you said it was late to be checking the traps," said a soldier.

"Not sure what the point is," said another.

"A scrawny old pigeon and some rancid rat meat."

"You want we should throw it back?"

"They might do for a dimmest snack."

The Gansevoort Goons wore black brimmed caps with little skulls sewn into them, and whatever else each member could afford – battered denim, sleeveless shirts, and boots with holes in the toes. They carried brick bats and cheap hatchets. They were gods over six blocks between Bethune and West Fourteenth.

"Feed you franks," Ariadne said, tight in her fighting crouch, steel bristling. "Feed you beans."

"Before resorting to castration..." Gillian reached into a pocket of her trench coat and came back out with her badge.

"What's that?" asked one of the Goons.

"It's pretty," said another.

"Are you trying to bribe us?"

"'Cause we'll just take it off your corpse."

"The badge means I'm here on Council business," Gillian explained.

"Oh."

"Eh."

"I don't see the Council around, at the moment."

"You got anything else in there?"

"Just this," said Gillian, now holding a small revolver.

There was silence, followed by general laughter.

"What scrap heap did you get that out of?"

"I know a bodega sells them in a bin next to the hard candy."

"I bought one last dim for my nephew."

"The one you gave your nephew didn't have any boom," Gillian said.

"Yours doesn't neither."

"No one has any boom," promised the Goon's War Chief, though he began to reconsider the matter when Gillian set her barrel on him.

"Shooting you is expensive," Gillian said, "and I'd prefer to avoid it. Back out of here slowly, take your boys, and you might live to see bright."

A stressful silence followed. The War Chief had not yet come to a decision when Gillian, feeling the pause had extended too long, decided unilaterally to end it, with a loud bark and an accompanying puff of brain.

A Goon howled, two Goons shrieked, several thought seriously about fleeing. A lieutenant, hoping to be made War Chief and thus largely indifferent to his predecessor's aeration, decided to play heavy. "Be cool! She's only got five more shots!"

"You just signed on for number two," Gillian said, swiveling the gun to meet him. "Who wants to be three through six?"

But before anyone got to drawing lots, the action was interrupted by a loud burp from the alleyway.

"That boom is coming out of your cut," Gillian declared, putting the gun back into her shoulder holster.

Swan[22] had acquired a robe, sandals, a sword, and a bottle

---

22 The deadliest man in the World-Writ-Large.

of distil since Gillian had last seen him. He had not bathed. A black leather hood covered his eyes and his ears and his nose, but it left his mouth free for speech. "Let's talk about my end. It's a peculiar coincidence that I ran out of money the exact moment you required my services."

"Hell and High Towers," said one of the Goons. "It's him."

"You ran out forever ago," Gillian said, "I been floating you since so that I'd know where you were when I needed you. And now I need you, and you were late."

"I passed a bar," said Swan.

"Who gave you money for the liquor?"

"No one did; I just grabbed it and walked out. Terrified people are generous, you ever notice that?"

"I had."

Swan tippled his spoils, clear liquor running down his unshaved chin. "Are these the guys?"

"Obviously," Gillian said.

"By the Queen in Yellow," said one of the guys.

"By the Bull and the Bear!"

"Aren't you ecumenical," said Swan.

Interlude: A Happy Couple

Once, there was a happy couple. The husband was dark haired and broad shouldered and had a good job in a stable counting house. The wife was fair and bright eyed and laughed often. There seemed much to laugh about. They were young, they had the other to hold, and last but not at all least, they expected a child. No lump of flesh in its fleshy cradle, no protrusion beneath a dress, had ever been anticipated with such joy.

Happiness like that, a place like the Island... it was asking for trouble.

And trouble came for them one warm brightest, with the light shining through the funk. Swelled as she was, she ought not have gone outside, but the weather was so lovely, and they were such fortunate people – the sort of people to whom bad things don't happen. They took a pedi out to Carl Schurz Park, to promenade beside the East River. Their rosy future seemed close, the funk very far.

Never trust the funk, little grinder. Don't trust nothing and no one, but never trust the funk.

The oystermen noticed the change in the wind, and everyone else followed them inland, through the park and west into the Island, out of reach of the suddenly voracious funk. He could have made it, if he had left her; instead he was lost somewhere by the quay. She, stronger, managed to stumble all the way to East End Street, by which time her body had turned tumescent, a bubbling stew of flesh. She collapsed, lifeless, but the screaming continued from inside her stomach. The sawbones needed a hatchet to cut through all the extra meat, raising the still-mewling orphan to the funk-ridden sky.

-01:07:34

"It's probably not him," said a Goon.

"I didn't think he was real." said a Goon.

"By the Queen in Yellow!' said a Goon.

"This is what you brought me all the way out for?" Swan asked.

"You're awful pompous for a man with vomit on his bathrobe," said Gillian.

"It's not mine. Not my vomit, I mean. It's my robe."

"Is that supposed to be better?"

"I'm not sure," Swan admitted. He hocked a wad of yellow and spat it at the phalt. "Who's the rat?"

"This is Ariadne. She's tagging along a while."

"You smell like…" Swan's leather cap was thick over his nose. "Dade! You kin, or…?"

For the first time, Ariadne had gone meek. They had heard of Swan in the dark as well. "Mate," she said finally.

"Tell him I say 'hey'. For a fellow that ate human flesh, he wasn't so bad."

Interlude: An Unfortunate Child

Swan bemoaned his introduction to existence with such unceasing bitterness that his grandmother, mad from lack of sleep, tried one dark dim to smother him. He stilled quickly, but roared back when, conscience stricken, she removed the pillow. A bit of experimentation led to more elaborate sets of protection: bandages and masks, cotton wads and wax molds, though even with his head swathed, a distant laugh or the sudden scent of garlic was enough to send Swan into spirals of agony. He spent his youth looked after by a series of soft-voiced tutors, his physical genius undiscovered until a spring evening in his early adolescence when he killed a man.

Two of them, practiced burglars who had worked up and down the Enclave without even the Force grown wise. Swan, maddened by the sound of glass being cut, found them rifling the desk in his grandfather's study. They had only intended the knife as threat, but it made Swan uncomfortable, and so he took it away, then gave it back. The partner's screams were so agonizing that he ended them reflexively.

-00:22:07

Swan rubbed a dirty sleeve against a snotty nose. "Can't they just run away or something?"

"No."

"The guy you shot in the head isn't punishment enough?"

"No."

"One or two, then?"

"It's business."

"Oh, it's business. That's fine, then. It's business; don't let it weigh on you."

"You want your money, you'll do what I told you," Gillian said.

"You're a sick person, Gillian," Swan's cutter looked like any other, single-edged and swinging lazily from a shoulder strap. "There's something really wrong with you."

Interlude: Mortal Combat

There had always been a particular 'sound' that Swan could not account for, a distant, buzzing something, and he decided to investigate its origin before turning his new knife on himself. He left his UES estate for the first time and without difficulty, slipping over the Enclave walls and into the city proper.

Sometime later, Swan sat on a bench overlooking the river, a few blocks from where his parents had died, and where he had been born. During his walk, Swan had *seen*: the outline of a corpse, a whore beg for customers, the rot grow in tower and phalt and bone; and *heard*: a rat feast on another rat, a child weep uncomforted, the retort of flesh against flesh; and *smelled*: feces, human feces and dog feces and rat feces and mice feces, and the waste of a thousand separate animals, not to discount every other sort of effluvia – hot breath, menses, and bitter urea. And he'd *discovered*, or *decided*: that misery is life's binding thread, and thus, his personal despair commanded no early claim on death's attention.

Though he would fight countless battles after, this was the closest Swan ever came to violent death. Bright rose over the East like the blinding white of blessed nothing, and he wandered off to find breakfast.

00:00:00

Swan drew his sword...

+00.00.17

...through epidermis, dermis, hypodermis, arteries, capillaries, periosteum, marrow, periosteum, capillaries, arteries, hypodermis...

+0:02:33

...from the shoulder, a smaller spray from the arm itself, Swan shifting, grimy bathrobe whiplashed, the knife turning end over...

+0.04:82

...tip nicking his spinal column, living flesh turned to dead weight, screaming, screaming, screaming, Swan facing the sure trajectory of the knife...

+0:07:12

...pink flushed intestine become visible, "Bridge and–"

Swan's strike severing words, breath and jaw, knife gone *thunk* in the back of the final fleeing Goon...

+0:07:83

"Phalt hide me," Ariadne gasped. "Maze keep me safe."

Swan cleaned his cutter with a rag. There was blood on the phalt and on the walls and on and near everywhere else, but there was none on Swan. "Yup, that's how they look on the inside." He found where he had put his bottle of distil, and he took a long swig, neck bobbing. "It's odd how often you need reminding."

"I told you, this was business," said Gillian.

"Get a new line of work."

"If I did that, who would keep you in flower and spoor blossom?"

"Speaking of which, that's... nine, at whatever the going rate is. Credit my account, I'm going back to bed."

"Eight. I shot one of them."

Swan burped. "Fine, eight."

"I'll pay you when we're through."

"Cash on the barrelhead."

"If I pay you now, you'll be too stoned for when I need you next."

"Don't rile me," Swan said. "I did what you asked. Now Daddy wants his medicine."

"A little longer."

"It's loud out here, Gil," Swan said. His bottle was empty. "I swear it gets louder every time."

"Just a little longer, I promise." Gillian handed him some scrip. "This should keep you going."

Swan snatched it out of her hand and shoved it into a pocket of his robe. "You hollow, Gillian," he said. "You empty straight through." He turned sharp to Ariadne. "How long you tanned that mole you're wearing as a shirt?"

"A... a while," Ariadne managed finally.

"Wasn't long enough," Swan said, stumbling east without further comment.

Most of the Goons were in so many pieces as to make a search impractical, and so Gillian started with the man she had shot. In his pants pocket, she found an overlong coil of flattened discs with 🐍 on the front.

"How you think these losers got to carrying a fortune in change?" Gillian asked.

"Ask one of them faces," Ariadne suggested.

"You're catching up."

16

Bedtime Stories

Fran was gray and squat and had lasted longer than any of Newton's[23] other nannies. She was from Morningside Heights, and she made very good apple dumplings, and roasted rather bland dog, and had never once beat him. There was no one in the world to whom Newton was closer, even though the stories she made up from his panel books were not nearly as good as the ones Newton himself made.

"...so then this one, with the claws, he gets put to sleep by this other one, this one who he thought was his friend."

"But wasn't."

"Guess not, 'cause there she is, standing on top of him and laughing."

"So, the bad guys win?" Newton asked, neutrally.

"Looks like it. She's got the skull and crossbones on her chest."

"And those eyes," added Newton, "those mean eyes."

"You can always tell the villain," Fran agreed. She closed the panel book and put it on a pile with his others. "And that's two," she said, "and two is what you get before you go to sleep."

Newton knew better than to argue. The nanny before Fran didn't even tell him one story, and if he complained, she would pinch him with her savage little nails.

---

23   Unpopular orphan.

"Don't forget, your uncle is coming for supper," said Fran.

"Oh."

"Won't that be nice?"

Newton reminded himself to smile. "Yes."

"You want I should leave the door open a crack?" asked Fran, turning off the juice.

"No, thank you," said Newton. "I prefer the dim."

17

Several Floors of Vice

Downstairs

The Lower East Side was a madhouse just then, everyone at war with everyone else. You passed half a dozen borders on the way to your bodega, and not even the hippest grinder could have known the parole for each, a different clique every block, children with scrap-metal knives and eyes ignorant of sin.

Best parties, though; on that, there was universal agreement.

Most of the windows in the pointed house on Henry Street had been broken, but there were some ones near the top that were very fine, and the juice light passing through them bathed the dance floor prismatic. The organ's great brass wall pipes made a sound that was less a sound and more like a change in the weather. On stage, a boy in girl's clothes and a girl in boy's clothes keened sharply. Below them, two hundred of the Island's brightest young things bobbed and juked and shimmied, rubbed flesh, and howled themselves voiceless. In the center of this ebullient mass, Ael cut himself a fine rug, large enough even outside of his battle-leathers to earn space to move. The song hit its climax, and then the song hit its denouement, and then Ael and everyone else howled approbation and made for the bar.

Kyra made sure to get behind him in line. "Nice moves," she said.

"Thanks!"

"What's that for?"

'That' was a rabbit with its eyes crossed out, tattooed on his bicep.

"The Dead Rabbits," Ael said.

"Never heard of them."

"They're not around anymore."

"What happened to them?"

"I suppose I did."

"Huh?"

"Well, we weren't ever a very big gang, you know; just a couple of blocks around Pearl and Coenties Slip. But we were tough! I mean, Cleon was tough. Cleon was War Chief. Trained me up – knives, footwork, the whole bit."

"And?"

"So one dim, I decided to find out if I was better than Cleon, and afterward they went and made me War Chief."

"What's so bad about that?"

"Who wants to be War Chief? Terrible job. "Ael, what's the parole? Ael, are we going to take the Widow Makers up on their offer? Ael, should we break Old Man Kramling's fingers because he's late on his tariff?" Not for me. I realized I didn't want to be War Chief; I just wanted to war."

"So?"

"I told them they had the wrong guy, and that actually, maybe I wasn't cut out to be in a clique at all. They took that kind of hard."

"So you…"

"Not all of them, but enough that they kind of stopped existing as an organization."

They arrived at the counter.

"Distil with honey," said Kyra.

"Tap for me," said Ael, slipping off a spot of change. "Keep the tip."

Kyra leaned a little closer. "So what do you do now?"

"It's kind of complicated. But the short of it is, I'm trying to kill my hero."

"Oh," said Kyra. "Cool."

"Yeah, Swan. You know Swan? Of course you do."

"With the mask?"

"Yup!"

"You're going to fight Swan?" Kyra asked, laughing. "You're too much, man."

"What's so crazy about that?"

"He's not even real."

"Oh, he's real!" Ael said happily. "Believe me!"

The Madison Monsters were the official hosts of the evening's entertainment, but Lewis Street were planning on making a raid dimtime next, and Powel, being a Lewis Street lieutenant, thought it was probably okay to throw his weight around a bit, especially with a couple of friends behind him and a shiv he'd taken through security. And Kyra was his third-best girl, after all.

"This guy bothering you, Kyra?"

"Finally," Ael said, shaking Kyra's hand off his arm and cracking the joints in his fingers. "How long were you louses going to keep me waiting?"

Upstairs

The Kid was just below the steeple what was just below the funk, sitting on his fire escape and exhaling neat rings of smoke. Tobacco was an expensive crop; it could only be grown in Uptown hothouses, and the graveyard of butts at his feet represented fifteen shifts for a JuiceTown pedaler. When he saw her bike turn onto Henry Street, he tamped one more to their number and went back inside.

The Monsters let the Kid use the room in exchange for some things he'd helped them with. The Monsters wouldn't be around much longer, but by then the Kid wouldn't need the room. It had been a very long time since the Kid had slept in the same place twice. He took his shaggy black jacket and hung it on a wire.

After a shambling ascent up the fire escape, Chisel threw a leg through the window and came inside. She had sweated through her work clothes on her journey out from the bridge. "You just let me up here?"

"I knew it was you."

"And why would you trust me?" Still standing, Chisel pulled off her boots and threw them in a corner. Then she started on her pants. "Maybe I'm coming to ambush you."

"Maybe I laid you a trap."

"Maybe," Chisel said. "I was promised a hundred bulbs, and I only got ninety-seven."

"I'll tell the Frenemy to make it up for you next week." The Kid took his shirt off and hung it neatly over a chair.

"She's taking advantage of you."

"That's what bean counters do. So long as they keep their grift to a reasonable level, there's no point in making an issue out of it."

"We'd throw someone off the bridge for that kind of nonsense."

The Kid removed his pants and laid them on the chair. "The Island doesn't run like your bridge. It's a chaotic environment; you have to allow a certain amount of leeway."

Chisel sat cross-armed, naked and impatient. Her breasts yielded little to gravity, and the hair on her thighs lay thick and dark. "Sounds like a comfortable excuse for weakness."

"But I don't care about your opinion," said the Kid. He folded his silk underwear with all appearance of care, though he had started to sweat and was hard as a stone. "You're an employee, and you do what I tell you."

"Do I?" Chisel asked, then slapped him across the face.

He smiled at the first, but he blocked the second, bending her wrist. Beneath his loose shirt he was coiled muscle, and after a brief struggle he forced her onto the bed. With her remaining hand she struck him, closed fist, hard enough to bruise his temple. He winced but twisted her against the mattress.

Their breath commingled.

"You gonna rut me, little man? You gonna to do me proper?"

"What you biked up here for, wasn't it?"

"Doesn't mean you can do it."

He snarled. She opened for him without effort. They grunted along a while. Her eyes closed, sometimes, but his never seemed to.

"Enough for you?"

"You don't have enough."

The music started up once more, eclipsing her moans. The bed hammered against the wall unevenly, as if repudiating the rhythm below.

"What are you thinking about?" the Kid asked afterward.

Chisel lay beside him, but they did not touch. "I'm thinking there has to be a way of cutting down on the smoke from my cannon, some alteration in the mixture. A finer grind, maybe. I'll set Adze on it. What were you thinking about?"

"Some guys I have to kill."

"Where are my pants?"

"Wherever you threw them."

Chisel rose, found her pants, then put them on along with the rest of her kit. "Don't smoke before I come next time," she said, heading out the window. "It's disgusting."

"Who said there would be a next time?"

She didn't answer. He waited until he couldn't hear her on the fire escape, then went outside. Dimmest had turned to less dim. The Kid lit a cigarette. Chisel pedaled hard for the Ring, turning onto Gouverneur Street without looking back.

Brighttime Next...

18

A Tourist in Times Square

Just before first bright, the Island flooded the Square, every species and subspecies to be found in the surrounding ecology come to wander through its maze of stalls. Here an oysterman bartered his catch for resoled shoes and patched pedi tires, there a majordomo from some Enclave estate poked through the scavenge for bulbs or silk or, praise the Tiny t, coffee. A mother inspected a basket of battered dolls, brightly-colored and missing limbs; an Aquarian checked the tang on a second-hand cutter. Hawkers sold popcorn, rat fritters, skewered shroom, house brews of a dozen different sorts, fry bread in honey, flower loose, flower pre-rolled, and shots of distil, two bits to fill the tin cap chained to the kettle.

"Having a bad run?" asked a greasy man in heavy furs. "No wonder! The Bear walks behind you, roaring woe! A modest donation to the Bull might be just the thing to…"

"Boys who follow the Queen in Yellow do not swear or gamble or take strong drink. Girls who follow the Queen in Yellow dress with modesty and speak when spoken to." Beside the preacher, an unsmiling woman passed out fliers showing 🐝 ❤ 📖.

"What time is it?" asked a spindly youth.

"Showtime!" asserted his friend, upside down on a cardboard mat.

"Quit gaping," said Gillian. "You'll swallow a fly."

"So much," said Ariadne, "everywhere."

"Midtown sucks," Gillian agreed.

Above and all around them, vibrant wreckage of the ancients decayed, long dead heroes looking down on their descendants, gigantic screens gone gray like the blind eyes of forgotten gods. Every spare inch of stone, concrete or plastic had been marked, painted, and inked, and staring you could almost convince yourself there was some pattern, as if the ancestors were trying to tell you something, some warning or secret.

"The ancestor's language could only be understood by the initiated," explained a new friend, appearing suddenly beside Ariadne, "but with it they could send a whisper anywhere in the Island, quick as..." He snapped his fingers.

"Talk rot," said Ariadne.

He laughed and gestured upward. "You stand in the shadow of their works, yet doubt their power?"

Ariadne followed his gesture to the towers looming over them, grander in Midtown than the rest of the city. "How high?"

"Above the funk – to where our ancestors wait, hoping ever to bring us home."

"What?"

"That's why they built them, of course. The ancestors knew the funk was coming, and they built the towers to take shelter above. They went first, and we were supposed to follow, but the funk came too quick, and now you can't talk to them, unless you're using one of these." He took a green lump of plastic out of his coat. "Cells, they were called, a straight line to the ancestors–"

"Quit trying to trump my tourist," Gillian snapped, threatening the mountebank with the back of her hand, "or I'll break your teeth down your throat."

"Wouldn't want to share heaven with no rat anyhow!" shouted the man. "Ought to follow the Honey Swallowers lead, do them all like they did the Orange Line!"

Ariadne started after him, but the Square was its own burrow, and he was gone up a hidey-hole an instant later, Ariadne left to simmer.

"Your own fault," said Gillian. "Sidewalk's got simple rules: never stop moving, never make eye contact."

A sadly cynical guideline, though a necessary one; for as meat draws maggots, so does the fecund loam of honest commerce attract its own parasites – pickpockets and three-card dealers, unlicensed hetaerae, sellers of false flower, flim-flam men, rooks, and, of course, bankers.

"This is us," said Gillian, stopping in front of a narrow building with 🙂 painted bold above the entryway. A cat scowled at them from a trash heap.

The established houses – Goldman, Sax, Madoff – possess a certain regal threadbareness, as if they didn't really need your business but would take it if you insisted. Newcomers to the high ranks of Capital are not allowed that same luxury, however, and as the Frenemy had only recently bought her way to legitimacy, her shop was everything expected. The floors were marble and smelled of polish, security wore livery and carried halberds, withered men at wooden tables pushed silently at counting boards. Even the secretary was frowsy, if competent, rising even before Gillian could introduce herself. "I take it you're here to see the boss?" And without waiting for an answer, she led Gillian to an open elevator. "She's on the eighth."

"I remember," said Gillian.

Ariadne reached for her hook as the doors began to close.

Gillian cackled. "Simmer, now. No trouble here. Frenemy is a friend."

"Crone have friends?"

"Sure. Everyone loves the crone."

The Frenemy's office overlooked the Square. This was its only nod to luxury. Inside there was only a desk, and two chairs for Gillian and Ariadne, and one chair for the two of *them*. They were not quite identical: Right's eyes were crow-lined, Left's were careworn. Right had a small beauty mark that Left lacked. Still, you could be forgiven for mistaking them.

"Gillian," said Right, half-smiling, "what an unexpected surprise."

Left was busy sketching out symbols and did not pause to offer greeting.

"You couldn't have been that shocked," Gillian said, "waving me in like that."

"We've all heard of your recent appointment. Re-appointment? In any event, congratulations. Of course, we wouldn't dream of making the Sheriff wait in the lobby."

Left hocked with her half of the throat, then spat into a wastebasket.

"Can I get you anything?" Right asked. "HR came back from market this morning with a bag of beans…"

"Whole beans?"

"Whole beans."

"If you're going to twist my arm over it," said Gillian.

"And your… friend?" Right asked.

"I doubt she'd–"

"Rat try," said Ariadne.

"Lovely," said Right. "How do you take it? Honey? A few grains of sweet?"

"Black," said Gillian.

"Black," Ariadne echoed after a moment.

"Somehow I guessed," said Right. Left smirked. Right rang a bell and gave her assistant their order. Left set aside her note and started moving stones on her counting board.

"Now," Right asked, "what is it that we can do to for the Council?"

Gillian tossed a coil of the Frenemy's change onto the table.

Right looked it over a moment. "Not to seem ungracious, but really, this is something one of our cashiers would be better equipped to help you with. Our rate in seed and rat meat is posted outside. Were you thinking of swapping the whole chain, or...?"

Left laughed.

"I took this off some people paid to kill me," said Gillian.

"I'm not sure what this has to do with–"

"People paid by the people who killed the I's."

Left set down her quill and scratched Right's elbow. "Anyone can use our change."

"I'm afraid I have to agree," Right said. "We obviously can't be held responsible for what happens once our coin leaves the office."

"They're in sequence," said Gillian. "And there were more. Someone bought a bulk lot."

"Gillian, please. Our currency has become popular exactly *because* we make no effort to determine who uses it. Ours is a judgment-free means of exchange, one which doesn't care about where you father was born, one that–"

"Who got you the right to mint that currency?" Gillian snapped. "Who got you a share of Capital, one-seventeenth of a Council seat, just like the big boys?"

"You were compensated for that," said Left.

"Wasn't for me, you'd still be offering short-term loans to shift workers. You think they wanted to sell? A freak like you, and a woman?"

"We paid you for that," said Right.

"You think I didn't have to step on some throats to get your share? Bury some bodies? Put some skeletons into closets? Dig some skeletons out of your closets, put them in better, safer closets, closets only I got the key to?"

The secretary opened the door, distributed her coffees, and left.

Gillian took a sip. "It's lovely."

Ariadne sniffed suspiciously at her mug.

"How long do you expect us to compensate you for your… services?" Left asked finally.

"Forever, obviously."

"Nothing's forever," said Right.

"Nothing and no one," Left agreed.

"Was that a threat?" Gillian asked.

Right didn't answer, and neither did Left. Ariadne sipped at her drink.

"If so, it was a fool one. Because even if you did manage a lucky shot, it wouldn't help you, believe me. It would only make things worse."

Ariadne spat onto the carpet. "Mole piss," she said. "Bog water."

"I never thought very much of the two of you," Gillian admitted. "Apart from your polyphonic gimcrackery, you're a second rater; it's always short money over long. That's why I put you where you are: because I knew you'd be easy to bully. But you aren't being easy bully, and for the life of me, I don't understand why. Who cares about this customer? Why are you even putting me through this trouble? Hand them over and I'll let you keep whatever is left in their accounts as a happy bonus. Unless of course, this is some issue of professional ethics…"

Right and Left pondered this a moment, then split a grin.

"Gillian, please–" Right began.

"No trouble," Left assured Gillian, holding the coil close to her eye. "Now that you mention it, this was that one that…"

"Wanted a thousand in newly minted change," Right continued, "and he also wanted us to get him some scattergun."

"And boom," said Left. "Enough boom to make trouble."

"What did he look like?"

"Couldn't tell you," said Right, "we did everything by courier."

"Drink tainted?" Ariadne asked.

"It's not poison," Gillian assured her. "Who was he fronting for?"

"Can't say," said Left.

"Not our business to ask."

"That's not enough," Gillian said.

"What if it was all we had?" Left asked.

"Then I'd say you were pretty well-rutted, 'cause I'm going to need to feed the Council someone soon, and that someone's likely to be the last person I talk to."

"It isn't all we have," Right assured Gillian.

"They wanted something besides the boom and the scattergun," added Left.

"What?" Gillian asked.

"We're not sure," Left admitted, "but they wrote a chit to some Force in East Harlem as deposit."

"Topsiders mad," Ariadne said, rubbing her tongue. "Topsiders bug-sick."

19

The Nine Lives of Nelly Karrow

What did the men and woman of Yorkville eat? Dogs – both domesticated and wild – pigeon and pigeon eggs, smoked rat, dried rat, boiled rat, ground rat, rat made into pies, rat made into dumplings, rat made into fritters, rat raw if you couldn't stand to wait. Potatoes, corn, wheat, apples, plumcots and sweet cherries, mushrooms of all sorts and sundry, unlabeled pre-funk tins. In short, the people of Yorkville ate everything that the people of the rest of the Island ate, which was anything they could – with one exception. No one in Yorkville, however hungry, however desperate, would eat a cat. From 79th to East 96th was a virtual feline paradise, near on thirty blocks full of fearless clowder, ignorant of cruel children or unleashed dogs. What divine protection draped itself over this demesne, what force ensured the amity of Yorkville's human population towards their kitten compatriots?

Her name was Nelly Karrow, and just then, she was sitting at the back table of her local café, scratching the ears of a black cat, her journal open beside her. She was also…

…napping on a bright-lit ledge in the East Village…

…rubbing her ears against her fingernails…

…at the window of the Bowery dive bar where Swan was passed out on the floor…

…outside of the castle on 6th Street, where Maryland Slim made his final goodbyes…

…yawning…

…snapping…

…stretching…

…and sitting on top of a trash heap on West 46th Street, observing Gillian and Ariadne flag down a pedicab.

Nelly took a sip of her tea, frowned, and made a note.

"More milk," she said with no particular sweetness when the serving girl returned.

20

A Thin Blue Line

"Feel free to try one," Sergeant Pell told the mirror. "Feel free to try one. You want to try one? Feel free to try one. You can feel free to try one." He scowled a moment longer at his reflection, then left the bathroom.

Alvarez and Enzo and Bryant and Kim waited for him in the bullpen. Kim had a cannon, standard, with three boom left in the clip, but the rest were carrying short cutters, and Alvarez was even leaning on his pike.

"Put that away," said Sergeant Pell, "you're going to knock something over."

"I'm better with my pike than I am my cutter," Alvarez said defensively.

Sergeant Pell's once promising career with the Force had taken a miserable detour after punching a Captain in a bar fight. After which, he'd been detailed to the 18th Precinct, all the way up in East Harlem, a colony of third sons and freed slaves tearing down houses and putting up crops. Joining him in exile were four patrolmen who could not be stuck anywhere worse: Bryant smoked flower on shift, Kim once wasted a shot of boom on a fleeing thief, rumor had Enzo fiddling an underage suspect, and Alvarez had once asked Pell, "Why'd they call it the East River?"

It was grim material with which to be committing a crime against the state, but then, needs make must. "Just set the spear down, " he said.

"What time is it?" asked Bryant.

Kim took his hand off his cannon long enough to check his watch. "12:23."

"They're late."

"Not long."

"Any late is late."

"We've got the two-fifty already," said Alvarez. "Why don't we just..."

"Walk away on the other five hundred?"

"Put your pike down and find your stones." Kim had got boom-brave. Pell had seen it before: fill a grinder's cannon and all a sudden he was tall as a tower.

"Let's everybody just simmer," said Pell. "No one's doing nothing but sticking to the plan. Think on your split; it's the difference between doing another tour in the Force and buying your own diner."

"A nice one," Kim added, "with lace curtains, and fritters like your momma used to make."

Alvarez blushed. "There'll be a seat waiting for you guys any time."

If Pell had his way, he'd never see any of them again, but this was not then relevant. There was a bang on the door. Everyone looked at Sergeant Pell.

He gave the nod. "Open it."

But before Kim did he put his hand on his cannon, and despite orders, Alvarez had not set down his pike.

Ael came in smiling as soon as the door opened and took a quick look around. "You're going to knock something over with that pike if you're not careful," he said to Alvarez.

"You the Kid?" asked Pell.

"Nope! I'm Ael," said Ael. Ael was wearing his walking-around clothes, black denim and red leather. Two cutters crossed his back, and he carried a black suitcase. "This is the Kid."

The Kid came in.

"Makes more sense, doesn't it?" asked Ael.

The Kid looked thin and irascible, and he was huffing through his eighth cigarette since rising from a sleepless bed.

"Tiny t," Enzo said. "What are we doing?"

"This is the buyer? He isn't old enough to shave."

"You're late," said Sergeant Pell.

"What?" the Kid asked.

"You're late. I said 12:00."

"You think I pedal a stationary? This isn't the Enclave, no one cares about your fancy new clock. I said I'd be here before brightest, which puts me at perfectly punctual."

"Where's our change?"

"Half broke my back lugging it up here," Ael said, opening the suitcase.

Sergeant Pell grew vertiginous. Bryant began to slaver.

"Your turn," said the Kid.

Pell nodded to Bryant, who took three boxes from the ground and set them on the desk, then opened one. Inside were four chunks of solid green, each about the size of a fist.

"How do I know they work?" the Kid asked.

"Feel free to try one," said Sergeant Pell.

"Groovy," said the Kid, reaching for a pin.

Enzo gasped. Alvarez dropped his pike.

"They work!" Kim yelled. "They work."

"We've kept them in storage since the funk came," Pell promised. "If they don't work, it's on the ancestors."

"And no one's going to notice them gone?" asked the Kid.

"The storage room got flooded, another case got ruined. We swapped these."

"That'll be a fun surprise for one of your comrades."

"You talk big for a little boy," said Enzo. "Ought to put you over my knee."

"Yeah, I bet you'd like that," said the Kid, looking at Enzo till Enzo blushed. "Anyway, it's nothing to me. Ael, if you'd shoulder the boxes, I'm going to hold onto these myself." He picked up two superbooms.

The hypebird hidden in the rafters began to squawk. "Done and done, done and done!"

Kim was halfway to his cannon when Ael waved him off.

"Chill, it's just my hypebird."

"A what?"

"Damn, you Enclave flunkies don't know nothing 'bout nothing."

"What's a hypebird do?"

"It tells the truth," said Ael.

"Ael's the greatest!" squawked the hypebird. "Ael's the fastest, Ael's the strongest, Ael's the–"

The Kid snapped the case shut and shoved a superboom into his jacket pocket. "Can we get a move on?" he snapped. Ael opened the door and the hypebird lilted out, but the Kid tarried a moment before following. "Congrats, boys," he said, "you've got everything you've ever dreamed of."

"Good on you!" said Ael, shutting the door as he left.

Celebration followed a brief pause.

"Tiny t, I can't believe it…"

"Did you see the shine on that change?"

"Rich, rich, counting-house rich!"

"Never need to work again."

"Biggest diner in Midtown!" Alvarez swore, once again holding his pike. "And you guys can eat for free!" He reached over to touch the suitcase, but Pell grabbed his hand.

"Nobody's buying nothing," said Pell. "Not yet. Not until we're good and sure no nosy quartermaster is going to come counting."

"I know the plan," said Alvarez, "but still… it can't hurt just to look at it?"

Sergeant Pell didn't see how it could, and in truth he wanted to take another look himself, run his fingers round the coils of change, feel them grow warm with his touch. He opened the case.

21

The Eight Lives of Nelly Karrow

She was not a very nice girl, the serving girl; Nelly did not care for her, not her clever tongue or the little flip of her wrist when she poured milk. In Nelly's time, a menial knew their place. Nelly was thinking of having a word with the owner, and she was also…

…lounging contently in a corner of Tompkins Square…

…tormenting a mouse with one cruel paw…

…watching Maryland Slim enjoy a shave at a LES barbershop…

…deciding not to eat the meal left out for her…

…waiting for Swan to, at some point, waken…

…pursuing a lover, barbed penis erect…

…fleeing the aforementioned…

… seated on a windowsill on East 119th, as Gillian and Ariadne got out of their pedicab, door opening when–

Nelly screamed and overturned her teapot.

22

A Thread Abruptly Severed

A tongue of fire shattered the windows of the 16th Street Precinct, obliterating Sergeant Pell and his subordinates.

The pedicab driver screamed. The smoke from the explosion rose seamless to the funk.

"Next plan?" Ariadne asked, after the ringing in her ears had subsided. "Or can Crone talk to corpses?"

"Raising the dead is my other plan," said Gillian, scowling, "and I had good reason for not putting it first."

23

The Last King of TriBeCa

Their pedicab driver, already pretty spooked from the explosion, would not take them south of Broome Avenue, and so they had to walk the last few blocks. Though still technically in Soho, the streets were empty, nothing but cracked phalt and bits of plastic blown by a suddenly strong breeze.

"Stay here," said Gillian when they got to Canal Street.

"Dade said–"

"Dade doesn't know about this," said Gillian. "Up to me, Dade never learns – but if he did know, he'd say 'simmer.'" Gillian took out her flashlight and handed it to Ariadne. "Hold my torch."

"Why?"

"The King don't like them," said Gillian, setting a frown on her face and heading south.

Of course, Ariadne did not listen; she counted ninety and then hid Gillian's flashlight behind some cardboard, adding hers as an afterthought, and passed into ruined TriBeCa.

The funk fell jagged and uneven; on Broome, the bright had reflected off the glass towers, but Canal Street was all gloom. By the time Ariadne had made it past Varick, it was nearly as dark as the tunnels, which should have comforted her, but didn't. The doom what had ravaged TriBeCa had broken every window and burnt all the towers that could be burnt. The funk was thick as stew, but it carried the conversation, and Ariadne followed it until she found them.

The man was tall and stately and watched intently as Gillian continued her story: "...then you clapped your hands three times and the floor opened, and below the dance floor was a pool."

"Magnificent."

"Some felt so."

"And what did I do?"

"You jumped in, laughing."

"And was it not the most exciting thing that had happened on the Island in a thousand dimtimes? And was my suit not the snazziest, and my cravat the most shapely? Be honest now; I'll know. Lies taste of quim."

"Personally, I thought it was garish, like the cravat, and there was some general feeling that it was too cold to swim. Where is my enemy?"

"In his office downtown," said the man. "He's trying to figure out who you are. He knows there's someone doing something, but he doesn't know who. He's unconcerned. He doesn't take you seriously. He doesn't know who you are, but he doesn't take you seriously. What happened at dimmest?"

"Outside, great kettles of distil had been set at every intersection, for any and all to try, and jugglers with hatchets—"

"I don't care about the distil, and I don't care about the jugglers, and if you don't start telling me what I want to hear, you'll go back to Soho disappointed. Now tell me, what happened at dimmest?"

"The virgins filed past," said Gillian, "and you chose the ones that pleased you."

"Fortunate souls, to serve as my holiday lovers!"

"Where is my enemy from?" Gillian asked.

"Poughkeepsie. Did I take a boy or a girl?"

"I don't remember. How long till the tunnel opens?"

"You're no fun anymore," said the man. "It's like you only come here to ask me things. It's like you don't even enjoy our chats."

"How long do I have?"

"Tell me about the ban."

"I need to know how long I have."

"Then you had better... tell... me... about... the... ban. I have forever, Gillian, or several generations at least. I suspect you're operating on a tighter schedule."

"The Widow Makers[24] hated you because you dressed better than they did, and threw better parties, and your champions always bested theirs."

"Yes, TriBeCa had some very fine soldiers."

"The Force[25] would take any excuse to pounce on a clique, and they wanted to let the Honey Swallowers[26] know they still had plenty of boom."

"Trivial plotters. What about you, Gillian? Remind me of your reasons."

"You thumbed your nose too long at Capital[27], and so–"

"Out with it!" shrieked the man, the man and everything else, the funk and the phalt and the broken walls of TriBeCa, everything except Gillian and Ariadne. "You, not the rest of them. You. Tell me why you put the ban on me, tell me what you learned when you were here as our guest, tell me what it was you sniffed out. Tell it to me, and tell it to me slow."

"You huffed funk," said Gillian.

"Huffed it! Huffed it, she says! I *was* the funk! I breathed it, caressed it, preferred it even to air–"

"Worshiped it, gave it to children, to their pregnant mothers."

"My children, in the bellies of my wives!"

"Fed it to them and bred your children against one another."

---

24 Lords of Wall Street and the surrounding territories, worshipers of the Bull and the Bear.

25 The Enclave's security force.

26 Followers of the Queen in Yellow, whose Empire runs from Midtown to the Upper West side.

27 A rotating spot on the Council filled by one of the officially recognized counting houses.

"Gods and Goddesses, they would have been, and me their father! The things I saw in the funk, Gillian, the things I learned there–"

"And when I found out what you were doing, I ginned the Council into being my sword, bent their arms and prodded their asses, and we came down here and slaughtered our way to the Huddy, you and all your kinfolk and your soldiers, after which we divvied up your civilians and burnt everything that you ever cared for. And now you're caged in the ruins, diminishing bit by bit, your only release when an old enemy comes to stir at the ashes of your consciousness for her own selfish ends. That's the story of the ban," Gillian said. "Now – do I smell of quim?"

"Actually, occasionally someone is foolish enough to sneak in here and I get to play with their brains a while. But in principal, you're right," conceded the dead ruler of TriBeCa. "It's a miserable thing I've been reduced to. And all because you didn't like my cravat."

"You were always trying too hard," Gillian said. "How long before it's done?"

"Three turns. Maybe four."

"What does my enemy fear?"

"Failure. That was such a bad question I won't even charge you for it."

"Which of us wins?"

"Too vague, you could define victory all sorts of ways."

"Which of us lives?"

"Now, now, Gillian, you know I can't see the future; only feel the funk. How do I know what will happen? Maybe you both live. Maybe you go on to be best friends, and get a duplex together on the Lower East Side."

"I doubt it."

"No, probably not."

Ariadne made a slight sound and Gillian's eyes flickered towards her, and the King's did the same, his eyes which were not eyes and his face which was not a face but the funk... *are you sure you are not the funk* "Now who's this one, coming in here so quiet?" *how would you know if you weren't the funk* "A slippery one, is that because of the tattoos?" *wouldn't you maybe like to be the funk* "How peculiar." *have you really thought about it* "Of course, now that I've seen you..." *you can do anything you want in here anything you want do it and feel it at the same time you the lash and you the flesh you the knife and you the chest you the violator you the violated you the violation forever and ever and ever and–*

"You've an heir!" Gillian screamed.

Ariadne crumpled to the phalt.

"Boy or girl?"

"I'm owed another question," said Gillian.

"Boy or girl?" the Last King of TriBeCa asked, and Ariadne screamed once more.

"Boy," said Gillian, "and that's as much as you'll get, however loud you make her scream."

It was dimmest dim just then, black as a buried coffin. "If he is mine, he will find me," said the Last King. "TriBeCa will rise once more. Ask your questions."

Gillian looked at Ariadne, frowned, then said, "What was it got sold Uptown?"

"Superboom."

"And where is it headed now?"

"Stuy. Anything else?"

"Nothing, for now."

"Marvelous," said the Last King of TriBeCa. "Absolutely wonderful." Then the funk thickened around him, and then there was nothing but funk.

Unspeaking, Gillian helped Ariadne to her feet, and they stumbled east to 6th Street, at which point Ariadne collapsed once more.

"Where did you put my flashlight?" Gillian asked.

"Behind the cardboard."

"Gone now," Gillian said, after checking.

"Crone angry?" asked Ariadne.

"I think you've paid enough," Gillian said, pointing at a scarred woman reflected in the metal girder of the ruined tower.

24

After Math

"That's nice," said Mariann, but she had to say it a second time for Newton[28] to realize she was speaking to him, because people so rarely said things like that to Newton.

"Oh," said Newton. "Thank you." "What is it?"

"The one with the sword is named Cinder," said Newton, "and the rest are his noble companions."

"Why is his arm like that?" Mariann asked.

"Because his father cut it off when he was a kid, and it got replaced with living flame."

"How does he carry a sword if his hand is on fire?"

"It's only hot when he wants it to be."

"Draw a pecker," said Kev, appearing suddenly.

"Go away, Kev," said Mariann.

"Draw a pecker," said Kev.

Newton had been having that peculiar ticklish feeling he got sometimes. Not like a pain, exactly, just a sort of prickliness, as if you all of a sudden remembered that you had skin, when normally it was something you took for granted. "Always peckers with you, isn't it, Kev? Peckers, peckers, peckers. How about I draw some for a while and then after we go behind the shed and I show you mine, maybe let you put it in your mouth? You figure that game out yourself, Kev, or was there someone that taught it to you? A cousin, maybe, or even a–"

---

28 Schoolboy, occasional artist.

It did not seem that Kev would ever stop hitting him, even after Mariann's screams alerted the teachers.

25

Below a Noodle House in Gramercy

"Look, man," said the very skinny guy, "your friend has got to go."

"Your friend has got to go, man," said the guy in very skinny pants. "Your friend has for real got to go."

"How much did all this paint cost?" asked Maryland Slim[29].

"A lot," said the very skinny guy.

"A ton," said the guy in very skinny pants. "Which, also, if this dude's your friend–"

"If this dude's your friend, you owe us for all the punch he drank."

Swan[30] was unavailable to defend himself, being then catatonic on the floor, though his holding an empty bowl was itself fairly damning.

"I've been eating here forever; I had no idea there was a club in the basement," said Slim.

'Here' was 🐎 🥟 , in Gramercy, and below it was, as it turned out, a sprawling meat locker in which a pair of entrepreneurs were preparing for a dim full of remunerative revelry. The walls were brightly painted, and a bar had been recently erected.

---

29 Stylish psychic.
30 Melancholic super-killer.

"And everyone has to go through the kitchen?" asked Slim.

"There's a password," explained the guy in the very skinny pants.

"You gotta know somebody," explained the very skinny guy. "Word of mouth."

"What is it?" asked Maryland Slim.

"We can't tell you."

"Blueberry cobbler."

"Wacky," said Maryland Slim. "And what's with all the soap?"

"We fill the room up with suds."

"Around dimmest."

"What happens to your clo... No, wait, I get it, I get it. I guess that might be fun, if you were high on spoor blossom punch."

"Which, again–"

"How did your friend even know it was here?" asked the very skinny guy.

"He's got a nose for trouble," Slim said. Then Slim laughed.

"Was that supposed to be funny, man?"

"We've got two hundred people going to be here after dimtime–"

"Maryland Slim, you old dog!" Swan said suddenly. "Sneaking in all quiet like! Join me in a cup of kindness, why don't you?"

"He can't drink any punch, man, 'cause you killed it," said the skinny man.

"You killed the punch," said the man in the skinny pants.

"We already sold tickets."

"We pre-sold the punch, man."

"How much?" Slim asked curiously.

"Eight bits a cup."

"Eight bits a cup!" Swan pitched backward, staring at the ceiling in wide-eyed disbelief. "That's theft! That's outright robbery!"

"There were thirty-seven mushroom caps in that bowl–"

"Thirty-seven caps, man, no lie. I cut them up–"

"If there were thirty-seven caps of spoor blossom in there, I'm the Pope!" Swan said. "No way that was worth eight bits a cup."

"That includes the paint–"

"The rent, the suds, the fee to the 18th Street Boys for security–"

"Which, shouldn't they be here to like, get rid of this guy?" said the skinny man.

"Go find them and complain," suggested his partner.

"First time I drank spoor blossom, do you know how much I paid?" Swan asked rhetorically.

"Was it sixteen-hundred bits? Because that's how much you owe us."

"Two bits! Two bits for a full ladle. Got it from some Aquarians, used to have a loft above Bleeker. I was fresh Downtown, barely had so much as a glass of distil; didn't know what I was in for."

"Sure, man, but–"

"Gillian?" Maryland Slim said. "Yeah. I found him, but he won't be much use for a while. I don't know what to tell you, better unpack your back up plan."

"The room starts spinning," Swan continued, "and I figure these yippies must have poisoned me, and I'm getting ready to kill them with the tips of my fingers when all of a sudden, a man in the wall starts telling me to simmer, 'cause everything's going to be fine."

"You gotta pay us, man," said the very skinny guy to Slim.

"You gotta get your friend out of here," said the guy in the very skinny pants.

26

A Life Well Lived

Sordo of Peter Cooper Village

Sordo's world was bound by 1st Avenue and the outer ring, by East 23rd Street and the no man's land of 20th. On one side of that line was strength and honor, upright men and decent women. On the other side of that line – and directly south of it, in particular – was darkness, filth, and corruption. Only twice in his life had Sordo ever left Cooper Village: once to execute the ban on TriBeCa, and once to try a boy the dim before his wedding, and on neither occasion had he enjoyed himself. The Coop was enough for anyone, and better than most deserved. Its preservation had been his sole concern since he had first taken up his spear.

"Chief," said his lieutenant. "A scout just reported in. The juice in one of their towers went out."

"Every window?"

"Yeah."

"Okay," said Sordo.

South on the Eff-Dee-Ar

They hurdled towards Stuyvesant, four stout Boromen[31] to pedal, Hope[32], Ael, and the Kid in the back, along with the merchandise.

---

31 Refugees from the far boroughs, forced to wander the Ring forever.
32 Mind like a cannon. Playing with her nose ring.

"Say, Kid!" Ael said. "Hope told me you've got your six-thousandth dim coming up."

"Did she?"

"Got anything fun planned?"

"I'm going to start a war."

"No cake?"

Of Further Concern

"Chief," interrupted the Lieutenant.

"Yeah?" asked Sordo.

"Stye just got a convoy. Big pediwagon, looked like it was Boromen driving it."

"Boromen?"

"Looks like it."

"Send a runner out to Tower Four," said Sordo. "See who's around can shoulder a pike."

"Will do," said the Lieutenant. He was a brave, plain-faced man who reminded Sordo of his dead son, long lost in a skirmish with Stuy.

"And while you're at it," Sordo added, "send a runner out to Tower Three."

Reserved Parking

The gates of Stuy closed behind them, and they pulled their wagon into the turnaround. The Kid sat on top of a crate, hands cupped around his cigarette as if sharing a secret. Waiting for them were Stuy's War Chief, looking the same as the rest of Stuy but bigger and meaner, along with two dozen soldiers wearing kettle-caps and carrying pikes. The men the Kid had met with the previous dim were nowhere seen.

A Second Plan B

"I already tried one back up plan," Gillian said to Maryland Slim, "and it didn't run so hot."

"Talk twice," Ariadne muttered. Her lank black hair was tinged with gray, and the skin of her neck had grown mottled.

Gillian returned to the present, and her partner. "You need a break?"

"I'm fine."

"No shame–"

"I'm fine," Ariadne repeated, more firmly.

"As you like," Gillian said. The 1st Avenue gates had been built atop the great chassis of a rotted eighteen-wheeler, and it took four stout men to move it. A dull-looking soldier, broad shouldered and bullet-headed, stared down at them. "Who's you?"

"The Sheriff," Gillian said, "and co. Go get whoever you need to get to open the door."

The Most Troublesome Woman on the Island

"Chief?"

"Yeah."

"There's a woman outside wants to get let in."

"And?"

"Says she's the Sheriff."

Sordo cursed, then grabbed his pike and headed into the courtyard. With last bright closing on first dim it was busy, Sordo smiled at a young mother bobbling a square-headed child on her knee, and a toothless grandfather who had once been the fiercest fighter in Peter Cooper Village. The towers were hung with crushed cans, reflecting light onto rows of crops, mushrooms and maize grown high. More than their walls, more than their pikes, it was the green that kept Coop safe, that allowed them to make their own destiny, free of the Enclave or anyone else.

Coop would be a heaven, Sordo often thought, were it not set beside a hell.

"I don't care spoor about your badge, Gillian," he announced upon arrival at the west gate, "and this isn't a good time for a chat."

"What's wrong?" Gillian asked. "Nervous about that shipment that just came in to Stuy?"

Introductions

"I'm the Kid," said the Kid.

"We know who you are," said Stuyvesant Town's War Chief. He was an unpleasant man in general, made more so by having barely survived a coup the previous dim. He had a spear and a big beard. He was twice the Kid's size and three times the Kid's age.

"Then you know what I'm carrying."

"We know."

"Twenty scatterguns," said the Kid, "with ten shots each. More boom than you'll find outside of the Enclave, enough to march straight through the Coop, finally put paid to this whole will-they/won't-they thing."

"Just rut and get it over with," said Hope.

Reasonable Skepticism

"So Stuy is getting some weapons," Sordo asked, "so what?"

"Scatterguns and boom, enough to end the feud right now."

"Every word from you is crooked, Gillian. Was always that way. Why should I trust these?"

Firm Proof

"How do we know that your boom even–" the War Chief began.

The Kid grabbed a scattergun from the box and fired it into the air.

A Preemptive Strike

"You hear that?" Gillian asked.

"Issue pikes to anyone what cares for the Coop," Sordo yelled at his lieutenant, "and bring out any cocktail we've got!"

Show Your Hand

"That first is on me," said the Kid, tossing the scattergun to Ael, who racked it on reflex.

"And the superboom?"

"The superboom is good," promised the Kid, smiling nastily. "I tested it myself. Where's your end of the deal?"

A Desperate Muster

They came streaming out of the neighboring towers and into the courtyard, a scratch force, but speed mattered more than numbers; and anyway, they would never have enough soldiers to make a direct assault on Stuy anything but madness.

"What are you getting out of this, Gillian?" Sordo asked. "Why are you so keen to make sure the Coop stays free?"

"It doesn't mean a lot to me either way," Gillian admitted, "but I am curious to know what Stuy is using for barter."

What Stuy Was Using for Barter

The War Chief signaled, and two soldiers appeared from one of the towers, carrying what looked like a very heavy trunk. The Kid opened it.

Ael whistled. Even Hope seemed impressed.

"Beautiful," said the Kid. "Let's get this on the pedi and you can go conquer the Coop."

"Not quite yet," said the War Chief. "We need to discuss our deal."

"We've already came to terms."

"Them you came to terms with have been shaved and sent to the basement. They won't be fit for nothing but a suicide charge."

"I'm not sure they could even manage that," said the Kid, "letting themselves get outplayed by a withered gray halfwit."

"I thought you might come in here with enough muscle to force my hand, but seeing as how you didn't, there's no deal. We keep everything, your bit and ours. You're lucky we're leaving you your wagon, and your heads, for that matter."

"Perfidy! Deceit! Oh, how I wish I'd thought up some defense against this eventuality," said the Kid, pulling a superboom from out of a pocket of his coat.

Hope popped her bubblegum at the square jaw of a standing Stuyman. "You know you all look alike?"

A Forlorn Hope

There weren't enough of them, weren't close, not for an assault across 20th Street. Forty men, but only half were soldiers, the rest elders what hadn't held a spear in who knew how long and boys what had only hoped to shoulder one.

They would have to do. "For Coop and freedom!" Sordo roared, and went charging into the street.

The Art of the Deal

The tocsins broke the stare down, alarums going off throughout the Stuy.

"Sounds like Coop is making a visit," said the Kid. "Bet it would be useful to have a whole bunch of boom right now."

What was the Kid against the feud? What was anything against the feud? The War Chief sent twenty men to stem the assault and threw his back out helping to load up the wagon.

Aristeia

Like a fork through pudding or a knife through most things, so did Sordo's charge tear past the roundabout. Stuyvesant Town gathered to repel them, but too slow, too slow. Coop become a steel-tipped current forcing its way forward.

A Satisfied Customer

Ael held on to his scattergun until they were through the gates, and then he tossed it to a guard. "One more makes twenty!"

"The Kid is a man of his word!" the Kid roared.

Evens

"Stuy strong!" screamed the soldier as he sprinted out of the doorway, spear fixed on Gillian's back.

Ariadne batted the tip aside with her hook, tripping him as he passed. After a brief tussle she looked up at Gillian, knife-bloodied, and said: "Square."

Heading Towards the Ring

The Kid allowed himself a cigarette and a smile; his seventeenth and first since waking.

Sordo's Last Stand

Sordo punched straight through to the east gate and would have carried on into the river if it hadn't been for the boom, the first of which struck Opie of Tower Three in the face just then.

The Coopers dropped against a convenient wall, Stuy cheered and continued arming themselves from their new stash.

"We have to pull back!" yelled Sordo's lieutenant.

But to do that would only give them more time, and to argue would do the same. And so without further word, Sordo lit the neck of his cocktail and went sprinting up from cover. There had been no boom in Stuyvesant Town for generations, and the shots from their scattergun clattered against Stuy brick and through Stuy glass and into Stuy bedrooms, Sordo surviving untouched until he was only a few steps from the shipment, and then one more *boom* tore through his chest and his neck. With his last flickering shred of consciousness, Sordo dashed his cocktail against the crates, the scattergun and the boom and, unbeknownst to Sordo, the superboom itself.

Thus was Sordo of Peter Cooper Village carried to his grandfathers, having been victorious against hated Stuy, keeping his home free for another bright, at least.

Call no man happy till their death!

27

An Aesthetic Dispute

A scrawny bird, Old Lady Whimple, but there was power in those spindly arms and a weight of lead sewn into the bottom of her clutch – or at least this was how it felt to Mr Pedigreaux whilst being struck by it.

"I thought you was a decent gentleman!" she roared.

"Ms Whimple–"

"You said you was a god-fearing man!"

"All of them, I assure you–" said Mr Pedigreaux.

"Service every dim, you said!"

"More when I can manage it, which is–"

"Come in to see if you wanted a cup of tea, and what do I find? What do I find?"

What Old Lady Whimple had found, upon entering uninvited the attic room which she had been renting to Mr Pedigreaux, was a folder of stock that Mr Pedigreaux had been about to put into his briefcase.

"Art, is the word you're looking for–"

"Smut!" roared Whimple, starting in again with her makeshift sap. "A smut peddler, worse than one what huffs funk!"

"Ms Whimple," said Mr Pedigreaux, drawing himself up as high as his modest frame would allow, "as I said, I am an *agent*, and my business is to assist my stable of artists–"

"Don't talk to me about art! That thing that woman's doing right there isn't art! I don't know what that is!"

"There is nothing about the reproductive process which ought to be considered in any way *shameful*, Ms Whimple, and–"

"Reproductive process! Five boys I brought to the Island, and I never once needed to bend that way!"

"None the less–"

"And what's that one supposed to be doing with that aubergine?"

"I rather gather he intends to–"

But Ms Whimple was in no mood to listen. "You're on the phalt come first bright, Pedigreaux! I'd put you out this tic if it weren't for this soft heart of mine. The t bids us be tolerant, but it also tells us to terrorize those who transgress!"

"I'm paid through till–"

"You'll be out at first bright, or I'll get the Lewis Street Boys to show you why I pay them protection!" Old Lady Whimple roared before slamming the door with such vigor that it seemed the house might cave in around her.

And a fine thing for everyone that would be, thought Mr Pedigreaux miserably. He sighed. He took his hat off and put it on the hook, which was the room's only furnished article besides the bed. Bones in the basement, to be reduced to arguing with a bitter old harridan over a few bits! But then, it had been a run of hard luck for Mr Pedigreaux; the Bear had been savaging him for the better part of forever, and despite what he had told Old Lady Whimple during his preliminary interview, the Bear was the only god in whom Mr Pedigreaux believed.

"At least she didn't destroy the stock," Pedigreaux consoled himself. Besides his suit, a battered boot knife, and one other thing, the crumpled sketches and worn panel books were his only possessions. Two weeks now, he'd been trying to sell them up and down the LES, to every juke joint and dive bar, every brothel and most of the bodegas, without much luck. Lately, everyone had to have color; weren't interested in honest etchings, didn't matter how filthy.

"Less dim comes after dimmest," Pedigreaux reminded himself. And then, as if to prove it, he went and opened the window. The Downtown scuzz flushed in, the smell of rotting trash and simmering mushrooms and tightly packed flesh, accompanied by the usual tenement sounds: farting and rutting and screaming. Pedigreaux went to his battered suitcase and pulled out a length of telescoping pipe with a mouthpiece at the end. "Thank the Tiny t she didn't see this one," said Pedigreaux. Then he went back to the window and stretched his instrument until it reached deep into the surrounding funk.

Pedigreaux took a hard whiff.

Then Pedigreaux put the pipe on the ground and rattled his head about as if searching through a tin. "Nothing here."

And so saying, he took the knife from his boot and brought it swiftly across his throat, spraying blood across his stock, a scattering of crimson to color the grayscale.

28

A Battery

The Swellest Guy on the Lower East Side

The funk turned warm while Maryland Slim was in the basement, and leaving 🦄 🐚 , he took his coat off and folded it neatly over one arm.

"How you doing there, Slim?" asked a passing pedaler.

"Right as the river," said Maryland Slim.

"Looking good, Maryland Slim," said a stoop dweller nursing from a bottle. "Looking pretty."

"Back at you, boss man," said Maryland Slim. Maryland Slim bought an apple at an apple cart, tipped the homely vendor a wink and two bits. His boots held a bright sheen, his bowtie was neat, and he twirled a new cane as he crossed over 1st Avenue and into Stuy, the guards opening and closing the gates for him.

Interlude: Everyone Called Him Slim...

...though his real name was Charles. It was a source of neighborhood speculation how a woman so poor could have a child so fat. His elder seven siblings, all appropriately spindly, had been passed over swiftly, but the confessor stopped when he reached the youngest of the brood.

"High Towers! What have you been feeding him?"

"How old is he?" asked the other confessor.

"Five," said Slim's mother. "Six, maybe."

"No way."

"By the Bull and the Bear," swore his mother, "by the–"

"All right, all right, enough with the god babble."

One of the confessors stared very hard at Slim. Slim felt a tickle round his temples. "Eh," he said.

"What, eh?" said the second.

"He could go either way."

"Let me look."

That tingle again.

"See?"

"You going to take him?" asked Slim's mother. "He's a good boy, never gave me a moment's trouble."

"No, just swallowed every rat bone and all the seed corn," said a confessor.

"It's a mean joke to play on our pedaler." said the other.

"He's getting paid. Besides, we needs porch sweepers just like we do cardinals."

"Cash his mother out, then."

"Thank you, by bridge and tunnel, by bacon and bliss, by the highest of all the towers–"

"Yeah, yeah. You want to say goodbye?"

Slim's mom held Slim tight against her breasts, a tiny woman whom he didn't know well and would never again see. "You do what they tell you now, hear?"

Slim nodded dully and climbed into the waiting pedicab. One of his siblings said goodbye. Another began to wail uncontrollably, but that was on account of the heat. The pedaler cursed as he headed north.

Phrenology

What was it that the confessor saw? Simple: Slim had a big brain. This was not to say that he was clever; he was clever, but that was unrelated to his having a big brain. Having a big brain meant that and nothing more, a mind a little too large for its case, one that could, with some effort, be sloshed over onto other people, people with smaller brains. This was what Slim was doing as he walked through Stuy, leaning on the folk around him: on a woman lost in the memory of a dead lover, on two Stuy brothers what began to scuffle with even less excuse than usual, on a soldier snoozing over his pike. With the citizens and soldiers of Stuyvesant Town proving serendipitously distracted, Maryland Slim strutted across the courtyard and into one of the towers.

Interlude: A Priceless Education

They called him Slim at the Cloister also, according to the same sadistic instinct shared by children across the Island and the World-Writ-Large. He proved an easy target, large but gentle, or quiet, at least, though those are not always the same thing. Only with great difficulty did he manage to acquire the basic skills of the order: to listen to two conversations at once, to simultaneously tap out a separate rhythm with each hand, to soak in the feelings of a neighbor. They'd have called him 'broom sweep', if he hadn't already had a nickname.

Then, one bright, he did something that no one in the Cloister had ever done before, just *woosh,* sat there and did it. Then he did another thing, and a thing after that, and it turned out his brain wasn't weak, exactly, only crooked, and this crookedness let him think around corners where others blundered straight through. Cardinal Ransom said that he had always seen the genius beneath the boy's portly exterior, while Abbess Wahman[33] claimed flat out to have inspired it. And so quiet, so docile! What a fine confessor he would make them, what a useful tool!

Until the bright he did not show up to breakfast, and his bed was found empty.

---

33   At current, Pope.

As for the Competition...

Stuy grew their own crop and pedaled their own juice, but Stuy still had a confessor, like every other clique which could afford it. An unpopular equilibrium, but preferable to getting knocked over by everyone who had ponied up. Stuy's confessor was named Sartwell, and he was just then in the third tower, him and two spearmen watching over the thing that the War Chief had asked them to watch over, thinking about... oh, nothing much really; the weather, what he would do when his shift was over, the time he had jerked off a dog. No, he wasn't thinking about that, *hahaha*, he certainly wasn't thinking about that, couldn't have been, since he had never done it, not out back of the Cloister on a dare once, a slimy bright red, the five bits proving poor compensation against the memory of its bark, as if in appreciation–

"Huh," said Slim.

He closed the crate and left.

Interlude: Charles Was a Dancer

Charles was a dancer; in that mental space in which he resided, in his soul, if you accepted such a concept, Charles was a dancer. Locked in his fleshy cage, Charles was footloose, Charles was light-boned, Charles could keep a perfect rhythm. Charles knew this to be true. He held this certainty against the circumstances of his birth and his time of bitter tutelage, and for the rest of his life it would carry him smiling over the vagaries of ill-fortune and cruel fate, buoyant as a bird in the sky.

"What's your name?" asked the pedicab pedaler.

"Slim," said Charles.

"Just Slim?"

"Maryland Slim."

"What's 'Maryland' mean?"

"No idea," said Maryland Slim, "but it sure sounds pretty."

When the Boom Went Off...

Slim was sitting at the patio bar at ☺ 🍸 . "This is a fabulous highball, Jerry," he said after an appropriate pause.

"That means the world to me," said Jerry.

"Best on the Island. Top three, at least." The patio bar at ☺ 🍸 overlooked 14th Street, and so Slim got a nice view of the competition as they scurried past on their pedicab, a red-haired punk and a feisty looking grinder with a lot of metal and a very handsome young woman chewing...

"Nice bubblegum," remarked Maryland Slim.

Jerry came back, and Maryland Slim ordered another highball, and one after that, and then he ate a dozen oysters real slow, taking time with each, and then he had another highball, and then Gillian showed up.

"A battery," Maryland Slim told her whilst dabbing at his chin. "A great big battery."

29

Family Ties

"Hello, Newton[34]!" said Newton's uncle as Newton sat down to dinner.

"Hello, Uncle," said Newton.

"Where did you get that shiner?"

"I fell playing stickball," said Newton.

"Boys will be boys!" said his uncle, then he turned to the meal. Newton's uncle did not like him very much. That was something that Newton was not supposed to notice, or at least not supposed to comment on, like the fact that his uncle was always attended by scowling men carrying cutters and even cannon, and also that men similar to these waited by the exits to Newton's house and walked Newton to and from school.

"How's math class?" asked Newton's uncle.

"It's fine," said Newton.

"Learning to use your counting board?"

"Yes."

"And catechism?"

"Very good, thanks," said Newton.

"You ask me," Fran[35] said, serving Newton an intimidatingly large slice of mushroom casserole, "instruction in the Tiny t is the only education a young man needs!"

---

34 Unhappy child.
35 Newton's longest tenured nanny.

"May I go to the bathroom?" asked Newton.

He tarried coming back. Newton often did this during dinner and school as well; sometimes he wouldn't even use the toilet, just sat quietly away from everyone until he started to worry they'd notice he was gone.

They mostly did not notice, however, nor did they that evening. By the time Newton returned, his uncle was on the porch, talking to one of the men whose job it was to watch him. Newton did not know the man's name. The man had made a point of not telling him.

"Same as ever," the man was saying. "School, home, school, home."

"Anything... strange?"

"Like what?"

"Anything you can't account for?"

"He's the weirdest little runt ever been spat out a womb, but nothing apart from that. It's a dull detail you've got us on."

"Pray it stays that way," said the man Newton called Uncle.

30

R & R

Idle Hands

A Widow Maker came signifying down the Bowery, beating his buckler for all to hear. And when they reached Elizabeth Street, Ael dropped off the back of the pedicab.

"This is not part of the plan," said the Kid.

"I'll catch up with you."

"Ael–"

"I haven't had anything to do in a while," Ael said. "I'm getting antsy."

In pleasant weather, Downtown lives outside, pretty girls gossiping on stoops, JuiceTown pedalers sharing some distil before starting off for the third shift, hawkers with dried shrooms and fry bread. The Widow Maker was tall and handsome, and his hypeman carried his two-handed sword as if it was a holy relic.

"With your cutter, with your fists, with your pecker," the hypeman roared, "there ain't no one in all of Downtown can match Saski!"

"Talk louder," said another member of the entourage.

"We can draw a ring now or we can take it to the Mad, don't matter none to Saski. The Bull can't help against Saski, and the Bear spoors when he hears his call! From Battery Park to–"

"You're Saski?" Ael interrupted.

"Who's asking?" asked Saski.

"Ael."

"What crew you in?" asked one of Saski's people that wasn't Saski's hypeman. "You got some nerve walking solo up to–"

"Hush up a tic," said Saski. "Ael, like the Ael what did Cleon what led the Dead Rabbits?"

"You've heard of me?"

"I heard you wasted your clique 'cause they tried to make you War Chief."

"Yup!" "Heavy," said Saski admiringly.

Ael pointed at Saski's sword. "That seems longer than it needs to be."

"No such thing," said Saski's girl.

Saski's hypeman laughed.

"I never knew anybody good who used two same-sized cutters," said Saski. "Never. That's strictly for amateurs."

"I got this trick I do," said Ael.

"Word," said Saski. "You want to send for someone who can stand as second?"

"No need."

The hypebird had been pecking away at some corn fallen onto the phalt, but he took to the air just then and began to squawk. "Ael the unmarked! Ael without scars! Ael prettier than your girlfriend, Ael take him home to momma, Ael dyes his clothes in the blood of his enemies!"

"Not literally," said Ael.

"Bliss and bacon!" Saski exclaimed. "Is that a hypebird?"

"Yup!"

"Gorgeous," said Saski. He took his sword from his second. It was indeed very long, but he held it nimbly above his head.

Ael took his baldric off, then took off his red leather jacket and handed it to one of Saski's entourage. Then he put his baldric back on, and unsheathed his cutters. "Say when."

A Clean Break

Adze[36] and a few of his boys were waiting at the abutment. They transferred the Kid's new battery to their own wagon and started funkways up the fortifications. It was a development greeted with enthusiasm by the three pedalers who had only been expecting to be paid for their expedition with hard coin.

"You just going to leave me here?" asked the Boroman who had been rubbing Hope's feet the dim previous, and pedaling her bike just prior, and had shared her bed in the interim.

"Don't make too much of it," said Hope. "I'm sure you'll find someone else to have sex with."

"Maybe we could see each other again?"

"I don't think so. There are too many names to remember already."

"When"

The thing about having two cutters is that one of them is almost certainly not necessary. Even on the Island, there are not many things which remain so indifferent to being struck with one sword as to stick around for a second. Ael's trick was to stand in a certain way as to make it unclear which hand his strike would come from, so that when his opponent should have been watching the muscles in Ael's left elbow, he was watching the muscles in Ael's right shoulder, and by the time he figured out his mistake, it was too late.

Ael still only hit him with the one sword though, a neat slice through the fat center of his thigh.

"So sweet you could drain him and flavor your distil!" the hypebird roared. "No one to touch him, no one to stop him, tell your grandkids you saw him, Ael, Ael, Ael!"

"Shucks," said Ael.

---

36 Hammer-holding head of Security for the Bridge Brides.

Saski was on his knees. "That was..." he began, but didn't finish.

"Thanks!" Ael cleaned and sheathed his swords, then took his coat back from the guy he had given it too. "You really might want to think about shortening your cutter."

"Saski?" asked Saski's hypeman. "You all right?"

"He's fine, it's just his leg. There's a pretty good sawbones on Allen, it's only a couple–"

"I think you nicked his artery!"

"Ho boy," said Ael.

A Blunt Welcome

"Where's Chisel?" asked the Kid.

"Working," said Adze.

"Working where?"

"Don't worry about Chisel," said Adze. "Chisel's busy. I can handle the delivery."

"That's now how this works," the Kid explained. "You hop when I tell you how high."

"Where's the one with all the weapons? The one whose job it would be to stop me from hurting you, were I so inclined?"

"It's a mom-and-pop operation," said the Kid from somewhere near Adze's stomach. "We each wear a lot of hats."

"Is that stew I smell?" Hope interrupted.

"What?" asked Adze.

"Or is that top secret likewise?"

"It's in the dining hall," said Chisel's Null. "I'll take you."

"Fabulous," said Hope. "And you, big man," she ran an appraising eye over Adze, "how about you walk my cousin over to wherever your boss is, real careful like, so you can make sure he don't break nothing."

A Change of Leadership

"When did this become Widow Maker territory?" Ael asked, backing his way towards Broome.

"Since the I's got ended," answered one of an increasing number of Widow Makers what had arrived since Ael had killed their champion.

"Oh," said Ael, "right."

"Numbers don't mean nothing to Ael!" squawked the hypebird. "Not ten to one, not twenty to one, not thirty–"

"Thirty to one might do it," said Ael.

In The Lab

On the floor in front of Chisel were hoses and shafts and screws and washers, indeterminate bits of metal, spokes, lots of rubber, many other things at which she scowled fiercely.

"We have it," said the Kid.

"How did you get back here?" asked Chisel.

"Adze let me in."

"Adze shouldn't have done that."

"You afraid I'm going to steal your secrets?"

"You wouldn't understand them," said Chisel. She picked up a spring, then sat it back down.

"We got it," said the Kid again. "A proper tower battery, should be able to hold enough juice to–"

"Did Adze look at it?" Chisel interrupted.

"Yeah."

"Then I'm sure it's fine." She compared one gasket against another, found neither to her liking. "What? You want me to tell you how clever you are?"

Up Top

"How high up you guys get?" asked Hope.

"High."

"But how high?"

The Null giggled. "I never had flower like this."

They sat in the rigging above the dormitories, watching some commotion taking place around South Street Seaport, a whole bunch of Widow Makers flooding the streets, occasional bursts of screaming.

"You locals don't even know what good flower is," said Hope. "This is my personal strain; took a cutting from my grandmother."

"It's..." But the Null forgot to finish.

"How long you been with the Brides?" Hope asked.

"A while."

"What was your name?"

The Null giggled. "Not supposed to remember."

"You can't make yourself forget a thing," Hope opined. "It's not possible."

The Null giggled again.

"Have some more flower."

"We used to call it 4:20."

"Huh?"

"Like the time."

"Like Enclave time?"

"Yeah."

"Why?"

"Dunno."

"Huh," Hope said. "Have another puff, why don't you?"

"If you're going to insist."

An Uninvited Guest

They had kitted out the courtyard in grand fashion, strung streamers and hung pinwheels, brought out the all the high relics, not to mention a vat of distil and a keg of house brew, a tray full of flower, the whole bit. Wasn't every dim a squire got promoted to soldier, and the War Chief's nephew, at that.

"Five Points is strong because Five Points is family," said the War Chief. "This blade was carried by Tomes's father, my brother, to TriBeCa and to a hundred separate scuffles. On his death bed, I swore I'd make sure his son would grow to be man enough to wield it. I'm proud to say, I kept that faith." The War Chief had tears in his eyes as he handed Tomes the cutter. "To Tomes!" he roared. "May he live to pass his sword!"

"To Tomes!" the assembled agreed.

Tomes was all set to say something sweet when Ael hopped over the fence that separated the courtyard from the courtyard beside it, carrying his jacket like a banner, his hypebird gusting bright above. He sprinted past Tomes lifting his new cutter in what might have been considered a threatening gesture, and on joyous instinct Ael caught his head with the jacket and dragged him *smack* down against the phalt, leaving both and continuing up over the fence and into the next courtyard.

The Five Point Felons had been unprepared for Ael's arrival, but when the Widow Makers arrived in pursuit, they received a warmer reception.

Still Higher

"You do it in the dorms in front of everybody?" Hope asked.

"There's a room away from the corridor, and you just kind of know not to go when people are inside," said the Null.

"Never work for me. I'm a screamer. Besides, I need some space to get tossed about in. Like that Adze of yours..." Hope gave a false shiver. "He looked like he'd give you a good throw."

The Null blushed.

"You want a guy you aren't worried you're going to break, you know? That's my thing, at least, but you know, everyone has theirs. There was this guitar player from Meat Packing I used to run with, wanted me to let him call me Mommy and walk him around on a leash." Hope exhaled flower. "No thanks. Whose mom walks them like a dog? It was conceptually muddled."

"Yeah," said the Null.

"What about the senior members?"

"Senior members have their own quarters."

"Like   Chisel?"

"Yeah," said the Null. "Hers is at the bottom. No one else goes in there but me, though, and that's just to pedal her juice."

"None of you strapping young fellows warms her cot?"

"Chisel doesn't rut," said the Null. "She's giving birth to the future. She's going to be the mother of tomorrow."

Hope took the joint back. "You've had plenty," she said.

In a Basement Below 🦄 🐾

When Swan woke, the bubbles were up to his chin; a little longer and they'd have succeeded where numberless toughs had failed. Blitzed brainless, he fought his way to his feet – no easy feat, but he managed it.

"Weird that feet and feat are the same word," said Swan.

"Huh?" said a reveler.

"Never mind."

The party had hit some snags in the early going, but they'd righted the ship, moved Swan to a corner, and found enough spoor blossom to get a second pot simmering. Half-naked beauties gyrated above the cresting foam, broad shoulders and bouncing breasts, paint on the wall and on their skin. On a stage above the soap, someone played a mammoth melodica while on either side, a man and a woman pumped the bellows and sang along.

"Yeah!" said Swan, who found he didn't mind the noise so much as he normally did. "Yeah!" He bobbed along awhile, lost in perfect rhythm, then went to steal more punch.

The Kid Alone

The Kid dangled his legs over the East River. When one cigarette went out, he lit another.

The Enemy of my Enemy

"Ael's the fastest!" the hypebird squawked from high above Bayard Street, dodging out the way of a javelin. "Can't none of you lay a finger on Ael!"

"Kill it!"

"Get it down!"

"Murder it!"

"Forget the bird, get the man!"

"Close off the back!"

"Someone find a slinger!"

There had been blood shed, there had been bones broken, there had even been feelings injured before the Widow Makers and the Five Point Felons found common cause against their shared enemy. They had managed it, however; after which, the swelled mob had cornered Ael atop a townhouse overlooking Columbus Park. There were soldiers coming up the fire escape and soldiers coming down the hallway, and Ael yelled, "Sore losers, the lot of you!" before leaping into the green below.

Pillow Talk

Gillian lived in a penthouse overlooking Union Square, and dimmest turning to less dim, Ariadne met Daedalus in its basement. A symbol scratched beside a sewer grate had been enough to get him word, but he'd had to wait since dimtime and the anticipation had done him no good. He rose when she came in and gasped when he saw her face: where her ink did not run, the skin had colored, as if of a burn long healed.

"By the labyrinth," he began.

"Ain't nothing," said Ariadne, turning away.

"Crone?" he asked, growing furious.

"Not Crone," said Ariadne. "Rat chase cheese. Rat catch snare."

Subterraneans were hard folk, not given to emotion; but still, Dade held her face a moment before continuing. "What's the scuttle?"

"Quarry's clever. Smelled spoor, but no meat."

"And Gillian?"

"Crone clever too," said Ariadne grudgingly.

"Crone cleverer than anything," Dade said, "and worse than that too. Follow her, keep a close watch, but come back to clan. Better swallow poison than trust Gillian."

"Rat hear," said Ariadne. Then, against herself, though she did not want to know, she asked, "Dade peeped TriBeCa?"

"Dade peep."

"What... was it?"

"Dunno. Funk, or a ghost, or nothing. Dunno. Stay out of TriBeCa," he said, pulling her close. Then, because he could not stop himself, he added, "Don't trust Crone."

Obligations of Leadership

When Chisel left the laboratory, it was deep dimmest.

"Done?" Adze asked.

"If I had another week, it would be better," said Chisel.

"You could add that sentence to the end of every other sentence you'll ever say."

"Where's Hope?"

"Passed out in an extra bed," said Adze.

"And Ael?"

"No word."

"Let the guards know he might slip in," said Chisel.

"I already did," said Adze.

This far funkways, the bridge seemed like a tunnel; they were surrounded by thick gray in all directions.

"And?" Chisel asked finally.

"This is getting worrying."

"What is?"

"You are a relentlessly unsubtle person," said Adze.

"You're not exactly spy material neither."

"You shouldn't be rutting this child."

"Since when is it your business who I rut?"

"Since I swore an oath to do what you told me."

"I know you don't like him," said Chisel.

"He's Belleview," said Adze. "He's blood simple."

"Nothing simple about the Kid."

"He drops more bodies than he does cigarettes."

"Isn't like we haven't made our share," said Chisel.

"You can kill a man with a screwdriver, but that's not its purpose."

"With the loot he's given us, we'll be able to advance our timeline by–"

"Where does all that scrip come from, you ever wonder? You know he smokes straight tobacco, no flower, goes for twenty a tab. Who in the Island has that much money?"

"Whoever he's working for."

"You come to any conclusions about that?"

"No," said Chisel, "which is why I'm going to need you to figure it out."

Late Arrival

It had certainly born all the signs of a raid, the Widow Makers and the Five Point Felons armed and enraged and sprinting towards Two Bridges. And so the Twins met their invaders as they always had: with shiv and brickbat, with hatchet, with cutter, with chain and spear, with rocks dropped from high windows.

Ael jogged up the Brooklyn Bridge Walkway, limping slightly but smiling. He didn't even get annoyed when a guard with an X-bow challenged him.

"Who you?"

Turning circles in the air above, the hypebird was swift to answer: "Ael the swift, Ael the clever, Ael what can't be caught..."

31

Boy with Horn

Goldman showed up at ♥ 🎁 just before it closed, with the stage dark and the bouncer ushering out the last customer, and Antony making a vague show of cleaning.

"Were you been at, Enclave?" asked Antony. He had owned ♥ 🎁 since he'd mustered out of the Anarchs; purchased it with the loot he'd taken from ruined TriBeCa.

"Had a set at Money Talks," said Goldman, trying not to sound proud.

Antony whistled. "Coming up in the world. You want a house brew?"

"I wouldn't mind," said Goldman, though he barely drank any, nursing it while Antony put the chairs on the tables and began a vague feint at cleaning the counter.

Dumaille and Nina wiggled in then.

"How you doing, Enclave?" said Dumaille.

"Looking sweet, Enclave," echoed Nina.

"Howdy," said Goldman, making sure not to blush. "Good evening?"

"Usual Uptown crowd," said Nina, "no offense." Antony brought her over two shots of distil, and she took both in rapid succession. "Won't dance no matter what you do for them."

"You'd be better off playing Downtown," said Yancey, who had slunk in all of a sudden.

"They don't pay," said Dumaille.

155

"But they listen to the music," said Yancey. He took a seat at the bar but didn't get a drink. Yancey didn't drink, and he didn't even chase much tail. About the only thing Yancey really did was play his accordion better than anyone who had ever lived. "Why you keep letting Enclave in here?"

When Antony or Nina called him Enclave, it was a nickname, but when Yancey did it was a threat, or maybe a challenge.

"Because it's my joint, and I let in whoever I want," said Antony.

"Where is Reed?" asked Yancey.

"He's got that girl he's seeing in Greenwich," said Nina. "Hill woman, something like that."

"How the hell we gonna play we don't have a horn?" asked Yancey.

"Enclave's got a horn," said Nina.

"Yeah, he's got a horn; don't mean he can play it."

Goldman had been waiting for this moment since Yancey had walked into the bar, and for most of his life before that. He pulled the trumpet neatly out from his case, bringing it to his lips and letting loose. Dumaille tapped his foot for a moment, and then went to find his guitar. Nina headed over to the house piano, and finally Yancey stopped staring at Goldman like he was going to kill him and instead he took out his great big accordion, fingers falling into place perfectly.

And for a while afterward, there was nothing but the *groove*, Goldman's god and the god of all the musicians that played at ♥ 🎁 after closing, which the hip cats and only the hip cats knew was the tightest band on the Island.

"What you stop for?" asked Goldman, after they had stopped.

Yancey laughed. "How long you think we been going?"

♥ 🎁 was on the third floor of a building on Houston, above a bodega and a smoke shop, and when Antony opened the window, Goldman could see less dim turning to first bright.

"Getting late," said Goldman.

Dumaille laughed.

"Enclave can blow," said Nina.

"Enclave can blow," Yancey agreed.

Goldman smiled shyly but didn't trust himself to speak.

Antony came back from the window with a metal object the shape of an egg and the size of a small melon. "Huff?" he asked.

"I'll take a quick one," said Yancey.

"If you're going to twist my arm," said Nina.

Yancey held the egg to his lips. "Barry Gordy's Ghost," he said passing it on to Dumaille, who took a huff and passed it on to Goldman. Goldman had tried a bit of flower once at a party, but he hadn't liked it and he hadn't tried it again. And for that matter, he wasn't such a big fan of distil or even house brew. But that was hardly the point. Having proven himself on the horn, was Goldman going to fade now? No, Goldman was not. Goldman brought the egg to his mouth and took a shallow breath.

"I guess we can tell Reed he don't never need to come back from Greenwich," said Antony, laughing.

"No help here, either," said Goldman, getting up and heading to the bar.

"They say those Aquarian girls have all kinds of tricks," said Dumaille. "Say they can do things drive a man mad."

"You'll believe anything," said Nina.

"Like you know."

"One licked me out once, and I can tell you it wasn't nothing special."

"Maybe it just works for guys," said Yancey, laughing, just before Goldman hit him in the head with the knife he had taken from behind the counter.

Dumaille screamed and Nina screamed and Yancey collapsed onto the ground and Goldman laughed and was set to continue his slaughter when Antony, who carried a ratchet on his hip from long habit, got up and stabbed him in the chest.

The scene at ♥ 🎁 never really recovered after that.

The Bright After That…

32

Before Class

"You shouldn't smoke," Newton told the man behind the fence.

"Probably not," agreed the man. Young man, really. Older than any of the boys in Newton's school, but not by much. He was thin and dark and red-haired and cruel-eyed, and Newton thought him the handsomest thing he had ever seen. He pointed at the sketch Newton was drawing. "Who's that?"

"His name is Cinder," said Newton.

"Why is his face like that?"

"That's the living flame. It used to be just in his arm, but now it's spreading to the rest of him. The living flame is the only thing in all the World-Writ-Large that can defeat the First Wyrm, what overthrew Cinder's father, Virgil the Wise. Cinder needs to defeat the First Wyrm so he can put his father back on the throne."

"Why?" asked the Man.

"Why, what?"

"Why would Cinder put his father back on the throne?"

"His father's the king," explained Newton.

"His father *was* the king. Now the First Wyrm is the king. If Cinder kills him, Cinder should be the king. That's the way kings work."

"Who are you?" asked Newton.

"A messenger."

"For who?"

"As in, 'who sent the message?' or 'who is the intended recipient?' "

"Who sent the message?"

"It doesn't matter."

"Who is it for?"

"You."

"Me?"

"You and your parental guardian."

"I'm an orphan."

"Is that right?"

"What's the message?"

In the dust of the phalt, the man drew a ▼.

"Okay," Newton said. "I'll tell him."

33

The Seventh Life of Nelly Karrow

"I'm sorry," said the sawbones, "when the funk gets into their lungs like that, there's really nothing to be done."

"Butcher!" roared Nelly Karrow. "A cough, she had! Come in with a cough and you... you... oh!" Nelly Karrow sputtered speechless. This man did not know who Nelly Karrow was, clearly! Nelly Karrow had friends in high towers, friends who knew the worth of Nelly Karrow when held against some Alphabet City sawbones. Idiot with a hacksaw, more like. By the Tiny t, Nelly Karrow would give him a piece of her mind, while also...

...mewling piteously in anticipation of the diminution of 12.5 % of her consciousness...

...breathing out its last on the gurney in front of the useless sawbones...

...savaging an antique sofa, great white rents of cotton...

...screeching in an alley off the Bowery...

...sniffing the Huddy's tang from a roof in meatpacking...

...micturating fiercely on a beloved family heirloom...

...watching Gillian at the window of a café across from JuiceTown...

34

The Great JuiceTown Robbery

Inside

Van didn't actually see much, on account of Simmons was out with fever and the foreman had given Van his stationary in the back corner of the second level, far from the door with the hum of wheels so loud that it blotted out your very thoughts. Besides, midway through a shift, you weren't paying attention to anything but the pedals turning, which was to say nothing at all, trying to keep your mind blank till they blew the whistle. Though he drank for a generation off what he pieced together afterward – the giant in red armor, his desperate struggle with the Force – the honest truth was that the first that Van was even aware anything was going on was after all of the guards had already been slaughtered and a kid leaned over the railing and yelled, "Quit your pedaling! This is a robbery!"

Outside

Gillian watched from the patio of a café across the street, drinking a weak but enormously expensive cup of coffee. Maryland Slim was having the same along with some fried pigeon eggs. Ariadne sat at the table but had resolutely refused a second coffee and was making do with a glass of water. Swan was passed out on the pavement, naked except for his mask and a loin cloth, sallow skin painted in garish red and green.

"What happened?" asked Ariadne.

"They don't have drugs in the dark?" asked Maryland Slim.

"Dark got shroom wine! Dark got everything."

"Ariadne, does the Green Line run below here?"

"Crone knows so," Ariadne said. "Rat peep?"

"Rat peep," confirmed Gillian.

"Dig," said Ariadne. "Rat bored of simmering."

"Ariadne!" Gillian called back, "Peep, don't claw. This is just a guy; we want the guy behind him."

Ariadne nodded and flitted off to find a sewer grate, or a manhole cover, or just an honest subway entrance. With her gone, only Gillian and Slim were left conscious.

"That's quite a scar on your girl," said Slim.

"Yeah?"

"Yeah."

"Where did she get it?"

"Did you ask her?"

"I'm asking you."

"Why ask anyone, if you already know the answer?"

Inside

Moze was the name of the second shift supervisor, and he was upset. "You're insane. Every clique in the city will be after your head! It'll be the ban for sure! And there isn't even anything to steal! What are you going to do, walk out with our stationaries?"

"Nope," said the Kid, "just your juice. Ael, if you'd be so kind."

Ael wore his full regalia, spiked battle leathers, a dozen different means of homicide and a bandolier of nasty looking black spheres, one of which he lit and tossed off the balcony. It exploded with more smoke than fire, but it was sufficient to get Van and all the rest of the pedalers on the second shift sprinting madly up the stairs.

Outside

The explosion jolted Swan awake. He rubbed at the black cap which covered his head and most of his face, and then he moaned a while. "Where am I?"

"Outside of JuiceTown," said Gillian.

"Oh," said Swan. "How did I end up here?"

"I had Slim get up in your mind and walk you over."

"Is that why my head hurts so bad?"

"The drink probably didn't help," said Slim.

"Probably not. How's it going, Slim?"

"I get by. How about you?"

"There's an ice pick in my skull," said Swan, "and this paint itches like you wouldn't believe."

"Sorry to hear that."

"Where's your sword?" asked Gillian.

"I dunno," said Swan, "you're the one what brought me out here."

The mob of JuiceTown pedalers reached the exits just then, hundreds of men with wide thighs and narrow shoulders bottlenecked into the double doors of Rockefeller Center.

"We gonna tell anyone about that?" asked Slim.

Gillian sipped her tepid coffee. "You don't think they'll hear?"

Inside

Moze was not sure when exactly the frightening woman and her slightly less frightening accomplice had come in. Also, he wasn't sure which one was which, just that they'd appeared all of a sudden while he was occupied by the Kid, a rounded woman carrying a cannon and a scenester with a nose ring.

"Where's the tricycle?" asked the Kid.

"In the service elevator," said the woman with the cannon. "Send Ael down after it." She turned hard eyes on Moze. "You must be our host."

Moze decided then that she was the more frightening of the two.

Outside

They did learn. They learned pretty quick. Rockefeller Plaza is just outside the gates of the Enclave, and it only took a few tics for the Force to arrive, a detachment of cavalry galloping down 5th Avenue, blue pennants fluttering in the breeze. They were joined not long after by the Commissioner[37] and every patrolman the Commissioner could scrounge, followed closely by the Mayor[38] and a dozen armed aides. Gillian went to the toilets, leaving behind Swan and Maryland Slim and a flask of distil that Maryland Slim had in his suit pocket.

"What was the name of the gang she had you kill?" Slim asked.

"The Blades? Or maybe the Orphans?"

"What was their sigil?"

"I don't remember; something stupid. Skulls, or something." Swan took a guzzle, then returned the flask. "Anyway, I don't think they're that important."

"Huh," said Slim, pondering.

"So that bunch in there killed the I's," said Swan, "then got a battery from Stuy, then come here to fill it up?"

"Apparently," said Slim.

"And Gillian is chasing after them?"

"That's what she says."

"Why is the rat girl here?"

"I'm not really sure."

Swan took the flask from Maryland Slim. They watched as the Mayor and Commissioner gesticulated at one another in increasingly excited fashion. Another wave of Force arrived.

---

37 Head of the Force.
38 Upright as any of his predecessors.

"You know she's Dade's mate?" asked Swan, after another guzzle.

"Didn't Gillian try to kill Dade, once upon a time?" asked Maryland Slim.

"Other way."

"You sure?"

"You ever know Gillian to leave someone alive?"

"Good point," said Maryland Slim, retrieving his flask before Swan could finish it outright.

Inside

Dark inside, but the dark was comfort. You can't see in the dark, but they can't see either, and you can smell at least, better than them. Hear better than they can; how couldn't you, yelling and talking all the time, loud words and too many of them, like they never learned to listen, or forgot how. Ariadne wiggled through the crawlspace, not fast but faster than anyone wasn't raised in the dark could hope to move. Her hook hung on her back.

Outside

"Stand down, Mayor," said the Commissioner, "this isn't your concern. The Force are responsible for security in JuiceTown."

"And a bang-up job you're doing," snapped the Mayor. "Who was it slaughtered their way through your entire guard?"

"That would be me," the Kid yelled from a window on the second floor.

Inside

"I won't tell you anything," Moze[39] said to Chisel as she prodded

---

39 JuiceTown Foreman, not anticipating this when he clocked in.

him towards the back rooms. "I swore an oath to JuiceTown, and to the Tap, and you'll never have me break it, never."

"No?" asked Chisel.

"It wouldn't matter to me if you tied me up naked and whipped me with a length of wire, or tied me down, naked, and stepped on my scrotum, or–"

"I doubt it will come to that," interrupted Chisel.

JuiceTown was three floors of stationaries, hundreds of bikes on each floor, every one attached to a length of wire which ran to a battery the size of a small room: the Great Tap, the source from which nearly all the batteries on the Island were recharged. Of course, it was useless unless you were Moze or one of his fellow guildsmen and had been initiated into its secrets, a vast sum of esoterica impenetrable to outsiders. "This is the wonkiest set-up I've ever seen," said Chisel, after a brief inspection. "What kind of electrode are you using?"

"Magnesium," admitted Moze.

"Magnesium!" Chisel shook her head. "I can't believe you haven't blown yourselves up already. Which, by the way, what do you suppose would happen if I were to take one of those big metal spears my friend was carrying, wrap some wire around it and…"

Outside

This was the first sight that the Mayor or the Commissioner had gotten of their adversary, and it was not a particularly prepossessing one.

"Hell and High Towers," said the Mayor, "how old are you?"

"I've started finding hairs where there weren't no hairs before," the Kid admitted, "but that's not really the point right now."

"No," the Mayor agreed, "it isn't. Look, kid–"

"It's the Kid, actually."

"What?"

"As in singular."

"Right," said the Mayor. "Look, the Kid, if you supposed we were going to keep you alive because you're holding some JuiceTown functionary hostage, you've made an error in judgment. The Commissioner here is not a fellow renowned for his squeamishness, and I confess, I myself am thinking more of the Island's well-being than any collateral damage required in its service."

"Curse my naïveté!" said the Kid. He flicked his cigarette onto the street below and started immediately on another. "Fool I am, to trust my safety to your soft-heartedness!"

"It's a bomb!" Moze screamed as he came sprinting out of the doors. "They've rigged the Great Tap into a giant bomb!"

This revelation caused the predictable stir among the gathered crowd, the Force and the mayoral aides and the mob of potentially unemployed pedalers and just your usual gawking passerby, nothing better to do than mill about in hopes of seeing something bad happen. The Kid disappeared from the window.

Gillian arrived just as the mob began to turn. "Commissioner. Mayor. Might I be of service?"

Inside

"It's not that the Force can't fight; it's that they can only fight when you warn them ahead of time." Ael had pushed the tricycle into the main lobby, where it shared company with half a dozen corpses and Hope, who was flipping through a nudie book she'd taken off one of aforementioned corpses, drawings of ladies in black leather, holding chains and utilizing various sorts of thrusting machines.

"Not really," said Hope.

"They're all reaction. If you surprise them, or show them one hand and give them something else, they just fall right apart."

"I could do that one," Hope said, flipping a page, "but this I don't really have the build for."

Outside

"What do you mean, they're going to turn it into a bomb?" asked the Commissioner, in the sort of voice that had, back when he'd just been a patrolman, generally preceded a suspect being beaten about the face and neck.

Moze was pretty shook, what with everything. "Only the wisest of JuiceTown sages are even aware that such a thing is possible, let alone that–"

"Then how the hell did he–"

"She, not he! And someone must have taught her," Moze continued, "it's the only way that she could have–"

"A big bomb, you said," Gillian interrupted. "How big?"

"Huge," said Moze. "If they rigged the Tap to blow, it would wreck half of Midtown."

"Hey, Gillian," Swan interrupted, arriving just then, "how long is this going to take?"

"It depends on whether or not the Commissioner decides to play hardball and get all of us killed."

"Oh," said Swan. "Do I have time to go grab a bottle?"

"No," said Gillian. "Just chill a bit, okay? Doesn't Slim have something?"

"He did."

Inside

"That's him?" Hope asked.

"Yup!" said Ael.

"With the paint and no pants?"

"Yup!"

"Huh," said Hope.

"What do you mean, 'huh'?"

"Nothing, nothing."

"What?" Ael asked. "What is it?"

"He's kinda fat."

"He's not fat!"

"For a guy you're telling me is the best killer on the Island…"

"He does have kind of a paunch," Ael admitted. "Say, Kid?"

The Kid was down by the stationaries, fiddling with an alarm clock and some wires. "Yeah, Ael?"

"You sure that's Swan?"

"Yeah."

"Swan, like the Swan who killed every grinder in Chelsea that time?"

"Yeah."

"Swan who slew TriBeCa's champion, though they was taller than a lamp post?"

"Yes."

"You sure, sure?"

"Yeah, Ael," said the Kid, growing annoyed. "I'm sure."

"I still say he's eaten a few too many poodles," said Hope.

Outside

The Pope[40] arrived with six confessors and three bishops and even a cardinal. Having hurried all the way down from the Cloister, she took a surprisingly long time to alight from her pedicab, even with the gentlemanly assistance of the Mayor.

"I gather there's something of a problem," she began, eventually.

"Sad to say," said the Mayor.

"Don't the Force handle security for JuiceTown?" asked the Pope.

"Bacon and bliss," the Commissioner began, "We–"

"Indeed, they do, Pope, indeed they do," the Mayor

---

40   Head of the Cloister. Big brained.

interrupted, "and we'll have to discuss that matter in thorough detail at some future moment. But for now, other considerations must dominate the conversation."

"You want to keep warm in that stone palace of yours?" the Commissioner interrupted the Mayor. "Then jiggery pokery these idiots in range of our boom."

Inside

Unable to stand the sound any longer, Chisel looked up from where she knelt by the Great Tap and said, "Chew that gum somewhere else."

"We need to have a chat," said Hope.

"Hurry up, then," said Chisel, going back to her work.

"I don't like you."

"Okay."

"I don't trust you either. None of you Brides, your weird nicknames and all that nonsense talk about the future."

"If you're so suspicious," Chisel asked, "why don't you root about in my brain a while, and figure out whether I'm on the level?"

"That's not the way it works; I can't read your mind. I can do a lot of other things, though. Like, if you were for some reason to betray us, I could have you leap off your bridge, or choke on the barrel of your cannon. Something to think on."

"I'll add it to the queue," said Chisel, fiddling with a dial on the machine. "Anything else?"

"You know it's Kid's six thousandth?"

Chisel stopped what she was doing. "He didn't mention it."

"How many dims you got?"

"Dims are a useless unit of measurement."

"You think we call him 'the Kid' because he's so old?" Hope replied.

"Are you coming to a point?" Chisel asked.

"You break my cousin's heart, and I'm going to put your

mind inside a cage and rent your body to a whorehouse. Then I'm going to I'll let you back out again, so you can see what's been done to you."

Standing, Chisel was quite a lot bigger than Hope. "You come at me, you best put me in the East River," she said. "Anything short and you'll spend a long time regretting it. You don't have the slightest conception of what I'm capable of doing, and there are a lot of ways to ruin a person don't have nothing to do with magic."

Outside

The arrival of the Pope and her colleagues had not gone unnoticed by Maryland Slim. They were too far away to hear the conversation, but Slim knew what they were saying. Arrogant Uptown idiots. Even being allied to them by default was enough to get Slim grinding his teeth.

"High Towers," Swan said. "You get made fun of a bit in school and it's mortal combat for the rest of time."

"Weren't you supposed to be getting a sword?" Slim asked.

"Yeah, thanks for reminding me." With his usual superhuman celerity, Swan pointed abruptly to a pasty-looking Anarch in the crowd nearby. "Gimme your sword!" he yelled.

The Anarch tore the seat of his pants in his haste to unbuckle it.

Inside

The Kid was putting together the device Chisel had given him when he felt the first tingle. "Right on schedule," he said.

Outside

The Pope did not bother to do anything herself, nor even to

use her cardinal, leaving the confessors and a single bishop to cordon themselves around the entrance to JuiceTown. At the café across the square, Maryland Slim kept up a contemptuous commentary for an indifferent Swan.

"No artistry, no style – spokes in a wheel, every one of them."

"This cutter is bent," said Swan, inspecting his newly acquired weapon.

"It's like listening to someone play an untuned guitar."

"And it doesn't even have a tang," Swan exclaimed, still fixated on his weapon. "They like... glued the blade to the handle."

"They shave their heads every bright, most of them," said Slim. "Every bright! Can you imagine someone telling you to do that and then you actually doing it?"

Swan set his sword back in its sheath. "You and Gillian, you just can't let anything die."

"Some grudges aren't meant to die."

"Everything dies, Slim – or hadn't you noticed?"

Inside

"Hope!" the Kid yelled down. "I'm feeling a tug."

"I got it," Hope yelled, but she and Chisel remained eyeball to eyeball a bit longer. "You just remember, the Kid isn't the mean one in the family."

"You are?"

"No," said Hope, "but I'm bad enough." And then she closed her eyes and fell silent.

Outside

One confessor screamed as if he had put his hand in scalding water. Another spoored his pants so violently that it was noticed in the distant reaches of the crowd. The bishop fell flat backward, slammed his head and began to fishtail across the phalt.

"Walk to Jersey!" Slim cheered. He'd have jumped right out of his chair, had he been more of a jumper.

Somewhere Else Altogether

"You got some heat on you, girl, by the Towers."

"Who are you? How did you get through my shield?"

"Oh, Slim's got as many cards as he's got sleeves. And in here, you can have all the arms you want."

"Those are bad last words."

"Be cool, be cool, I'm not with them."

"You don't sound like it. Look like it. Feel like it. Whatever."

"Feel like it; you had it right the third time. Maryland Slim, at your service."

"OK."

"…"

"…"

"*The* Maryland Slim."

"What?"

"That is to say, I'm the real and true Maryland Slim, not someone claiming to be me."

"Why would someone want to pretend they were you?"

"I'm famous."

"Apparently not."

Inside

Chisel came back from the Great Tap, saw the Kid still fiddling with some wires attached to the chronometer, and said, "Get up."

"Is the battery charged?" the Kid asked.

"Obviously. Get up."

"Ael," said the Kid, still trying to puzzle through his task, "go get the battery."

"Now that I think on it," Ael said to his hypebird, "he wasn't really in great shape."

"Had a paunch," the hypebird agreed.

"Ael!" said the Kid.

"All right, all right."

"You're making a mess of it," Chisel snapped.

The Kid stood reluctantly, and Chisel took his spot.

Outside

"They've got someone in there," announced the Pope, as her underlings dealt with the wounded.

"Seems like it," said Gillian.

"Not one of ours," the Pope continued, turning ferocious eyes on Gillian. "An apostate."

"Don't look at me; my apostate is over there," said Gillian, pointing to where Maryland Slim sat in the shade of the café, choking back laughter.

"Someone else, then," the Pope acknowledged. "At any rate, it won't matter long. Now that we know they're in there, we can adjust to compensate." "I'm sure that will work," Gillian said, not meaning it.

"What's the alternative?" asked the Mayor.

"Give them whatever you have to give them to get them away from JuiceTown, and then kill them and take whatever you gave them back."

"Actually," the Mayor said, "that's not a bad idea."

Somewhere Else Altogether

"Seriously? Maryland Slim? The Foremost Apostate? The Dropout?"

"Doesn't ring a bell."

"The Cloister sent six confessors and a bishop after me before they finally gave up."

"I'm not real impressed with what I see of your locals, apart from the robes."

"How is it that the Pope didn't pick you up at some point?"

"On the Ring, we don't sell our children to old women in stone castles."

"An admirable policy. Though, if they did, you might have a little more technique to you."

"Doing well enough so far."

"So far. You hear that?"

"No."

"Listen harder."

"You said you can't listen here."

"It's a tactile equivalent. There?"

"Yeah."

"That's them. They'll be here soon."

Inside

"Say, Kid," Hope began. A chaw of pink sat forgotten in the corner of her mouth, and she tugged anxiously at her nose ring. "Is this going to take much longer?"

No one noticed the rustle in the vent.

Outside

"Nearly there," said the Pope. Her scalp glistened keenly. "Whoever is inside might have some... raw potency, but they lack discipline."

Somewhere Else Altogether

"All you need to do is ask."

"For what?"

"Maryland Slim's assistance."

"Huff funk."

"You got spine girl, but they're going to eat you soon enough."

Inside

Ael was strapping the battery into the truck bed. Chisel was in the driver's seat, wearing a set of leather goggles. Her cannon was stashed beside the battery. Hope was chewing her bubble gum like the bones of a sworn enemy.

Outside

The Pope and all the rest of her people that could still stand locked hands.

"They don't need to do that," said Maryland Slim. "They just think it looks cool."

"That pocket square of yours isn't exactly functional neither," said Swan.

"But it's pretty."

"I guess. I should probably go find another sword."

"Rut it," Slim said, coming to a decision.

The confessor on the far left tripped. A minor thing, but it seemed to affect the balance of all the rest, the one next to her dropping suddenly likewise, the Pope going down on one knee, a cardinal vomiting up all over his mink.

Somewhere Else Altogether

"Wow!"

"Told you."

"How did you do that?"

"I'm Maryland Slim, baby girl. I can do all sorts of things."

Inside

"They're down!" said Hope, "Let's mosey."

"Groovy," said the Kid from where he sat beside her. "Chisel?"

"Where's my cannon?" asked Chisel.

The answer arrived just then, Ariadne popping off with one chamber from her stolen weapon. It went high, puncturing a hole in the ceiling, and Ael was turning enthusiastically to deal with her when the Kid yelled, "Forget about her! Floor it!"

Outside

The autocycle smashed through the JuiceTown doors, plunging down the marble steps, passing the broken chain of confessors and the loose cordon of Force and mayoral aides. Its chassis was welded together from a pair of busted motorcycles and an acrylic blue sedan with white wingtips, and its three fat tires had come off a maintenance vehicle from all the way up in Manhattanville. The wagon bed was just a wagon bed, you could get that anywhere, but underneath it was an engine incomprehensible to anyone else on the Island or the World-Writ-Large, save Chisel herself. A soldier shot a hole in the fender before Ael, standing on the back running board, skewered him with a neat cast from a javelin, and then they turned onto the phalt and headed west on 49th Street, the crowd making desperate way before them.

"Interesting," Gillian said. Gillian had found herself, potentially even by coincidence, standing beside a cavalryman, who stared open-mouthed at the rapidly receding vehicle before finding himself on the phalt, Gillian astride his mount a moment later. "You coming?"

"I'm not so big on chases," admitted Maryland Slim. "I'll be at the Magic Box; come by and let me know how it goes."

"What about you?" she asked Swan.

"I hate horses."

"Then steal a bike," she snapped, then slapped the rump of her horse and galloped towards 5th Avenue.

The autocycle surged passed Radio City Music Hall, silencing the performers begging for change on its steps. Crossing the blessed Way, it sent pedestrians into doorways and pedalers into street stalls and merchants into fits and a pregnant woman into labor. Turning south on 9th Avenue, they passed a handsome Uptown girl in a pink dress, and the Kid pointed at her, winked, and said, "Boom."

Had they actually made a bomb out of the Great Tap, as the Kid had threatened, it would indeed have turned most of Midtown into a crater. As it was, the black powder rig that Chisel had put together was only enough to shatter every window and destroy most of the bottom three floors of JuiceTown, rattle crockery in Harlem, give a bean counter in FiDi a heart attack, set children weeping on the LES, and so startle Swan that he crashed his stolen bike.

It was likewise loud enough to reach the elevated platform running between 10th and 11th Avenues, from one end of Chelsea to the other, the most peculiar swathe of green to be found in the city. For what purpose had the ancestors put a park in the sky? Who could say? Way things were, to kip so high unprotected, you'd have to be mad – or at least fearless of the funk. Amid the overgrown grass, a line of eyes opened, bright against the gloom, not all of them in pairs.

Two blocks east and fifteen north, the Kid watched as Gillian followed in the autocycle's wake, the trumpets of the Force cavalry echoing close behind her. "This is slower than advertised!" he yelled to Chisel.

"There are a lot of people on it!" Chisel snapped, moving her pool-cue sized stick-shift into a higher gear. From his spot on the running board, Ael shadowed Gillian with a javelin, who waited just out of range, likewise holding the fire from her cannon.

"Cut underneath the High Line!" said the Kid.

"That's a very bad idea!" said Chisel.

"We'll never have time to unload the battery, we have to shake them loose."

When the funk stopped being a habit and became a compulsion, when your kith ignored you and even your kin closed the door, you went to the High Line, to drink rainwater and huff funk and eat anyone fool enough to come close. Up and down the green, carried by shrill hymn and rattling sternutation and wet fart, the Funkees spread word they were having visitors for supper.

A troop of cavalry had passed Swan while he was recovering, but he soon pulled ahead of them, pedaling so swiftly he seemed sure to break his battered scrap-metal bike. Ten blocks south, Ael and Gillian continued their stand-off as they passed through Chelsea.

"Take your shot!" Ael roared, beating his chest. "Take your shot!"

But Gillian ignored him, past 23rd Street, past 22nd Street…

Chisel twisted the wheel and the autocycle, rattling right onto 21st, crossing beneath the shadow of the High Line.

Before the funk kills, it rots – nose, eyelids, ears, tongue, the tips of your fingers, other appendages – so it wasn't quite three Funkees that dropped just then, more like two and six-tenths. The first misjudged his target and was crushed beneath the wheel of the autocycle. The second landed squarely, the vehicle bobbing from its weight, a putrescent howling biped whom the Kid knifed and dumped overboard. The third, Ael took care of with his predictable competence, and then they were through, heading west towards the Huddy.

Gillian proved less fortunate, a Funkee belly-flopping *splat* onto her horse's head, the beast tumbling, Gillian herself thrown clear. The nearest of the Funkees turned on the downed animal, as happy to slake their hunger with horse meat as human, weak jaws tearing at raw flesh. With the trough over-crowded, the rest of the Funkees turned to Gillian, who was bloodied and woozy, but upright and somehow still holding her cannon. *Boom*, one down, *boom*, another, but more of them were coming than Gillian had boom.

So it was well that Swan arrived then, angry as he had ever been in his bitter and long-seeming life. Leaping from the bike, he drew his stolen cutter and brought it through one of the

Funkees and then another one after that, moving through unhindered as water through a crack in the phalt.

The autocycle turned onto the Ring. Ael smacked the side hard enough to leave a dent and roared, "Fat, she said! Fat!"

"Second best killer on the Island!" the hypebird squawked before they disappeared from view.

How many Funkees lived on the High Line? How many lost souls are there on the Island, how many desperate fools, rejected spouses and mistreated children? Some multitude, surely, but then again, what quantity of wheat would be sufficient against the scythe? The Funkees searched for Swan like an ugly man for love, and with as much success, their rotted teeth and twisted claws and makeshift weapons useless. A glint of bright off Swan's cheap sword and a Funkee was unseamed at the waist, a second strike, too swift to follow, and a pair of Funkees were obviated in one economic motion.

It would have all been over in a few tics if the Funkees' champion had not then arrived, an elephantine teardrop falling from the High Line and crushing several of her soldiers, though Swan moved neatly clear. She was mostly tumor, a pyramidal mass of pockmarked meat with boils the size of pumpkins. Her arms were stubbed and multitudinous, and shared space with a menagerie of malformed half-hands and unnamable fleshy protrusions. One eye was pinned shut by a cancerous, bright-purple growth, but the other was a lovely light blue. She carried no weapon; perhaps none could be found to fit her, perhaps she could not be made to understand its purpose, perhaps she understood the purpose but did not see its necessity.

"Hell and High Towers," Gillian cursed.

The Funkees scattered. Swan sighed and pulled off the top of his mask and threw it onto the phalt. Below his eyes and ears remained wrapped in thick cotton, the surrounding skin a sickly pale. "This one will cost you extra."

Her war cry was a quivering soprano, and her asymmetrical breasts tumbled helter-skelter as she charged. Swan was motionless until she seemed sure to crush him, and then he was not where he had been. Again, the soprano, but this time agonized rather than ferocious, provoked by a flash of steel and a burst of red. A tremulous, shuddering twist, her limbs reaching out in desperation for their tormentor, a closing wall of tissue but Swan shivering through the cracks. Another cut, another splash of pink, sufficient to paint a studio apartment. With the next, however, Swan struck a goiter which proved not meat but cartilage and dense bone, his cheap sword shattering in two. Looking down at the handle of his weapon, he was caught by what was either one of her handless, ram-like surplus arms or the eruption of a boil, either case delivering sufficient force to send Swan flying over the phalt and into an iron fence.

Had Swan lay stunned a few more tics, Gillian would have fled without compunction, being a practical woman above all else, but he rose just then, furious, screaming, for the first time interested in the results of the engagement. He broke a sharpened length of metal from off the fence as easy as if it were matchstick, and then he beat his chest with it. Once more, the high-pitched wail, almost piteous, once more the charge, Swan waiting, motionless, back turned until it seemed certain she would reach him, and then he was gone, three steps straight up the side of a wall before launching himself high into the air. She followed his rise with her blue eye the size of a dinner plate, blinking once before Swan skewered it with his makeshift spear, into her brain and neck and further still into an undifferentiated swath of fat until she burst like an overripe berry, flinging Swan and a gelatinous shower of pink and red across 21st and 10th.

Silence.

The cavalry arrived to interrupt it in neat formation, pennants fluttering from their lances. Gillian stepped gingerly over the thing's remains and went to check on Swan, who lay where he had landed, breathing heavily and contemplating the various errors in judgment which had brought him to his current predicament.

"I am pretty insanely angry at you right now, Gillian."

"I didn't tell you to lose your sword."

"Is there intestine in my hair?"

"Cords," admitted Gillian.

"I'm going to go take a bath in the Huddy."

"That's a good idea."

"They got away," said Swan.

"I noticed," said Gillian.

Somewhere Else Altogether

"Thanks."

"Don't mention it."

35

A Matter of Time

"Yes indeed, I have heard of the Enclave's 'master clock'!" Ragman informed the sky. "The hope of fools!"

Ragman was where he usually was when brightest turned to less bright, on top of an abandoned building in the Garment District making his casts. He wore a battered top hat and a heavy coat and a lighter coat and a blazer, and all sorts of other clothes as well, matted down nearly to a second skin.

"So far as I'm concerned, Enclave time is like Enclave law: bunk past Enclave walls. Who could hold faith with such foolishness? They say they have five men in five rooms keeping five separate clocks running, but I say funk does as funk likes!"

Ragman reared his fishing pole above his head, then sent his tackle sailing square into a particularly juicy-looking gust of funk. The oystermen might dispute the matter, but in fact there was not a finer caster anywhere on the Island than Ragman. His line caught in the thick chunks of gray, while far below, the pedestrians went about their business.

"No, I'm not for these new-fangled notions. Dim and bright were good enough for my parents, and they're good enough for me."

Ragman reeled in his line. This was another difference between Ragman and the oystermen: Ragman always caught

186

something; Ragman's luck never failed him. He pulled the egg-shaped sieve off the end of his line and held it, masklike, over the bottom of his face.

Then he dropped the egg, peered over the edge. "Nice view," said Ragman, "but no dice." He waited for a pedi to pass, and then leaped free.

36

Big Promises

"A new life awaits you!" roared the barker. "A new life in the North!"

The official scuttle had yet to reach the Square, but even before the explosion, prices on full batteries had doubled and redoubled and doubled once more, rumor traveling faster than even Senior Newsboys. The mood was tense, which the barker blamed for the fact that he hadn't had a single volunteer since bright, and why he puffed up so quick when the Null[41] and Adze[42] stopped in front of him.

"You interested in the future, lads?" he asked.

"Very much, in fact," said the Null.

"Then what are you doing in Midtown? Let me guess: wasting your life clerking at a counting house, or stocking shelves in some bodega? Fine for now, but what about next bright, my friends, and the bright after that? The future is Uptown! Where a man can still get a condo for himself, not need to kip with a dozen others. Where a man can grow his shrooms, raise his own dogs! An impossible dream? Far from it! They're giving out land in the North, lads, free and unentailed! And, as part of the Mayor's new reclamation project, I'm even authorized to

---

41 Chisel's servant, nameless slave in service of tomorrow.
42 Head of security for the Bridge Brides, on a mission to discover the Kid's secrets.

pay you a signing bonus! That's right, a free plot of green and fifty bits in your palm. All you have to do is make your mark!"

"Sweet deal," said the Null.

"Now, I won't say life up there is easy," the barker continued. "You're a hundred blocks from civilization, and the row and the hoe are no easier than the stationary! But at least at the coming of every dim you'll be able to look over your piece of green and know that your work didn't go to make some Enclave fat cat richer, but rather to your own–"

"Where's the land?" Adze interrupted. He was wearing his thick leather apron and was wide enough to interrupt the flow of pedestrian traffic.

"Excuse me?"

"This green I'm going to love so good, where is it?"

Behind them, a presumable shoplifter sprinted past holding a left shoe, a cobbler cursing and hurrying after him. Normally, the Force patrolled the square thick as lice on a dog. But looking around then, it occurred to the barker that he hadn't actually seen one in a while.

"Say," said the barker, "you're one of them Bridge Brides, aren't you?"

"You figure that one out by yourself?" asked Adze.

"Why are you even interested in turning farmer? I thought you were all about building things and stuff."

"We are. You've got some of us whose job is to design the thing, and some of us whose job it is to hammer the thing together." Adze leaned over the barker. "Which do you suppose I am?"

The barker sweated some. "I don't have the location," he admitted. "If you sign up, you'll be assigned a plot by–"

"East side? West side? You got a street? An avenue?

"To the North. Near Fort Tryon."

"Where's Fort Tryon?" asked Adze.

The barker shrugged. "To the North."

"This might go on for a while," said the Null.

"Not a whole lot longer," Adze answered.

"Tell you what," said the barker, "let me get you in touch with my boss; he's the one you really ought to be talking to about all this…"

37

Heavy is the Head

Unhappy Constituents...

The Mayor had changed his suit since the explosion outside of JuiceTown, and he was smiling his old smile when Nelly Karrow[43] walked into his office and tossed the charred corpse of a cat on to his desk.

"Vengeance!" she shrieked. "Vengeance for Fluffy!"

"Believe me," the Mayor continued, "the man responsible for killing, at this point, several dozen people as well as, apparently, a cat–"

"Five cats!" Nelly had her small hands up around the Mayor's tie, a silk red number which generally inspired great confidence. "Each of them a precious jewel, pure innocents, brought low by that hell-spawned monster!"

"Get off me I'll break your thumbs," the Mayor muttered, assuming a most ungentlemanly demeanor.

Nelly sat.

"As I said," the Mayor continued, "whoever is responsible for the destruction of JuiceTown, and the immolation of your feline companions, will suffer a fate of savage severity just so soon as we find out where he is. To that end: are you still keeping tabs on...?"

"Of course, I am!" said Nelly. "Not that there's much point, her being right out there in the hall!"

---

43 Ailurophile and intelligence agent.

"There's something else I need you to look at."

"With who? I'm running out of cats!"

Faithless Subordinates…

When they shuffled Gillian in, the corpse of the cat had been removed and the Mayor had retied his tie, though not quite so neatly as previous. "Sheriff."

"Mayor," said Gillian.

Less bright turned towards early dim. The order had gone out to conserve juice, and so their interview was being conducted by candlelight. "Would you like to tell me what you were doing outside of JuiceTown just before it was robbed?" asked the Mayor, once the wax had dripped a while.

"Waiting for it to be robbed, obviously."

"So you knew that was coming?"

"I wasn't there at random."

"Had you thought on informing the Council of your suspicions?"

"So you could come in and botch my play?"

"What were we supposed to do? Let them destroy JuiceTown?"

"You did let them destroy JuiceTown," Gillian snapped. "At least if you'd listened to me, we'd have some idea where they went after they destroyed it. As it is, we've got no juice and no leads."

"And where does your investigation go from here?"

"That's a very good question, Mayor," said Gillian. "Do you have any thoughts?"

"I don't want to know about it," the Mayor said anxiously.

"No, you wouldn't, would you?"

"Any hint of collusion with… even to acknowledge the existence of the thing in TriBeCa… the slightest involvement…" The Mayor shook his head. "I'd be tainted forever."

"I know what it would do; that's why you pay me, to make

sure it doesn't." Gillian was up from the chair. "So let me do my job, and stay the hell out of my way from now on. By bliss and bacon, if you muck up the trail again, you can find yourself another sheriff." A pause before reaching the door, "And I'll keep the ten thousand."

Quarrelsome Rivals...

The Mayor shut his desk drawer just as Alvin, War Chief for the Honey Swallowers,[44] came into his office. He chose not to sit, and the Mayor chose not to quibble with this decision.

"It's been a trying bright," the Mayor began, "if you could get to the purpose of this unscheduled visit, I'd deeply appreciate it."

"I've less taste for this conversation than you do, and your pleasantries only prolong it."

"I'll dispense with them," said the Mayor, falling silent.

"The Yellow Empire is indifferent to the destruction of JuiceTown," said Alvin. "We have wax enough for candles and no need for the frivolous pleasures the rest of you deem so important. 'The honey of the Hive is enough for any honest bee,' so says the proverb."

"Don't quote scripture," the Mayor grumbled. "Just tell me why you're here."

"Do you know why I agreed to give Gillian the badge a second time?" Alvin asked.

"Because she's such a trustworthy, upright woman?"

"Because I knew I had nothing to fear from her."

"The virtuous take comfort in their innocence."

"I'm not so fool to believe that," said Alvin. "Your Council is a rotten thing, and you worst of all. Blasphemers, enemies of the Queen in Yellow, sybarites, drunkards, and secret worshipers of the funk."

---

44 Servants of the Hive, slaves of the Queen in Yellow, may your soul taste sweet upon her tongue!

"I forget sometimes what a keen diplomat you are."

"Perhaps not, but I've a very fine head for strategy. The Honey Swallowers are the only things stopping the Force from making the entire Island their personal property; without our muscle to keep them honest, they'd eat you like a skewer of rat."

"If you know all of that, then why did you waste your time coming down here?"

"I wanted to make sure your sense of self-interest hasn't dulled."

"Sharp as ever," the Mayor promised. And after a moment, Alvin nodded and left.

A Superior's Displeasure

Before meeting with his next visitor, the Mayor drank the rest of the bottle in his desk drawer, and some of what was in the bottle in his hidden drawer, and then he went to his bathroom and tossed some water on his face, and then he went back to his chair. With no juice, his speaker was off, and so he had to yell through the door to his secretary. "Come in!"

He looked like any other Downtown soldier, except that he wasn't flagging any colors, and he had a whole jaw full of teeth, and he initially forgot to take his cutter off before sitting in his chair.

"Dallas," said the Mayor. He kept his voice steady. "This is unexpected."

"You think we wouldn't notice half of Midtown getting blown up?" Dallas asked, trying to find a comfortable way to hold his sword.

"Barely that."

"Mr Simpson[45] has concerns."

"We're handling it."

---

45 Who knows?

"He disagrees. He wants a meeting. You and the other two."

Outside, the weather had grown fierce and stormy, the temperature dropping and great gusts of funk striking against the windows. "I'll alert them," said the Mayor after a moment.

"Tomorrow at noon."

"What?"

"High bright," Dallas said, sighing, then got up and left.

Family Troubles

The Mayor was staring out at the funk, eyes red and veiny, and it took his aide three tries before he answered. "What? What is it?"

"We've got a situation, sir."

"Really? Who's left?"

"It's about your nephew. Something strange happened to him at school."

For the first time, the Mayor looked frightened.

38

The Magic Box

What Do You See in Her?

It had sat in the corner of the bar since before the funk. It had red plastic buttons on the front, and speakers on the sides, and a viewing window in the middle with who-knew-how-many black plates inside, and a slot where you could put in the discs you needed to work the thing. Saul sold these at the counter, five bits for one gray token, the face on the front shaved blank from time. Slim slipped one into the slot and waited; a click, a whirr, a spin, and then an angel cooed from beyond the grave.

"Do it to me, girl," said Maryland Slim, shifting his great bulk from right foot to left in even time. "That's right."

Taste of Cindy

Legend held that when Saul's grandfather had run the place, there had been a way to choose what song you wanted to hear, but most of the locals regarded this as blasphemy. The box played what it wanted to play, what you needed to hear. That was what made the box magic.

"You know how to use that?" Slim asked. He was rolling a joint of some West Village flower he had picked up two dims prior.

"Rat puzzle," said Ariadne, inspecting her new cannon from various angles.

"You're going to blow your face off if you aren't careful."

A hand inside the box picked up the disc and replaced it with another. A young man began to shout over the speakers. He could not play his instrument very well, and seemed quite unhappy about something.

"What are you doing up here, anyway?"

"Clan business," said Ariadne.

"That's it?"

"Line call, rat answer," said Ariadne. She set the cannon down and began to nod, in rhythm or just in general agreement. "What's he wailing over?"

"What's anyone wail over?" asked Maryland Slim. "Heartbreak."

O! Sweet Nuthin'

"Funk hunger," Ariadne explained, the smoke from Slim's joint mixing with the smoke from the candles. "Funk see, and funk hunger and funk eat. Labyrinth hides rat from funk." Ariadne traced a finger on the tattoo curled around her face. "Funk hungry, but funk curious; funk follow labyrinth and forget about rat."

"I've heard worse," Slim said, taking the joint back.

Swan walked in just then, wearing a chartreuse leisure suit.

"Bliss and bacon," Slim said, "who been dressing you?"

"A guy what owns a stall in the West Village."

"What'd you pay him with?"

"Threats of violence, obviously. I was bare naked. How's the color?"

"Do you see colors?" Slim asked.

"Not in the same way you do," Swan admitted.

"So how am I supposed to answer that question?"

"What does it make you think of, when you look at it?"

The guitar jangled and the man's voice droned along with it, gaining momentum with each word and verse.

"The last bit of bright before dim," Slim said.

"Cool," said Swan.

"It's certainly an improvement on the loincloth."

Ferris Wheel

There was always a crowd of regulars in Saul's, lost souls sipping the house brew and staring blankly at the walls and hoping to whatever gods they held the box would play *their* song, the one they heard a thousand dims back but still can't forget.

"Worse than huffing funk," Slim observed quietly, staring at the other patrons.

"Always liked Dade," Swan told Ariadne. "For a man what ate people, he was all right."

"Topside legend," Ariadne admitted.

"You never ate anyone?"

"Kettle an honor," said Ariadne, "for best friends and worst enemies."

The song the magic box was playing just then made you think about the past. Not past like the ancestors – past like *your* past, like how it was, remember? Like how it used to be?

"Say, Swan," Slim began, after they'd sat in silence a while, "what was the name of that girl you used to dance with sometimes at that bar in the Alphabet City what burnt down?"

"The one with the hair?"

"Yeah."

"Martha."

"Martha, right," said Slim. "Whatever happened to her?"

"She died," said Swan, "in that fire that burned up her bar."

"Oh," said Maryland Slim.

There was a question that Ariadne had been wanting to ask for a while. "Gillian and Dade?"

"A while," said Slim, "until Dade went back under."

"They close?"

"I guess you'd know better about Dade than we would."

"And the Crone?"

"Close as Gillian gets," said Slim, which wasn't much of an answer.

Lucinda

Swan was waiting out front as Gillian got out of the pedicab. She looked haggard. She looked meaner than usual.

"Why do you think it is I kill for you?" Swan asked.

"Money," said Gillian.

"Lots of people would pay me to kill for them."

"But you'd have to go find them, which you don't want to do, and you'd have to deal with them, which you wouldn't like doing."

"I don't like dealing with you."

"You'd like dealing with anyone else less."

"That's kind of my point. You're a little bit better than the other people who would pay me to kill for them. Very slightly, but still."

"Thanks for the pep talk."

"It's not a pep talk; it's a dressing down. Why do you smell like TriBeCa?"

"I don't have time for this," said Gillian, heading into the bar.

When Swan decided to do a thing, he seemed already to have done it, his hand at his side and then two fingers pressing against Gillian's chest, the intervening motion impossible to perceive. "Amid an overlong life of pointless idiocy, one small spot of pride remains: that I was the one what put the ban on TriBeCa."

"I recall."

"Do you remember that monster I killed there?"

"Yes, Swan, I do."

"Made that thing below the High Line seem human."

"Are we approaching a point?"

"I opened with the point: what were you doing in TriBeCa?"

"He knows things."

"*It* knows things," corrected Swan, "but you'd be a fool to listen to them."

"You think I'm a fool?"

"That depends on what you gave it in return."

Gillian brushed aside Swan's hand. "You must have stones the size of pumpkins, second-guessing my moves while you can barely keep yourself clothed. Just be happy you don't need to do anything but show up where I tell you and kill who I point at."

"That's a neat little trick there, making your sin seem like virtue," said Swan. "You practice that a lot?"

The music drifting out from the bar sounded like something you might still have heard on the Island, a twangy guitar, a lonely soul, a bad life ending bitterly.

"What I did in TriBeCa was necessary," said Gillian finally. "Everything I do is necessary. If I don't explain some piece of my plan, it's because I know you're too soft to handle it."

"Yeah, Gillian," said Swan, "you're the meanest thing alive. And look at all the good it's done you."

Shakey Dog

Gillian entered, went to the bar, ordered a shot, took that shot, ordered another shot, and while she was waiting for it to come, said, "We've got a lead."

Swan had rejoined Ariadne and Maryland Slim at the counter by this point. The magic box barked a perfectly syncopated anthem of war, juveniles with scatterguns prepping for a ride-along. Not everything had changed since the coming of the funk.

"I'm all out of swords," said Swan, pouring himself another glass of distil.

"Slim?"

Maryland Slim looked at Gillian for a while, then he shook his head. " Normally when you play me, I don't notice so much, or at least I don't mind."

Gillian accepted the betrayal of her two oldest allies with apparent indifference. "As you like." The second shot came round then, and she drank it. "Rat?"

Ariadne looked at Slim and Swan, then back at Gillian. "Rat with Crone," she said, grabbing her stolen cannon from where it hung on the chair beside her.

Gillian didn't thank her, didn't nod, just turned and walked out of the bar, Ariadne following a few steps behind.

"You're just as bad as the rest of them!" Swan yelled at Gillian's back, though she did not pause or even flinch in response. "You're not the tiniest bit better!"

39

A Concerned Guardian

"Tell me again what he looked like," said Newton's uncle.

"I told you already," said Newton.

"Just one more time," said Newton's uncle.

They were still at the dinner table. They had been at the dinner table since Newton had come home from school and drew Fran[46] the sign that the man had drawn for Newton, and then Fran had showed one of the men what guarded Newton, and then that man had sent for Newton's uncle, who had arrived smelling of toilet water and of things toilet water could not mask.

"He had red hair and he smoked," said Newton. "His coat was too big."

"How old did he look?"

"Younger than you. Older than me. Can I go read a panel book now, please?"

"Just another toc," said Newton's uncle, who got up and left the room, leaving Newton in the care of Fran and Fran alone.

"What's so bad about the sign, nanny?" asked Newton.

Fran's eyes had that mist they often got after dinner. "Don't you worry yourself none about that. If you need to know, your uncle will tell you."

Who returned then, having re-applied his smile. "Well, Newton," said Newton's uncle, "it seems clear this whole thing

---

46 Nervous nanny.

is a big to-do over very little, some neighborhood transient muttering nonsense."

"He knew who I was," said Newton.

"Such an imagination! Do you get that from those panel books?"

"I don't... *think* so," said Newton, pondering the matter.

"No, surely just some unfortunate funk-huffer. A sad place, the Island, object lessons and so on. Nothing to worry about. But all the same, I'm thinking it might be safer if you moved in with me a while."

"But you just said there was nothing to worry about."

"I said there was *probably* nothing to worry about."

"No, you didn't," said Newton.

Newton's uncle laughed, though Newton had not thought he was making a joke. "Yes, just some drunk, surely, but if you were to see him at school again, make sure to tell an adult you can trust."

But all during bath time, and even as he went to bed, Newton found he could not think of one.

40

The Ties That Bind

You Can't Go Home Again

After they had hid the autocycle in the basement of a ruined warehouse in South Chelsea; and after they had met the boat halfway down Chelsea Pier, a paddlebarge crewed by a half-dozen of Hope's[47] kin; and after they had finished their combination parole and familial greeting; and after they had dropped anchor and floated south towards Battery Park, hugging the shoreline; and after the other Borofolk had floated over, and after they had started to grill the dog haunch, and after someone had rolled some flower, and after a guitar had started to play, but before supper had been served, Ael was reenacting their escape.

"...and I thought for sure this lady on the horse was aced, right, but then Swan shows up and just starts wrecking them! Left and right," Ael made sword-fighting sounds, "like it was nothing!"

"Gosh," said a Borogirl.

"Fastest thing I ever saw," said Ael. "And I don't just mean the fastest human – I mean the fastest thing I ever saw, like faster than a cat on a pigeon, or a rock dropped from a tower."

"Not so fast as you!" said the hypebird.

---

47 Daughter of lost Brooklyn, whose extended family of exiles travel in a great loop around the Island.

Hope slavered beside the grill. "It's done," she said.

"It's not done," said Flushing, who was Hope's uncle the way the Kid was Hope's cousin.

"You leave it on any longer and the skin's going to char."

"The skin is supposed to char some," said Flushing. "You think this is the first time I ever cooked a collie?"

Chisel was at the stern, down on her knees with a torch trying to puzzle out the ship's workings. "You rigged it so the wind spins the paddle?"

"The paddle and our juice besides," said the first mate. "Don't got a stationary on board, and we don't trade with JuiceTown, neither."

"Fascinating," said Chisel. "But why didn't you make the sail bigger?"

The success of this latest stage of his great, if opaque, endeavor seemed to have brought the Kid little pleasure, the waves of frivolity breaking against him like the Huddy over a stone. He leaned at the railing and scowled at things he saw.

"It's overcooked," said Hope, after taking the first bite.

"Eye of Coney," Flushing exclaimed, "if it was up to you, we'd be eating the thing raw."

Hope licked juice off her fingers.

Supper was an informal affair, the assembled stopping over to snap a cut of flesh. Ael ate half a haunch himself, re-enacting Swan's adventures with a femur. Hope and another Borogirl got into a heated dispute over whose strand of flower was the more potent, one which remained unresolved three joints later. Chisel had a plate but mostly forgot to eat from it, busy questioning Flushing about the ship's engines.

The Kid smoked.

Bright had been warm enough to go shirtless, but a chill crept up around dimtime and everyone gathered round the fire, huddling beneath thick blankets, kept warm by distil and house brew and the flesh of a neighbor.

"When I was born," Flushing was saying, "Nan Toni took

a look at my future and gave me a number. Twenty-seven circuits – that's how long she said I had."

"And you just believed her?" Chisel asked.

"Nan Toni had the knowledge. There was more to Nan Toni than there was to the rest of us. She had some of what Hope got."

"I wouldn't trust Hope if she told me bright came after dim," Chisel muttered.

"I didn't think much about it till my twenty-fifth circuit or so, but then I started thinking about it hard. A sin for a Boroman to stay in one place, to get a condo and live like a local! Worse than death. But, then again, death is pretty bad."

"So?"

"I fixed up the barge. The current never circles the same way long enough to finish a full spin around the Island."

"Never?"

"Once, we got all the way to Highbridge Park; that got me nervous, you'd best believe. But then, the water turned and we hustled back downtown."

"Gimme the ban," the Kid cursed as he saw Hope return to the firelight. "Send me to Jersey."

She was carrying a chunk of honey-battered cornbread and a single candle stubbed in the center, and when she started singing everyone, barring Chisel, joined in. Their rendition included, at various points, two guitars, an accordion, and a flute. Ael tapped a perfect rhythm on his knee and Hope roared loud enough to be heard in Harlem and the Kid blew out the candle with a distinct lack of enthusiasm.

"I don't like cornbread," he said.

"You don't like anything." Hope handed him a package. "Happy thousandth."

"What is it?"

"If I wanted you to know that right out, I probably wouldn't have wrapped it."

It was a burnished silver cigarette case with 💣 on the front.

"From Don DeAndre's," she explained. "Flushing did it up with your symbol."

The Kid didn't smile, but there was a tic when it looked like he might. "Thanks."

"Sweet as honey, the two of you!" said Flushing. "You'd never think the first time they met I had to pull him off her, and Hope bleeding worse than a stuck dog."

Chisel snapped her head up.

"They never told you that one? Why do you think her nose has that dent in it?"

"I like the way my nose looks," said Hope.

"Kid always was wild," said Flushing in friendly conspiracy with Chisel. "You said the least little thing to him and *wham*! His eyes would roll up in his head and he'd just start swinging. One time – Nan Toni was alive, so he couldn't have been but a child – he got it in his head to see the canal on Canal Street. I told him there wasn't one, but he didn't believe me. Said he was going to head off and find it himself. I said go ahead, have fun – boys that age will say anything. Come dimtime, he still wasn't back, Nan's howling at me, all of us searching round the Ring, and the boy headed so deep into Morningside we had to loose the dogs on his bedsheets to find him!"

Even some of the crowd that heard the story laughed. The Kid's head dropped lower over his shoulders. "I still say it's a stupid thing to name a street."

"But that's the Kid for you," Flushing continued. "Temper like a cornered raccoon, and nothing's too grand for his ambition. Got that from–"

"And you were always a loud drunk, who never knew when to keep his mouth shut," said the Kid, shoving his cigarette case into his pocket and standing. "Enough with this back-when-we-were-young nonsense. I hated it here then, and I'm not any crazier about it now. Up to me, you'd have let your dogs stay sleeping and we'd have said our last goodbyes ages ago."

"Moody, likewise," Flushing said to Chisel as the Kid stomped off.

A Singular Ambition

After the Kid had left in a huff, and Hope had taken Flushing aside and yelled at him a while; and after the weather worsened into a slushy drizzle; and after most of the Borofolk broke off to return to their own houseboats or to the safety of the Ring, Ael and Hope were in one of the guest cabins, listening to the rain rattle against their tin roof. Hope lay on her single bed, blowing rings of smoke, while Ael bounced around the small cabin which they shared, engaged in fierce combat with his shadow.

"He's faster than me," said Ael.

"I don't believe it!" said the hypebird, perched in a corner.

"No, he is; he's faster. I'll have to time it perfectly if I'm to have any chance," said Ael, slipping smilingly into southpaw.

"Bronx Zoo, this is exhausting," said Hope.

"I got a lot of energy," Ael admitted.

"How about you knock that off and we can rut a while?"

"Not interested," Ael said.

"Men more your thing?"

"Nah. I mean, one time, just to see what it was like, but as it turned out… nah."

"What is it, then? You'd really rather dance with yourself than let me touch your pecker?"

Over upraised fists, Ael shot Hope a glance of withering contempt. "You know what, Hope? I pity you."

"Do you?"

"I really do. I pity all of you. You just drift along, no goals, no drive, no purpose."

"The Kid has purpose," said Hope.

"You're right," Ael conceded, "The Kid has purpose."

"Straight as an arrow!" the hypebird agreed.

"But the rest of you – getting high, getting laid, no direction, one dim the same as the next. I want to be the greatest killer on the Island, okay? That's all I ever wanted to be. Soon, I'm going to get my shot. My whole life, all that work, all that training, all of it winnowed down to fifteen tics, maybe less! And you want me to waste my energy in bed?"

"Swan's not here right now, you know."

"If there's one thing I learned from old Cleon, back before I killed him, it's this: you don't rut before a fight."

"Whatever," Hope said, popping her bubble. "Where's the Kid?"

"Somewhere making it with Chisel, if I had to take a guess."

"You knew about that?"

"I can count to twenty with my shoes on," said Ael, slipping a phantom right and letting loose with a flurry that would have downed any corporeal opponent.

Somewhere Else Altogether

"Hey."

"Howdy."

"How's it by you?"

"All right. Getting chilly."

"How's your lunatic with a sword?"

"Comatose. And he lost his sword."

"Mine will be disappointed to hear that."

"Yeah?'

"Yeah. He's real, real excited to meet yours."

"We'll see how that goes for him. You wouldn't want to tell me what's going on, from your perspective? Maybe we could pool information?"

"And ruin the surprise? Sorry. And shouldn't you be out chasing me? Following up leads, sniffing after my scent?"

"It's looking like any further pursuit will be of a purely personal nature."

"That's too bad; I was anticipating getting to see which of us is better."

"I am. And anyway, I wouldn't rest so easy, if I were you. I'm sweet as honey, and even Swan's not so terrible neither – Gillian's the one to worry about. She's still on your trail, and she makes the rest of us seem like purse dogs."

"Ha!"

"You scoffing?"

"Quite the reverse, in fact."

A Little Death

After Hope had finished her otherworldly conversation with Maryland Slim, and smoked enough flower to send her to sleep; and after Ael had gotten into the bed across from hers, to stare open eyed at the ceiling and dream on the coming bright; and after the rain had turned to snunk, falling in gray drifts on deck, Chisel went to find the Kid.

"Why didn't you tell me it was your thousandth?" she asked.

He was in his cabin by the stern, smoking a cigarette and staring out the window, shirtless despite the cold. "It's an arbitrary measurement of time."

"Still."

The Kid shrugged.

"What's got you?"

"I'm fine," said the Kid. He flicked his cigarette into the water, though it was only half done.

"You worried?"

"Why would I be?" asked the Kid. "So long as your machine does what you've promised, the thing will go soft as rotted wood."

Chisel bristled. "My wagon works fine."

The Kid lit another cigarette.

"I never thought of you as having a family," said Chisel.

"You thought I sprung out the phalt?"

"I just never thought on it."

"I have a family," said the Kid, but nothing else.

The wind bruised against the cabin, howled through the window, rustled the sleeping bag on the small cot which was the room's only furniture. Chisel looked at the Kid a while, puzzling, like she had earlier with the paddleboat's machinery.

"You botched rigging that bomb," she said finally.

"What?"

"Setting the bomb in JuiceTown. You botched it."

"I'd have finished it," said the Kid.

"When? After the confessors had eaten through your cousin's brain and killed us all?"

"I was almost done."

"I showed you the set-up three separate times, and you said you had it down, and then when I came back up, you were still–"

"I was under the time limit," said the Kid. He turned smoldering eyes onto Chisel. "Three hundred tics, that was what we planned for it, and I was barely at two-twenty–"

"Three-hundred tics! I have a Null that could have managed it in a hundred! Maybe you should give up on your current line of work, come and pedal my stationary for me."

"Get out of here," said the Kid.

"Screw up like that come bright time and we're dead as our grandmothers."

"Shut up."

"Maybe it's just time to admit you've gotten in over your head?"

"Shut up."

"You got a good growl, I'll give you that," said Chisel. She stood between him and the bed. "Roar like a mastiff from a few blocks off, but up close, you're a lost pup keening for its mammy."

The Kid snarled and pounced on Chisel, bearing her down against the edge of the cot. Her struggles were ceremonial, but the Kid was so choked with rage or lust that he struggled to disrobe her, tearing the buttons of her shirt because he could not manage their complexity. She gasped when he entered her and he closed his mouth around hers as if to catch it, the two of them a closed circuit, impervious to the world. She grappled her legs around his waist and pressed herself further against him, and he touched the small of her back gently. He bit her neck, her shoulders, the tops of her breasts. She held his forehead in her hand, curled his hair around her fingers and shook herself into orgasm, a shuddering gasp setting him to the same, existence blanked away in a perfect instant of oblivion.

Afterward, they even cuddled.

41

Stake Out

Gillian's crew, now reduced to Ariadne alone, sat by the window of an abandoned house at the intersection of West End Avenue and 71st Street. It was dimmest and they were deep in Honey Swallower territory, and so the streets were empty, the diligent sons and faithful daughters of the Hive sleeping soundly, their rest undisturbed by juke joints, street parties, distilleries, houses of ill repute – revelry, generally speaking.

"Yellow headdress?" asked Ariadne.

"A grinder in a yellow headdress," agreed Gillian. "That's who we're looking for."

"Why?"

"Because he's going to lead us where we need to go."

"Says who?" asked Ariadne.

Gillian didn't answer.

"Says TriBeCa?" Ariadne asked.

But Gillian remained silent.

"What is he?" asked Ariadne.

Gillian sucked a tooth.

"Rat owed answer," Ariadne said, running a finger over the peculiar, puckered scar on her face.

"Told you not to follow," Gillian said.

"Still."

Gillian looked at Ariadne a while. "Part what was the last

ruler of TriBeCa. Part the funk, or part of the funk, or a friend of the funk. Dunno."

"He hip you to the trail?"

"Something like," said Gillian.

A tabby cat skulked across the street. It was as much action as they'd seen in a long time.

"In exchange for?"

"The King's fading," said Gillian, "turning to straight funk. Nostalgia's what keeps him solid. I let him pick through my old memories, and he gives me what scuttle the funk whispers to him."

"That all?" asked Ariadne.

Gillian didn't answer.

"Swan, Slim..." Ariadne began.

"Pink-livered, milk-fed. I can't kill with my mind, and I ain't faster than death." Gillian turned a blunt finger on Ariadne. "Big bucks are allowed a pretense of righteousness, but a doe doesn't have any illusions. The Island's hard. You want to survive it, you'd best be harder."

Ariadne pondered this bit of wisdom as they waited for the man in the yellow headdress to arrive.

42

An Idiot Every Block

Some of them knew as soon as they came inside the shack, saw Gregor and bolted; Sanza and Baron had to catch them as they ran outside. Others figured when Gregor locked the door behind them, or during the long descent into the basement. But all the time they'd been running the scam, Gregor could not recall getting anyone all the way to the cellar, a windowless, stone chamber with blood stains on the floor, and still needing to maintain the deception about Fort Tryon and a promised plot of land.

"One every block," said Gregor.

"What was that?" asked the idiot.

"Nothing," said Gregor.

"Do I get tools, for my Uptown plot?" asked the idiot.

"Yeah, sure," said Gregor.

"What kind of tools?"

"Huh?"

"To tear up the phalt – what kind of tools do I get?"

"Uhhh… you know, hoes, and shovels, and all that stuff. Post-diggers," said Gregor, in a sudden moment of inspiration. This was normally the point in the proceedings where Sanza and Baron came in holding clubs and chains, but they must have been smoking some flower or something, because they were slow on their cue.

"And seed, right?" asked the idiot. "To grow the crops?"

"Yeah, lots of seed. Potatoes and… onions."

"Garlic?"

"Sure. All kinds of stuff."

"I love garlic!" said the idiot.

"It gives me heartburn," admitted Gregor. Gregor liked to wait until they had the dupe surrounded before showing his hand, but Gregor had a long knife in his belt and a date that evening with an 8th Avenue Ogre, for which he didn't want to be late. There was a trunk in the corner, and Gregor opened it and pulled out a manacle and threw it on the floor in front of the idiot. "We'll just have to get started the two of us."

"Sounds good!" said the idiot.

"Your momma drink a lot of grain liquor when she was pregnant?" asked Gregor.

"Huh?"

"Never mind." He pointed at the chains. "Put those on."

"Why?" asked the idiot.

"Because if you don't, I'm going to beat you up and then put them on you myself."

"Why would you do that?" asked the idiot.

"Because I've got to deliver you to the worksite."

"Why?"

"Because I get a hundred in bonds for every one of you idiots that I bring over there."

"Why?"

"I don't know," admitted Gregor. "Because they need you for something. They'll let you know once you're over there."

"I'll make sure to ask!" agreed the idiot, with all appearance of good humor.

Gregor started to get worried, then, because it was looking like the idiot wasn't an idiot – the idiot was a lunatic, and these are two entirely different categories of creature. So he was pleased when he heard the door open behind him, Sanza and Baron finally finished with their delay. "You go ahead and do that," said Gregor to the idiot, "but in the meantime, put the chains on."

The idiot looked at the manacles for a while, then shrugged. "They look kind of heavy."

"Spoor of the Bear, will you–" but turning, Gregor discovered neither Sanza, nor Baron, but only a massive, scowling man with a hand the size of Gregor's chest holding a maul with a bloodied end. Gregor reached swift for the knife at his belt, only to discover the idiot had his wrist locked tightly.

"Let's the three of us have a conversation," said the idiot[48].

---

48   Chisel's Null, in fact.

43

Market Volatility

"Tiny t, that's good," said the seventh richest man on the Island, pulling himself up off the egg.

"I've an engineer in JuiceTown who rigged up the filter," said the fourth wealthiest man on the Island. "It gives a purer shot."

"Does it ever," said the seventh wealthiest man on the Island. "Take a toot there, angel."

Angel took a toot. Angel's name was Esme. Esme had the sort of beauty which would attract the attention of the fourth and seventh wealthiest men on the Island; Esme had other qualities as well, but since one of them was intelligence and another candor, she could admit these mattered little to the fourth wealthiest man on the Island, nor to the seventh.

"JuiceTown," said Four, taking another huff, "can you believe?"

"The Commissioner ought to be replaced," snapped Seven.

"I'm sure the Mayor thinks something similar."

"The Pope, too."

They were at an orgy being thrown by the eleventh wealthiest man on the island, in one of the back rooms. They were supposed to be wearing robes and masks – not Esme, obviously, just the guests – but they had taken those off to rut and huff funk, respectively.

"Strange times on the Island," said Seven.

"Strange times," Four agreed.

"Have another huff there, angel," said Seven.

Esme had seen enough peckers in her time to know that they mostly all looked alike; it was the rare bird indeed that attracted more than a moment's attention. The fourth richest man on the Island had one like all the others, but something was up with Seven's; it was a tiny little nub of a thing bumped back against stones the size of pool balls. This was, Esme supposed, why he was constantly drawing her attention away from it and towards his funk-huffer. Esme did not particularly like huffing funk. You never knew what you were going to think about after. Could be bright and blissful, could be a straight descent into despair. Esme did not particularly like swallowing semen, either, but she did it, and for the same reason: because she was being paid.

"Who's behind it?" asked Seven.

"Honey Swallowers?" guessed Four.

"Why? What do they get out of shutting off my lights?"

"Who knows? Maybe their Queen in Yellow told them Juice was a sin, like using the counting houses or dancing or every other thing on the Island."

"Have another toot, angel," said Seven.

Esme did so, then gave her head a vigorous shake, then wrapped her mouth around Seven's pecker.

"You think Alvin[49] arranged some secret hit on the I's? You can say whatever you want about the man, but he doesn't fake his fanaticism," asked Four.

Seven took a while to answer. "Anything which weakens the Enclave strengthens his hand."

"Early," said the fourth richest person on the island. "Much too early. They don't have the numbers to go up against the Force, let alone the whole–"

Seven interrupted Four just then with a scream that bounced off the walls and reverberated throughout the mansion, and then Esme spat a wormy protrusion onto the plush carpeting.

---

49   War Chief of the Honey Swallowers.

"There is nothing in the World-Writ-Large more worthless than a banker," Esme said through a red-spattered mouth.

"B-b-b-bones in the basement!" shrieked the fourth wealthiest man on the Island.

Standing to flee, he tumbled over the length of his robe, lying supine as Esme retrieved a bronze figurine from where it was displayed in a wall sconce. A thump and Seven jumped to Six, though bleeding from his stump, he did not long enjoy the promotion.

44

A Jaunt Through Ruined
TriBeCa

Chisel was snoring when the Kid slipped from their bed, pulled his clothes on, and went down to the deck. He removed a kayak from its moorings and set it into the uneasy waters. The weather had turned vicious, clouds of snunk falling on the Huddy and the Island itself. The boat was anchored, but the current turned downtown, and setting himself adrift, the Kid sped past Chelsea and the Village and southward still, not turning to shore until after he had passed Pier 25. It would be impossible to make his way back until the current reversed itself, though beaching his craft in Rockefeller Park, the Kid wondered seriously if this would be a problem.

It was black as pitch until he made it over West Street, and then it turned not brighter, but clearer, somehow, as if the Kid could see through the dark. A man was waiting for him on a bench in Washington Market Park, wearing a top hat and a very fine suit.

"There was a time," said the man, "when TriBeCa was renowned as much for its hospitality as for the beauty of its women and the ferocity of its soldiers, and a visitor could be assured a hearty greeting and a twist of flower."

The park looked as it had during the golden age of old TriBeCa, children playing merrily in a gazebo, lovers canoodling on the green, the surrounding buildings yet whole.

"After everyone was slaughtered, however, we were forced to alter our policies on uninvited guests."

Washington Market Park turned monstrous, children grown feral and their slaver-parents holding the leash, the lovers merged into one hideous bifurcated beast, the buildings themselves yapping for the Kid's blood, mouth-doors gnashing, eye-windows red-veined, the man turning to face the Kid, *what a handsome little boy you are what fun we'll have together in the funk together forever–*

"He's small for his age," gasped the Kid from where he lay doubled-up on the phalt.

"Who?" asked the man.

"Your son," said the Kid. He got to his knees, and then he got to his feet. Then he reached into a pocket of his coat and took out his cigarette case. "That was a freebie; you'll have to pay for the rest."

Washington Market Park went naked then, stripped of its illusion, revealing its ruined self – the bodega ash, the surrounding buildings long devastated, even the ground itself sandy and lifeless. "You'll have to forgive me," said the Last King of TriBeCa. "I had assumed you were one of these neighborhood idiots sneaking in on some dare, not a gentleman come to discuss a matter of importance. I'm afraid that even still, I have little by way of refreshment to offer you; the only thing left in TriBeCa is the funk."

"That's cool," said the Kid. "I ate before I came."

"I'm the Last King of TriBeCa," said the Last King of TriBeCa.

"I gathered," said the Kid.

"Of course you had. But still, there's a certain form to these things. And you would be…?"

"The Kid," said the Kid. He tapped the end of his smoke twice against the 💣 symbol on his case, and then he lit it.

"Just 'the Kid'?"

"It's what my mammy named me," said the Kid.

"You've a familiar look; have we ever met before?"

"I think I'd remember."

"Probably. In any event, tell me all about him!"

"There's a form to these things, like you said. And 'tell me all about him' is not a question."

"No, it isn't. Clever boy. Let me play fair: Where does he live?"

"A condo."

"Does he know of me?" asked the Last King of TriBeCa.

"I can't see inside his brain. How do I know what he knows?"

"How was he saved from TriBeCa?"

"Can't say," said the Kid. His cigarette smoke, white and crisp, contrasted starkly with the surrounding funk.

"Who saved him?"

"Someone who thought to make use of him."

"And why are you telling me about him?"

"The same reason."

Once, when the Last King of TriBeCa had just been the King of TriBeCa, he had had a servant flayed alive for spilling coffee on his lap. Being dead his temper had not improved, though he managed, with great effort, to hold onto it just then. "You've got an… aggravating conversational style."

"He likes to draw," the Kid said, as a sop.

"An artist, of course he would be! I've always fancied myself the same, though on a far grander scale; my work is not with paint on paper, but in flesh and marrow, my canvas the Island itself!"

"I gather he mostly just draws panel books," said the Kid.

"Panel books?" The Last King of TriBeCa seemed disappointed.

"Yeah, panel books. You know, like they tell a story as you go through them. Usually there's a hero and a–"

"I know what a panel book is," snapped the Last King of TriBeCa. "How old did you say he was?"

By then, their constitutional had taken them over Hudson Street. "I dunno. Three, four thousand dims?"

"Isn't that kind of old to still be looking at panel books?" asked the Last King of TriBeCa.

"Is that one of your questions?"

"No, no, just commenting. At that age, I'd killed my first man and bedded my first woman – though, admittedly, both were tied up at the time. Anyway, something to talk to him about when we are finally reunited. Which, Mr The Kid, is our next topic of conversation."

"It's just the Kid," said the Kid. "And what's in it for me?"

"Anything," hissed the Last King of TriBeCa, "anything that you want."

"You say that," said the Kid, "but what if what I want isn't in TriBeCa? 'Cause I don't see much here worth hanging on to."

The Island-wide search for his lost heir had drained much of the Last King of TriBeCa's strength, and rather than maintain his usual illusions, he had allowed the neighborhood to look as it actually did: well-ruined, the glass broken and the buildings ravaged. "My reach is not limited to TriBeCa alone. Anywhere the funk goes, I can be – not as easily, true, not without some personal cost, and my resources are far from infinite. But you bring me my heir, and they'll all be at your service. I'll drive your enemies mad with fear and hate, I'll crush their bones. Whatever you wish, anything you dream, I can do. Just bring me back my son."

"Cool," said the Kid. By then, they had walked all the way to Vestry Street, close to the boundary with Soho.

"Only fair to warn you," said the Last King of TriBeCa, "you have a competitor. And this is the sort of deal that only has one taker."

"Got it," said the Kid.

"But, in the meantime, you deserve just compensation for the information you've provided me. Ask away! The funk whispers its secrets to me, from the far reaches and darkest corners of the Island, from first bright till deepest dim. To me is known the most wretched secrets of the high, the noblest impulses of the basest born, the–"

"I'm straight," interrupted the Kid. He crushed his cigarette beneath the heel of his shoe.

"Excuse me?" asked the Last King of TriBeCa.

"I don't have any questions."

"Everyone has questions about *something*."

"I kinda figured it all out already."

The funk rose suddenly so thick that the Kid could not see the top of his boots, and the Last King of TriBeCa stopped looking like what he looked like when he was alive, and started looking like what he really was, the corners of a disordered mind given sludgy shape, putrefaction personified. "This is a matter of honor," he hissed. "I've accrued a debt, and a gentleman does not allow a debt to remain unpaid. To insist otherwise is to insult me, my magnanimity and generosity of spirit, my–"

"Fine man, cool off. I'll come up with something if your ego is so fragile." The Kid thought a moment. "Why do they call it Canal Street when there's no canal there?"

"What?"

"Canal Street. Why do they call it Canal Street when there's no canal there?"

"I don't know," admitted the Last King of TriBeCa.

"A lot of use you are," the Kid grumbled, setting off into Soho.

45

A Poisoned Pawn

Sin seldom sleeps, nefariousness never naps, badness knows no bedtime, and so neither could High Inquisitor Dak allow himself a moment's respite, not even as dimmest rolled towards less dim.

The Hive was protected from attack by its walls and its Paladins, but danger did not come only from beyond the gates, did it? No, the true threat was already inside – false followers of the Queen in Yellow, faithless servants, hornets masquerading as bees. Not a dim passed when High Inquisitor Dak was not forced to bust up an unlicensed still or shut down a ring of nudie-book dealers. It was a heavy responsibility, but it was one that High Inquisitor Dak met proudly.

The note had arrived just after dimtime prayer, Dak met outside the temple by one of his subordinates. It read:

Dak distrusted anonymity on principle – nothing in the Hive should be hidden; there ought be no subterfuge between siblings! – but Dak was a man more practical even than he was fanatical. It was not uncommon for one wasp to sting another to death, and even evil men could unwittingly serve the Queen in Yellow.

And there was that worrisome first symbol. Impure brethren and those sad souls what lived outside of the Queen in Yellow's kindness, clinging to their dead idols and their false gods, these were to be treated as disobedient children – sternly, forcefully, but still with hope that they might learn the error of their ways. Not so a funk-huffer. To make common cause with the funk, to ask for its blessings, was to put yourself outside of even the Queen in Yellow's magnanimity. The two Inquisitors who followed behind Dak carried cutters and materials to make a cleansing fire, and if what they found at the address was anything like what the missive suggested, whoever was inside would be lucky to find themselves dead by the first.

West End Avenue and 71st Street was a distant corner of the Hive, only recently incorporated and yet to benefit from the Queen in Yellow's influence. At first glance, the building looked abandoned. But upon closer inspection, the side-entrance showed recent signs of use. Dak gave the word to his two underlings, and they unsheathed their cutters and busted through the half-rotted door.

An anti-climax, empty inside except for a table and a bulletin board, and on both, maps and drawings and charts of the Island. Before he could try and make sense of them, there was a noise, and Dak and his men turned to discover a scarred subterranean girl standing in the doorway. Dak did not give the order, but he did not need to; a rat was near as bad as a funk-swallower, and this could only be some treacherous trap of those what lived below. Dak's soldiers rushed forward until the thing in the girl's hands *boomed!* and one of them died, and then it *boomed!* twice more, and the other dropped likewise, only Dak left to revenge them, pulling his knife and then one final, different-sounding *boom!* and High Inquisitor Dak went to bask forever at the boots of the Queen in Yellow, singing backup in her joyous choir, an eternal life of bliss unknown on this bitter, mortal plane.

Presumably.

The Target

"Nice shot," said Gillian.

"Pulls right," said Ariadne.

Gillian looked at her revolver, and sighed. "I need to stop using so much boom."

"Carry a cutter," suggested Ariadne.

"People treat you different when they see you with a cutter." She took a look through the documents on the table. What was nonsense to Dak was immediately legible to Gillian, and even Ariadne only took a moment to follow along.

"Stuyvesant?" Ariadne asked, pointing at one of the schematics.

"Yup," said Gillian.

"JuiceTown?" Ariadne asked, pointing at another.

"Yup," said Gillian.

On the bulletin board was a map of the Island, with a stretch of the Way circled in red. Pinned beside it was a sketch of a dark-skinned man with thick glasses and no smile.

"Who's he?" asked Ariadne.

"I would very much like to know that myself," said Gillian, unpinning the drawing.

And the Bright After That...

46

A Stranger in an Unfriendly Land

Mr Simpson awoke in his windowless cell to the tinny bleep of his digital alarm clock. He turned that off and turned on his table lamp. He made his bed. He took a clean wipe from a box, ran it across his face, then below his arms, then over his genitals. He dowsed his hands with more sanitizer than the back of the bottle recommended. He took an omelet and ham MRE from beneath his bed, opened it and ate it cold. Then he put on his clothes, a drab, gray suit with a battered trench coat and an automatic in a shoulder holster and went to meet Dallas by the stairwell.

"Morning, Dallas."

"Good morning, sir," said Dallas.

"Not really morning, is it, Dallas?"

"No, sir, not really. Best get your other coat; it's a cold one."

"But yesterday was—" Mr Simpson choked off his complaint, went back inside, put on his heavier coat, then returned to the stairwell and began their descent. "I'm running very low on clean wipes."

"I'm sorry to hear that, sir."

"I don't suppose there's any chance to get some from the savages?"

"I doubt it."

"I miss showering, Dallas."

"Me too, sir."

"And coffee. I would shoot a man in the head for a decent cup of coffee."

"Would that it were so easy, sir," said Dallas.

The building had been the NSA's back in the day, whatever day that was – what was time without a moon or stars, what was time without fucking seasons? But the point being, it had been the NSA's originally, fifteen prison-like stories in the center of Manhattan. Deep inside one corner of that building, however, there was a wing no one went to, and that was the Shop's. Of course, the Shop had their little piece of it, as they had their little piece of every government bureau, NGO, and banana republic – a cache of small arms and ammunition, body armor, surveillance equipment, along with comms devices which the funk had rendered useless.

"No clean wipes, though," grumbled Mr Simpson.

"Sir?" asked Dallas.

"Nothing," said Mr Simpson as they reached the lobby.

Outside was the most miserable February morning that Mr Simpson had ever seen, except even in a February snowstorm, you knew there was a sun somewhere above and the snow was snow, not whatever the hell was falling on the asphalt in gooey gray piles like dried spunk. Awaiting them was Mr Simpson's armored pedicab, four Neanderthals to pedal, and a team of his own people riding on top, plus their cavalry escort looking like second-rate LARPers, leather armor and old tennis shoes.

"Good bright to you, sir!" said the Captain. "There's some trouble along the Ring; Stuy and Coop have revoked passage. We'll have to take you up the Way."

Mr Simpson shrugged and entered the pedicab, Dallas closing the door behind him. Like he gave a rat fuck about their route. The escort of Force was just for show; security was the responsibility of Dallas and Dallas's men, and on his infrequent excursions into the city, Mr Simpson often dreamed of some episode which required their vigorous assistance, *Black Hawk Down* on Bowery, a Midtown My Lai Massacre.

No sign of such good fortune as they began their procession north into the cobbled street of Soho, five blocks of vice so vicious it made the Reeperbahn look like Vatican City, an army of malnourished whores chomping toothless mouths in enticement, lip sores which might have been herpes or might have been the bubonic fucking plague. In front of what was once a Chipotle, a knock-off Viking with a battle-axe and a shirt advertising a generations-defunct insurance agency ate rat on a skewer.

Mr Simpson closed the curtain. "You know this was my first posting out of the academy?"

"You've mentioned, sir," said Dallas.

"I'll tell you something: the apocalypse improved it."

"Ha ha," said Dallas. Dallas had heard this joke before.

"Hot in the summer, cold in the winter; if you wanted to go somewhere, everyone was there already, and the wait was forever and the drinks were twenty dollars. The subway didn't work, the cab drivers were surly, their pizza was not as good as Chicago or Detroit, and don't get me fucking started on Brooklyn."

"I dunno," said Dallas. "I took my wife here for the weekend once. Didn't seem so bad. Climbed the Empire State Building, saw *Cats* on Broadway. There was... something about the place. A buzz."

"What does that even mean? Nothing. One idiot started saying that and that another idiot started agreeing, and pretty soon it hit moron critical mass and entered the common wisdom. 'Buzz', Dallas, is a bunch of assholes bumping against another bunch of other assholes on a narrow sidewalk." Mr Simpson waved in contempt at the world about him. "Manhattan, the tip of modernity's spear, an enormous engine of excess swallowing everything you gave it and shitting garbage out in the Hudson. How long you think it would have gone on, even without the funk? Climate change would have put it under water in thirty years anyhow, and good riddance."

Like poking at a loose tooth, or drunk dialing an ex-girlfriend, Mr Simpson opened the curtain of his pedicab once more. They were rattling through NoLita, handsome brick buildings infested by degenerate mongoloids. Half a dozen dogs hung butchered from a stand on Canal Street, Fido and Rover slit throat to crotch, wide-eyed and drawing flies. A gaggle of children threw handfuls of not-snow at each other, the off-white ooze splattering against their faces, inhaling who knew what sorts of toxins. A rail-thin street preacher ran along beside them for a quarter of a block, close enough for Mr Simpson to smell the stink of his rotting teeth. "Your wealth will not matter when the Yellow Queen calls you to her bosom!" he yelled. "The souls of the sweet rise, but the bitter unbelievers will fall forever from her light! Repent! Repent! Re–"

Harris, riding up top, struck the street preacher in the face with the butt of his SMG. Mr Simpson smiled and let the curtain close once more.

"I'm kidding, of course," he said.

"Of course," said Dallas.

"New York was the shittiest place in the world, and I did service in Kabul and in Pittsburgh; but everything's relative, isn't it, Dallas? There is no bottom to the hole, always somewhere worse, down and down and down and down. I would cut off a pinkie and eat it like a raw carrot to be drinking a beer in Times Square Chili's right now."

The curtain was closed, but still the place filtered in on him, hawkers offering cast-off clothing in their gutter dialect, a high-pitched whine, loud and growing louder, the smell of dung fires and of the endless waste, but mainly of the funk itself.

"And the so-called Council, worse than any of them. Let me tell you something, Dallas: the only thing worse than a dog is a dog that thinks he's a man, drinking rainwater out of garbage pails with its pinkie up. All these Notting Hill Napoleons strutting around like–"

"Do you hear that?" Dallas interrupted.

But before Mr Simpson could answer 'yes, actually, I do', the sound was drowned out by screaming, and then by *boom boom boom boom* coming so fast and so loud that all conversation was impossible, and then Dallas came tumbling into Mr Simpson, and then they were upside down and then rightside up and then upside down once more.

Impact

The warwagon split Mr Simpson's pedicab in two and continued out of control over the Way, heading towards a warren of merchant stalls until Chisel pulled a hard right and put them straight into a wall. It would have shattered the previous version of the autocycle, stripped down and built for speed, but its replacement had scrap-metal plating and barbed wire round the windows, and the impact only burst their front tire and ruined the engine and sent Ael tumbling from the cannon which was built into the top of the frame. The cavalry rallied in pursuit, half a dozen lancers and even a bugler charging boldly at the immobilized vehicle. But Ael was back at his gatling gun just as the first spear seemed sure to reach him. *Boom boom boom,* and the charge dissolved to scrap and bone, white ossein and pinkish tendrils of bloodied meat.

Violent Delights

Climbing out of the cabin, Mr Simpson felt that fuzziness which suggested a concussion, but he drew his pistol from a shoulder holster with a smile. A field man, obviously, but still a planner, not a hitter, and Mr Simpson had never felt the joy of firing off a gun in a crowd. His first shot went wide, a woman wearing a Versace hat and surplus army gear screaming and dropping to the ground, but the second two were on target, ricocheting off the back of the car and sending the gunner into cover. "Dallas!" Mr Simpson yelled, "get the fuck out of there and let's do some killing!"

In His Sights...

With his door jammed from the crash, the Kid had to kick out his window to escape, dropping onto the phalt carrying one of Chisel's cannon. A dismounted cavalryman came at him with a saber, and the Kid fired from the ground, *boom*, the top of his head went pink, the Kid on his feet by then, running back towards the Way. The tourist stood by his ruined pedicab, and there was a broken instant in the chaos where they both stared at one another, and then the Kid sighted down the barrel of his rifle and *boom boom boom*!

Near Miss

Mr Simpson screamed and slapped at his neck, but somehow he didn't think to go to his knees, standing stunned, a corpse for certain if Dallas hadn't pulled him to the ground.

"Sir!" Dallas yelled, loud enough to be heard over the Kid's cannon. "Willis and Smith are dead, sir! We need to get you out of here!"

"But–"

"That was not a suggestion!"

Two of Dallas's men held position by the pedicab while Dallas and the last hustled Mr Simpson towards Prince Street.

The Driver

Pedestrians fled screaming east and they fled screaming west, they took shelter in alleyways, they ran each other down in their haste to escape. A gut-shot soldier collapsed facedown, the final flailing of his limbs leaving angels in the gray snunk. A riderless mount galloped back and forth, gone mad from the noise or its wounds. Getting out of the warwagon, Chisel's nose was broken and there was a bit of white protruding from her wrist. The fighting had moved south, the Kid and Ael in pursuit of the fleeing target, but Chisel declined to follow them. "Rat-rutting idiots," she cursed, climbing aboard the back of her warwagon and reloading the automatic cannon – no easy task, one handed. "Bury your bones in the tunnels and take your skin to off to Jersey."

Surveying the Scene

In every condo on both sides of the Way from Broome to Bleeker, tenants were cowering in back rooms or inside bathtubs – save only 318 Spring Street, 4C, where Hope watched smiling from an open window, just then starting to peak on the three or so fistfuls of spoor blossom which she had swallowed sometime earlier.

Boom! Boom! Boom!

Hope giggled and watched the fireworks.

A Fighting Retreat

Hurrying down an alley towards Mercer, Dallas caught sight of a faded Mermaid decal. "Hold position!" he yelled to his single remaining soldier before kicking open an access door and hustling Mr Simpson into the Starbucks beyond.

Long years a killer, the soldier did not need to be told twice, training his SMG on the mouth of the alley, ready to ventilate any would-be pursuers. His movements were neat, spare, stripped of any excess, like a carpenter hammering a nail. In the World-Writ-Large, for men like this, war was not chaos but comfortable routine, something close to a science.

On the Island, however, it was an art. A cheery roar was the last thing the soldier heard, followed by a terrible weight on his back, and then long nothing.

Loot

Ael cut loose the SMG with his bloodied knife. "Upgrade!" he announced, before hurrying into the building.

Reinforcements Arrive

Tocsins beat across Downtown, every clique within fifty blocks preparing to repel this desperate assault. A scratch troop of Force hurried south down the Way, huffing, pikes aloft. Chisel waited until they were midway across Houston before letting loose with her cannon. Operating it one-handed, she couldn't aim, really, but the boom was so large and there was so much of it that this proved not to matter, half the Force slaughtered and the other half retreating madly back the way they had come.

Chisel sucked a tooth and spat blood into the snunk. "Come on, Kid," she said, "hit him and get back here."

Trigger Control

The elation caused by the unexpected violence and his moderate concussion had worn off, and Mr Simpson was now only frightened and nauseous. It was everything he could do to maintain pace with Dallas, who rushed them through the building's warren-like partitions, occupied by the usual sub-human peons. Mr Simpson assumed the big man who appeared in the hallway behind them was one of these, until he noticed the SMG.

"Howdy!" said the man, leveling the barrel.

Common wisdom to the contrary, nothing of any profundity ran through Mr Simpson's head just then, his presumable final thoughts being equal parts resentment and rage at the absurd series of events which were about to see him killed by a man wearing football pads wrapped in dyed dog skin.

The safety clicked. "Huh," said the man.

More practiced in the complexities of 21st century firearms, Dallas let off a quick burst with his own weapon, and it was only by diving shoulder-first through the glass windows of the second floor and out onto into the street that their would-be assassin avoided swift death.

Surviving Contact With The Enemy

The Kid remained on the Way, pinned down behind an overturned apple cart, two of Mr Simpson's men letting off if he dared to rise out of cover. He held his superboom in one hand and his cannon in the other, and he looked, for the first time, slightly worried.

From the railing of her apartment Hope watched the bullets strike against and around his position. "He's such a good dude," she said, very much enjoying the way her fingers felt when they touched her other fingers. "We need to find him a decent girl."

"I'll keep him covered," said one of the men shooting at the Kid. "Flank him!"

"Got it!" said the second man shooting at the Kid.

"Stupid future cannon, doesn't even boom when it's supposed to," Ael said, appearing from behind them just then, "gimme a good sword any time!"

An Instant's Hope

The Kid noticed that no one was shooting at him, and looked up to see Ael cleaning his blade. "Did you–?" the Kid asked.

(Interruption)

Boom! Boom! Boom! Chisel could keep the Force bottled up behind their barricade till dimtime, or till they brought in their own cannon; that was not her problem. Her problem was the squad of Bowery Boudiccas slinking along Houston, daughters of the bow, the best shots on the Island. Fierce isolationists, still they had been drawn from their roost in Roosevelt Park by the unheard of attack on the Way, ducking behind merchant stalls and down alleyways, popping up only to send an ever-increasing number of arrows in Chisel's direction. One *tinged* off the guard below her cannon and she swiveled it as best she could in the direction of the Brides, cranking and hoping for the best. *Boom! Boom! Boom!*

Swiftly Dashed

"...near as hair on a nipple!" said Ael. "But no dice."

Never Reinforce Failure

Chisel ducked, and the arrow flew through the space she had just then vacated, the Boudiccas getting closer. The bravest of the Force prepared a charge across the open killing ground of Houston. A mixed mob of Sacred Band and Devastators roared north up the Way. Eastward along Prince, the SoHo Sublime did the same, all of Downtown making common cause against the invaders.

"Rut a mutt!" the Kid roared, then pointed caddy-corner to the balcony of 318 Spring Street, 4C.

Exit Strategy

"Hey, cousin!" Hope waved.

The Kid did not wave back, sprinting towards the crippled warwagon, firing his rifle as he ran. That was okay. Everything was okay, so far as Hope was concerned: the screams of the dying, the red-spattered snunk, the certain eventuality of her own death. Three caps of spoor blossom running through her and things were fine and better than fine, things were *downright fabulous,* and that kind of feeling shouldn't be kept to oneself, that kind of feeling had to be spread; at least, that was what Hope thought, leaning back in her chair and letting her brain expand, bubbling out of her condo and into the street, past the carnage on the Way and the wounded taking shelter in the tenements and so on and so forth, a great crescendo of bliss like an orgasm, but it didn't end and it went up your whole body, up your spine and into your brain and then back down again, through to the distant tips of your toes, sparing only Ael, the Kid, and a wounded Chisel, who swiftly made good their escape.

47

Another Piece of the Puzzle

Adze and the Null lay prone on the roof of a warehouse at the far end of Pier 26, staring north-east, back towards the Island. The far-seeing glasses were too small to cross the great bridge of Adze's nose, and he had to keep transferring it from one eye to the other.

"Who is it even owns that section of Canal Street?" he asked.

"Nobody," said the Null. "It's fallow. Too close to TriBeCa, no civilian will kip there."

"Then what's all that smoke from? And the guards? And who built those barricades?"

"Dunno," said the Null, taking the glasses.

"What in the name of tomorrow is going on in the Holland Tunnel?"

48

Aftermath

By brightest, the snunk had melted, puddles of red staining the heretofore sacrosanct phalt. From Houston to Canal Street sawbones tended to the wounded, wives wept over the dead, children ran their hands over boom holes in brick walls. The Downtown cliques swaggered left and swaggered right, bragging of the great victory they had won against strange weapons and overwhelming odds. On each neutral corner stood Force with pike and cannon, as if to remind everyone that however many soldiers they had lost, the Enclave had yet plenty to spare. Street preachers prophesied apocalypse, and for once, they did not struggle to drum up an audience; the I's being murdered was business as usual, and JuiceTown could afford new bikes, but once broken, a taboo can never be restored. Violence... on the Way? It was like feeling the phalt buckle beneath your feet.

Amid such epistemological tumult, the Mayor stood steady, offering a word of succor here, the odd remonstrance there, comforting the small with the knowledge that the great had noticed their misfortune. It was an impressive display of equanimity, though it slipped a bit when Gillian arrived.

"This habit of tardiness is growing frustrating," he said. "Too late to keep JuiceTown intact, too late to stop... whatever the hell happened here."

"I assume it was an attempt to assassinate this man," said Gillian, handing the Mayor the sketch.

The Mayor looked at it for a moment.

Gillian looked at the Mayor. "Do you know him?"

"I've never seen him before in my life," lied the Mayor. "Who is he?"

"I have no idea," said Gillian, "because it isn't my job to find out, like it wasn't my job to protect him, like it wasn't my job to stop JuiceTown from getting blown up, like it isn't my job to scrub your toilet. Twenty thousand in scrip to uncover the party behind the murder of Don DeAndre; that was what we agreed. Call the Council together," she said. "I've arrived at my recommendation."

"About time," said the Mayor.

49

Emancipation, etc.

Woes of a True Domestic

Fran[50] fumed her way up the stairs towards her quarters. All that time, looking after the boy, and now she was out with the rubbish! She would like to see them find another nanny half so caring as Fran! How many had they gone through before they had found her, how many other women had shirked from even spending a few dims with the boy?

Nor did Fran blame them. He was an odd one; so hard as she tried to keep it from her face, she could not keep it from her mind. Fran had been a caretaker since a slate tile had fallen on her mother when she was just a girl, Fran left to take care of her younger siblings while her father pedaled and drank, and in all that time, she had never known a child so strange as poor Newton. That way he had of staring sometimes, as if he didn't recognize her, and that thing with the gardener – how had Newton even heard the girls were missing? And after, when they had dug up the rose bushes, and the menfolk were dragging the gardener away for his justice, and Newton's uncle asking if he had seen the gardener bury them, and Newton shrugging and shaking his head 'no', he just knew.

Fran unlocked the door to her room and went inside, then locked it behind her. It was cozy, even spare: a small bureau,

---

50   Underappreciated domestic.

a table with a candle, a Tiny t hung over a bed. Fran ignored all of these and headed for the window. "Uncle, indeed," Fran said. Then, "Ha!" as if she hadn't voted for him herself, put her chit below his sigil. The window was well-oiled and opened easily. Fran reached outside and pulled a worn egg from where it sat on the windowsill.

"Just as well, anyway," Fran said. "I'll get a position with some nice new family; girls still in pigtails, won't be any trouble. Don't need to worry about making stories from panel books, or how it is the boy came to know the things he knows." Fran rapped the egg against her bureau once, twice, the motion pleasant and practiced.

But what would happen to Newton, away from her? There was sweetness in girls, or at least there was less capacity for cruelty; but a boy needs to be taught to be decent. Left to their own, they rot into brutes. And who would school him? Not his 'uncle'; Whatever relationship he had with the boy, it was far from avuncular. Those guards certainly couldn't be trusted. They didn't know Newton's name nor hers, and looked at Newton like he was – not an animal, more dangerous than that, more precious, but still not like a man should look at a child.

"In the t's hands now, I suppose," said Fran, taking her huff.

Provisions

Inside Newton's bag were: thirty-seven bits that he had saved or scrounged from various occasions; the penknife which Uncle had given him for his three thousandth dim what had a compass on the pommel; some rat jerky; all of his pens which had any ink, two empty notebooks, and a couple of doodles he had liked; three changes of underwear, two pairs of socks, several shirts; the panel book what showed the champion with the shield, the panel book with the nasty looking bald man, the panel book which had a picture inside of a woman not wearing a shirt.

"Ready," he said, zipping it closed.

Due Severance

"I don't get what's so special about this kid," said Duncan.

"Oh, you don't get what's so special about him?" asked Gerry.

"So special that it needs five of us with boom to escort him six blocks?"

"Well, if you don't understand, then we ought to scrap the entire operation," said Gerry.

"All right."

"Let me call up the Mayor, tell him Duncan don't understand, ask if he'll come up here to–"

"Like you aren't curious."

"I know the Mayor sent five of us out here with boom, and I know the Mayor doesn't do anything foolishly. And I know the Mayor doesn't want us to know who the boy is, and if the Mayor doesn't want us to know who the boy is, there's probably a good reason for that likewise. Especially if we have to…"

"You think it'll come to that?"

"Nah. An armored pedicab, and straight through to the Enclave? Who would try to make a grab? Still," said Gerry, "that's no excuse to drop your guard. Until we're inside the walls, we'd best keep our eyes on him like he was–"

The door opened and Gerry went silent, Newton's nurse entering with a tray.

"No thank you, Madam," said Duncan, playing the beau even to this fat old woman, "we've ate already."

But she set the tray down on the table all the same, a pot of stone root tea and some napkins and something next to it, which only after it was in Gerry did Duncan realize was a knife.

Hearing the Screams...

Newton jumped, and since he was just then climbing out the

window, that meant that he struck the top of his head against the frame and landed squarely on his testicles, before slipping slowly into space, down two stories, and into a nest of bushes.

It was a bad beginning to the affair, and Newton spent a long few tocs groaning among the gardenias. More screams, then three loud shots of boom, then more screams, and then, against the knot of pain in his lower torso, Newton forced himself upright and towards the back corner of his garden. There had been snunk in Midtown, but Uptown the weather was quite temperate, the funk giving as the funk liked, no care for neighborhood nor block. The walls around his house were too high to be scaled, and the tops were covered with barbed wire and broken glass, but there was an oak tree beside it from which a brave soul might make an escape.

Newton could not manage to be such, just then, straddling a branch and willing himself to make the jump down to 81st Street.

"I know you're scared right now, Newton," said Fran, "but you don't need to be. This is the start of a new life for you, better than anything you could have dreamed."

Newton thought: Fran believes it. And then he also thought: That is not Fran.

He turned to find Not Fran coming down from the house. She carried one of the guard's cannon and the knife that she had used to take it.

"Everything they ever told you is a lie, Newton," said Not Fran. "I know that's hard to understand right now, but it's true. Everything. Your name isn't even Newton; that's a lie too. In TriBeCa, of which you are heir, we named our children after the great heroes of old: Arvis, Warren, Sean, and Todd. And when you come to your rightful inheritance, you'll take on one of those."

The house was on fire, Newton noticed then.

"I'm sorry, I must sound like I'm talking nonsense. It's a strange position to be in. Here's the important thing: we need to get you out of here. Those what have been trying to keep you from me, they're going to be back, and back soon. We need to bring you to TriBeCa before they can kidnap you again. When we're there I'll explain everything, I swear, but we don't have much time. Please, come down."

Newton stared at the face of Not Fran, and then back over the wall, weighing competing terrors. "What did you do to my guard?"

"You mean your captors? I killed them, Newton, and lament only that the aforementioned demands of time meant they suffered less than their due torment. They didn't care about you; none of them did. None of them ever cared about you; they were just using you. They were frightened of you, Newton, and they should be, the way a rat is frightened of cat, as a boy would be a man, as a worshiper ought a–"

But before Not Fran could finish this last bit, there was a *boom*! and then she stumbled off the porch, choking on blood for a bit and then expiring.

The man who had shot her came into view. He wore red leathers and carried a long cannon with several chambers. "I really hope that wasn't your mom or something."

"I'm an orphan," said Newton, from the tree.

"That's a relief," said Ael.

50

A Jury of Peers

Legend held that the mirrored black building on 42nd Street and the East River had been used by the ancestors for the same purpose as their descendants, as a neutral territory for the peaceful assemblage of great powers. If so, the World-Writ-Large must have been very much bigger than the Island, ten or even twenty times so large, for there was room for hundreds of people in the main hall, though the High Council needed only eight seats, and of these, only seven were in use, Don DeAndre's[51] spot remaining vacant.

"I've completed my investigation," Gillian[52] announced once the last Councilmember had arrived and their various lifeguards had finished eyeballing each other.

"Took you long enough," said Gecko, War Chief of the Widow Makers[53].

"Four dims ago, a band of assassins, with cannon and inside knowledge of the I's set up, slaughtered Don DeAndre."

"Not to mention my confessor!" said the Pope.[54]

---

51 One-time head of the Eternal I's, currently residing in the stomachs of various East River aqua life.
52 Sheriff.
53 Owners of Downtown from the Battery to Canal Street, worshipers of the bull and the bear.
54 Hairless head of the Cloisters, psychic adversary of Maryland Slim.

"I followed their trail to a band of cut-rate killers," Gillian continued, "bought off with a long chain of scrip."

"A tragic circumstance all around," said the right half of the Frenemy[55], who was, by presumable coincidence, filling Capital's[56] seat just then.

"Whose scrip?" asked the Mayor.

"There's no need to get bogged down in details," insisted the left half of the Frenemy.

Gillian seemed to agree, because she did not stop to answer the Mayor's question. "From there, our mystery assassins bought some superboom from a band of Force[57] uptown."

"Impossible!" roared the Commissioner,[58] "as if a member of the Force would ever stoop so–"

"With their new weapons," Gillian interrupted, "they led an assault on JuiceTown, further crippling the Island's ability to defend itself."

"So I recall," said the Chief Engineer[59] of JuiceTown.

"The violence on the Way was caused by the same band of perpetrators, who intended to–"

"We know all of this," the Mayor[60] interrupted. "By the gods of our fathers, just tell us who's responsible."

"The Honey Swallowers, obviously." said Gillian, with as much passion as she'd have shown ordering a plate of rat meat.

Several members of the various lifeguards gasped. The Pope rubbed her bald head vigorously. The Mayor frowned.

"The hitters were outside muscle," Gillian continued, "but it was the Honey Swallowers that armed them, backed them,

---

55   Bifurcated banker.
56   A consortium of counting houses.
57   The Enclave's muscle, more men and more boom than any clique on the Island.
58   Leader of [58].
59   Smarting pretty hard over the destruction of his home and life's work.
60   Shady elected official, anxious to keep Gillian from finishing her sentence.

and gave them a hole to hide in. I found these in a basement on the Upper West Side, protected by a High Inquisitor." Gillian snapped her fingers, and a servant began to distribute the plans and schematics she had found, a folder to each of the parties. Then she pulled the badge from inside her coat, and held it up in front of her. "As Sheriff of the Island, I formally recommend the ban be put on the Honey Swallowers; their soldiers to be slaughtered, their property to be looted, their crops to be razed, their houses burned, their phalt split and broken, their kingdom to lie fallow until all who ruined it themselves lie dead."

"Harlot!" Alvin[61] roared. "Funk-huffer! Eater of unripe fungi! You... you... you... you Becky with good hair!"

His lifeguard gasped in horror at the enormity of the insult.

"That's not much of a defense," said the Commissioner.

"What defense would be needed against the obvious lies of a false-hearted woman? *She* says that she found this evidence in the Hive, but even if it were true, it would prove nothing. The Yellow Empire runs from Midtown to Washington Heights, and we cannot be held responsible for the goings on of every room in every shack from–"

"And yet, I'm convinced," said Gecko. "The Widow Makers agree to the ban. I've always wanted to get one of those pretty gilded pictures you like to carry – give me something to wank to."

"I'll see your pecker stuffed into your mouth before you die," Alvin raged.

"For too long, we've known the Honey Swallowers were not to be trusted," said the Commissioner, smiling, "but even I could not have imagined such perfidy."

"Tunnel-dwellers! Maze-wearers!" Alvin continued.

"What else can you expect from these fundamentalist freaks?" asked the High Engineer rhetorically. "JuiceTown gives its agreement."

---

61 Leader of the Honey Swallowers. Upset.

"The Hive will not forget this; the Queen in Yellow's memory is long and her vengeance is–"

"As is that of Capital," said the Right side of the Frenemy. The Left side stared hard at Gillian for a moment before echoing, "Agreed."

"Filthier than Borofolk! Lower than those what live below the phalt!" said Alvin. "Beckys with good hair, the lot of you, and your punishment is sure to come!" He turned then to the Mayor, whose vote would determine whether or not the ban would be leveled. "As for you, think hard on what the Island would look like without the Hive to balance out the rest of these animals. If justice does not sway you, bow to self-interest."

The Mayor had been uncharacteristically silent since Gillian had offered her recommendation, his attention taken up entirely by a small note, drawn on the folder he had been given.

"Guilty," said the Mayor finally, adopting Alvin's suggestion. "Guilty."

51

The Last Lives of Nelly Karrow

Nelly Karrow sat at her table in her Yorkville café looking harder than a stepfather's hand. Concern furrowed her brow, and her downy lips drew downward. It was not the loss of her beloved feline familiars which pained Nelly Karrow just then, nor even the reduction of her consciousness their loss had entailed; it was something else, a faint sense of unease, like spoor deposited just left of the litterbox. Who was bankrolling the Kid? What was the point of the battery they had stolen? Why would the Honey Swallowers want to have blown up JuiceTown? How was it that both Gillian and the Kid had gone to visit damned TriBeCa?

So distracted was Nelly Karrow by this cacophony of concerns that she didn't notice him until he was already beside her: a Downtown grinder in red, the sort of person who didn't belong north of 42nd Street.

"Ms. Karrow?" he asked pleasantly, though before she could answer, there was a swift sudden pressure, and Nelly Karrow's dress front grew damp. She gasped out her final breath a few tics later, while simultaneously...

...howling miserably atop an armoire in Murray Hill...

...expiring as Maryland Slim entered a building off Union Square...

...tumbling off Gillian's window ledge in the same building, six stories, though dead long before it struck phalt...

"Never once left a tip," said the serving girl when she came back from the kitchen and found what remained of Nelly Karrow. "Not one single time."

52

'X X X'

As always, Abner[62] was first out of the Times Building, but already the tocsins were ringing across the city, in Lenox Hill and in Turtle Bay, in the Garment District and Chelsea and East Harlem. Outside of JuiceTown a pack of out-of-work pedalers disputed how the news would affect their prospects for future employment, and further south a priest of the bull offered an impromptu service, pious mothers and obedient children on their knees surrounding him. The bars were offering discounts on distil and house brew, and the brothels did a predictably brisk business. At the corner of 38th Street an industrious insurance seller offered death benefits to soldiers of any officially recognized clique – two-hundred and fifty to your family in exchange for fifteen perfect of any loot, should you survive. He was far from the only man wagering on the outcome: in Madison Square Park a dozen bookies waited to take money wherever you sought to place it; on the number of gangs that would gather, on where they would be sent and who would lead them, on which crew would come away victorious and who would end next dim nothing but a memory. Abner flew down the Way swifter than he had ever managed, past Soho Sublime making common cause with their neighbors north of Houston, cutters in pink and grinders in grim turquoise

---

62 Times Senior Newsboy.

spitting on palms and swearing oaths and talking about the war to come. Crake[63] was at his usual spot below the arch in Washington Square, but Abner flat ignored him, leaping atop the news crate and bellowing with lungs still strained from his sprint, "The Ban has been passed! The Ban has been passed! The Honey Swallowers are outcast, by word of the Council! At bright, the Island goes to war!"

---

63 Beloved Broadcaster.

53

Councils of Battle

"Let me know if you need help," said the Kid.

"Nah," said Ael, keeping even time with the oars, "it's fine. Those last two weren't barely any trouble. You all right down there, Newton? You look a little green."

"I've never been on a boat before," Newton admitted. The current ran swift uptown, away from the pier and towards where Flushing's[64] boat lay moored just south of the Queensboro. Last bright moved swiftly to first dim, the funk darker and meaner than normal, rumbling like it had supped on spoiled shellfish.

"You're the man from outside of my school," said Newton.

"Yup," said the Kid.

"Could you tell me what's going on, please?" asked Newton.

The Kid finally managed to light a cigarette, and he puffed at it a while before speaking. "It'll take a while, and I have to tell someone else what's going on first. I'll try to catch you up later."

"Adults often say they'll tell you something later," said Newton, "but they rarely do."

"I'm not an adult," said the Kid, but he seemed uncertain.

---

64 Boroman, aquatic exile of lost Brooklyn, knew the Kid back when he was a kid.

Reunion

Swan was the last to arrive at Gillian's penthouse. He wore some of the suit that he had been wearing before, as well as some other things that did not match it.

"This better be good, Gillian," he said. "This better be walk-up-ten-flights-of-stairs good."

The juice was off in Gillian's building, as it was everywhere else on the Island. Gillian hung Swan's coat in the hallway closet and handed him the weapon that rested there.

"I got you a new sword," she said.

It was a beauty, hand made by an Uptown smith, long and single-edged, and with a pommel worked intricately in sterling and black leather. Swan accepted it indifferently.

"Aren't you going to say 'thank you'?" Gillian asked.

"Are you going to ask me to kill someone with it?"

"Yes."

"Then I don't really think a 'thank you' is warranted."

Analgesic

Chisel lay on a cot in the visitor's cabin, having her arm tended by Flushing, who was the ship's sawbones just as he was its mechanic. The room was made from a rusted cargo container, and the top of Adze's mohawk brushed the roof.

"My favorite halfwit," said Adze when the Kid came in.

"How's your wrist?" asked the Kid.

"Fine," said Chisel.

"Very badly broken," corrected Flushing. "Have a sip of this," he pulled out a small flask, "it'll dull the pain."

"I don't want it," said Chisel.

"Suit yourself," said Flushing.

"A real bust-up plan you had there, Kid," Adze said. "I can see how you got your reputation."

"She was driving," said the Kid.

"This will hurt a lot," said Flushing.

But Chisel didn't scream, only winced for a tic and drank what was in the flask.

"Have a sip, I said," said Flushing, as he bound Chisel's wrist against her chest. "Not the entire bottle. While you're sleeping, I'll make you a plaster. Keep it on and you might be able to use your hand again… eventually, for simple tasks that you don't need to perform very competently."

"I'll manage," said Chisel.

Flushing slipped outside, around Adze who was blocking most of the doorway.

"Did you get the guy you were trying to kill?" Adze asked the Kid.

"Didn't she tell you already?" asked the Kid.

"Sure she did, but I want you to tell me; that way, it'll feel more humiliating."

"Adze, get back to the Bridge and make sure the crew has executed on our prototype," said Chisel.

"The Null can handle it," said Adze.

Hopped painless on Flushing's concoction, wrist broken, Chisel still had a scowl to peel paint.

"All right, all right," said Adze, letting it force him out of the room.

Then it was just Chisel and the Kid. "Where did you go?" Chisel asked.

"Ael and I had to take care of some things."

"What things?"

"A kidnapping and a murder," said the Kid. "Don't worry about it."

"No?" Chisel asked. She stared at her working hand as if to familiarize herself with each digit.

"I've got some things to tell you," the Kid said.

A Parlor Scene

From the windows in Gillian's living room, Union Square

looked all a bustle, the market frantic with soldiers wanting to spend their last bit of scrip. It was a logical spree, for by the morrow, they'd either be dead or flush with their spoils. Daedalus sat on a pre-funk settee, and Ariadne sat beside him, stroking the arm above his severed hand, offering comfort or clarifying her ownership.

"Hey, girl," said Swan. "Good to see Gillian hasn't gotten you killed."

"Crone came close," said Ariadne.

"And you brought company!" said Swan, grinning from below his constant hood. "I was wondering if I'd get to see you again, Dade."

"How you been, Swan?" Dade said.

Swan walked over to Gillian's wet bar, set his sword down beside it, opened a bottle of distil, and took a lengthy swig. "Just rosy, thanks. How about you? I hear you went all establishment."

"Dade conducts Green line," Ariadne interjected.

"That sounds like a dog's job. Authority! Who would want it." Swan burped loudly.

"Clan comes first," Daedalus said after what seemed a long time.

"What's going on, Gillian?" Maryland Slim asked. "The Aquarians are having a pre-ban shindig, and I want to make an entrance before their berserkers get started on spoor blossom."

"Slim settle," said Ariadne. "Crone's got words."

"You've gotten real lock-step all of a sudden for a mole girl used to threaten to eat people a lot," said Slim, but he fell silent.

Gillian paused a tic. "It's time I told you what's been going on," she said.

The Big Reveal

"A while back some sort of ship berthed near Forty Tryon," Chisel said. "Men from the World-Writ-Large got off. They cajoled or threatened the Mayor into helping to rebuild the Holland Tunnel, using slave labor from downtown folk desperate enough to sign on for land in the far north. It was that man that we were trying to kill on the Way, before he can open up the tunnel and bring in the rest of his people. That everything?"

"Most of it," the Kid admitted.

Reaction Shots

Slim laughed.

Swan laughed also, but bitterly.

"Maze hide us," said Ariadne.

Daedalus said nothing.

Strategy

"You had your giant snooping after me?" asked the Kid.

"You're not the only one can play a thing sideways," said Chisel. "What don't I know yet?"

"Come bright, while the rest of the city is killing each other, we're going to fight our way into the Holland Tunnel."

"Who's 'we'?"

"Me, you, Ael, Hope. The foursome that's been chasing after us."

"They're in on this?"

"Yeah."

"And what do we do once we get in there?"

"We use that battery we got from Stuy to blow the thing to hell."

"And that's everything, then?"

"The relevant bits."

The Kid could tell from the way she dipped her shoulder that she was about to hit him, but he sat still for it anyway.

Casus Belli

"You got the ban put on the Honey Swallowers, brought war to the Island worse than anything been seen in a generation, just as... what? A distraction?" asked Swan.

"Pretty much," admitted Gillian. "Also, I figured it would pay them back for what they did to the Orange line."

Daedalus didn't rise to this, pondering the matter a while before speaking. "It was you backing the boy keeps blowing things up?"

"Yeah."

"Meaning it was you what sent him through the tunnels? Meaning it's your fault for bringing us into this to begin with?"

"You're into it already – everyone is; every man, woman and child on the Island, plus anyone who doesn't fit into the traditional rubric. There's only one reason anyone from the World-Writ-Large would come back to the Island, and that's conquest."

"After what happened," said Swan, "don't you think this... tourist of yours will be wary?"

"They've got a complex set up around the mouth of the tunnel," Gillian said, "and a team of people he brought in from outside."

"Confessors, too, I'd bet," said Slim. "He'll have had to make some deal with the Pope."

"Probably," agreed Gillian. "Probably a big mess of them."

"And a lot of soldiers likewise," said Swan, "cast-off killers and what reinforcements he could get from his allies."

"Not as many as they'd have if the Island wasn't going to war," said Gillian, "but still a lot more than we'll have."

"Why not let him take it?" Dade said after a moment.

"What do you mean?"

"This tourist – if he wants the Island so bad, why not let him have it? You think he'll do any worse a job than the Mayor, or that High Council of yours? Who knows what tech they might have–"

"Don't talk rot," Gillian snapped. "Look around you – the ancestors were mad, and we live among the evidence of their madness. Towers stretching to a sky we'll never see, wonders squandered and worse than squandered. Whatever the funk is, they brought it, with their pride and their foolishness. Better off groping blindly towards our own future than taking part in the past they ruined. They are our parents," she continued, "and they cannot be forgiven."

A sudden gust of funk sprawled against the window. Swan made an admirable attempt to finish the rest of what was in his bottle.

"Now," Gillian said, after a tension-building pause, "who's with me?"

Why Slim Agreed

The whole bit about the tourist seemed solid. Gillian could be trusted to know what she was up to, even if she couldn't be trusted to tell the truth about it. Because he genuinely kind of liked Gillian. Because, whatever the case, this was clearly the biggest thing that had happened on the Island since the coming of the funk, and something so extraordinary would be, obviously, incomplete without the attendance of Maryland Slim.

"I'm in," said Slim.

Why Swan Agreed

Momentum, mostly, because he'd already gotten this far. Also because Gillian had never asked him for a favor before, not once in all the time they'd known each other. Also, Swan was not sure that he could be killed, and anyway would not have minded so much if he was, and so it wasn't as big of a deal for him as it would have been for most people.

"Why not?" asked Swan.

Why Daedalus Agreed

Will be discussed later.

"Green Clan roll," he said.

Why Chisel Agreed

"You are a limp-peckered, egocentric fool," said Chisel.

"Okay," said the Kid.

"You're no kind of nothing."

The Kid got up off the floor.

"Why wouldn't you tell me?" asked Chisel.

"There was no point in you knowing."

"All the time we've been…" but she didn't finish. "Who else knew? Did Hope know?"

"Hope's family."

"And Ael?"

"Ael's too stupid to try and cheat me."

"Ael's not stupid, he just doesn't care about the things other people care about. He's lucky, that way." The narcotic had started to kick in, Chisel's eyes going wide and almost soft. "What do you care about, Kid?"

"What do you mean?"

"What do you care about? I care about the Bridge, and the people on it, and tomorrow. Ael cares about being the best killer on the Island. Hope cares about you, and the other Borofolk, and having fun. What do you care about?"

"Power," said the Kid, but he didn't seem sure.

"Power is a thing you get to get something else. It's not an end by itself."

"A lot of people don't think that."

"A lot of people are fools. I didn't think you were a fool."

The Kid didn't answer.

"You are, though, and I guess I am too. I think I thought maybe I could get you to care about me, that if I poked down hard enough, long enough, I'd find something there. But there isn't anything," said Chisel. Her eyes were closing, and she had a faint smile on her face. "You're hollow, straight down through. What was it made you like that?"

The Kid didn't answer.

"Probably we'll all die trying to blow up this tunnel," said Chisel, yawning and stretching herself in the bed she and the Kid had just recently shared, "but if we do survive, I don't ever want to have to look at you again."

"I can sympathize," said the Kid.

But she was already asleep.

54

Strangers

Dimtime, and the Island was in an uproar. Every clique from the Devil to the Battery had begun their pre-war rituals, praying or drinking, but mostly drinking. Anyone who wasn't in a clique was holding up wherever they could find shelter, barricading their hovels and nailing shut their doors. As if reading the mood of the Island – or perhaps due to some other, unrelated disappointment – the funk had turned fierce, dimmer than dimmest and the wind howling hungry. On the High Line and in the far reaches of the Island, Funkees beat bruises into their breasts and gnashed their teeth as if to sever their tongues.

Gillian sat on a bench in East River Park and thought thoughts.

Gillian – 3,150 Dims

"They're so tall," said Gillian, looking up at the walls of the Enclave.

"Wouldn't want to storm those," said Gillian's papa.

"It's not nearly so green as Governor's Island."

"No, it isn't."

"But the funk ate Governor's Island," said Gillian.

"North to south," said her papa.

"And now we're going to the Enclave, so you can be master of arms for a great gentleman."

"Something like."

"And I'll be a proper lady."

"Maybe."

"I don't want to be a proper lady."

"I don't want to raise one," said her papa.

Gillian – 4,015 Dims

"I'm better than all the other boys with the cutter," said Gillian.

"You are now," said Gillian's papa. "You won't be much longer. Maybe you can get the drop on some fool doesn't give you your due, but you'll never be big enough or strong enough to take anyone competent. Open your present."

Inside was the cannon. Gillian lifted it gingerly.

"It was my father's, and now it's yours. I'll show you how to clean it. And come bright, I'll show you how to aim."

"Have you ever fired it, Papa?"

"Twice."

"Did you hit anything?'

He laughed. "It's a hundred bits a shot! You're damn right I hit something."

Gillian – 4,745 Dims

"Don't go," said Gillian.

"Have to go," said Papa. "Ate the man's bread."

"You're just another servant to him."

"That's not the point."

"Who cares? He's not a soldier, just some blue blood wants to seem brave."

"That's his business."

"At least take the cannon."

"No."

"Take the cannon."

"No!" snapped her Papa. "I go, the cannon stays. End of

conversation." He turned softer. "Don't worry yourself so. This isn't the first scrap I've come through."

Gillian – 5,474 Dims

"Hello, Gillian," said the gentleman. "Thanks for coming to see me." He was middle-aged, red-headed, and handsome.

"You're welcome," said Gillian.

"I know it's been a long time since we've had a chance to chat. How have you been?"

"I'm fine."

"The work in the stables suits you?'

"Suits me fine."

"If you had some other request, I'd be happy to–"

"The stables are fine," said Gillian.

"I had very great respect for your father," said the gentleman, eventually.

Gillian didn't say anything.

"Of course, you've heard the story of how he saved my life."

"I've heard stories before," said Gillian.

"Such heroic loyalty demands… obligations beyond the normal," the gentleman said, looking Gillian up and down. "And thinking on it, I can't escape the fact that I've been negligent in my duties. It's time we found you work in the main house, where I can attend more closely to your education."

Gillian – 6,171 Dims

"Gate closes at dimtime," said the guard.

"It's not quite dimtime, looks to me," said the girl.

"Why do you need to be going out of the walls now anyway? It isn't safe outside the walls, not after last bright."

"My lady says…" but she couldn't finish.

"Out with it."

"My lady says if I don't bring her back a new hairbrush before she goes to bed, she'll take the old one to me so hard I won't sit right for a dozen dims."

"You've got a nasty mistress to be sending you beyond the walls after dark."

"She might have mentioned it to me at brightest."

"Ha! Didn't think to start with that one, did you? But I have to close this gate in a few tocs, and so even still, you won't be able to get her the brush."

"I could go out through here, then sprint down to the Square, then back up the Way and use the main gate – that one stays open, doesn't it?" "It does indeed. You're a bold little thing, aren't you? Well, I won't hold you up any longer. Be brave, girl! And be careful!"

"Thank you, sir! Thank you!"

The alarums sounded soon after, the doormen at each tower passing it downward. The clatter of hooves signaled a detachment of cavalry, trotting briskly towards the gate. "Did she come this way?" one asked.

"Who?"

"Who? That maid what's got the whole Enclave in an uproar, that's who! Slit her master's throat like you'd shuck an oyster…"

Gillian – 6,273 Dims

"I told you," said Gillian, "my mother died before she could teach me the lore."

"She looks local to me," spat a Boroman. "I say be off with you."

"What you know about anything?" snapped Nan Toni. "Boro is Boro by blood; doesn't matter if no one taught them the old ways."

"Anyone can come in and say they're Boro. Doesn't make them–"

"She's preggers, you halfwit," Nan Toni said. "If she's lying, it's 'cause she's got nowhere else to go. You want to kick a woman bubbled up like that to the phalt?"

Presently

The Kid sat down beside her. "Hello, mother," he said. "Been waiting long?"

Gillian – 6,534 Dims

"Who are you?" asked the Widow Maker.

"Who else would be sitting on a bench in Clinton Park after dimmest?" Gillian responded.

"Didn't think you'd be a woman."

"And I didn't think there would be three of you."

"Dangerous thing, a meeting like this," said one of those three.

"Is it?"

"We don't know you, you don't know us. Who's to say we all play fair?"

"I prefer to believe that like calls to like," said Gillian, "and that an honest soul will find the same." It was too dark to tell when Gillian had pulled her cannon, only that it was out, and that it was staring at one of the three Widow Makers.

"Hold on now, we weren't–"

"Of course you weren't," said Gillian, "and I wasn't neither. No one was. Perfectly friendly folks, the lot of us. I don't mind that there are three of you; the more the merrier, the way I see it, especially because three of you means it'll cost you triple."

"That wasn't the–"

"Or there could be two of you, and I could charge you double."

"Triple is fine!" said the third Widow Maker. "Triple is totally reasonable."

Gillian – 7,220 Dims

"Isn't right," said Nan Toni. "A child ought to have a name."

"What's a name?" Gillian asked. "A handle to grab hold of, nothing more."

"He's old enough to start asking questions. About his momma, his daddy–"

"He'll learn when he needs to."

"Give the boy a name," Nan Toni all but pleaded, "for both your sakes."

The Kid – 1,420 Dims

"I told Hope to quit poking at my brain," said the Kid.

"I know, child," said Nan Toni.

"I told her last bright, and she didn't listen."

"Still, you oughtn't have hit her," said Nan Toni. "She is kin, after all."

"What's that got to do with it?" asked the Kid. "Kin hurt you worse than anyone."

Gillian – 7,986 Dims

"All their promises aren't worth a rat's tail," snapped Gillian. "Pay me, or your skulls will be decorating the I's doorstep. Salvation is a seller's market, and I got it cornered. Yes, or no?"

He said yes. They always said yes.

The Kid – 1,815 Dims

She arrived the morning they put Nan Toni into the Huddy, an unsmiling woman with streaks of gray in her brown hair, and empty holes for eyes.

"I'm your mother," she told the Kid by way of introduction. "You can call me Gillian."

Gillian – 8,345 Dims

"Got stones, for a chick," said a Murray Hill Murderer.

"Got stones for anyone," said another. He was sharpening a knife.

"Sure, stones for anyone, but especially for a chick."

"Didn't do her much good, though," said the War Chief.

"No, it didn't do her much good; but that's not the point. No backing, no clique, just her mouth and that cannon, and who knows if the cannon's even loaded?"

"Cannon's loaded," said the Murderer what was inspecting Gillian's gun.

"More than I can say for either of you," said Gillian. "What the hell kind of War Chief are you, doesn't show his face until the fight's done?"

"A clever one," said the War Chief. "You think I don't know there's a bounty on me?"

"Not that clever," said Gillian. Then, "You're late."

"Sorry," said Swan,[65] entering the room just then. "You ever try spoor blossom? It is dee-lightful."

The Kid – 2,178 Dims

"Five tics," said Gillian.

"Fish, dog, two knives, first dim, the funk, the Council, apple, mushroom, cannon, a tower–"

Gillian reached out and thunked the Kid in the forehead, rocking him back and forth slightly.

"Why did I do that?" said Gillian.

"I answered wrong."

"No. You weren't concentrating. If you concentrated and got it wrong, I wouldn't be angry. But you didn't even try."

"I hate you," said the Kid. "I wish I had never met you."

"Yeah," said Gillian.

---

65   Younger, thinner, sometimes smiling.

"I wish I had never been born!"

Gillian flipped over the next card.

"Five tics," Gillian said again.

Gillian – 9,075 Dims

"Why does the Kid need to leave?" asked Hope.

"He's going to go to an Uptown school," explained Gillian, "so he can learn to be a gentleman."

"He doesn't want to be a gentleman."

"I don't want him to be a gentleman either, but I want him to learn to pretend."

"He doesn't want to go," said Hope, as if this was a secret.

"I know he doesn't," said Gillian. "We all have to do things we don't want to do."

"He's just a kid," said Hope.

"That don't excuse him neither," said Gillian.

The Kid – 2,569 Dims

The Kid had never seen bar soap before, or a fresh towel, or running water. The rest of the boys had been there longer and were familiar with the set-up.

"Doesn't spoor go in the toilet?" asked one.

"Who just plopped one here in the showers?" asked another.

"Wait, that's not a raw turd; it's our new cadet!"

"Sorry, new cadet. It's that Downtown stink, smells just like spoor."

The Kid wet his towel in the basin.

"Be careful with that soap, cadet."

"Gotta hold on to it."

"Big trouble if you drop it."

The Kid closed the towel around the bar of soap and wrung it out.

"How you like it up here, cadet?"

"We don't get a lot of Downtown trash."

"What's it like downtown, cadet?"

The Kid looked up a while at his tormentors. Then he rooted around below the sink until he found an empty wooden crate, and then he took it out and set it on the floor.

"They teach you to suck pecker downtown?"

"Who put you in here, cadet?"

"Your father?"

"Your mother?"

"Your mother!"

"Why'd she put you in here, with all of us?"

Standing on the box, the Kid was only a head shorter than his tallest antagonist. Six teeth came loose with the first *whoosh* of his makeshift sap, and the second turned the boy's eye forever cloudy. The Kid dropped the bar of soap from his towel, then tied it swiftly around the boy's throat.

"Because she hates me," said the Kid. His enemy's face grew red, his compatriots fearful. "What's your excuse?"

Gillian – 9,075 Dims

"Captain Bulver of the Force owes a thousand in scrip to Madoff, and he's looking to make good any way he has to," Gillian said. "Lieutenant Gecko of the Widow Makers has been rutting his War Chief's mistress. The Honey Swallowers have entered into negotiations with the Columbia Lions over Morningside Park. What should the Lions ask for?"

"Nothing," said the Kid. "They give a finger and they'll lose a hand."

"The Hive is too powerful for the Lions to buck outright."

"They'll only get stronger. If I was in charge of the Lions, I'd pick my top five men and walk into the Hive, start killing until I found someone important."

"Would that work?"

"Of course not," said the Kid. "But at least they'd go out swinging."

Gillian nodded in agreement. "How's the man-at-arms in here?"

"Thoroughly sub-human."

"He teaching you?"

"He insists I'm quite the prodigy."

"Don't get a swelled head. I was the fiercest swordswoman on the Island, till puberty hit and I started fighting folk twice my size. And you aren't listening to any of this other nonsense they talk, about the Tiny t, or civilization and the Enclave, are you?"

"No, mother."

"'Cause they don't mean that for you. You're Boro trash, so far as they're concerned."

"Don't worry, mother," said the Kid, "I hate it here very much."

The Kid – 3,312 Dims

"He fell three floors," said Professor Bottoms.

"Gosh," said the Kid.

"The sawbones says he'll never walk again."

"Golly," said the Kid.

"Where were you last dim?"

"At catechism, of course," said the Kid, wide-eyed and innocent. "Ask the rector, he'll remember."

"The rector is drunk after dimtime."

"Insobriety in a clergyman? I don't believe it."

Professor Bottoms stood up from his desk and pulled the paddle off his wall. "Twenty-five licks," he said, "so you learn respect for your elders."

Though, they would prove insufficient inspiration.

Gillian – 10,192 Dims

"Experiments," Gillian said, "or rituals, maybe. They huff the funk, they swallow it, bathe in it, deliver it in suppositories. The King's been giving it to his children, and then... breeding them against each other."

"By the Tiny t," said the Commissioner, "that's the most terrible thing I've ever heard."

"No, the terrible part is that it's working. I've seen the King do... impossible things. Horrible things. Impossible things." Gillian pulled the badge from inside her coat, held it up as if aegis or evidence. "As Sheriff of the Island, I formally recommend the ban be put on TriBeCa; their soldiers to be slaughtered, their property be looted, their crops to be raised, houses burned, phalt broken, their kingdom to lie fallow until all who ruined it themselves lie dead."

"Affirmed," Alvin[66] said. "The Hive will muster its full levy and march upon TriBeCa at first bright, irrespective of the Council's decision. By the Queen in Yellow, such blasphemies cannot stand."

"You'll be behind us Force, then," barked the Commissioner.[67]

"I know you and the King are close, Mayor, but–" Gillian continued.

"To my shame and lamentation," said the Mayor.[68] He shook his head sadly, though his eyes were bright. "I affirm the ban."

The Kid – 4,002 Dims

"You should have picked a dim to try and run when I wasn't on chaperone duty," said Professor Bottoms. He had the Kid pressed up hard against the barbican wall, but he had started to sweat, and his skin was growing pale.

---

66 Having recently joined the council.
67 A different commissioner than the one you met, but then, all commissioners are pretty much the same.
68 Same mayor.

"You think I'd bust out before looking at the watch schedule?" asked the Kid. "Everything that's happened so far has gone exactly according to my plan. Right now, for instance, you're putting together that I poisoned your flask."

"You… little…"

"And now you get to find out what this shiv is for," said the Kid.

Gillian – 10,830 Dims

"It won't work," said Gillian.

"It might," said Daedalus, "if you helped."

"Not even then," said Gillian. "Who's going to want to go to war against the Honey Swallowers to defend the Orange Line?"

"Anyone who cares about justice."

"Expect to be outnumbered."

"What the Honey Swallowers do to us at first bright, they can do to anyone next dim."

"Then next dim will be when everyone starts worrying about them."

Daedalus slammed one of his two fists against the table. "You play at rebel, but in the end, you're nothing but a cog in the wheel."

"You're wrong," Gillian said sadly. "I'm just working on a longer time frame."

The Kid – 4,874 Dims

"Not good enough," roared Caul. Caul was a towering mountain of meat, three times the size of his cupbearer, with speckly foolish eyes offset below a forehead like a cinder block. He beat the table as he had been taught. "I want three hundred by dimtime next, or I'll sell the spears to the Bruisers. Unless you feel like going to battle holding your peckers in your hands, you'd best find a way to get my scrip!"

The War Chief for the Anarchs and two of his companions skulked out furiously. When they were gone, the Kid leaned over to refill Caul's booze.

"Very good," said the Kid, "but remember next time not to look in my direction."

Gillian – 11,774 Dims

Caul stared face up at the ceiling, a hilt protruding from his breastbone. Gillian had one hand on the Kid's lapel, and with the other, she slapped him silly. "You muscling in on my turf with this weak play?"

"Just trying to get your attention."

"What happened? Too slow to graduate?"

"Higher education isn't in my future," admitted the Kid, smiling below a blackening eye. "I want to join the family business."

The Kid – 4,439 Dims

"You wanted me to incite conflict between the Honey Swallowers and the I's," said the Kid. "Getting rid of the Monsters creates a vacuum in Midtown, which both sides will be anxious to fill."

"You threw a brick at a wasps nest. There were ways to do this that didn't involve wrecking half the Island."

"Of course there were," said the Kid, lighting his cigarette, "but they weren't near so much fun."

Gillian – 12,177 Dims

"From where?" Gillian asked.

"From outside," said the Last King of TriBeCa.

"Outside like, outside?"

"The World-Writ-Large."

"What's he want?"

"That's a question we can get to after you remind me of the beau that I took to my soiree," said the Last King of TriBeCa.

Gillian sighed. "Personally, I prefer my men with a little more grit to them, but if you're into boys who look like girls, I suppose he wasn't altogether appalling."

The Kid – 5,904 Dims

"What are you doing up there?" asked the girl what Kid had met at the club.

"Slowly dying," said the Kid, looking down from the edge of the roof, "like everyone."

Gillian – 12,323 Dims

"He's from outside," said Gillian.

"Outside of what?"

"The funk."

"That's a good con," said the Kid. "I'm sort of surprised I didn't think of it."

"If it's a con, it's one he can back with tech better than anything the Island has seen since before the funk."

"And what does he want?"

"The same thing everyone wants: more."

Presently

"I gather those drums deserve congratulations," said the Kid.

"They wouldn't be necessary if you had taken care of your end," said Gillian. "I ask you to kill one man, and you can't even manage it. What about all those new toys your fat friend had?"

"Obviously, mother, if Chisel's cannon had been effective, we wouldn't be having this conversation."

"That's your answer?"

"We never had an entirely accurate notion of the tourist's forces," the Kid snapped. "I played the hand I was dealt as best as I was able."

"That's a lot of words to say you failed."

The Kid laughed and started on another cigarette.

"How many of those have you smoked since first bright?"

"I lost count," said the Kid.

"It's costing us a fortune."

"One that pales beside what you've boomed through your cannon lately. Could you try going through a dim without shooting anyone? There is a reason we invented knives."

Gillian stretched a wide hand around a weary forehead "What about the Brides?"

"They're in."

"You're sure?"

"Super sure," said the Kid. "Absolutely positively, a hundred and ten percent."

"You think rutting their leader has affected your judgment on the matter?"

The Kid did not know how Gillian had learned this information, but he was not particularly surprised that she had. "What's wrong, mother? Don't you approve?"

"It's idiocy to mix business with pleasure."

The Kid's cigarette had gone out, and he stopped to relight it. "I'm touched by your concern. Though, as it happens, Chisel and I recently decided to retire our relationship to a strictly professional realm, so you can allow any concerns to return to their happy slumber."

"Fine," said Gillian. "Then I'll see you next bright."

"Just one more point," said the Kid. "I'm letting Newton go."

"Negative."

"We don't need him anymore, and I've got enough to worry about without playing babysitter. Might as well send him back to the Mayor."

"And give up our leverage? Not executing the ban is a

bannable offense. So long as we've got the boy as proof, the Mayor won't dare–"

"He won't dare either way. You think he's going to go in front of the Council and say that you played him? It's one of the joys of blackmail that the victim has as little incentive to publicize the matter as the perpetrator."

"Stick to the plan."

"Why do we need him?"

"Don't worry about what I need him for," said Gillian. "You just bring him along."

"I suppose his father would make a useful ally."

Now it was Gillian's turn to go silent, pale-faced, uncharacteristically anxious. "

"Ugly place, TriBeCa," the Kid continued. "I bet it was ugly before it was ruined. Being left alone there for so long, the Last King proved anxious to talk. Wouldn't shut up, to be honest."

"You fool," said Gillian. "You've no idea what you've done."

"Why do you want Newton?"

The waves lapped against the shore. Gillian recalled that she had not slept for several dims, but soon forgot it. "Because you rutted the dog, boy," she began, any trace of softness altogether absent, "because you couldn't complete the simple task that I asked, and now I have to come in and clean up your mess. Don't worry about what I need Newton for; Newton is my responsibility. You just soldier and keep your mouth shut."

The funk drew mad squiggles over the East River, drew forward and pulled back, a swirling tempest of subdued violence.

"Of course," said the Kid, rising finally. "The obedient son, as ever."

Gillian – 6,603 Dims, The Kid – 0

"You did wonderful," said Nan Toni, "just wonderful. As easy a birth as I've ever seen.

He mewled as soon as they set him in Gillian's hands, a mouth that seemed to take up all his face, from his button chin to his few strands of red hair.

"He looks just like you!" said Nan Toni.

"No," said Gillian, "he doesn't."

55

Crossfire

"Gonna be a rough one," said Flushing as they rowed towards shore.

"What?" asked Chisel, struggling to be heard over the roaring funk.

"I said, it's gonna be a rough one!"

Sister's Keeper

"She's not as clever as she thinks she is," said Adze.

"No," said the Null, though, whether he was agreeing or disagreeing or just making conversation was unclear.

"It's hard for her to keep that in mind, and she seems so sure of herself that everyone usually just goes along because they don't want to upset her, or they don't have any better ideas."

"Maybe talk a little quieter," said the Null.

"I know they say she was the one who started it, but it isn't true; there were always folk living on the bridge, grinders what couldn't get along with their cliques back home or just liked having the air beneath them, and since we had to build everything ourselves, I guess we got some sort of a reputation for being fix-its. Back when I joined, the top mutt was a fellow called himself Engineer Ed, though really, he didn't know much more than a Null."

The Null did not take offense. "What was Chisel doing before she got to the bridge?"

"You ever ask her?"

"Once."

"Did she tell you?"

"No."

"Probably she had a reason. Anyway, once she showed up, you could see the rest of us didn't know what we were doing, even ones like me who were pretty good with our hands. She'd look at a thing a while and figure out how it would work, how to make it better. You know how she is."

"She's clever."

"But not as clever as she likes to think. I kept telling her Engineer Ed would rather be first in a shack than second in a mansion, but she didn't listen, not till one dim when Engineer Ed and a couple of Engineer Ed's idiots went to visit her while she was putting together our first water pumps."

"What happened?" said the Null, checking his sights.

"I happened, long story short, and then Engineer Ed didn't happen anymore. That's what I'm saying: she's not so clever as she thinks she is. That's our one problem. Our other problem is, she's the cleverest thing we've got."

The Trap is Sprung

It wasn't that they couldn't manage it with two men, it was that doing it with two men offended his professional sensibilities, and Dallas[69] was nothing if not a professional. But with everything going on at the tunnel, they couldn't afford to use any more of their own people for a simple snatch. And so far as Dallas was concerned, the locals were worse than useless, swaggering around with their scrap-metal broadswords and

---

69 Mr Simpson's second-in-command, soldier from the World-Writ-Large.

desiccated pistols, as likely to blow up in your hand as it was to fire. And the ones that had led them here were worse, albinos with hooks and strange tattoos...

Carson signaled from the other end of the alley, and Dallas signaled back. For the tenth time that hour and the ten thousandth time since coming to this godforsaken hellhole, Dallas wished for a functioning radio. He had wished for functioning radios almost as often as he had wished for the sun, and with as much success. Half the time, you turned it on and you got nothing but static, the other half, you got who-the-hell-knew-what, play-by-plays from when the Dodgers had still been in Brooklyn, musical recordings in languages Dallas couldn't recognize, and that one thing that only Simmons had been able to hear and that had made him pull his combat knife against his wrist, then write on the walls in his draining life's blood *the funk the funk the funk the funk the fu...* only stopping once he was fully exsanguinated.

The funk fucked visibility like it did comms, and Dallas didn't see her until she was already on the pier. He slipped the safety off his weapon. A quick burst around the kneecaps; they wanted her alive, for a little while at least, though Dallas didn't fancy the poor girl's chances, not with the way the boss was acting lately, fucking lunatic. Being smart was all fine and good at the academy, or when you were a thousand miles removed from any killing, but to Dallas's mind, there was nothing so great about being clever. The clever ones were the first ones to lose it, fragile sorts, minds like–

BOOM! BOOM! BOOM! BOOM!

Good for the Goose

Chisel reacted to nearly dying, and then not dying, with predictable equanimity. "The wounded one had better live," said Chisel.

"Calm down," said Adze, holding a smoking cannon. "I got him in the knees."

56

Q + A

It was well past dim when the Kid finally made it back to the Boroboat, tying his kayak against the craft and climbing on board. He found Newton and Ael still awake, the former practicing cuts with one of the latter's swords.

"How was that?" asked Newton.

"That was terrible," said Ael, but he said it in a nice way.

"Why?"

"Everything about it was bad, to be honest. You look like you just grew a pair of feet and this is the first you've gotten to try them."

"No chance for improvement?"

"A little, maybe," Ael said, "but not a lot. I don't think you've got it in you to be much of a killer, anyhow."

"We've all got it in us," said the Kid.

"Hey, Kid," said Ael.

"Chisel get off okay?" the Kid asked.

"Flushing dropped her on shore a while back. What's the news?"

"It's on. At bright, the Island goes to war."

"Boy, I'd sure like to be in on that scrap," said Ael. "Maybe if we get finished up early, I could swing by for something?"

"I doubt it," said the Kid. "And anyway, you'll get your share of trouble."

"Swan will be there? You're sure on it?"

"I'm sure."

Ael whistled. "You know who Swan is?" he asked Newton.

"Best swordsman on the Island."

Ael held his hand out, and eventually Newton managed a high-five.

"Ael," said the Kid, "do me a favor and find something you need to do that doesn't involve you being here."

"Okey-doke," said Ael. "Be seeing you, Newton."

Ael headed off to his quarters.

"I guess it's time to answer some of your questions," said the Kid.

"Okay," said Newton.

"I can't tell you everything," said the Kid, "but I promise I won't lie."

"If you were going to lie, you'd probably promise anyway."

"Probably."

Newton thought for a long time before beginning, the Kid starting on a cigarette in the interim. "Who am I?" he began. "Who was the man pretending to be my uncle? What was the symbol that you drew for me that frightened him so much that he decided to move me? What was it that possessed my nanny? What did it want from me? Who exactly are you?"

"That's not a question other people can answer for you," said the Kid, "the Mayor, the sigil for ruined TriBeCa, can't tell you right now, don't know, and I ask myself that a lot."

Newton took a moment to digest this. "My nanny – the thing that looked like my nanny but wasn't, actually – she kept talking about TriBeCa also."

"Did she?"

"Yeah."

The Kid grunted.

"They put the ban on TriBeCa, didn't they?" Newton asked.

"They did."

"Who?"

"Everyone, but my mother, mostly."

"Why did they do that?"

"Everyone or my mother?"

"Both."

"Different reasons, and I'm not sure."

"You're not very much use," said Newton.

"I gather everyone rather hated TriBeCa," said the Kid, "or at least they all had a good reason to want them dead. My mother prefers the official version, which was that they experimented with the funk, gave it to their servants and children."

"And that's so bad?" asked Newton.

"You really don't know much."

"I know they say it's bad," said Newton, "but they say a lot of things, and they don't mean most of them."

"That's true," admitted the Kid.

"So, what's so bad about the funk?"

"It changes you," said the Kid. "It makes you something different than you are."

"Do you like what you are so much?"

"Not really." The Kid flicked his cigarette into the water. "Any other questions?"

"Are you going to kill me?" asked Newton.

"I'm not sure yet," said the Kid.

The Last Bright

57

An Incidental Slaughter

Bright rose – presumably, though it was hard to tell with the funk hanging dark and thick as deepest dim – and the Island prepared for battle.

6th and West 9th

The ones who liked to rut had rutted. The ones who liked a smoke had smoked. The ones who liked to swallow spoor blossom were deep in the midst of their trips, foaming teeth tearing at strips of leather. They sat encircled on the front lawn, beating their drums in an enthusiastic if uneven rhythm, Mountain Girl[70] voluptuous in the center, calling down a prayer.

"It's a long trip, sisters and brothers, and it's a strange trip, but it's our trip and we'll ride the bus to the very end! Are we going to let some bunch of monotone Uptown reactionary zealots muscle us out of the Village?"

"No!" yelled an Aquarian.

"Heck no!" yelled another.

"The funk is made of egg yolk and mushroom strudel!" yelled a third. "And rats nest inside my skull!"

Overcome with inspiration by this last piece of doggerel, a fierce giant with a matted beard and eyes wide from

---

70 Maryland Slim having left her bed sometime earlier.

hallucinogens leaped upright and began to howl at the funk. A second berserker rose to do the same, and then they were all doing it, barking and hustling out of the compound.

Beneath their flag of a thousand colors, marching to a disordered beat, the Greenwich Village Aquarians rose to war.

7th and Christopher

Rembrandt leaned against the stone wall, smoking a twist of stemmy flower. The door to the bar opened and Stag came out, a bear of a man wearing a small leather cap.

"Nervous?"

"About what?" But his voice cracked saying it.

Stag laughed.

"Maybe a bit," admitted Rembrandt.

"You stay on my hip when we get there," Stag said, "and don't get caught playing hero on the first charge." He leaned in and caressed Rembrandt with one thick thumb. "You're too pretty to die young."

In black leather and silver chains, bound by the unbreakable bonds of love, the Sacred Band rose to war.

Lenox Avenue and 125th

"He'd be proud of you," said Owen's mother, handing him his father's sword.

"Thanks, Mom," said Owen.

"You were better with it than he ever was."

"Thanks, Mom."

"He'd have been the first to tell you that. He'd be so proud of you."

"Thanks, Mom."

"Bring it back bloodied," said Owen's mother, "or don't bring it back at all."

Lords of eight Uptown blocks, dying as pawns in a game they never understood, the Hurricanes rose to war.

Bowery and Hester

"I don't give a rat turd for the Honey Swallowers," said Boudicca Blonde, "and I don't give a rat turd for the Council, neither. Don't let yourself get caught up in any of this nonsense, and don't be one of those fools gets themselves sacrificed for the glory of the Enclave. On the other hand, I hear they have some nice stuff on the Upper West Side."

"Gonna get me a slave does nothing but keep my clothes cleaned!" laughed Big Boudicca. She held aloft a longbow too tense for anyone else to draw, and her wig was perfect.

"Gonna get me a girl to live between my legs!" yelled Brutal Boudicca, smashing her fist against her open hand.

Sincere in their sisterhood, with sharp arrow and keen eye, the Bowery Street Boudiccas rose to war.

53rd and 3rd

Jeter checked his paint in the clubhouse mirror, then grabbed his war club and jogged up the stairs into the street, DiMaggio close behind. The whole team followed him up from the basement, breaking into a fast jog, harlequins carrying war clubs, eyes gleaming in the funk.

Mute, their only sound the perfect rhythm of their steps against the phalt, the Pinstripes went to war.

The Brooklyn Bridge, 3rd Strut

"Don't do this next time," said Adze, holding the Null's hair back.

The Null wiped a string of bile off his lip. "Next time?"

The door to the cell was half open, and on the floor inside

of it was a thing which had at one point been Dallas.[71] He whimpered in the corner, too weak now even to scream.

"Tomorrow don't come easy, and not all of us will make it; and some of those that make it won't deserve to see it. But it's gotta come," said Adze. "It's just got to. Now, get up."

The Null got up.

Adze pulled a flask from his leather apron. "Swig."

The Null swug.

Chisel came up from the laboratories.

"Are the warwagons ready?" Adze asked.

"Near," said Chisel.

"Good," said Adze, "'cause it's a lot worse than we thought."

Whitehall and Water Street

There was the statue for the Bull, of course, but no one really had any idea what a Bear looked like, and so the costume which the bum wore looked a little bit like a cockroach and a lot like a slug and a fair bit like the corpse of a Rottweiler. The bum did not mind; blind drunk on distil, blind generally from the way the costume hung over his eyes, he had no notion whatsoever that Gecko, himself wearing the ceremonial horned headpiece, was about to trample him.

"The Bull will run forever!" roared Gecko, knocking the bum off his feet and hurrying onward.

"Short the Bear!" roared Gecko's lieutenant, just behind him.

"Short the Bear!" roared the rest of the Widow Makers, following in their leader's footsteps.

They sprinted up Whitehall and over Bowling Green, cutters and hatchets and clubs and even the occasional scattergun lofted funkward, each making sure to touch the Bull's horns as they passed.

---

71 Unfortunate soldier of the World-Writ-Large.

Arrogant as gods, merciless as children, the Wall Street Widow Makers rose to war.

Strawberry Fields

"Do not forget what you fight for!" rasped the preacher. "Not only for your wives, for your mothers, and your children; for…"

"A bit of something to warm you?" Reynolds asked from atop his mare.

"Don't mind if I do," said Baldur, taking a sip from Reynold's flask. The Force had taken hard losses that week, as bad as anyone could remember, but still their cavalry stood in perfect formation, pennants fluttering from their lances.

"…for the Island itself!" the preacher continued. "Remember that the Tiny t stands for 'truth', and also for 'talent'! Though the horde bays ever at our walls, still we keep alight civilization's dim flame!"

"You think they'll send us in to star?" asked Baldur.

"I imagine they'll give them a bit of cannon first," said Reynolds.

"Just so long as there's a few to play with."

"My thoughts exactly," said Baldur.

Brutal, blue-clad, bourgeois brutes, the Force rose to war.

Columbus Circle

"She played me from the beginning," the Mayor said. "The assault on the I's, JuiceTown, all of it. She knew we were watching, and she made sure to go through the motions, all the while smashing us against one another like we were puppets, like we were toys. She must have found out about Mr Simpson somehow, and this is her plan to take care of him."

The Mayor was talking to no one, or the Mayor was talking to the bottle on his desk.

"By the Tiny t, I hope she wins," he said, taking a drink.

The door to the Mayor's office opened, and an aide came in. "Sir? They're waiting for us."

The Mayor rose and fixed his tie.

Adrift, uncertain, reduced, the Mayor went to war.

Riverside Drive and West 96th

As the high priestess gave the benediction, her sisters passed through the long lines of kneeling soldiers, holding trays of wax cups brimming with shots of yellow.

"There can be no forgiveness without admonishment!" said the high priestess. "And betrayal demands punishment! Did she forgive her consort for his infidelity? Yes, but first he was made to suffer, as the Island must suffer before they can be brought beneath her banner! Redemption comes after vengeance, and the vengeance of the Queen in Yellow is a terrible one!"

"Hail the Queen in Yellow!" roared Alvin.

"Hail the Queen in Yellow!" roared everyone.

United below their savage goddess, innocent only of the crime for which they were sentenced, the Honey Swallowers went to war.

Shaggy Dog

Not everyone answered the Ban. Neither the Coop nor Stuy rose, their own enmity overriding loyalty to the Council or any promise of geld. The I's were not around to add their axes, nor the Gansevoort Goons their knives. The Lower East Side, bereft of leadership, trickled in desultorily.

Still, what a sight it was! They were the Burners, the Bulls, the Brawlers, the Bullies, the Alphabet City Anarchs, the Raiders, the Ogres, the Lamplighters, the Maulers, the Harlem Hellions, the SoHo Sublime and the NoHo Knockers, the Saracens, the Destroyers, the 9th Avenue Avengers, the

New Murray Hill Miscreants, dozens more. Up the Way they marched, a hundred colors and ten thousand men, carrying barbed wire clubs, carrying knives that had been sharpened and re-sharpened, carrying pikes, if they were lucky to have them, carrying short cutters and longs cutters, carrying singled-bladed cutters, carrying double-bladed cutters, carrying axes, carrying any cocktails they could get their hands on, carrying cannon, carrying boom.

It was quite a spectacle, the War of the Upper West Side, though one which, being only the third most important event which would occur on the Island that bright, will be largely ignored from here on out.

58

A Grand Alliance

Hope came in next-to-last, feeling rested as an innocent man on the morning of his execution, feeling rested as someone who had eaten three caps of spore blossom and slept for a very long time. "Auntie," she said, "we've missed you out on the Ring."

"I'll come for a visit when this is all over," said Gillian, nearly smiling.

They were on the ground floor of a sleek, sprawling building slightly east of the entrance to the Holland Tunnel. Once upon a time, it had housed the hottest restaurant south of the Village. But after the ban, there were few willing to venture near TriBeCa for a plate of fried dog in fresh mushroom, and it had long been shuttered, furniture scavenged away, fit habitation only for roaches and rats.

"How's my cousin?" Hope asked.

"Grumpy, as usual," said Gillian.

The Kid smoked a cigarette on a bench, next to Newton.

"Who's that?" asked Newton. Newton had not slept as well as Hope. He was pretty anxious about being murdered.

"That's Hope," said the Kid. "She's like a confessor, but meaner."

"Oh," said Newton. "Same as the big guy?"

"Maryland Slim, yeah. Like him."

"Which side is Hope on?"

"We're all on the same side."

Newton looked around for a moment. "Are you sure?" he asked, skeptical.

Daedalus leaned next to a fire door, restlessly scratching the stump of his right hand with its still-extant twin.

"Conductor quiet," said Ariadne. She was sharpening her hook, though it was plenty sharp already.

Dade didn't say anything.

"What's the scuttle?"

"Rat stay cool," Daedalus said, "come whatever."

Beneath his customary hangover, Swan could feel Ael giving him a lot of long, lingering looks, of the kind overweight boys give pretty brunettes in quiet cafés. "Can I help you with something?"

"I'm Ael!" said Ael.

"Ael the ferocious, Ael the feared, Ael the fast!" the hypebird squawked.

Given the reasonable suspicion that he would not see another dimtime, Maryland Slim had decided to pull out all the sartorial stops, coming clad in a speckled blue double-breasted suit, wearing a matching pocket square and other accoutrements of which tailors and Maryland Slim knew the proper names.

"I'm going to go out on a limb, here," said Hope, "and guess you're Maryland Slim."

Maryland Slim doffed an impeccable fedora. "At your service."

"You look a lot different than I thought you would," said Hope.

"You look exactly the same," said Maryland Slim.

You wouldn't have known Gillian was nervous. You wouldn't have known anything about Gillian; that was just how Gillian was. "You're missing a piece," she said.

"She'll be here," said the Kid.

Newton looked down at his feet, then up at Ariadne, then

back down on his feet, and so on for a while before asking the Kid, "Why do they have mazes on their body?"

"They say it keeps the funk from eating them."

"Does it work?"

The Kid shrugged. "It has so far."

"How can you move in that suit?" Hope asked.

"Oh, girl," said Maryland Slim, "Maryland Slim is smoother than silk."

"Who was it told you that mentioning yourself in the third person all the time was charming?"

"Maryland Slim is mostly self-taught. Never had much use for a classroom, maybe you heard. Broke out of the Cloister when I was only–"

"Hell and High Towers, you're worse than the hypebird."

Which was turning frantic circles amid the cavernous interior, winging back and forth from the darkened corners of the room.

"I just want to let you know," Ael said, "I'm a huge fan."

"Of what?" asked Swan.

"Of you!"

"Of me?"

"Yup!"

"Why?"

"'Cause…" Ael blushed. "I mean… 'cause you're Swan."

"Yeah?"

"You're so good at killing people."

Swan shuddered and returned to his headache.

"Dade," said Gillian.

Dade traced the lines of his maze tattoo absently.

"Dade!"

"What?"

"Your rangers ready to swarm? Or are you going to bail on us like the Bridge Brides?"

"That was charming, mother, thank you," said the Kid, rising to stand in the corner.

"Clan come on call," Daedalus said.

Tuckered out, the hypebird alighted on Ael's shoulder. "Ael swallows shoe leather! Ael, deadlier than the funk! Ael, meaner than your step-momma!"

"What in the Towers is that thing?" Swan asked.

"It's my hypebird! Like a hypeman, but, a bird. There's a woman in the Square breeds them. You like it? She was part of what I got from the Kid."

"In exchange for?"

"Killing a lot of people."

"I think you got trumped."

"The hypebird was only half the payment."

"What's the other?"

"You!" Ael said.

"Come again?" Swan asked.

Hope took the seat the Kid had emptied. "Who are you?" she asked.

"I'm Newton," said Newton.

"What are you doing here?"

"I got kidnapped," explained Newton.

"Bummer," said Hope. "You want some bubblegum?"

"I've never had any before. What's it taste like?"

"It doesn't taste like anything, it's just fun to chew on."

"Oh," said Newton. "Sure."

Daedalus propped the fire door open.

"I'm pretty good with a sword, see? Like, maybe the best ever," Ael explained. "The 'maybe' is the thing. The 'maybe' drove me mad. The Kid said if I helped him out a while, he'd make sure that you and I got to run into each other. And the Kid is slippery as an eel, but doggone if he didn't make good!"

"You want to fight me?" Swan asked.

"Not now, of course," Ael assured him. "We'll take care of this thing with the whatever and whatnot, and then it's you and me, buddy! One on one, steel against steel! I been thinking about how I was gonna do it since I saw you fighting Funkees, and I think I've got a shot."

"Best of luck," said Swan, meaning it.

Gillian triple-checked the boom in her cannon, then shut the chamber and put it in her pocket. Then she cornered the Kid in the corner where he had gone to brood.

"What a surprise," she said. "You were wrong about something."

"She'll be here," said the Kid, though even he was beginning to doubt it.

"If she was coming, she'd have come already. We'll have to get started without her. You're in charge. Have Slim and Hope batter their way in as best they can, and have Swan sneak through any side-corner you can find."

"That's a heck of a plan, mother," said the Kid. "I can see where I get it."

Gillian narrowed her eyes to black specks. "Give me Newton, and five tocs, and then go do what I told you."

The Kid reached into his pocket and took out the case with 💣 on the front. The Kid removed a cigarette and lit it. The Kid's hands did not shake. "There's been a change of plan. The kid stays with me."

"The Kid doesn't make that decision."

"Are you going to try and take him?" asked the Kid, squaring up.

"If it comes to that."

"You so sure you can count on the rest of your companions to die so you can feed the king of old TriBeCa his child?"

Gillian was yet taller than her progeny, and as she dipped her forehead against his, a single drop of sweat came loose. "Of course not," she hissed. "That's why I'm in charge, and they aren't. That's why we're in charge. I don't want to do what I'm going to do to Newton, but I'm going to do it anyway, like I've done a million other things I didn't want to do. I'd assumed you'd be able to understand this by now, as long as I've been trying to teach you."

"What can I say? I'm a terrible disappointment."

They were interrupted by a high-pitched, barely audible whine, and almost immediately after by an altogether audible scream, Swan shoving his hands against his hood and dropping to the ground. The front door flew open and a fist of metal came flying in but Ael, as surely as if he had known and planned and practiced for its arrival, caught it and sent it spinning back to its original owner, a brute in camo carrying a cannon from the World-Writ-Large.

There was a very bright light and a very loud noise, and Ael came fast behind it, grabbing the half-corpse of his assailant, spinning him around to face his comrades. "Sons of rats! Funk swallowers, dog-rutters, and lice pickers!" A body is a soft thing, and a bullet from an automatic weapon will go right through it, but even a hardened killer will generally prove uncomfortable aerating a friend. And during the short interlude in which his enemy was hindered by an excess of humanity, Ael tossed a bit of metal through the man's helmet, shattering the plastic and intruding on his brain.

Ael had spent much of the previous dim figuring out how to work his assault rifle. He fired a quick burst, which pinned the reinforcements at one end of the hallway before disappearing down the other. "If you kill him before I kill him, I'll kill you!" he screamed. "Kill you all dead, you hear me? You keep him alive!"

Newton swallowed his gum.

Gillian was slower than Ael – everyone on the Island was slower than Ael, save perhaps Swan – but still it wasn't more than a tic or two before she had her cannon out and trained on the doorway. *Boom* and a soldier went down, *boom* and the next feared to enter. "Slim!" she yelled. "What the hell is going on?"

But Slim didn't answer, caught up as he was in an unanticipated bout of psychic combat, titanic forces raging against one another on a metaphysical plane.

"Out the fire door! Now!" Gillian yelled, two more *boom* to keep their attackers honest, and then–

And then she was on the floor, a strange interplay of colors stretching loose across her vision. Dade stood over her, his hook in his one good hand. Past him streamed a line of well-inked, claw-wielding rangers, bearing down on Hope and Maryland Slim, both already supine, bearing down on an unresisting Newton, bearing down on the Kid.

"Sorry, Gil," said Daedalus. "Clan come first."

59

Uptown Interlude, Part 1

They came howling west down 87th Street, bearded giants geeked from their leather sandals to their long, knotted locks, berserkers swinging two-handed cutters and weighted chain. The Paladins were all defending the main gate, and these distant flanks were protected only by the Hive's shield-bearers, youths with nothing to defend themselves but stout cudgels and their faith.

"Stand firm!" roared their leader. "Remember the Goddess with every breath!"

60

An Ebb

The Flynn Effect

"Are you familiar with the Flynn Effect?" asked Mr Simpson.

They had taken Hope and Maryland Slim somewhere. They had chained and carried Swan somewhere else. They had put Newton in the room next to the room in which they had brought Gillian and the Kid. What exactly had happened to Daedalus and Ariadne was as yet unclear.

"No," said Gillian.

"No," said the Kid.

"Of course you aren't," said Mr Simpson. "It was a rhetorical question. The Flynn Effect is the term used to describe the phenomenon by which successive generations test out as smarter than previous by a small but statistically significant measure. Up till now, no one has been able to figure if it's random noise, or evidence of people getting better at answering test questions, or if it actually means what it looks like it means: that your grandkids will be smarter than you are, that the species is improving."

"Up till now?" asked the Kid.

"Turns out it's all bullshit, though. If it were true, we'd be on opposite ends of the conversation. Six, seven generations since the funk came, maybe more, should be plenty of time for all of you to have turned into geniuses. But here you are, stupid as rat shit, about to get dumped dead into the river. How was it you managed to find out about me, anyway?" Mr Simpson asked.

"A little funk told me," said Gillian.

The Kid laughed.

"It gets less funny once we start snipping off toes."

"I just told you," said Gillian. "The funk told me."

"How'd you guys get the Mayor to throw in on the Ban?" Mr Simpson asked.

"It's a long story," said Gillian. "You don't really care about it anyway."

"No, not really," Mr Simpson agreed.

"And Dade? How did you get him on your side?"

"That was pretty simple, actually. We have this gas that's poisonous and heavier than air–"

"What?"

"Sorry, I forgot that I'm dealing with illiterate monkey children for whom even the simplest scientific or cultural concept is as impossible to comprehend as the sky would be to a suckerfish."

"Don't worry about it," said the Kid.

"Anyway, when we got here, we dropped one of these beauties into one of those troglodyte tunnels, or whatever, and then we told them we'd drop another if they didn't snap to."

"If you knew what we were up to," asked Gillian, "why'd you let it go so long? Why let us set the Island against itself?"

"Why do I give a fuck if you savages want to slaughter one another? Once that tunnel opens, we're going to send a division of marines in here to wipe out everyone that looks at us funny. The two of you have been doing my work for me."

"You're welcome," the Kid said.

Alone Again

Logically speaking, being captive to this new set of people was not really worse than being captive to the Kid, nor, for that matter, being subject to his uncle, or whoever his uncle had really been.

Newton felt worse about it, however. "I liked the Kid," he said to the single window in his cell. It faced south, towards Canal Street and the ruined land beyond, as dark a bright as Newton had ever seen.

Detention

It took ten confessors to keep watch on Hope and Maryland Slim. At least, there were ten confessors watching them just then, scowling from far corners of the room, bald men and bald women staring at the captives like they might, at any moment, explode. The door opened and the Pope and two cardinals slipped in. For once, their heavy furs were appropriate to the temperature, and it must be said that the Pope cut a fine spectacle as she descended on Maryland Slim.

"Such is the fate of all apostates."

"I'm surprised you've the stones to keep me alive this long," admitted Maryland Slim. They had knocked off his fedora and there were some scuff marks on his pants, but apart from that, it was hard to tell he was in the hands of his bitterest enemies, so cool was his demeanor.

"A favor to our foreign friend. He's keenly interested in what exactly it is that allows us to do the things we do, and happy to have someone to... how did he put it? 'Dissect like a grammar school frog'?" The Pope shook her bald head happily. "I'm not exactly sure what that means, but it sounds unpleasant." The Pope turned her attention to Hope. "As for you, daughter, though your sins are manifold, and egregious, we are not heartless, no matter what Slim has told you. There is still time to make good on your misdeeds, still time for redemption." The Pope had a face meant to frown, and a voice tuned to lecture. "You have great power in you; were it properly trained, you could make great contributions to the Cloister, great enough to, perhaps in time, outweigh even the evils you have thus far committed."

Hope seemed to be chewing over the question, but then she blew a bubble, and it became clear it was only her gum. "I could never keep up with all the shaving. I tried it for a guy once and the itch was insane. I kept scratching myself in public; people thought I was a degenerate."

Maryland Slim laughed and the Pope gnashed her yellowed teeth. "Foolish girl," she said. "You'll have a long time to lament your idiocy when the outsiders are poking at your brains."

"Still better than moving uptown," said Hope.

The Pope scowled and took her exit, leaving behind Maryland Slim and Hope and the aforementioned ten confessors.

"It probably won't be better, actually," said Maryland Slim.

"No, probably not." Hope said. "Any way you see us getting out of this?"

"There's always an out," Slim said. "The question is, can you squeeze through the door?"

"I'll avoid the obvious response."

"I very much appreciate it."

Fanfare

Two Bridges was all but empty, every grinder worth the name waging war uptown and their civilians taking shelter from the funk raging turbulent all across Downtown, and so the only witnesses were a pair of gutter transients sitting on Frankfort Street, passing a bottle of distil back and forth. The warwagons came rolling past the abutments and into the city, four scrap-metal monstrosities, all pointed edges and rotating cannon, and on top of them were twenty hard-looking Bridge Brides, savage men and ferocious women with chambered cannon and enough homemade boom to split the Island half open. They trundled past the besotted bystanders and towards Houston, one after the next, salvation come ever so tardy.

A Master's Class in Misery

Swan knew pain. To a certain extent, everyone does, of course, but Swan particularly did. He was, if not an aficionado of agony, at least an expert, so he could say with certainty, had he then been able to speak, that nothing in his long association with misery had prepared him for being set in a room beside a speaker playing a high-pitched buzz at a low volume.

He vomited up blood.

Provincial Arrogance

"Can't you see I'm trying to do you a favor?" asked Mr Simpson. He pulled a pill bottle from his suit pocket and dry-swallowed a pair of whites.

"Thanks," said the Kid.

"This hill you want to sit on – it's made of shit. It's a shit hill, from top to bottom, and all of you vile little fuck-monkeys fighting to get to the top. What did you have for breakfast, Mr Kid?"

"I skipped breakfast."

"What was the last thing you ate, then?"

The Kid thought a moment. "I had a skewer of rat last dimtime."

"This would be my point. Believe it or not, outside of this happy little society of inbreds, we don't eat rat meat as snack food. We don't normally peg our currency to it either. What I'm trying to say is, you have the shittiest life on the fucking planet. There are cripples in the Third World begging for change in train stations who have it better than you. It's not your fault. I tell myself that a hundred times a day, and I know it's true; but I'll be honest, I still blame you for it. It's not rational, but there it is. Looking at you makes me sick. Your idiot hieroglyphs, sacrificing chickens to posters of dead movie stars, Jesus-fucking-Christ. If it were up to me, we'd come in here with napalm and just start the whole thing over."

"If you hate it so much, then why don't you just leave us alone?"

"The funk, of course," said Mr Simpson. "It turns out it has some fascinating effects on people. Your two friends downstairs, the fat one and that one with the nose ring, we're very interested in them. The very, very fast one also, though less so."

"What are you going to do with the rest of the Island?" Gillian asked.

"Turn it into a zoo? Charge the citizens of King's County a buck and a quarter to come gawk at their feral descendants? Toss you peanuts and see you jump? I don't know, and frankly, I don't care. As soon as that tunnel opens up, I'll walk to Jersey and never look back."

Last Request

Having had a few tocs to review his life, Maryland Slim was feeling pretty okay. There had been missteps, errors, even outright failures. A girl in a bar on Bowery that he had seen but never spoken to – a redhead, as it happened, and Maryland Slim liked redheads. Who knows what happiness their union might have fetched him, had he been a bit bolder? Also, there was this place in Turtle Bay that did the best fried oysters on the Island, and Maryland Slim had been telling himself for a long time that he was going to go back there and eat some. But he hadn't, and it was looking like now he would never get to.

Still, all in all, Maryland Slim had few complaints. He was what he wanted to be; how many men could say the same?

"Will you do something for me, Hope?" he asked.

"Depends what it is."

"Speak well of me."

"I'm not sure I'll get the opportunity."

"But elaborately," Slim continued. "Really lay it on thick. I was the smartest man you ever met, and the most virile. Never dropped my fork, never missed a dance step, never failed at an endeavor, never had my tie crooked."

"Your tie is crooked right now."

"That's what I'm saying. That's why it's a favor."

Hope thought this over. "It's a big ask."

"It is."

"Let's see how the rest of this goes."

"Just watch," said Slim, straightening his tie.

The Loneliest Boy on the Island

"I don't suppose I'll ever have a friend," said Newton, feeling very glum. Outside his window, the funk writhed and the funk wriggled, the funk stretched and the funk strained, the funk roiled, the funk pulsed.

"That sounds about right," said the Kid. "Head back to Jersey with your tail between your legs."

"Kid," Gillian warned.

"Excuse me?" asked Mr Simpson. He pulled his automatic pistol from its shoulder holster .

"You heard me fine," said the Kid. "Like some shuttered Enclave clerk, spends a dim Downtown then runs home to brag about about all the local color he saw."

"Local color? You live in a latrine!"

" 'It's dirty, the food sucks, there are too many people.' " the Kid mocked. "Quit beating around the bush and be man enough to admit you weren't man enough to hack it in the big city."

"I'm man enough to conquer it," Mr Simpson snapped. Mr Simpson's eyes were small and nasty. Mr Simpson's opiates had kicked in.

"Kid," warned Gillian a second time.

"You can keep telling yourself that," said the Kid, "but it don't make it true. You could put a soldier on every block and it wouldn't be yours. You're a tourist, and that's all you'll ever be." Mr Simpson considered this for a moment, and then nodded in agreement. "You're right. I can never really own it. But I can ruin it, and that's nearly as good."

The automatic bucked.

Maryland Slim's Last Tango

This is how it went.

One on one, Slim ate confessors like he did fried mushrooms. And even doubled up, they weren't much of a challenge. But ten confessors was a lot of confessors, ten people standing around you with cannon, all waiting to fire.

And what if you ducked?

This was what Slim did just then – metaphorically speaking, obviously. The entirety of the combat took place in a realm which has no physical analog, where the most concrete notions of existence – distance, direction, momentum – are without parallel. In this sideways sphere, a being of pure thought, will, style, Maryland Slim walked up and smacked one of the confessors, the biggest of the confessors, then ducked and let the return blow strike another in the chest.

Again, not really, but it was something sort of a little bit like that.

They were half-expecting it, but even so, the confessors weren't swift enough to respond, lumbering buffoons waddling across the mindscape. They howled and swore, they threatened, they pursued Slim like a pack of pugs swarming after a greyhound, and with as much effect.

And as for Slim? Slim pirouetted and Slim briséd, Slim cambréd, Slim chaînéd, and Slim chasséd. If you went left, Slim went right. If you went right, Slim went left. Also, because again, this is not reality we are talking about, there were other directions to go in and he went in those too, shivering sideways past his waddling assailants, leveling his sting as he passed, and smiling, always smiling, or just existing in a way that made it clear he was enjoying himself. The confessors toddled in his wake, rotund and endlessly off-footed, careening into one another, screaming soundless expulsions of pain. It seemed at every instant the dance would come to its end, the trap would slam shut around him. But somehow, he continued, boogieing his way through infinity, Maryland Slim the divine, Maryland Slim untouchable.

Until they touched him finally, a searing mental blow and he tumbled like a wounded bird, but still smiling, landing hard in their midst, cratering among the crowd, shards of Maryland Slim sent spinning through the tissue-paper minds of his enemies.

Mama's Boy

The Kid screamed.

"Don't be such a baby," said Mr Simpson. "It's not like you liked her anyway."

Promise Kept

Back in reality, there were eight confessors staring fuzzily and forever at the ceiling, or the wall, or wherever their bodies had happened to fall, and one confessor who had bitten free her tongue and then choked on it, and there was Maryland Slim. Blood leaked out of Maryland Slim's nose and stained his bright suit. Maryland Slim took a silk handkerchief from his pocket, wiped away the spot of crimson, folded it neatly, and returned it to where it had been. Then he rose onto his great fat legs, took two steps forward and collapsed, the floor shuddering with his weight.

"By the t," said the last confessor. "By the Tiny t and everything holy."

As far as last words went, they weren't terrible. Perhaps with more time, the confessor might have come up with something better, but the confessor had no more time, a jut of steel pressing through his robes just then.

"Maryland Slim was the greatest lover in the history of the Island," Hope said, letting the confessor slip off the knife and onto the floor, "and he did the two-step like a living god."

A Dying Request

The door opened and one of Mr Simpson's soldiers barged in. He glanced at gut-shot Gillian, but didn't comment. "We have a situation downstairs," he said.

"I'm pretty busy here," said Mr Simpson.

"It's with the confessors."

Mr Simpson sighed and returned his warm automatic to its shoulder holster. "Don't go anywhere," he said. "I'll be back to continue this in more detail."

Gillian had pitched backward in her chair and she lay on the floor, bleeding, though not sobbing. As soon as the door closed, the Kid joined her.

"Don't try to talk," he said, "conserve your strength, we'll–"

Her eyes were very white and her breathing had gone shallow. "You have to kill him."

"I will, Mom, I swear to all the gods. I'll get him and I'll murder him slow, cut him up till he can't remember being human, cut him up till–"

"Not that idiot," Gillian said. "Newton. You have to kill the kid, Kid; that was the part of the plan I couldn't tell you. I was gonna crawfish on the King, get him to wreck the tunnel and then put some boom in his son's brain. They have too many soldiers. You'll never break in, even if the Brides come. You've got to get the King to do it for you, and to do that, you have to give him Newton." She strengthened suddenly and grabbed the Kid's shirt. "But you can't give him Newton. If he gets his heir, he can do anything he wants. Do you understand?" Blood bubbled out of Gillian's mouth, and her grip began to weaken. "Whatever happens, don't let his father have him."

A Wish Granted

The funk danced midway across Canal Street, then danced back. Eyes seemed to form inside of it, eyes and great, gaping maws.

Newton paced across the floor of his cell, kicking at the stone and saying mean things to himself. "Stupid Newton. Stupid Island. Stupid World-Writ-Large. I'm not so terrible. I'm pretty awful. I'm not any worse than anyone else. Everyone else is horrid, though. But still! They have parents, and friends. Why don't I? And now I'm probably going to be killed and I don't know why I never got to have a sleepover or kiss a boy. It isn't fair. It isn't fair."

Outside his window, unnoticed in the depths of Newton's despair, the funk formed a vast hand, fingers the length of lamp poles, a palm the size of a square city block.

"I wish someone would come and take me away," said Newton, miserably.

The funk fist forced its way across Canal Street, ruptured steel and pulverized concrete, the borders of old TriBeCa expanding over the southern half of the building, a thick curtain of dim which seemed to swallow up everything.

61

Uptown Interlude, Part 2

Rembrandt would try always to remember Stag as he was in those final moments, first in the van, snarling his way up 122nd. Stones struck and boom exploded all about him, but his steps neither faltered nor sped, not till just before he reached the barricades, which he surmounted in a running leap, landing among the Honey Swallowers, pretty as porcelain in their bright gold, and they broke just as easy.

The Honey Swallowers fled, and the Sacred Band pulsed after them, Stonewall victorious, the cost not clear until Rembrandt saw Stag strung out in the mud, his comrades taking swift advantage of the triumph their War Chief had purchased with his flesh.

"No," said Rembrandt, falling to his knees, "no, no, by every god and every saint, by all our brothers what come before us–"

"Hush, now," said Stag. His grip was still strong as he pulled Rembrandt into a final kiss. "You be a man, like I showed you."

62

Cavalry, Belated

When Chisel finally showed up with her warwagons, Hope was waiting outside chewing a fat wad of bubble gum and spinning her bloodied knife. Swan leaned against the wall beside her, recovering slowly and thinking savage thoughts.

"Thank the Bull you're all right!" Ael said, leaping off the front of the warwagon before it had come to a complete stop. "Did they hurt you? But not bad, right? Like, nothing that should slow you down too much?"

"I'm touched by your concern," said Swan. "You got anything to drink?'

"Where'd you find him?" asked Hope.

"He was waiting for us on 7th, getting ready to make a suicide charge single-handed." Chisel looked at the billowing gray mass which had fallen like a curtain halfway across the buildings, the borders of TriBeCa proving ravenous. "What happened?"

Hope shrugged. Hope was having trouble following all of these new developments herself. "The funk, I gather."

"What about the tourist? And his men?"

"I think they skedaddled back to the tunnel," said Hope, "but I was pretty busy pulling Swan out."

"Where's the Kid?" Chisel asked, finally giving voice to it.

Hope made swift, thoughtless passes with her knife, a murderous instinct vented unconsciously.

"I'm sorry," said Chisel.

"I'll be sorry later," said Hope. "Right now, I'm angry."

"That's good to hear," said Chisel. She had her arm bandaged against her chest, and a pair of heavy goggles, and a chambered pistol, and twenty souls similarly attired, ready to kill for her. "Because they're going to know we're coming."

"It turns out they knew we were coming already."

"Give me a distraction," said Swan. He took the leather cap off his head and stuffed it into the pocket of his robe. "Give me enough of a distraction to get inside, and I'll flood the Huddy red." His ears were packed with cotton, and there was a long black ribbon wound inch thick around his eyes, which he began to slowly unwrap.

"Oooh boy," Ael said excitedly. "Count me in."

"We need to get into the into the tunnel proper if we want to bring it down," said Adze, leaning one massive arm out the window of the warwagon he was piloting. "The deeper, the better."

"How are you going to set it off?" asked Hope.

"You let us take care of that end," said the Null from behind a swiveling cannon mounted on the back of Adze's warwagon. At this point, the Null had really done enough to warrant a name, but there hadn't been time to go through the official ceremony.

"That's a big cannon," said Hope.

"Ain't it just?"

"All right, then," said Chisel. "We'll go straight up the exit, hit him hard enough to get some attention. Swan – you are Swan, yes?"

"I am," said Swan.

"Swan the all-swift," said the hypebird, "Swan the all-seeing, Swan meaner than–"

"Don't forget which of us you squawk for," said Ael.

"Fine," said Chisel, "Swan goes in through any side-entrance he can find."

"I'm with him," Ael said. Ael was carrying his matching

twin cutters and a bunch of smaller weapons and the future cannon he was very excited to try out some more.

"Whatever," said Swan. A thin wisp of ribbon was all that protected his eyes from the things they might see, and he held the sword Gillian had given him sheathed in his off hand. "Just make sure and stay out of my way once we get in the dark."

"Heroes united, a desperate gamble, vengeance for the fallen!" preached the hypebird.

"And keep that thing silent," Swan said, wincing, "or I'm gonna split it in two."

63

Uptown Interlude, Part 3

Their losses had been bad, worse even than the Commissioner[72] had expected, the Honey Swallowers fighting fanatically for every block, foot, and inch. But the Force were not pussy cats neither, and for that matter, there were still a few grinders downtown who knew which end of a cutter to hold. With their heavy infantry pushing at the main gates, the irregulars and cavalry had executed a vast envelopment, rupturing the flanks, piercing the Hive at all points.

A runner approached their position from the north. "The 102nd Street gate is breached, sir," he said triumphantly. "The Widow Makers are streaming into the Hive."

"Late as ever!" the Commissioner laughed. "All that talk, but they take second to our boys in blue!"

Yes, it had been a close-run thing, but a hard victory is worth more than a soft. And who knew that this was to be their last? Alvin had been right: with the Honey Swallowers gone the way of the I's, the Force would have a free hand on the Island; no other clique could hope to match them. The Commissioner was so caught up in his dreams of future bloodshed that he nearly lost track of the present slaughter, an exhausted runner

---

72 Leader of the Force, supreme general of the allied army, engaged in a combat largely ancillary to our actual story.

coming from the south, looking like he might pass out before giving his message.

"They breached the walls, sir!" he gasped.

The Commissioner laughed. "You didn't need to kill yourself getting that to me, son; the wall's been breached a hundred times by now."

"Not their wall," the messenger gasped. "Ours! A force of Paladins came streaming in from Harlem! They slaughtered the reserve guard and are burning their way down Madison! It was a ruse, sir, a gambit! The Honey Swallowers are loose in the Enclave!"

64

The Fate of the Island

Lost Amid the Funk

The walls of the building had disappeared around Newton, as had the floor and the ceiling. He was no longer in TriBeCa, or the Island, or even the World-Writ-Large; he was in the funk, thought and feeling and reality all muddled up together. How long did he wander? Who knew? Without tic or toc, without light or shade, there could be no conception of time. Newton was frightened. But, then again, Newton was always frightened. This is one of the few upsides of being weak: you grow accustomed to fear, if not a friend, then at least a familiar bully.

Finally, in the middle of all that funk, Newton met a man.

"My son has come home at last," said the Last King of TriBeCa.

Meanwhile, Our Heroes...

...prepared for their assault on the Holland Tunnel.

Sisters-in-Arms

They had arranged the war tanks at Varick and Watts, waiting for Swan and Ael to get into position. Chisel stared at the barricades with her far-seeing glasses.

"How's it look?" asked Hope.

Chisel shrugged and let the glasses hang by her wounded arm. "You're better off not knowing."

"Fair enough," said Hope. "I'm sorry I threatened to take over your body and use you as an unwitting sexual slave."

"That's okay," said Chisel. "I'm sorry I threatened to hook you up to a battery and juice you to death."

"I don't think you actually threatened that."

"Not explicitly, but it was what I had planned," said Chisel.

"I forgive you," said Hope. "He liked you."

"Did he?" asked Chisel, feigning indifference indifferently.

"I think so," said Hope. A wad of bubblegum sat forgotten in the corner of her mouth. "I guess about as much as he liked anything."

Hard Count

"Twenty-seven shots!" said Ael excitedly, caressing his future cannon. "The whole box carried thirty, but I burned three getting free of you last time. Still, twenty-seven! Can you imagine how many people I can kill with twenty-seven shots of boom?"

"Twenty-seven?" guessed Swan.

They were jogging across West Street just north of the Holland Tunnel, towards a gap which Swan had 'heard' in the phalt, a side entrance to the warrens which surrounded the tunnel proper.

Ael laughed nervously. "Of course, it's got nothing on a good cutter. I was just saying that. The hypebird heard me."

"Speaks the truth!" said the hypebird.

"I don't want you to think I'm running the sword down, at all. Nothing on the Island to beat a good cutter, and nothing in all the World-Writ-Large, for that matter! There's something perfect about them, you know? Something honest. A shot of boom could take anyone, but if you have a cutter and another guy has a cutter and you fight each other, then you've got an answer, you know?"

"There is something very seriously wrong with you," said Swan.

High Trump

On the back of the last warwagon, there was a heavy cannon, Adze, Chisel's Null, and the battery which they had bartered from Stuy and filled up with juice stolen from the Great Tap. It was attached to a peculiar, sting-like mechanism, a length of sharpened metal with a coil of wire attached.

"Hit the button," said Adze, "and run like hell."

"You don't figure a slow jog would do it?" asked the Null, slamming shut the breach on his cannon.

Reunion

The search for his heir and the expansion of the funk over Canal Street had left the Last King of TriBeCa a dim copy of what he had been several dims previous. He looked wispy, and faded, like a sidewalk drawing after the rain. He was smiling, though. "You've got your mother's eyes," he said.

"Do I?" asked Newton.

"I'm assuming. I don't actually know who your mother was, but my eyes were not blue."

"Oh," said Newton. "What color were your eyes?"

The Last King of TriBeCa's eyes were, just then, funk colored, as was everything else about him. "Brown, I think? It's been a while."

"And that would make you my father?"

"Yes, Newton, it would."

"Are you sure? Because you seem to be made out of funk."

"When the enemies of TriBeCa, traitorous, treasonous, fearful of our strength, made common cause with one another and marched on us—"

"Why did everyone want to kill you?"

"Because they were cowards, Newton, weak-willed and fearful, hypocrites, slaves to an outdated moral code which even they did not believe–"

"How did you get to be made of funk?"

"With our last bastions breached, with our enemies on every side, I was forced into a desperate gamble, melding my own life force with–"

"How can a person be made out of funk?"

"For a thousand dims, I studied, searching in the farthest corners of the Island, in the places where cowards feared to look. And in those abandoned places where–"

"I'm not made of funk," said Newton. "Or at least, I don't think I am, and I'm pretty sure I would know if I was. Am I made of funk?"

"No, Newton, you aren't literally made of funk, but the funk is your birthright, your heritage, every bit as much, even more so, more even than–"

"What have you been doing in TriBeCa this whole time?"

"If you let me answer one question before asking the next," said the Last King of TriBeCa, getting annoyed, "I promise I could explain this more swiftly."

"Sorry," said Newton.

"That's fine," said the Last King of TriBeCa, calming down. "Anyway, we'll have time for all of it, Newton, but for right now, the important thing to understand is this: you're special."

"I am?"

"Oh my, yes. You're the most special person on the Island. Before your birth you were chosen, your mother plucked from among all my subjects for her beauty and intellect – again, I can only assume because I'm not entirely sure who she was. In any event... the funk is yours, Newton, as it is mine. But where my power was hard won, purchased at the cost of my blood, body, and soul, yours is innate, the exercise of your powers easy as a light jog."

"I'm not much of a sprinter."

"As natural to you as something that you do find easy," said the Last King of TriBeCa. "Work with me a little bit, for the love of funk."

"Sorry," said Newton.

"My point is, whatever you want is yours for the taking," the Last King of TriBeCa hissed. "The funk can break bone and steel, the funk can twist minds, the funk can do anything you wish it too. Your only limitations are your imagination, and your hiddenmost desires."

"Newton," said the Kid, appearing from the funk just then. "Run."

While our Villains...

...prepared to defend themselves.

Dual Loyalties

Daedalus had not stayed to see what they did to Gillian, or the rest of his friends and associates, retreating to the tunnels below the Holland Tunnel to join the rest of the clans, not only the Green Line but Red and Blue and Purple and Orange and Yellow as well – even the pitiful inhabitants of the Silver Line, which ran only a few short blocks below Midtown. There had been nothing like it on the Island in who knew how long, all of the mazed come together for a single purpose. Then again, a lot of things were happening on the Island that had never happened before, and it was getting hard to be impressed by all of them.

Ariadne had watched Dade's betrayal in silence, and perhaps horror, and she had kept quiet as they had retreated to the tunnel, and as Daedalus had made his plans with the other clan leaders, and as the Green Line had taken their positions among the underground passageways and access tunnels where they expected their enemies, their friends, to strike.

But in a silent moment before the cacophony to come, she managed to steal a few words.

"Knew from jump?"

"Conductor knew."

"Couldn't spread the scuttle?"

"Crone savvy. Was savvy. Rat knew, would know. Better in the dark."

"Why cheat Crone? Why join tourists? Why any of it?"

"Green Line is all," said Daedalus. "Topside care nothing for below, never did, never will. Holland gets open, tourists leave. That simple."

"Crone saved me," Ariadne said after a while.

"Clan comes first," Daedalus answered.

The rangers were preparing for the battle to come, setting snare traps and sharpening their hooks, promising to watch over each other's pups, should the unfortunate occur, tracing the lines of their mazes nervously.

"Conductor carries," said Daedalus. "Rat was blind. Rat's blameless."

"Rat or topsider," said Ariadne, eyes hard and mean, "ain't none of us that."

Papal Infallibility

"Ten should have been enough," said the Pope.

"Ten was plenty," agreed her bishop.

The Pope and her surviving forces, half a dozen clean-shaven pates wearing finery of varying elaborateness, were deep within the Holland Tunnel complex, behind several barricades manned by soldiers with future cannon and a seemingly endless swarm of claw-wielding, tattooed tunnel-dwellers.

"Even for Maryland Slim, ten should have been plenty," said the Pope.

"Absolutely should have been," said her cardinal.

"Just bad luck," added the bishop.

"Could have happened to anyone," said a confessor.

"But we're sure he's dead?" asked the Pope.

"Absolutely," said the bishop.

"Quite confident," said the cardinal.

"Ehhh," said the confessor.

A distant moan could be heard from within the tunnel proper. The fight which was about to come was no excuse to knock off early; quite the opposite, in fact, the slaves pressed ever harder to finish their excavations.

"So it's just the other one? The girl? With the nose ring?" asked the Pope.

"Just her," said the bishop.

"Never even had any proper training," said the cardinal.

"Probably go easy," said the confessor.

"That should be fine," said the Pope, with somewhat less certainty than she had felt in some of her other decisions. "That should be plenty."

Rules of Engagement

Mr Simpson left Jersey with forty-two men: Edson had wondered into the funk the first day, never to return; Nance and Reese had shat themselves to death, something like cholera, though no amount of Cipro seemed to help; Alvarez had been knifed in a bar; Myke had gone native, started carrying a cutter and fighting for some gang in Alphabet City; they'd lost five men on the Way, plus the one who had gone with Dallas, plus Dallas himself – this last a particular lamentation, as Mr Simpson was no great tactician. Still, that left thirty soldiers for defense, thirty government-trained killers, thirty hard-bitten veterans with weapons no one on the Island had any notion existed. Thirty soldiers, plus the vast army of rat folk, plus the Pope and her people. And between outnumbering the enemy something like eight or ten to one, and having by then swallowed enough Oxycontin to stone a professional football team, Mr Simpson was feeling pretty good about his chances.

"They'll come straight in," Mr Simpson warned, "on these tank-like things with scrap metal for armor."

"Guns, sir?" asked Louis.

"Some sort of black-powder bullshit," said Mr Simpson.

"Still blow your head off if you stand in front of it," warned Adams.

"What about our allies, sir?"

"They're mostly carrying hooks and wearing mole skin," said Mr Simpson.

"Moleskine?" asked Louis, laughing.

"Don't be an asshole, Louis," said Adams.

"No one's going to get their pay docked for friendly firing a few of these troglodytes," said Mr Simpson. "But not the bald ones! Anybody greases a confessor and I'll personally see to it you end up cleaning latrines in some Baluchistani forward base."

"Hit a hairless monkey, lose a life," said Louis.

This time, Adams laughed also.

Justifications Inside the Brume

"If it isn't the Kid!" said the Last King of TriBeCa. "Oh, glorious life! Unlife."

"Get out of here, Newton," said the Kid again. "I'll keep him away as long as I can."

"I can't believe I didn't put it together earlier," said the Last King of TriBeCa. "That cast of your nose, the agonizingly annoying nature of our conversation – you are indeed your mother's son! Speaking of which, I can still feel her in the back there. She's in an incredible amount of pain, I thought you might want to know."

"Whatever he's told you, Newton, it's a lie. You can't believe him."

"He says he's my dad."

"That's true, but–"

"Why didn't you tell me?"

"It's complicated. I thought if you knew that–"

"Why did you steal me from the Mayor? Why did the Mayor have me to begin with? And what was the point of bringing me along?"

"Will you let me answer a question before starting another one?" the Kid asked desperately.

"I'll be surprised," grumbled the Last King of TriBeCa.

Hope's eyes flickered back into sentience. "Swan's in position," she said.

Chisel whistled between two fingers, and the warwagons rolled forward.

Frontal Assault

Mr Simpson's forces had been expecting it, but expecting it was not quite the same thing as being prepared for it. The strange whine of juice-powered engines, and then Chisel and her squad of warwagons came plunging through the first rounds of barricades. Subterraneans got crushed beneath tires, torn apart by heavy cannon, shrieked desperate pleas to their strange gods. From their fortified positions, Mr Simpson's soldiers plugged away with their assault weapons, tearing through the plate like it was paper, Bridge Brides bleeding and Bridge Brides dying, but still they plunged through the first part of the complex, past the slave quarters and around the vast mound of rubble which had been slowly, painstakingly pulled out of the tunnel itself.

They took their first serious loss just before they passed Washington, a bare block from the Holland, when the driver of the first warwagon, without warning or explanation, jerked her wheel leftward, upending her vehicle and hurling her passengers to their deaths. It was the last easy victory the Pope and her forces would enjoy – wrecking the warwagon had alerted Hope to their positions, psychically speaking, and she was not slow to pounce.

Vengeance for Slim (et al)

Anyone could be anything in the not-anywhere where they fought. Put another way, everyone could only be one thing, exactly what they were, without pretense or self-delusion. Hope was not a dancer. Or if she was, it was in a big scrum of people and she was throwing elbows. Hope was neither graceful nor poised. Hope was a cudgel, Hope was high tide in a bad storm, Hope was looking up and seeing an a/c unit come falling down from a high window knowing you should move but then not moving, and then *splat*!

The bishop screamed and Hope roared, "Slim, Slim, Slim!" his name echoing from every fragment of existence.

Fun With Future Weapons

With the cannon reverberating a few blocks over, Swan and Ael had climbed through the access vent and were heading towards the Holland Tunnel when Swan dropped to his knees and began to moan.

"Is it that thing again?" Ael asked. "That sound, thing? That thing that got you last time?"

Swan shoved his hands around his now unprotected ears.

"Don't you worry!" Ael promised, "I've got it! I'll take care of it! Just stay here and rest for later!"

"Ael got you covered!" said the hypebird, "Ael got your back!"

Ael hooted and ran forward, coming round a turn as the first rat popped up then and dropped back down as quick, the tiniest little depression of the trigger and *poof*, a skull exploded against a wall. The torch attached to the end of Ael's barrel lit on a pair of hook-wielding mazed, and then on two corpses slipping down into the muck.

"Twenty-four!" Ael yelled.

A ranger dropped from a depression in the ceiling, the hypebird giving warning just before he landed. Ael didn't bother to waste a boom. A swift moment's grapple, and then the butt of his cannon against the rat's face, once, twice, three times, and he hurried onward.

"Still twenty-four!" Ael yelled again, somewhere between reminder and war cry. "Still twenty-four!"

The Chosen One

"Look, son, don't let it get you upset," said the Last King of TriBeCa. "It's the way of the world! What did you expect him to do? Did you think the Kid was your friend?"

"I wasn't… I suppose I had hoped…"

"It's time to grow up, Newton. Everyone would do anything they wanted if they could, but they can't, so they make up a lot of reasons why they don't want to. That's what they call morality, understand? And it makes sense for them, because they're all so weak, and pathetic, and easy to break. But you aren't like them, Newton! You're special! You get to do anything you want, and that means you don't have to pretend!"

Newton had always secretly thought he was special. So had everyone else who ever lived on the Island, and the World-Writ-Large.

"The funk will do whatever you make it," said the Last King of TriBeCa. "Whatever you want, the funk will do."

"Funk," Newton began, "would you please–"

"Don't ask it," the Last King of TriBeCa hissed. *"Make it."*

Newton wiggled his fingers and found the funk wiggled with

him, not like an extension of his body but like an obedient servant. Like a perfect, willing slave.

"Oh, my," said Newton.

A Dream Deferred

After the twenty-seventh boom, Ael tossed aside his future cannon and drew his cutters. The rats were quick to react, converging on him from all sides, a multicolored subterranean swarm, rangers from every line, hooks gleaming in the dark. For a second time, Ael's dual swords proved no gimmick, beset as he was by the mass of mazed. He darted back and forth through the caverns and passageways, moving ceaselessly, never allowing a clump of the enemy to gather the courage to attack. He slipped hooks, he turned their numbers against them, he made clever use of every tactic and ruse his genius provided him.

But against so many, technique was insufficient, the rangers cornering him finally in a storeroom just below the Holland itself. The clamor of boom from the battle topside was ferocious, but Ael's scream echoed louder, an expression of pure and undiluted misery. Not fear of death, death was nothing to Ael, but to die with his dream so close in front of him? Against such agony even the strongest soul might break.

Standstill

The cannon they fired then was not like any cannon Chisel had ever seen; looked a little bit like an X-bow, and when its bolt struck the second warwagon, there was an explosion that not only destroyed it, but wrecked her own as well, a sudden flare of flame searing their armor and melting away the Bride they had on cannon and ruining the engines, the wagon gone stationary.

Hope Lost

Hope was terrible, but the confessors too knew power, and they yearned for their own vengeance, brothers killed and sisters left comatose. When Hope turned her great force on one, three fell on her flanks, and there seemed always too many of them. Only when she was already pinned did the Pope show herself for what was to be the killing blow, slithering upright and smiling expectantly.

Queen Sacrifice

"That's spoor," said the Kid, "that's nonsense. Some of us are rotten; that's no excuse for being the same."

"At least your mother wasn't such a hypocrite," said the Last King of TriBeCa. "She was the most traitorous, treacherous, serpent-tongued harlot that ever bedeviled man, but she wasn't a hypocrite. That was literally the only thing I liked about her."

"That panel book you were drawing that first time I met you, how was it supposed to end?" asked the Kid.

The funk stared back at Newton, echoed Newton, waved coquettishly at Newton, danced for Newton's pleasure.

"Cinder; that was his name, wasn't it? Cinder and his flame? The eternal flame?"

"The living flame," Newton said, turning from the funk. "He needed it to stop the Great Wyrm what overthrew his father."

"Why did he want to do that?"

"Because he was a hero," said Newton.

"Panel books are for children!" the Last King of TriBeCa snapped. "That's something we're going to have to talk about, actually–"

"You aren't like him, Newton," said the Kid, "and you aren't like me, either."

"That's enough," the Last King of TriBeCa said, turning himself on the Kid. "Watch this here, Newton. I'll show you a fun little trick. All you have to is look at them like this..."

and pop they fall right apart see have a gander at all the things going on inside this one he seems so cool but it's all a pose isn't it Newton it's all a pose for all of them they start screaming as soon as you poke at them you don't even have to try very hard like tearing up a pigeon carcass and look at that right there he was going to kill you Newton he was going to murder you and why because you're special that's why I told you Newton you should listen to your father he's been around a little while long enough to know that **an idiot who lives forever is still an idiot** *Gillian why there's some life in you after all perfect just perfect* **a cheap bully in a garish suit** *that's a question of taste isn't it Gillian oh happy fortune and kind fate I couldn't possibly have planned it better myself really I couldn't have your son here to witness your final failure* **twice the man you are and a woman** *or should I do him first and make you watch that might be the way to do it yes I think it just might* **scared little boy likes to hurt things to make himself feel brave** *actually I just enjoy it there was never anything more to it that than that I just enjoyed doing it* **mother should have broken you at birth** *sensitive subject Gillian I wouldn't be so quick to bring up motherhood if I were you shall we take a look into your mind Gillian shall we see what* stay out of there *I almost killed myself trying to find my son and you turned yours into a knife* **Island is hard he needed to be harder** *nothing to do with any of that nothing to do with any of that he had his father's hair and you hated the reminder* **I wasn't what I wanted to be** *take comfort Gillian I'll put him down after I put you down* **wanted him to be better you only want yours to be worse**

From inside them, Newton and the Kid watched as the words/memories/images that had been his mother reduced themselves down to a wisp, and that wisp evaporating into nothing, the Kid chasing after it futilely, then falling to his knees. He did not cry out, but he closed his eyes, and his face was all but empty.

Newton looked up at the funk, and then down at the Kid. "Your father seems pretty horrible," he said.

"I guess we have that in common," said the Kid.

"Yeah."

The Kid opened his eyes and looked up at Newton. "Good thing we're not them."

"Yeah," Newton said, after a moment. Then he smiled. "Rut them."

"Yeah," said the Kid.

Newton had never said 'rut' before, and he so enjoyed it he decided to say it again. "Rut them."

"Send him to Jersey," agreed the Kid.

The Most Incredible Thing That Ever Happened on the Island

This was more or less what he did, the Flynn effect in effect, young Newton effortlessly proving himself his father's superior, stretching out his hand and spreading the Last King of TriBeCa across the Island, from the Battery to the Devil and further still, to alien coasts, the names of which had long been forgotten. Pushed so far beyond its normal boundaries, there appeared then an aperture in the funk, centered over TriBeCa but visible from across the Island, through which a black sea extended on forever, or so long as you could look, interrupted by twinkling spots like gemstones, like a smile from a stranger, like a bit of sweet in your coffee, like nothing that anyone on the Island or their parents or their parents' parents or their parents' parents' parents or who knows how many previous parents had ever seen before, any of them, ever.

The Kid and Newton stared up at it a while.

"I'm sorry about your mom," said Newton.

"I'm sorry she was going to kill you," said the Kid.

"That's okay," said Newton. "She must have thought she had to."

"She was a difficult woman, my mother," said the Kid.

"I guess it's not such an easy thing having a kid."

"I guess not," said the Kid.

They looked again at the lights in the sky.

"She had her good points," said the Kid.

"I believe you," said Newton.

"She was funny, first of all. That counts for a lot."

"Sure."

"And she was tough. Funk, she was tough, tough as scrap iron wrapped in barbed wire."

"That's nice also."

"Another thing about my mom," said the Kid. "She really, really hated losing."

Deus Ex Nubes

The Last King of TriBeCa had been limited by the traditional boundaries of his old kingdom, but Newton had no particular connection to the triangle below Canal Street, and so he had no similar constraints, leaking a thousand tiny fingers of funk into the Holland Tunnel. Balking at murder, he plugged gun barrels, tripped ankles, turned blades, broke lights, guttered torches, and dismantled the elaborate speaker system which Mr Simpson, at great expense and with wise foresight, had rigged throughout the complex.

In the Dark

"Peep that?" asked Daedalus.

"Peep what?" asked a ranger.

"Gone quiet," said Ariadne.

The subterraneans thought themselves creatures of the dark, but really, they were only creatures of the very slightly light. For Swan, darkness was not simply his natural environment, but balm to his endless misery. More than indifferent, it was a positive kindness, and he spread it swiftly and without rancor. Lightless, it proved impossible to make out every moment of slaughter, each particular homicide. And just as well, for who would care to know all of them? Severed limbs stacked and the trickle of blood become a stream, crimson run-off rising ankle-deep in the tunnels, the full might of the underground nations insufficient to slow, let alone stop, Swan's assault. His eyes unbound for the first time since his infancy he slaughtered whole clans as easily as he might have single rats, saving Ael from his tormentors, continuing upward to where Dade and Ariadne and the other conductors waited.

"Hello, Dade," said Swan. And before Daedalus could raise his weapon or even speak, the right side of his body sundered from the left, a spray of blood which covered Ariadne and the wall, and then the two halves of Daedalus separated to the ground.

"Hello, Ariadne," said Swan.

Apostolic Turnover

Newton's assault fractured the Pope's concentration for an instant, and into that crevice of space-time Hope blossomed like shrooms after a rain, expanding and stretching until the Pope's mind was reduced to a child, and then a very young child, and then a dog, and then an insect, and then nothing, the other confessors fleeing, first in the not-space in which they fought, and then in reality, making desperate tracks for any far corner of the Island.

Sparking a Fuse

Three warwagons had been crippled. But the last, with Adze driving and the Null on back cannon, burst past the final line of barricades and into the Holland Tunnel proper. The slaves, Downtown citizens, half-savaged by nature, had taken the attack as an opportunity to slaughter their captors and were now hurrying to escape. Adze drove his wagon forward until they could go forward no more, come at last to the collapsed tunnel, largely rebuilt, a few hundred tons of rock all that kept them from the World-Writ-Large.

Adze had little time to appreciate the gravity of the moment. He kicked his door open, came running round to the back, wondering why the Null hadn't bothered to set the bomb off yet, learning swiftly.

"Hell and High Towers," Adze said.

The battery had survived, but the device they had rigged to detonate it was wrecked. The Null was desperately trying to unscrew the coiled spike from the machine. From the mouth of the tunnel they could hear soldiers coming with cannon.

"Just one more tic," said the Null, working at the spike.

Adze pushed him aside and ripped it free, one yank and the metal strained, and then it was in his hands. A raft of boom echoed just behind them.

"I'll do it," said Adze.

"I'll do it," the Null.

"You'll do what I tell you!" Adze roared. "You're not anything, I'm the head of security! For another twenty-five tics, or so. Then you're head of security." He shoved the Null off the back of the track. "Go!" he yelled. "Now! For tomorrow!" he added, the last thing Adze would say to anyone. As the Null scrambled for safety and the soldiers closed in, Adze plunged the spear into the battery, releasing a bright blue crackle of juice which stopped his heart before turning him to ash, dead in an instant, but the pierced battery continued to sweat and to bubble, and then–

Boom!
Boom!

65

Uptown Interlude, Part 4

When the funk opened above the Island, Owen had been engaged in furious combat with a Honey Swallower, his sword locked against the man's war club, their faces pressed so close that he could see the fresh acne on his chin, younger even than Owen, and Owen was a young man.

They stopped fighting when they saw the stars. Not everyone stopped, but many of them did.

"I'm going to go home," Owen said, after a while. "I don't want to do this anymore."

"I don't either," said the Honey Swallower. "I never really did."

66

Spoils of Victory

Leaving the Holland Tunnel, the former slaves found themselves intermingled with a great migration of soldiers then filtering back from the Upper West Side, walking listless, their cutters sheathed, their pikes forgotten, their eyes fixed to the sky. Across the Island, men kissed wives they had not thought to see again, held their almost-orphans, lamented the great foolishness of war, swore falsely never to forget this moment of salvation, to beat their blades into ploughshares and love their neighbors as themselves.

Bitter and Sweet

With some effort, they managed to get Chisel's warwagon moving again, scavenging pieces from the other vehicles to fix their engine. The Brides themselves were in little better shape than their rides – of the twenty-odd they had rode in with, only Chisel, the Null, and a few others had survived the assault. The Null had his head under the hood, working away at the battery, and so he did not see the Kid as he crossed over Washington.

Chisel saw him, however.

They did not run towards one another. They did not embrace. They did not smile, even. Chisel closed her eyes for a long time, but that could have meant anything.

"I guess you aren't dead," she said.

"Hell would be worse, probably."

"And heaven?"

"I don't think I'll see it," said the Kid.

"If you got there, would you kick your heels up? Or start plotting to overthrow the gods?"

"I should have told you about the plan," said the Kid. "I should have told you about a lot of things."

"Yeah," said Chisel, "you should have."

The Null finished what he was doing and shut the hood. "Ready when you are, Chisel," he said. He gave the Kid the eyeball. He was making up for Adze being gone.

"What do you think those are called?" the Kid asked, pointing up at the lights in the sky.

"I don't know," said Chisel.

"You look at a thing your whole life," said the Kid, "and you get to think you know what it is." It was most likely only the smoke billowing in from the ruined tunnel which seemed to strain his voice. "And then something changes, and you realize you're wrong. That you only saw the one part of it, and maybe not even the most important part."

Chisel looked at the Kid a long time. Then she climbed onto the back of her warwagon and slapped the fender twice. "The funk changes, but I don't think people do. I'm glad you're not dead, Kid," she said as the Null turned the warwagon around, "but I don't ever want to see you again."

The vehicle rustled east, back burst tire flapping black rubber against the black phalt. The Kid watched it until it was out of sight, but Chisel never turned to look at him.

"Kid!" yelled Hope, appearing just then. "Kid! You aren't dead!"

"Nope," said the Kid.

"Great!" said Hope. There was a pause. "You know we won, right? We blew up the tunnel?"

"I know," said the Kid, still scowling eastward.

"Saving the Island, defeating your enemies, our last-moment salvation, still can't get you to smile?"

"I can't really take credit for it," the Kid admitted. "Also, my mom died."

"Oh," said Hope. "That's terrible. But, also, I figured you were both dead, so this still feels like a win for me."

Then she threw her arms around him and burst into tears.

"You're getting snot all over my coat," the Kid said after a while, setting her gently aside. "Pull it together. We've got work to do."

"What's left?"

"I've got a few words I need to have with that tourist," said the Kid, pulling Gillian's cannon out of his jacket pocket and giving the chamber a spin.

Never Meet Your Heroes

After slaughtering his way through the Holland Tunnel, Swan took a seat on a bench in Hudson River Park. His blade was back in its sheath. Unblooded, unwinded, you would not have known he had drawn it, unless you had seen the great rotting mass of corpses in his wake.

"Perfect!" said Ael, who had indeed followed this trail. "This is absolutely perfect."

Swan didn't say anything. The window in the sky was shrinking, but still over the Hudson could be seen that lovely darkness, that darkness which was darker than dim, and also the twinkling lights interrupting it.

"Let's do it on the beach, yeah?" asked Ael. "It's better, don't you figure?"

Swan sighed and rose, and they headed over the service road and onto the narrow stretch of sand. Ael took his weapons off, and his armor, and took up position across from Swan, cutters drawn. "Okay if my hypebird says 'go'?"

"Are we really going to do this?"

"What do you mean?"

"Kill each other."

Ael shrugged. "I guess we could find an audience, if you really want to? But I don't honestly see the point. Who else could understand?"

"I didn't mean here, specifically. I meant at all."

But Ael remained confused. "Did you maybe get bumped on the head when they were taking you captive?"

"Maybe we could go find a place and get some pigeon eggs?"

"Pigeon eggs? Pigeon eggs?"

"Or oysters. In honor of Maryland Slim."

Ael took a deep breath. "I'm not sure you fully appreciate what's happening right now."

"Do tell."

"Just think about everything that got us here: the Kid and Gillian playing the Island off each other, setting up the I's and spinning everyone around. And then there was that JuiceTown robbery – did you see that cycle Chisel built? It was awesome. You weren't around for when we attacked that tourist on the Way, but trust me, it was wild, guns going off everywhere and the whole city coming to chase us down. And then the reveal at the end, where we were all working together to blow up the tunnel and save the Island. And that's not even getting into the war Gillian started, or whatever it was happened in TriBeCa that caused this whole hullabaloo with the funk! And now here we are at the end of it, grim survivors alone on a beach, the two greatest warriors the Island ever produced, as evidenced by the recent past, about to find out who is number one." Ael threw his hands up, trying futilely to convey the enormousness of the situation. "This is the coolest thing that ever happened! You know how lucky we are to be us?"

Swan turned his head to the fading night. "Eh."

Sorrow sat unfamiliar on Ael's tongue. "You're a real disappointment."

"I never wanted to be a killer."

"Then do something else!" Ael snapped, furious. "There are a million different ways you could spend your time, rather than carry around a cutter and complain. You could be... I dunno, a carpenter, or something."

"Be what you want to be!" said the hypebird, loyal as ever to its master. "Make your own choices!"

"But not yet," Ael said. "First, we're going to fight to the death. If you wanted to make a career change, you should have made it a few dims back. Now... are you ready?"

"As you like," Swan said.

The current lapped against the beach. The funk tightened its grip on the sky once more, the view of the beyond fading.

"Go!" the hypebird roared.

Footsteps in the sand. A sword unsheathed. A jut of scarlet.

"Huh," said Ael.

He collapsed against the beach. The waters of the Huddy caressed his corpse.

"Ael dark-haired, Ael courageous, Ael so lovely!" shrieked the hypebird, turning maddened wheels over his master. "Curse his killer, rot his bones, wreck his soul!" The hypebird was not a hunter, and its attack was awkward, but Swan allowed it to land a blow, in honor of Ael, or perhaps because he just did not feel like killing anymore. Though, if it was to be his last, he got over it quickly, the blade flashing one last time and all was quiet.

A While Later...

67

The Future to Come

First bright roiled over an uneasy Island. Things what had seemed certain for generations had been revealed as illusion. Alliances were overturned, empires crumbled, the powerful become weak and the weak begun to wonder if they might have misjudged themselves.

Shifting Sands

The Mayor sat in his office, drinking distil while an aide delivered a report.

"JuiceTown says they're ahead of schedule with replacing the bikes. It'll be a long time before they return to their previous capacity, but they should be up and running soon."

"You let the High Engineer know the first battery gets filled is ours," said the Mayor.

"The Cloister is still in mourning, but they're expected to announce a new Pope soon."

"It doesn't matter," said the Mayor. "The Pope might change, but the Cloister's interest remains the same. Stability over everything."

"The Commissioner insists the Enclave's damage was minimal, but our spies are reporting the Honey Swallowers managed to burn swathes of their fields before they were chased off – enough to affect the next harvest."

The Mayor sighed miserably and poured himself more liquor.

"Speaking of," the aide continued, "the Hive has allowed no one through their walls since the end of hostilities, not even civilians. I'm trying to get someone inside, but… it won't be easy."

"We're in for bloody times on the Island," the Mayor said, "bloody times. Any word from… her?" the Mayor asked.

"No, sir. Whatever happened with that mess down in the Holland Tunnel, it seems to have taken care of the Sheriff with it."

"Good," said the Mayor, though he sounded unsure.

Rat Queen

"One clan, one color, one conductor," said Ariadne. The surviving leaders of the subterraneans had met in the vast underground beneath Union Square Station, their numbers so reduced that the Red Clan had been forced to send a pup as representative and the Gray Line was absent completely. They were frightened, all but broken, and Ariadne's proposal had barely been discussed before taken up for vote. Even in the outermost reaches of the labyrinth, they had heard of the Green Clan's heir, and there could be no doubt that this was this great fate for which she had long been marked.

"One clan," agreed the representative of the Blue Clan.

"One clan," echoed Yellow's.

When each had finished swearing loyalty, she was officially supreme leader of the subterraneans. "Vengeance for Dade," Ariadne promised, loosening her claw. "Topside for kettle."

Back to School

2nd Adze[73] came late, having spent the morning vetting the new recruits, a dozen men and woman desperate to give

---

73   Once upon a time, Chisel's Null.

up their name to serve the Bridge, and only one certain spy between them, a dark-eyed grinder who might as well have come waving a flag of bright blue. Chisel and a few senior Bridge Brides were already waiting, slate and sharpened chalk in front of them.

At the front board was a man whom few would have recognized as Dallas[74], with his one eye ruined and leaning on a staff. "A is for apple," he began in a quavering voice, pointing at the letter on the board, "and for Alphabet City."

"A is for apple," the Brides intoned in unison, "and for Alphabet City..."

On the Shoulders of Giants

🪙 👛 's had not seen anything like it in a long time, the game gone straight through dimtime, fortunes made and fortunes lost.

"Raise fifty," said Shkreli.

Hope took a look at her hole cards. "That's a lot of change."

"Too much for you, little girl?" Shkreli asked. "Your knees getting week? Feel like dropping down onto them?"

"I'll raise you the table," Hope answered, smiling.

The New King of TriBeCa

"Four more come since bright," said Hem[75].

"We'll make room," said Newton. "No one will be turned away."

They had begun to trickle in as the funk had crept back over the Island, following the view for as long as they could: soldiers from ruined cliques, Uptown spinsters with slaughtered families and burned-out homes, oystermen, peddlers and

---

74 Formerly the leader of Mr Simpson's soldiers.
75 He kicked this whole bit off, remember?

pedalers, but mostly youths, girls and boys and young men and young women who had seen more in the sky than just the sky, who had seen the future. Hem was not young, but he was lost, and he had seen it as they had seen it, and been among the first to swear loyalty to a flabbergasted Newton.

"Of course, Brother Newton," said Hem. "All are welcome here."

Laight Street rung with the sounds of construction, people hammering planks for houses, people tearing up the phalt to make green, ruined TriBeCa beginning to blossom once more. They all stopped to wave as they saw Newton come past, grinders from all corners of the Island, from Harlem and from both villages, from Coop and Stuy alike, and every one Newton's friend.

Newton stopped in front of a three-story house which had not been there that morning, yelled to the man putting the finishing touches on the top floor. "How you doing, Swan?" asked Newton, smiling, as he had not previously been known to smile.

"Just fine, Newton," said Swan, turning briefly from his work. "Quite rosy, in fact."

The Kid and Mr Simpson

On the coast of Fort Tryon Park, the Kid, a handful of fierce-looking Borofolk, and several tourists walked towards the strange black ship which had brought the tourists to the Island. It had been a rough week for Mr Simpson. He stumbled some, and though he had no visible injuries, he was wearing a suit, so there might have been a lot of really nasty stuff underneath.

When they got to the beach, the Kid gestured to his cousins, and they undid the straps fettering Mr Simpson and his few surviving followers. "Why aren't I killing you?" he asked.

"Because you're a fool," said Mr Simpson. Having had his plans ruined, not to mention being tortured for a while, had not broken Mr Simpson, or at least it hadn't made him any sweeter.

"It's because I need you to carry a message," said the Kid. "Whoever it was that sent you, whatever they wanted, whatever they hoped to gain – tell them they can't have it. The Island is ours. Leave us alone and we won't bother to take anything else."

"I was right the first time," said Mr Simpson. "If you leave me alive, you're a fool. I'll come back and kill you, so help me God."

The Kid thought about this for a moment, then drew his mother's pistol from his belt and dropped a boom into the tourist's knee. "Just in case you're right," he said, "at least you'll be in a lot of pain at my funeral."

Long years of which did indeed begin for Mr Simpson just then, who began to scream and to shriek uncontrollably, to roll about on the beach like a fish stolen from water, blood roiling from his shattered kneecap, tears from his eyes. "I'll kill you!" he roared. "I'll kill you, Kid!"

"That's not my name anymore," the Kid announced, as much to the other Borofolk as to Mr Simpson. "From here on out, I'm the Man."

Acknowledgements

Thanks to Eleanor, Caroline, Gemma, Desola, Amy, and the rest of the crew at Angry Robot, for helping bring my formatting nightmare of a novel to fruition.

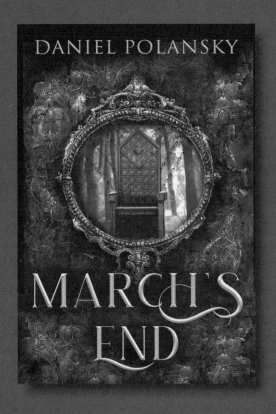

The children were in the attic. Mary Ann and John sat on the bed, with Constance in the big rocking chair beside them, flipping through the book. Watching through the window overlooking the old oak tree you would have thought she was reading them a story, but she was not.

"T is for the Tower," said Mary Ann. She was eleven, with red hair and a recently fastened set of braces. "From where the March is ruled with strength and wisdom."

"Good," said Constance, turning the page, "keep going."

"U is for Under the Mountain, the kingdom of the petrousian, carved from rock and stone."

The book was bound with something like leather and lacked title, author, or colophon. The pages were ancient but neither yellowed nor brittle, shades of colored ink depicting a vast subterranean city, gravelly humanoids smelting ore and carrying iron and carving stalagmite.

"From earth and stone," she corrected. Constance was thirteen, big for her age, frowsy haired and friendly.

"What's the difference?"

Constance wasn't sure, but as the eldest she couldn't say that. "It's in the book."

"From earth and stone," Mary Ann repeated unenthusiastically.

Constance turned a page to reveal a troupe of knights – fox knights and owl knights and clockwork knights and knights that looked like jellyfish but with fewer tendrils – all marching or riding or flying in spotless armor, carrying shining weapons and fluttering banners.

"V is for…" Mary Ann began but did not finish. "Oh, hell, I never remember this one. Can't we just go to the party?"

"Don't say hell," said Constance, "and not until we're done with the book."

"Hell," Mary Ann said again, "and who cares about the book? Why do we have to do homework on a holiday?"

"Because we're Harrow," said Constance, wearing what was Mary Ann's least favorite expression. "We're special. Go again."

"V is for very boring," said Mary Ann, "for vexing and for vile."

"You should know this by now. I memorized it when I was still in third grade."

"Of course, you did, you're perfect." Mary Ann crossed her arms.

"Mother says–"

"You're *not* our Mother."

"No, Mother is our mother, and she said we had to finish with the book before we went to the party. Do you think I wouldn't prefer being downstairs, rather than babysitting the two of you?"

"I think you *love it*. I think it's your absolute favorite thing."

"V is for the Valiant, who defend the March from evil," said John, turning from the window. John was eight; you could tell by his height and his baby face and the children's suit he had been forced to wear – but not always by his eyes, which were bright blue and strangely serious. "W is for the widdershins, nomads and wanderers, who walk with their hands and eat with their feet. X is for the xerophiles, lords of the western wastes, monarchs of the endless sand. Y is for the yearlings, the mounts of the mighty, who will not see a second spring. Z is for the zoaea, who guard the Southern oceans in argosy and galleass."

Constance turned to the final page of the book, which was black from margin to margin with something darker than ink. "What comes last?" she asked, with more than her usual seriousness.

Even Mary Ann knew this one. "The End," she said, matching her sister's tone.

Constance shut the book with a snap. "Now we can go to the party."

Which was already in full swing below, festive music echoing up the stairwell, the landing packed with revelers. Strings of colored lights twinkled over the mantle, a fire crackled in its corner, mistletoe hung hopeful over doorways, wine mulled, dips congealed. The Harrow's Christmas party was an institution across the neighborhood. The living room and the dining room and the fancy room in the back where no one ever went were busy with friends and acquaintances, people who worked with Father and people Mother had once gone to school with and everyone fortunate enough to live in their development; except for the Wolfes who were out of town, and Mr Crowley who never came to anything and turned his lights off on Halloween.

In the center of it, wearing a long evening dress with her hair up in a high crown, stood their mother. Sophia Harrow was a tall woman, with skin the color of fresh snow and the same blue eyes as her son. With effortless grace she greeted new arrivals, charmed strangers, filled cups, disposed of plates, always with a smile by turns welcoming and gracious, the very model of a genial host.

'It must be a terrible thing to grow up with a mother who isn't beautiful,' thought Constance.

'I'll never be so pretty,' thought Mary Ann.

It was hard to tell what John thought.

Sophia was busy but she broke away as soon as she saw her children, bending down to kiss them one by one, even Mary Ann who usually objected.

"Did you finish with your homework?"

"Yes, Mother," said Constance.

"Yes, Mother," said Mary Ann, an instant later.

John didn't say anything.

"There's food in the kitchen, and you can have some Coke if you want, but not too much or it will keep you up." Sophia patted Constance and rubbed Mary Ann's shoulder and fixed little John's little tie. "What did I ever do to deserve such lovely children?" she asked, not rhetorically but as if waiting for the answer.

There were fifty people at the party but when Sophia spoke it was like she was speaking just to you, and Constance beamed and John strutted and even Mary Ann looked pleased. Then Sophia was called away to deal with some minor crisis involving a chafing dish and the children were left to the interference of their elders. They congratulated Constance on her height, made John tell them his age and complimented Mary Ann on the dress which she hated, before – in the fashion of adults – forgetting about them completely, leaving the Harrow children finally free to go their separate ways.

Constance found her father in the kitchen, standing over a sudsy sink, hands sheathed in orange rubber gloves. Constance took a towel and started to dry a serving plate.

"Wouldn't you rather be enjoying yourself?" Michael asked. Michael had taken off his suit jacket to wash the dishes, and the muscles in his back and shoulders, and his stout gut, stood taut in his dress shirt. He shared the same genially unruly hair as his daughter. Sophia sometimes joked that it was the wildest thing about him.

"I don't mind," said Constance.

Her father smiled and Constance smiled back.

Mary Ann slipped out onto the porch to where Uncle Aaron leaned in the chilly shade of the December evening.

"Done with your lessons?" he asked.

Uncle Aaron was Mary Ann's favorite person in the world. He was terribly handsome, thin and dark with bright, striking eyes. He had lived in Europe for a while. He was also the only person Mary Ann knew besides their cafeteria lunch lady who smoked cigarettes, which was why he was outside, by himself, instead of inside, at the party.

Or so Mary Ann assumed. "Finally finished," she said. "Constance is such an apple-polisher – say 'a' instead of 'the' and you've practically got to start over."

"I used to hate the book when I was your age," said Aaron. "I could never get the V right."

"That's the one I missed!"

"Your mother could roll it off her tongue, of course," said Aaron, looking through the window at where Sophie stood over a tray of appetizers, pointing out various delectables to Mr Hoban.

Mary Ann took a firmer grasp on her uncle's arm. "I'm so glad you're back for Christmas this year."

"Yeah? Me too, Mule," said Aaron.

Mule was his special name for her, from when she was six and had refused to eat her broccoli even after the rest of the family had finished dinner and dessert and gone upstairs to wash up.

"Do you think you'll stick around after the holidays?" Mary Ann asked.

"Maybe," said Uncle Aaron, though he was staring at Sophia and did not look down.

John took a gingerbread reindeer from off a tray and went to stand in front of the Christmas tree, an overabundant Fraser Fir capped by a star which scraped the high ceiling. The base was bare, but in a few days it would be unapproachable with gifts delivered by an ageless Teutonic deity, tasked with dispensing punishment and reward among all the world's children. For John this remained a point of certainty; not once had he thought of poking around in upstairs cabinets for hopes of forbidden treasure. At eight, John still believed in magic.

"Finished with the book?" asked his grandmother, who sat by the fire with a quiet half smile on her face.

John took a seat on her lap. "Yeah," he said, "but it took *forever.*"

"Forever?"

"Constance and Mary Ann fight *all the time,*" said John. John had only recently been introduced to hyperbole and was losing no opportunity for practice.

"All the time?"

"Almost," he said, "Constance has to know better, and Mary Ann has to know best."

"It's part of having siblings," John's grandmother explained, "big table, lots of voices."

John swallowed this with his iced gingerbread.

Back in the kitchen Michael and Constance fought a desperate rear-guard action against the dishes, an endless horde of *hors d'oeuvre* plates, crystal glasses, serving trays and silverware. They fell into an easy, wordless rhythm, like dancing a tango or turning a double play in baseball. Constance would have preferred the second analogy.

"My loyal little soldier," said Michael.

Constance flushed proudly. "Somebody needs to help."

"Someone does," Michael agreed, "not everyone will."

Mary Ann had come in from the porch, and she watched as Sophia charmed Ms Alexievich and the Trevors with some or other sparkling observation, Mr Trevor smirking and Mrs Trevor giggling and Ms Alexievich laughing so hard that she coughed up most of her wine. Mary Ann wondered at how her mother had learned to hold her neck in that certain way, and to talk just loud enough that everyone had to lean closer to hear, and whether these were things that Mary Ann herself might learn with time and patience or if, like her blue eyes, they were a characteristic of her mother she could never acquire.

The fire in the great stone hearth – in previous years, reliably roaring – had burned down to hot coals. John's grandmother sighed.

"Do you miss him?" John asked.

"Of course," said his grandmother. "Every day."

This made John feel better. John missed his grandfather terribly – when Constance watched sports news, anytime he went swimming, sometimes for no reason that he could tell. Dead in his sleep earlier that summer, in John's mind he would remain forever a smiling, bushy-bearded giant, associated with the smell of wood smoke and motor oil, with a faded leather comfy chair, with a certain superficial severity, with safety and with home.

"No one loved the holidays like your grandfather," said his widow in the faded firelight. "He was like one of the kids, it was exhausting. Everything had to be exactly the same, every year – if you left out some tinsel or a plaster Santa he always noticed." She gazed into the dining room, where Aaron had come to join his sister as she held court around their makeshift bar. "He would have been so happy to see all of us together again."

Beginning as it did only a few years prior, John's sense of time was somewhat unreliable. Even still, he understood Uncle Aaron had not been to the house in a long time, a very long time, so long that John could only distantly recall having met him – at an outing to a fair, or someone's birthday. Too young likewise to be told anything, still John could piece together from the occasional strained silence and slammed door that however his dead grandfather might have felt on the matter, Aaron's return had not proved entirely easy for anyone.

"How come Aaron lives in Denver?" John asked.

"I guess he must like it there."

"It's far away, though."

Joan – this was the name of John's grandmother, though John was only dimly aware of this, her existence in his mind so entirely constrained by their relationship – sighed again and squeezed John tight. "Very far," she agreed.

So far that evening Mary Ann had eaten three buttered rolls and the crispy top off the creamed potatoes, and she was heading into the kitchen for another plate when she caught Uncle Aaron and her Mother engaged in the sort of conversation which children are not supposed to hear. She set herself against the wall and perked up her ears.

"I'm just suggesting you pace yourself," said Sophia.

"Thank you, sister," said Uncle Aaron, though not like he meant it, "but this isn't my first experience with alcohol."

"Yes, I think I recollect some of your earlier adventures. There was that Thanksgiving when you put most of Mother's turkey into the rose bush."

"Do you have these written down somewhere? Aaron's big book of failures? You could give it to the kids to memorize. 'C is for catatonic, a state of inebriation which Aaron reached just before we were supposed to take the family photo.'"

Against herself, Sophia broke into a slow chuckle. "You're such an asshole, Aaron, it's fucking unbelievable."

From the hallway beyond, Mary Ann's eyes went very wide.

"Don't let the kids hear you talk like that," Aaron warned.

"I never curse in front of the children," said Mary Ann's mother, "you entitled little cuntbag."

Uncle Aaron shook his head in confused dismay. "What would you even carry in that?"

"It's a portmanteau."

"I can't see it catching on."

Sophia laughed again, then drew closer to her brother, lowering her voice. "I'm glad you're back," said Sophia. "It's been...with Dad gone, I'll need your help."

Aaron set aside his towel, though there were still dishes wet on the drying rack. "We're on that again?"

"I can't be everywhere, and neither can Michael. Constance's young, and Mom's old."

"You think this was easier back in the day, when everyone had ten kids to help out with the harvest?"

"I think a lot of them died of cholera," Sophia pointed out.

Mary Ann tip-toed out of the kitchen and back to the living room.

It was *very* late, at least by Mary Ann's reckoning. Mr Isherwood, who was partner at her father's firm, snored unabashedly on their couch. Beneath a sprig of mistletoe Mr Trevor was whispering something to Ms Alexievich which she either did not like or did, it was hard for Mary Ann to tell. The Endos were arguing about something in the corner, quietly though not subtly. Mary Ann felt like when she had ridden the Tilt-a-Whirl at the spring carnival and gotten very sick, but like with the Tilt-a-Whirl she did not want to stop. The Rat Pack crooned dated carols from the stereo and Mary Ann began to dance, an arrhythmic shuffle which missed the beat while taking up a lot of space in the room.

This expression of merriment was, of course, Constance's queue to ruin everything. "You're acting like a child," she said, putting one hand on Mary Ann's arm.

Mary Ann pulled away. "Just because you can't dance."

"You can't dance either, you just don't know it."

"What does this look like?"

But executing a fancy two-step Mary Ann caught the corner of a side table, spilling a glass of wine. With the preternatural sensitivity gifted to parents of young children, Sophia arrived from the kitchen a moment later, pursing her lips unhappily.

"Good job," said Constance.

"Shut up!"

"Constance," said Sophia, "will you grab some paper towels and clean up that spill? And Mary Ann, why don't you help your brother off to bed, it's late."

Ms Alexievich had disappeared, but Mr Trevor was smirking, and the Endos had set aside their quarrel to bear witness to another.

"But, Mom, it wasn't my fault," Mary Ann hissed, conscious of the eyes on her.

"It's not a question of fault, darling, but John needs to get to bed."

Mary Ann swatted aside this olive branch like a hovering mosquito. "It's not late for Constance!"

"Constance is thirteen, when you're thirteen you can–"

"I'm almost as old as she is, and anyway it was her fault! You didn't see, she grabbed me!"

Sophia offered a quick smile to the too-curious Mr Trevor, then leaned down to scowl at her second child. "Don't raise your voice."

"Sorry," said Mary Ann, not really meaning it, a feigned retreat to marshal her resources.

"Now, we've had a lovely evening," said Sophia, "but all good things come to an end. Forget about the mess, I'll clean it. Just go to bed, you're tired."

Mary Ann wasn't tired, she was furious, her face flushed, every muscle in her small body tensed. The sheer *injustice* of it! If Constance had just left her alone, everything would have been fine, Constance who had to tell everyone everything, and who thought the two measly years between them meant everything in all the world. "But Mom–"

Bowing her head to meet her daughter Sophia Harrow resembled a whip crack or a lightning bolt. "You're embarrassing yourself," she said.

Cowed, red-faced, eyes flashing swift death on her tyrannical mother and sniveling sister and the sniggering guests, Mary Ann fled to the safety of the upstairs bathroom.

We begin as independent anchors of all reality, growing later to allow the introduction of a caretaker existing exclusively to service our own immediate needs, our perception expanding beyond that in time to encompass fathers, siblings, next door neighbors, so on and so forth. But the process is piecemeal and imperfect, and even the best of us regresses in moments of stress. Mary Ann was no more ruthless a sociopath than any other adolescent, and yet in her mind just then being sent upstairs early ranked high if not foremost in the grim and tedious annals of humanity's crimes.

A knock at the door did not improve her mood. "Go away!" she yelled.

"I need to brush my teeth," said John.

"Go away!" yelled Mary Ann, "I'm peeing!"

"No, you're not," said John.

The door to the bathroom locked but if you jiggled the handle the right way it would open, and John started jiggling it just then, one final indignity which Mary Ann was forced to suffer, lemon juice on her paper cut, salt in her wound. She wanted to scream but she couldn't so instead she did this thing which was like screaming but did not come out of her mouth, gathering up all her energy with her chest and her head and her throat, with her lungs, with something that was deeper than her lungs and for which she didn't know the name, wanting to go away, anywhere, it didn't matter, just away, screaming silently until she couldn't breathe and her vision was streaked with dots of color, John coming through the door just then, little brothers surely the curse of the devil himself–

–They were in a kitchen. Not *their* kitchen. Their kitchen only had one stove with four burners and an oven beneath, and this kitchen had many dozens of stoves running along the wall, and whereas their stoves ran on gas these stoves were kept hot by thick cords of sweet-smelling wood. Speaking of fires, their kitchen did not have a very large one in the center of it, nor had it ever been used to cook the skinned body of a cow, or perhaps it was a deer, or perhaps it was something altogether different. In fact, there were many ways one could tell that *this* kitchen was not *their* kitchen, not the least of them being the cook, who wore a chef's hat and a dirty apron and possessed a super-abundance of hands.

"Well?" he snapped two fingers at them, and with two more he tweaked his handlebar mustache, and with a hand he stirred thin soup, and with yet another he pulled a loaf of bread out from the oven and set it on the counter, and with another he cut the loaf, and with the rest he attended to the myriad of other duties required of him. "What are you waiting for? The fig aspic needs to get taken to the ambassador from the Faunae Palatinate, and this krill is nearly ready for the hydronese." The Man-With-Many-Hands sipped a tasting spoon of his stew. "Just needs some garum." He snatched up a bottle and added a few dashes of a thick brown sauce into the cloudy brine.

John gaped. Mary Ann gawked.

The Man-With-Many-Hands managed to find one to massage the sore spot which had formed around his temples. "Don't tell me – today is your first day?"

"We're new here," Mary Ann admitted.

"Of course you are! Why wouldn't you be?" The Man-With-Many-Hands threw himself back into his work, stirring a mix of indigo cake batter, thinly slicing a bit of beetroot, grinding an array of spices with a mortar and pestle. "I don't have enough to do feeding half the March, now I'm supposed to break in two new servers! On today, of all days!"

"What's today?" Mary Ann asked.

For a moment, albeit a brief one, all of the Man-With-Many-Hands's hands stopped what they were doing, so shocking was this question. "What's today? *What's today?* Don't they tell you anything in – wait, what are you?"

"Humans."

"Don't they tell you anything in Humanland?"

"Not a lot," Mary Ann admitted.

"Today is the Coronation. Why do you think the Tower is filled with guests? Why do you think we're cooking enough food to feed an army? Why do you think we were so desperate for help that we, apparently, hired the two dullest creatures in the March as servers?" Their conversation had interrupted the clockwork machinery of his kitchen, and the Man-With-Many-Hands had to rush to make up for it, limbs darting off in all directions. "Just fall in line and ask directions once you get to the throne room," he advised. "But hurry along – the faunae are friendly enough, but the hydronese get testy when they don't get their krill."

Not knowing what else to do, John picked up the tureen filled with tiny, listless, sour-smelling shrimp, and Mary Ann collected a gooey cube of brown, and then the Man-With-Many-Hands opened and ushered them out the door and into a great stone hallway. There they joined a menagerie of strange creatures carrying stranger dishes of food; an opossum with a vast brick of brie, a shambling, animate slow-cooker heating fondue on its back, four fluttering songbirds each holding a corner of a bread loaf wrapped in cloth. The Harrow children found themselves following the cavalcade down the corridor and into a stairwell which seemed to go up forever and down the same distance and packed into line there was nothing to do but follow the general ascent. Mary Ann had never in her life climbed so many stairs – then again, she had never smelled krill soup before, or met a man with more than one pair of arms, and so perhaps this was not the most noteworthy of the evening's novelties. Up and up and up they went, John and Mary Ann following along behind an elephantine sock puppet – another first – whose gray cloth exterior obscured their view of what lay ahead.

Mary Ann had begun to wonder if they would continue their climb forever, something which seemed less impossible just then than it might have earlier in the evening, when without warning the steady procession of servers reached the top of the staircase and entered a many-tiered hall. It reminded Mary Ann of the time her father had taken her and Constance to a baseball game, except that the walls were blue stone and the distant ceiling an elaborate dome of some substance clearer than glass which bathed the room in starlight. Also, in place of the baseball fans there were all manner of unlikely if vaguely familiar beings; awkward, strutting clockwork creatures; animals who were larger than animals were supposed to be and who also wore clothes, which animals generally do not; spindly humanoids in gigantic, impeccably painted masks; robed bipeds with polychrome wings and vivid coxcombs and sharp beaks; a cluster of upside down people with hands for feet and feet for hands and heads that nearly clipped the floor, dressed in colored caftans and burbling water pipes. Mary Ann had the strange sensation of seeing an old playmate or a distant relative she'd only known through pictures.

"We're in the March!" Mary Ann exclaimed suddenly.

"*Obviously*," John said. "I figured that out like a million years ago."

Then it was like seeing the reveal in an optical illusion or discovering yourself fluent in a language you have never spoken. There was no need to ask directions, Mary Ann recognized the embassy of the hydronese, diaphanous sylphs lounging in pools of tepid water impatiently awaiting their krill; and the gaggle of woodland creatures dressed in Renaissance silks which could only be the fabled faunae, sleek-furred lords and down-feathered ladies gathered in one corner of the terraced amphitheater. Their chief emissary, a severe looking sparrow, was just then returning to his perch after paying homage to the cathedra which filled the center of the room.

The chair was immense and fettered by a network of chains hung taught from the ceiling, like the struts of a suspension bridge. Each link was thicker around than a grown man and made of a myriad of materials – graceful argent, untarnished aurichalcum, grisly and misshapen iron, adamantine darker than ebony, luminescent crystal, a dense tangle of colored twine. The throne itself was enormous, so large and so grand that it ought to have dwarfed its single occupant, though in fact it served only to enhance her majesty. The Queen was tall and willowy and wore a long dress which seemed to be made not of cotton or silk but of the late evening sky, just before night has fully fallen. She wore a silver diadem which imprisoned a fallen star – the Bauble – and somehow, it was no shock to Mary Ann discerning her mother's face in it's cold, perfect light.

Standing beside Sophia, dressed in a suit of red and black armor, stood Mary Ann's father. Michael was bigger than Mary Ann could remember ever seeing him, hulking, as big as he had seemed when she was still a small child and he used to hang her upside down by her ankles. He leaned against a single-edged sword which was larger than he was, sheathed in a scabbard sealed by seven heavy locks. A ring of keys hung conspicuously from around his neck.

Uncle Aaron sat on a chair perched just below his sister, dressed all in gold and trying hard to look serious. Joan, their grandmother, sat beside him in a black mourning dress. Rounding out the three, wearing the same insignia as their father, was–

"What the hell is Constance doing here?" Mary Ann asked.

"*Shhhhh…*" John shooshed.

But it *was* Constance, the same wild hair, the same superior look. She sat primly, straight-backed, her gaze set on the creature then performing obeisance to their mother, a bipedal salamander wearing a headdress of maroon and cyan which contrasted starkly with her banana yellow skin. There were many thousands of – well, not people, but creatures of some sort – between Mary Ann and the proceedings, but by some strange artifice she could hear the supplicant's voice as clear as her morning alarm clock.

"The molluschites swear fealty to the Harrow, who keep the March at peace, and safe from what waits outside of it."

"In the name of the Throne, and of the Harrow, we accept your loyalty," said Sophia, in the same voice that she had used to welcome Ms Dermout to their Christmas party, "and we swear to uphold the ancient pacts, to protect and defend you until the last of our line."

"May that day never come," said the ambassador, who rose and shuffled her way back to her deputation.

"The new Queen is terribly beautiful," said an off-white mouse in checkered livery in the dense crowd beside them.

"She's too young," disputed an orange octopus through dangling chin-tentacles, "who can trust a Harrow without gray in their hair? Now, her father, that was a ruler. Great big chap, with a beard that ran all down his chest."

"Age isn't everything," said the mouse.

"Say that twice," muttered Mary Ann.

Back on the main stage a bullfrog in golden robes with a golden chapeau and a golden rod flared his neckflaps and bellowed an introduction. "Aetheling Calyx is called before the Gyven Throne."

The Aetheling was nearly, though not quite, a man. His skin was mossy green, his hair were tendrils of root curled into a tight chignon atop his head. He was dressed entirely in skins and furs of various sorts; a nubuck coat, a fine pair of smilodon breeches, a rug from an ice bear around his shoulders, a crown of antler horns atop his proud forehead. Alone among all the nations present, he had arrived without coterie or attendants. When called he rose from an empty suite of leather couches and approached the throne with the sharp, controlled steps of a dancer.

"The Kingdom of the Thorned Rose is in attendance," he announced.

"Has the Aetheling come to offer fealty?" the herald asked.

There was a brief pause, then the lord shook his head slowly. "He has not."

There was a sudden lulling from the vast assemblage; the hydronese stilled in their pools, the faunae cased their chatter, the molluschite ambassador, still returning to her seat, gasped and looked nervous. Drinks were set down, haunches of meat returned uneaten to their plates.

Sophia maintained her implacable smile. Michael pulled his key ring from off his neck and undid the first lock on his sheath, the *chink* echoing with strange clarity throughout the crowd.

"Much is told of the Kingdom of the Thorned Rose," began Sophia, in the same tone with which she had reminded Mary

Ann to clean her bedroom earlier that afternoon, "not yet have I heard them called oathbreakers."

"The word of a verdurite is more certain than the tallest redwood, or the growth of nettle come spring."

"And yet? When the End plagued your boundaries, warped the wood and corrupted your groves, did your pleas for help go unanswered?"

The Aetheling's face was hardwood but not unreadable, and Mary Ann saw him tense in indignation at the slight. "The wise reed bends to the storm, while the proud oak is uprooted."

"Fealty was the cost of that salvation – allegiance to the Harrow and to the laws of the Thousand Peoples."

"The verdurite have not forgotten their oaths," said the Aetheling, tossing a pointed look behind him, "alas that not all here can say the same."

"I object!" shouted the leader of the stony petrousian from where he waited to offer submission. Tall and stooped and crumbling, worn as a cliff face, he was assisted by two stout, stern looking children, rough and rigid as boulders. "If the north is in ferment, Under the Mountain is not responsible. The verdurites press our borders and harry our trade."

"What need has a tree for a cave? When we swore fealty to the Harrow we laid down our leather lassos and our spears of bone. For long years the Heartwood has thirsted, and our warriors lay awake in shame." The Aetheling turned squarely to face Sophia, his dark eyes stern and unbending. "But our faith has not been repaid. If the Tower cannot keep the peace, then the Kingdom of the Thorned Rose will be forced to make its own."

Sophia said nothing. Michael released another lock on his sheath. The mouse next to Mary Ann gasped. The cephalopod crossed its tendrils around its oblong eyes.

Mary Ann's grandmother, or perhaps only a woman who looked and spoke and acted like Mary Ann's grandmother, Mary Ann was not yet sure, rose from her chair. She wore a dress of shot silk and leaned upon an opalescent staff. "We have met, have we not, Aetheling Calyx? When I visited the north, in the days when your anther was newly blossomed."

"I am surprised you still remember, Queen Mother," said the Aetheling respectfully.

"I am not so old as to have forgotten my time beneath your boughs. I have hunted horned serpent and eaten flesh unblemished by salt. When your thanes went north I rode in the vanguard, fought the End beside your houscarls and great heroes, planted our fallen in the Heartwood." She took on a wounded, disappointed look. "I had not imagined their sacrifice would be so quickly dismissed."

For the first time the Aetheling seemed pressed. Mary Ann felt a peculiar pang of sympathy, having been on the receiving end of so many of her grandmother's chidings. "The name of the Queen Mother will be known among my people so long as seed takes root," he assured her, "but we cannot sit idle while our lands are occupied by these…these…tunnel dwellers!"

The petrousian bristled and would have argued if Joan had not continued on swiftly.

"Trust us now, as you did then," said Joan. "If there is a grievance between you and the sons of stone, it can be relieved; harms mended, injuries healed."

"You would come north once more, Queen Mother?" asked the Aetheling, with the faint trace of a smile.

"My journeys have ended," said Joan, "only the last remains to me, and I hope to put it off for some years yet. But I am not the only Harrow – and my son, newly returned to the March, might serve in my stead."

Aaron sat up uncomfortably, looking like Mary Ann when she was called to the board in math class. Sophia threw a quick, worried glance at her brother, then her mother, then turned back to face her subjects.

"A delegation from the High Prince," Joan continued, "to inspect the boundaries, and ensure peace in the north. Would that satisfy?"

The Aetheling thought this over for a moment. In his silence Mary Ann could hear, or perhaps feel, the crowd grow anxious around her; shuffling hooves, paws pressed together, serpentine throats cleared. The Coronation, a rote if ebullient ceremony, had turned pregnant with the potential for violence.

"It would be a start," said the Aetheling.

Joan nodded, and Aaron fidgeted, and the crowd calmed slightly. Sophia leaned forward from her throne, the Bauble in her crown like the gleam of a lighthouse. "Aaron will be sent north, to adjudicate any disputes between the Kingdom of the Thorned Rose and Under the Mountain, and the Harrow will do everything we can to ensure harmony between your peoples. We do not yet know each other, Aetheling, but you will find me as amicable as my mother." Sophia's face turned suddenly hard. "And as fierce as my father. The oath your people swore to my family does not require revisiting, and this coronation is a mere formality – but a necessary one. Refusal to bend knee to the Tower is treason, and jeopardizes the safety of our land, and that I will not abide, not from you nor anyone. Against such madness I would gather all the loyal forces of the Thousand Peoples and send them north, to hew your trees to stumps and turn your scared groves to charcoal. The Harrow set peace above everything save honor. Swear fealty or find yourself an enemy of the Throne."

Mary Ann's father wore a look of grim ferocity which she could not ever remember seeing before. Three locks hung loose off his sheathed sword, and the room, vast as it was, seemed to have grown warmer. Mary Ann did not realize she had been holding her breath until after a long moment the Aetheling dropped to one knee, and the Thousand People broke into rapturous applause.

And then another page – a sneering tin clown with a wind-up key in the back of his neck – pressed Mary Ann to her task, and the evening passed in a whirlwind of quotidian tasks in impossible surroundings. It was hours before the two Harrow siblings slept, amid the ranks of a towering bunkbed shared by the lower staff, each rung a small platform with a cheval glass and dewdrop wash basin, twisting chutes leading to the ground – but she woke in her regular bed, below the framed Joni Mitchell poster, with the morning light shining in through her window.

**For more great title
recommendations,
check out the Angry Robot website
and social channels**

**www.angryrobotbooks.com
@angryrobotbooks**

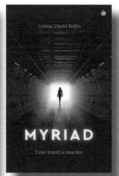

We are Angry Robot

angryrobotbooks.com

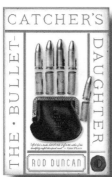

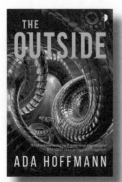

We are Angry Robot

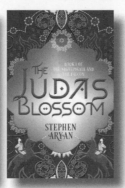

angryrobotbooks.com

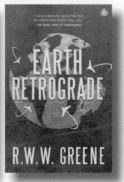

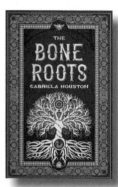

We are Angry Robot

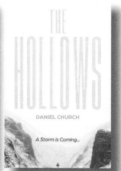

angryrobotbooks.com

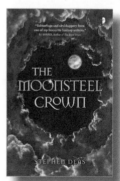
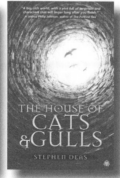

We are Angry Robot

angryrobotbooks.com